WHITE RABBIT: THE RISE

LONDON MILLER

Long live the Kingmaker!

 # L. Mil

LM Books, LLC

LM Books LLC

PO Box 1202

Lilburn, GA 30048

PRAISE FOR LONDON MILLER

"London Miller writes with both complex emotion, high paced intensity and a diverse cast of misfits that you can't help falling in love with."

— BESTSELLING AUTHOR, MARY CATHERINE GEBHARD

"This series continues to play out much like a chess game with all the players being moved around but with no known end ..."

— AMAZON REVIEWER, SANDY

"The way the Den of Mercenaries and Wild Bunch series are intricately woven into each other is impressive."

— EDGY REVIEWS, LILY

ALSO BY LONDON MILLER

Volkov Bratva

In the Beginning

Until the End

The Final Hour

Valon: What Once Was

Hidden Monsters

The Morning

Time Stood Still

Down the Line

Den of Mercenaries

Red.

Celt.

Nix.

Calavera.

Skorpion.

Syn.

Iris.

The Wild Bunch

Crooks & Kings

Shadows & Silence

Seasons of Betrayal

For Uilleam
Your time is here.

How much would you pay to be a king?

— UILLEAM RUNEHART

THE WOULD-BE KING

HEAD UP AND BACK STRAIGHT WITH HIS FEET SHOULDER-WIDTH apart, Uilleam Runehart awaited the inevitable.

He knew what came next if he didn't pass his father, Alexander's, inspection.

He knew the pain that came when he failed tests he sometimes didn't even know he was taking.

Every single part of himself and his bedroom had to be absolutely pristine. From his hair and starched clothes, to the sheets on his bed and the floorboards that didn't have a bit of dust on them.

Alexander demanded perfection in all things, even as it was impossible to obtain. Anything less and one risked his displeasure — and no one wanted to be on his bad side.

It never ended well. Not when his temper was notorious.

Weeks had passed since his last inspection, but Uilleam still had the bruises from the last time he failed to be anything less than the 'ideal son.'

But even as he stood there waiting — not daring to mutter a single complaint lest someone overhear — he had yet to hear the familiar thump of heavy footsteps coming down the hall or the scattering of servants that always accompanied Alexander's arrival in the right wing of Runehart Castle.

Something was different today though.

The castle was almost unbearably quiet.

And though some part of him should have been happy he had managed to make it this long into his day without hearing his father raise his voice, his mind wasn't at ease.

Standing there a moment longer, he fidgeted with the coin he kept tucked away in his pocket, trying to decide whether it was worth abandoning his post here, venturing out to find Alexander and get this over with.

On the one hand, it could buy him favor—what little would come of it—because Alexander would admire the initiative. On the other hand, should anything be out of place, a beating would surely follow.

But he couldn't let fear of what *might* happen stop him.

Before he could talk himself out of it, Uilleam walked out of the sanctuary that was his bedroom and ventured down the long empty hallway toward the west wing, briefly slowing in front of a closed bedroom door with the jagged crack that was impossible to miss down the very center of it.

Once, this room had been his very favorite place in the entire world—a room that had been his safe haven in a place that demanded one.

A room that had been vacant for several months now.

No matter how often he passed it each day, a pang still echoed in his chest. A pain he wished he could bury so deep he couldn't feel it anymore.

Because while he'd cried himself to sleep many nights when his brother had gone off and left him behind, that pain was starting to feel a lot like betrayal now, and *that* thought made him uneasy.

He loved his brother the most, and the thought of that love ever becoming tainted distressed him. Turning away, he put both to the back of his mind.

Runehart Castle had more than a dozen rooms, as many bathrooms, and looked as foreboding as most castles of old, save for the many modern amenities and the complete renovation the place had gone under after Alexander had bought it.

But as beautiful as it might have been, it wasn't *home*.

It didn't inspire warmth or comfort as a home should, and it certainly wasn't somewhere his friends, the very few he had, could visit.

It was too cold here. Too barren.

As if it were abandoned, even as they lived there.

Beyond the castle itself, it wasn't the only reason Uilleam spent much of his time alone. His father was too unpredictable.

Too easily riled.

He could be smiling one moment, charming everyone in sight, and then in the next, he became the tyrant so many labeled him.

And considering every inch of the castle was fortified—it was Alexander's pride and joy after all—no one wanted to be locked in here when he was on a rampage.

It was better he not condemn anyone to be in the presence of his father, he'd decided ages ago. He would suffer alone.

Much too often, he thought of burning it all to ashes to end this miserable existence.

Fire cleansed things. Purified them.

More than once, he contemplated just how long it would take for the centuries-old structure to collapse into rubble if he set flame to it.

How fast would the fire spread before it consumed every inch?

How long would it take before nothing was left standing but soot and old memories?

The thought shouldn't have comforted him as much as it did, but it got him through the day all the same.

He might have lived here all his life, but he felt no sentimental attachment to it. These walls had secrets, and he was growing tired of listening to the whispers.

Casting all thoughts of smoke and ruin aside, Uilleam descended from the second level, pausing in the oversized kitchen where two cooks were busy preparing for the night's events.

He didn't know who would be attending the party his mother was throwing or why—not that he cared either way—he only knew that he would need to look his absolute best for the guests and not embarrass Alexander in any way.

Mother's orders.

But even as he could see the two in front of him clearly working —neither truly paying attention to him beyond soft spoken greetings —the castle seemed rather empty. The servants *should* have been milling around, completing the day's tasks. Seen, but not heard as his father liked to say.

The fact that they *weren't* should have been the first indication something was amiss, and he should probably return to his rooms, but Uilleam rather enjoyed seeking out what he shouldn't.

Dangerous, curious things excited him. He sought them out as one would Pandora's box.

It was a compulsion he didn't bother to fight. He was his father's son, after all ... despite his feelings on the matter.

And that was no better reflected than right here where his family's legacy spanning generations hung on stone walls. War generals, a knight, and even an earl, his family's power was legion, but for the past few generations, the Runehart men had strayed from the public eye and political offices.

It was no longer prestige—*legal*, upstanding prestige—that they sought.

Now, it was something a little darker.

Something a little more wrong and forbidden.

And because of that choice, there was one unspoken rule in the Runehart family—what happened in the family, *stayed* in the family.

With the lives they led ... it was better never to speak of anything one saw or heard—a fact that should have alarmed twelve-year-old Uilleam, but he wasn't like other children his age.

His tutors liked to call him *special* when they thought he wasn't around to hear them.

He might've taken those words as a compliment had they not looked so concerned when they said it.

He wasn't sure what it meant, not yet, and no one would tell him when he dared to ask.

Soon, though, he would learn.

Very soon.

As he passed the courtyard with every intention of going up to Alexander's office, something out of the corner of his eyes stole his attention, bringing him up short.

He wasn't sure, at first, what he was seeing. Not when the huddle of men in dark attire blocked most of his view, but something caused them all to move at once. All taking a single step backward, and the gaps this caused allowed him his first glimpse of the bloodied man kneeling on the concrete.

One of the man's eyes was nearly swollen shut, nothing more than a narrowed slit. A deep gash bled profusely from a cut above his brow. Purple discolored bruises already covered nearly every inch of his face and upper torso.

Every breath had to cause the man tremendous pain.

But even as he was nearly beaten unrecognizable, the silver chain that dangled from the man's neck was all too familiar.

Peter, his name was, though it was one of the very few things Uilleam actually knew about him. Not his age or whether he had a family. Nor how long he had actually been working for Alexander.

Just a name.

And if he were being honest, he wasn't even sure if the man's name *was* actually Peter, but it was as good of a name as any.

From the looks of him, it didn't appear as if anyone would be calling him anything other than a distant memory very soon.

Standing above Peter with the sleeves of his silk dress shirt rolled up to his elbows and blood spattered across his severe face, shirt, and knuckles was a man who most, especially in this place, had learned to fear.

The man Uilleam called father.

Uilleam was tall for his age, though a bit thin, but Alexander was a bull of a man—as tall as he was muscled. He looked every bit the leader of a criminal organization no one could quite put a name to.

He was more akin to a savage than anything else.

Uilleam didn't think he'd ever even seen him smile before. At least not a genuine one.

His brother, Kit, far away now, would have turned in the opposite direction and ventured back to his room before any attention could be called to him, but Uilleam was too curious to move.

A fault of his he had yet to rectify.

So instead of disappearing before Alexander could see he was a witness to the brutal beating he was inflicting on the man sprawled on the ground, Uilleam drew closer to the glass, keeping his hands firmly at his sides instead of pressing them to the glass the way he wanted.

"Mercy," the bleeding man finally forced out between split lips, his one good eye going up to Alexander in subjugation. "Please."

"What's that?" Alexander asked, his voice like thunder.

The man didn't know how to speak quietly if he tried.

"Anything," Peter said before coughing violently, a spray of blood coating the snow in front of him. "I'll do anything."

Those words played over and over in Uilleam's head. His mind took them apart, put them back together again.

Understanding the implications behind them.

But he wasn't thinking about the brutal beating that had brought the man to this point.

He wondered what else could bring a man to his knees …

What else could make someone beg for their life?

What would a man be willing to offer if it meant his suffering would end?

How could *he* be on the opposite end of that?

Uilleam wasn't sure how long he stood there, watching as his father continued to rain down blows, not caring that the man had started to sob, holding his arm up in weak protest to protect himself, or that the gold engraved ring on his finger was leaving ghastly marks in the man's flesh.

No one stepped in to save him.

No one lifted a finger against Alexander at all.

They all stood silently as the man took his beating without fighting back. For fear of what would happen to them if they did.

Uilleam should have felt a stirring of disgust at the grisly sight before him, especially since he had once been on the receiving end of those very same fists, but he felt nothing.

Just the same curiosity that often got him into trouble.

Curiosity that made him wonder what it would be like to possess such power.

To be the only saving grace in a desperate man's pleas.

To become something feared and revered.

To never be weak again …

But it wasn't his fists he wanted to use to make people kneel at his feet.

He wanted them to quake at the very mention of his *name*.

1

A FIELD OF POPPIES

NEW YORK WASN'T JUST A PLACE—IT WAS A STATE OF MIND.

Karina Ashworth only knew what she had seen in the movies or read in the pages of a book. As she'd sat on a plane nearly a year ago today, staring down at the clouds beneath the wings, she had expected to find a bustling city.

One ripe with brutal confessions and endless secrets.

With more buildings than parks and the sort of air about it that said one needed to be resilient to withstand the brutality of it all.

It was vastly different from the town with rolling hills and sprawling trees she had grown up in. No matter where she moved to —and she'd moved quite a bit in her adolescence—her mother never settled on a house (whether the house, itself, was big or small) that didn't have a garden of some sort, with enough greenery around that spring meant it was always picture perfect.

She had known living in a big city would be a change from every- thing she knew, but she'd welcomed it. She'd looked forward to it from the moment the possibility had been put on the table.

And after nearly half a day on an airplane with little sleep, she had walked through JFK International Airport with a couple of suit- cases and stars in her eyes. She'd been eager to see the city her sister,

Isla, had talked so much about because, unlike her, Isla had actually traveled beyond the town they'd lived in.

From London to Melbourne, across the globe to California, then up to Canada and beyond.

It had felt like stepping into an entirely new world when she had arrived in New York.

Even as she had worried about how she would fit in with the sea of strangers around her, she had also felt a kernel of excitement about the fact that she was virtually unknown to everyone around her.

She could be whoever she wanted to be when no one knew who she was or the family she belonged to.

And that was exactly how she wanted it.

She hadn't minded moving into her one-bedroom apartment the size of a shoebox. It was *hers*. And her excitement at being away from home had only doubled once she got a job at the paper.

But if eleven months as a reporter for *The Gazette Post* had taught her anything, it was that most days in New York, beyond the glitz and glamor it was known for, were exceptionally boring.

If she wasn't sitting alone at her desk, plugging away at articles that needed to be edited and proofread before Jerry did the final inspection, she was at home working on her secret project. But no matter which she was doing, she was usually sitting behind a screen, the blinking cursor always reminding her of a new beginning.

During her first couple of months at the Post, she had written mostly about socialites on the Upper East Side. Their minor scandals didn't make first-page news but still deserved a place in the paper.

She hadn't minded, though that type of thing held no interest for her. She knew it was because she was new, that everyone had written a story or two they'd found tedious and uninteresting. She had to prove herself—show what she was capable of when given a blank page and a topic of interest.

Stumbling across a story that actually proven newsworthy had happened accidentally, but she was glad for it all the same.

Because without that day, she would have still been writing about what rich women liked to eat for dinner rather than something thrilling.

Except it had been two months since her big break.

Two months since anything had happened that was worth late hours and sleepless nights.

Now, she found herself staring at the phone on her desk, willing it to ring, anticipating a tip or a clue or *something* that would get her out of her chair and actually doing something.

Swinging around in the black swivel chair that was more comfortable than it first appeared, Karina propped her feet up onto the edge of her desk, briefly glancing over to check the time.

It was only ten in the morning—though it felt much later than that since she had gotten up at a quarter past five—and she briefly considered calling it a day and working from home. Greasy fast food and her favorite pajamas were calling her name.

"*Ashworth!*"

Karina perked up at the sound of her name.

Camilla stood in the doorway of her office, wearing her customary red dress that was vibrant against the backdrop of black and white furniture behind her. She gestured with a flick of her fingers for Karina to join her before disappearing to sit behind her desk.

"Looks like you're in trouble," Samantha, her friend and work neighbor, whispered with a nod of her head in Camilla's direction.

Between her time working and getting used to living in a new city—very different from the small countryside estate where she had grown up—Karina hadn't had time to actually go out and experience the city. Having a girl her age working alongside her had proven helpful where that was concerned.

It had only taken a couple of days and a love of morning coffee before they had their first conversation, and less than a day after that for them to exchange numbers.

Now, she was arguably the person Karina was closest to in this city, though they rarely spent time together outside of work. Something she *really* needed to work on.

The whole reason she had wanted to come here in the first place was because she wanted to step outside of her comfort zone. *Experience* a life that would otherwise be foreign to her if she gave in to what her mother, Katherine, wanted.

Expected was the better word.

"Whatever it is," Karina muttered as she stood, "I'm blaming it on you."

Sticking her pen in the messy bun on top of her head, Karina walked across the office floor, curiosity sending her thoughts scattering as she tried to anticipate what Camilla wanted to discuss with her.

It had to be about a potential case, if she were to wager a guess.

Certainly nothing about her or the lies she had told to get this job, even as that fear always lingered in the back of her mind whenever she was called into her editor's office for a private conversation.

Camilla was still on the phone when Karina entered the office, nodding along with whatever she was being told as she scribbled on a notepad. She didn't interrupt in any way, waiting silently until her boss ended the call and hung the phone up.

When she did finally look up, her expression was a mixture of intrigue and ... something else Karina couldn't quite put her finger on.

Though Karina had very little experience in the workplace—this was, essentially, her first real job—she couldn't imagine that Camilla was like any other boss out there.

Never mind that red was her signature color, and she wore it daily, but it was the way she carried herself. Her shoulders back and head up, her strut always confident and sure. Looking at her, one wouldn't have thought she was nearing her late fifties, or even that she was the editor in charge of a regional paper.

She could have been the editor of one of those glossy magazines Karina looked over when she was in the store, or the mother of one of the socialites she wrote about.

Her mother's words always whispered in the back of her mind: *Dress as if you want to conquer the world*.

Wise words to live by.

"I have a case for you," Camilla said, tearing the sheet from the notepad she'd been writing on before sliding it across the desk. "You know where the Paxton Industries building is?"

"The big ostentatious building near Times Square?" Karina asked, already picturing it in her head. "Yeah, I know it."

As well as the CEO it was named after.

Her morning was looking up.

"What about it?" she asked next, quickly scanning the note Camilla had passed over. "Wait ... someone found a *body*?"

"Police arrived fifteen minutes ago, so I need you there *now*. Get me everything you can."

"Of course."

"Good. And Karina?"

She had turned her back, all but ready to walk out the door and grab her coat before hailing a cab, but she paused and looked back at Camilla whose gaze was level on hers.

"I'm trusting you can handle this."

That was part of the job.

And more, this was her chance to prove herself. To show that she could do more and take on the important stories.

"I won't let you down."

A SEA OF BLUE AND RED LIGHTS WAS ALL KARINA COULD SEE AS she stepped out of the taxi. Yellow police caution tape stretched from one building to the next, dividing the police presence from the small crowd of pedestrians and reporters observing them with curious eyes as they worked.

Some actually took pictures, which was alarming in and of itself.

A police officer stood in front of the tape wearing a blue uniform, his hands clasped in front of him and his expression grim.

Officer Pinkerton was his name.

One of the two arresting officers of Rebecca McRalph, a rich girl from the Upper West Side, nearly a month ago. He was a rookie with less than a year on the job when he and his partner at the time had arrested her and booked her for a DUI.

Rebecca's father had tried to get the man fired because he'd believed the officer was out of line—though he had never acknowledged the fact that his daughter had, in fact, blown well over the legal limit and was only sixteen—but when Karina's article on the matter became public and drew a lot of publicity, the father had quietly backed away, and Pinkerton had been able to keep his job.

Afterward, he'd said he owed her one.

Keep friends in all places — one of the ten commandments her sister, Isla, lived by.

Tucking her hands into her bag, she felt the cool metal and leather that made up the camera tucked away inside. She didn't always bring it along — Camilla didn't require it since there was a photographer on the payroll — but she had started bringing it with her wherever she went as of late.

She wanted to capture her own vision to look over later.

To see what she might have missed the first time around.

It took a bit of effort to make her way to the front of the specta-tors, most graciously moving aside when they saw the name tag hanging around her neck, but unlike some of the other reporters who worked alongside her, she didn't try to venture beyond the tape to get that exclusive shot that would sell papers and create buzz.

It only made their jobs guarding the tape harder.

And she liked to think she erred on the side of caution.

Played by the rules.

A reason, she thought, that Pinkerton gave her a slight nod of acknowledgment once he noticed her and covertly took two steps to the left, blocking someone else's shot while giving her a good view of what was going on behind him.

At first, all she could see was the sea of red and green, the poppy flowers breathtaking in the bright morning sunlight. They swayed gently with the blowing breeze, beautiful if not impossible.

Poppies weren't in season, if she wasn't mistaken, but somehow, William Paxton managed to have a field of them outside his building. She could only imagine how much it had cost to have them imported and maintained.

Staring through the lens of her viewfinder, she captured a few images of the detectives talking amongst themselves; a medical exam-iner making notes on a clipboard off to the side; and the quiet, but intense, conversation between a detective she didn't recognize and a security guard. Only when she aimed her camera downward did her finger hesitate over the capture button.

She couldn't see the body, not when it was draped completely by a white sheet with a black body bag stretched out lengthwise beside it. It didn't matter that the woman's identity was virtually hidden beneath it. Or even that Karina had no idea who she was.

The sight still made the fine hairs along the nape of her neck stand up.

She swallowed, thinking back to the last time she had seen a dead body.

Even now, she could *almost* feel the chill on her face. The pain in her fingertips. How she hadn't been quite able to catch her breath before she'd taken a step forward into the blanket of snow where a harsh splatter of red clung to the ice ...

Shaking her head to clear the thought away, she forced herself to focus on the task at hand rather than distant memories. As the examiner gave the all clear for them to load the body up, she tucked her camera away.

Biding her time, she waited until some of the crowd had dissipated before walking over to Pinkerton. After ensuring her phone was clearly visible in her hand, she stood just out of view of the other officers.

"What can you tell me?"

Pinkerton was very good at keeping a straight face, and she might have thought he hadn't heard her if he hadn't finally whispered, "Not much to know, really. She didn't have anything on her that would give us an ID. I heard Peterson"—the lone female detective standing among the others— "say the vic was wearing pearl. La pearl?"

"La Perla," Karina corrected, thinking of how much the designer cost.

No ID. Expensive lingerie.

"Do you remember what she was dressed in?"

"Black dress. Heels."

An escort, maybe?

"What's the early report?"

He cleared his throat, glancing past her a moment. "Strictly off the record?"

"For you, yes." Whatever he told her, she would eventually learn anyway.

"They think she might've jumped," he said, a tinge of pity in his voice. "But she's got a few bruises, so the examiner is being thorough."

"And she jumped from Paxton's building?" she asked, though more to herself as she craned her neck back to look up toward the top of the building.

While it wasn't the tallest building in New York City by any stretch of the imagination, the top of it still seemed pretty far up.

"Any witnesses?"

"No one saw her come in, but when Paxton arrived at eight, she was there."

That was enough to make her blink twice. "The CEO found her?"

"Not really sure on the details. It might have been him or one of the security he keeps with him. Either way, he was there."

Interesting.

It wasn't every day that a billionaire CEO stumbled across a dead body, and while she couldn't be sure, she was sure she had heard Paxton's name recently. Though, for the life of her, she couldn't remember where.

But she would find out.

2

THE FIXER

ONE WEEK AGO ...

The pursuit of power was never an easy road, but it was one Uilleam was determined to follow through with all the same.

Which was why he was here at Paxton Industries, of all places, at four fifteen in the morning.

It was too early to be awake and too late to fall asleep, but Uilleam would have much rather been back in his bed rather than entering the chrome and glass building in lower Manhattan.

Frankly, men like William Paxton weren't worth much of his time.

The security desk to the left was vacant, despite the hour, and a glance up at the security cameras in the upper corners of the lobby showed they were all turned in opposite directions away from the front doors.

As far as anyone would ever know, his being here had never happened.

One of the many rules he abided by.

Swiping the plain white security card he'd been sent against the sensor, he stepped through the turnstiles, the mercenary that followed at his heels close behind and walked over to the bank of elevators.

They waited in silence until the mirrored doors slid open. One press of his finger took them up to the twenty-second floor where his newest client awaited him.

A client he'd fully intended on ignoring until he had learned of his connection to someone that *was* worth his time.

Which was why he had reluctantly agreed to meet on this cool, dark morning, but his mood wasn't completely grave. There was something about the promise of a new job that sent anticipation rushing through him. Puzzles had always fascinated him since he was a boy—the more complicated, the better.

He liked to analyze and decipher—taking two things that seemed opposite and bringing them together. And the more skilled he became at them, the better he was able to translate the same process over to people.

Taking what someone thought they knew and manipulating it into an image that better reflected what he wanted them to see.

That was what he did.

Who he was.

A fixer.

The fixer, for those of discerning means.

This was his pride and joy, but lately, he had begun to long for more. He'd reached the precipice and now he was ready to ascend beyond it.

But there was time for all of that later.

Right now, he had something else he needed to handle.

Twelve hours ago, he had received an encrypted email, sent through a number of proxy accounts that would never, if someone chose to track it, trace back to him. It was a summons, of sorts, from a man with far more money than he clearly knew what to do with considering he was requesting Uilleam's assistance for a potential job.

He'd hardly started reading over the simple inquiry—one that hadn't told him the full nature of what the job would entail—before a sizable retainer had come in the midst of it.

Two hundred thousand dollars, no questions asked.

Considering he didn't get out of bed for less than five times that, he'd elected to ignore the email. Except, before he'd had the chance to dismiss the letter entirely, another email had come in on the heels of the first with a single sentence.

Gaspard Berger suggested your name.

Now *that* had been enough to pique his interest, and without another request from the sender, Uilleam had agreed to the meeting.

He wasn't sure why Gaspard had bothered to drop his name—even how or when the opportunity had presented itself considering Uilleam had been trying to meet with Gaspard for more than seven months now without even a return phone call.

Had he not been the head of a vast criminal empire in France, Uilleam might have had the man killed for his insolence.

But there would be plenty of time for that later. He always gave those that opposed him a chance to come to their senses.

But whatever game the Frenchman was playing, Uilleam was more than ready, and willing, to play it along with him. And if that meant entertaining billionaires with seemingly too much time on their hands, then so be it.

He'd taken his jet from Wales at the earliest opportunity, using the hours traveling to the States to brush up on his knowledge of the man he'd been coming to meet.

No better time than the present to determine what sort of arrangement he wanted to make.

The doors slid open, a mute but pleasant chime signaling the end of their journey. Skorpion—named for the Russian made assault rifle he used to favor—stepped out ahead of him, dark eyes scanning the corridor before he gave the all clear for him to follow.

Unlike the lobby downstairs, they weren't alone on this floor.

William Paxton, the man who'd asked for this meeting, sat behind his desk, visible through the open door of his office, a cigarette pinched between his lips, the fingers of his other hand buried in the slightly graying hair at his temples.

He didn't look a day over forty, though he was closing in on his late fifties. With the sort of face that wasn't quite Hollywood but could still draw in the unsuspecting buyer, he was the optimal choice to be the face of a multi-billion-dollar company, as well as its CEO.

He was a man in a position of power and prestige, sought after by anyone who was worth knowing in the industry—both legal and otherwise.

Yet now his eyes were bloodshot and tired, his pallor sallow.

A haunted man, if Uilleam had ever seen one.

"Mr. Paxton," Uilleam greeted formally as he stepped inside the warmly lit room that smelled of the clove cigarettes the man was smoking. "I understand you have a proposition for me."

Paxton looked up, his expression anxious. "Are you really him? The man who can fix anything?"

Uilleam gave an immodest shrug before helping himself to a seat in one of the brown leather armchairs. "That's what they tell me."

He didn't miss the way Paxton glanced over at his personal security—who remained standing in front of a closed door with his hands folded in front of him.

While Paxton seemed almost relieved that he was still there, his guard was not.

It was clear he didn't trust them. And even as he had no idea why, he had every reason to be suspicious.

Uilleam could easily make Paxton's problem, whatever it turned out to be, go away without as much as a blink—that was how good he was—but only if it interested him enough to invest his time.

As he was known to accept the oddest of tasks, he also had a tendency to decline any job that bored him.

And boredom struck him often.

At this point in his career, whatever a person's proposition, it needed to be worth his time.

Paxton cleared his throat, trying to affect an air of importance, and even that he was in charge of this conversation—but they both knew he wasn't. "I have a problem."

"A two-hundred-thousand-dollar problem, by the looks of it," Uilleam returned, reclining back in his seat. "Though that amount only warrants me listening, you understand. I haven't agreed to anything."

"Of course. Yes, I understand." Paxton's throat hollowed as he dragged in a lungful of nicotine, letting the smoke billow out from between his lips before he continued. "But I'll pay whatever price you name."

"Then by all means," Uilleam said with a gesture of his hand. "Why don't you tell me how I can be of assistance?"

Paxton cleared his throat once more, grinding out the butt of his cigarette before reaching for another from the pack on his desk. Between placing the cigarette between his lips and lighting it, then standing and crossing the floor, gesturing for his guard to move out of the way, he seemed to make a decision.

One that appeared to be weighing heavily on him.

"It was an accident," Paxton explained quickly, practically tripping over his own words. "I was in the middle of something, and she interrupted me. We ... fought, but she was fine when I left her, I swear."

Uilleam found himself more curious than he had anticipated as he watched the man stop at the lone closed door in the room.

Skorpion didn't look nearly as at ease as he felt as he shifted his weight from foot to foot, ever ready for someone to make a move against them, but it was easy enough to guess what Paxton had hidden behind there, even without his near confession moments ago.

Uilleam could read people as easily as a book. It was all about foresight—anticipating the moves of his opponents before they acted. Like a game of chess.

It was what he did best.

So before the door even opened and he could see a hint of a pale arm stretched out across the floor, he had a good idea that whatever lay on the other side was something Paxton would pay an obscene amount of money to be rid of.

Whoever this girl was ... she was the source of Paxton's discontent.

Without waiting for an invitation, Uilleam got to his feet and moved across the room to stand behind the man, wanting a clearer picture for himself before Paxton could further paint his own narrative.

He couldn't see with the door blocking much of his view—the curl of fingers with neat, painted nails. The curve of a leg bent at an awkward angle. A heel resting on its side some feet away.

He saw the violence of it all.

"Who was she?" he asked. "And how long has she been here?"

"Her name is … was Miranda Abernathy. She was my … well …" He stumbled over his answer, clearing his throat again—a tell that was quite apparent.

As if Uilleam really had time to play word games. "Mistress?" he offered with an arch of his brow.

With one press of a gloved finger against the door, he sent it swinging wider, getting a better picture of the scene in front of him.

Early twenties, if he had to guess. Black hair that was slightly damp for whatever reason, eyes closed within a heart-shaped face.

A once beautiful girl.

The thought made him frown.

"Yes. Yes, she was my mistress, but I broke it off with her weeks ago. No one knew about her," he added on quickly, scrubbing a hand down his face. "Just my security, Phil."

And judging from the way that Phil had acted at the very sight of them, he hadn't opened his mouth to anyone about what had happened here. The sort of man who was loyal to a fault … even if that meant covering up a murder.

"My company is in the middle of a merger," Paxton went on in a frantic breath. "I can't afford for this to get in the way of that. Not right now."

Murder did have a tendency to end a business deal.

"So you're asking if I can get rid of this for you?"

"Your price, *any* price, just name it and it's yours."

There was always great business in desperate men.

Uilleam studied the body for another moment, wondering if he should have felt something more than casual interest. Repulsion, at the very least. Maybe even condemnation for the man who had so clearly committed the brutal act.

But he wasn't thinking of what was or what should have been.

He was facing the problem in front of him. All of it served his endgame.

He shifted his gaze from the woman to Paxton. "Let's begin."

Present Day ...

THERE WERE FEW LUXURIES MONEY COULDN'T AFFORD HIM.

Since he would be staying here in New York for quite a bit longer than he'd anticipated before arriving, that meant he needed to make his current accommodations suitable for his work.

It took no time at all to call down to the front desk with a list of his needs, and within the hour, two more flat-screen televisions were brought in and mounted to the walls opposite the one already present. Three brand new laptops came in unopened, as well as a number of burner cell phones should he have need for one.

As well as the treadmill he was currently running on.

And considering the sheer amount he was paying for not just the room itself, but the amenities it included, he didn't doubt he'd also have their discretion.

From the moment he had agreed to the job for Paxton—and given him his price (which had even made the billionaire blink in shock)—he'd been waiting.

For this very moment.

It might have been only ten in the morning—late considering how early he woke up everyday—but already, news of Paxton's lover's death was being broadcasted on every news station.

He should have been used to it by now, but it was always a little disconcerting knowing the intimate details of a person who was virtually still unknown by so many.

The details of their lives always played in the background of his mind when he watched these reports.

"Investigators have not determined how the mysterious woman fell to her death, but as of now, foul play has not been eliminated."

It would be by the end of the investigation.

Uilleam had seen to that.

What he did as a fixer wasn't a one-man job.

It involved various moving parts and a score of individuals who knew little more than the person who came before them.

And what had clearly looked like the murder it was a mere week days ago now looked like a suicide.

He would give it another day or two before news of her passing became a distant memory.

Before her tragedy became just one in a long line of them. Because that was the way the world worked.

Death came for everyone eventually.

The only thing Uilleam needed now was confirmation.

❧ 3 ❧

WHAT WASN'T SAID

Before moving to New York, Karina had always wondered how it was possible for the majority of the population not to own a car.

How did they get around at all hours of the night?

What happened when they needed to go grocery shopping?

She was used to the shops being farther away—where she could spend hours looking out the window at everything they passed whenever they ventured into the city—for it to be a *journey*. She hadn't realized just how close everything was—Manhattan, especially, wasn't as large as she had thought—or how she would become accustomed to taking the metro or a cab everywhere.

And with the way traffic was on most days, it always seemed faster to use public transportation.

Today, though, since she had time after the late lunch she had taken, she climbed into the back of a cab and let the sound of traffic be her background noise. She opened up the compact laptop she carried and went over everything she already knew—which was very little, she realized.

The reason she needed to make this visit to the police station to see whether she was seeing the ghosts of something that wasn't there, or if there was something to *really* pay attention to.

Earlier, she had shot off a text to a friend who helped her out with information that she couldn't get for herself.

This time, it had been a picture of the woman whose death she was looking into.

Twenty minutes later, a name was sitting in her messages.

She wasn't sure what program or software he used to find the information she needed, but she didn't ask either.

A name made it easier for her. Now whichever detective was assigned to the case wouldn't pretend as if they had no idea the victim she was talking about when she asked about the case.

Miranda Abernathy.

It was a ten-minute walk from the stoplight where she was dropped off to the 32nd Precinct.

The sidewalks weren't so crowded out here, making it much easier for her to walk without bumping into another person.

A flutter of anxiety always flitted through her whenever she passed a police station. Every time, she couldn't help but wonder if this was the day her secret was found out. Whether someone would run her license for whatever reason and find that under close scrutiny, it was fake.

And today, she was willingly going inside one.

The artist who had made her the fake license was one of the best, always making sure that it was as close to the real thing as possible.

So while she might not have enjoyed spending a time in police stations, today's visit was a must.

Though sometimes it didn't always pan out the way she wanted, she followed every case until the very end. And she would do the same for this one, even as there were already whispers that they believed it was a suicide.

Detective Bradon was the lead on her case, and an overall decent human being, though he had a tendency to be a bit blunt at times. She'd been trying to catch him for a couple of days now, but according to the receptionist she spoke with once a day, he was never there. Finally though, he was here at the precinct, taking a break from whatever had kept him away for so long.

Most people preferred to talk to his partner, but Karina had waited for him specifically.

He wasn't what one would call a "people person," but he was damn good at his job, so Karina was willing to put up with it.

Unlike Pinkerton though, she didn't have any favors she could call in with him. Instead, she had to hope he was in a sharing mood. Otherwise, she would be leaving here with nothing, and that wouldn't do.

She made it past the front desk with a flash of her press badge and a show of her license. The woman barely glanced at both before waving her on.

Bradon's desk was to the right of the bullpen. He sat in the short, uncomfortable looking swivel chair with his legs kicked up and a phone cradled between his ear and shoulder, oblivious to everything around him.

His expression remained neutral when she walked toward him as if he already knew why she was there and had prepared for it. The police were a close bunch, so she wouldn't be surprised if Pinkerton had given the man a heads-up.

Considering he wasn't shaking his head or sending her on her way just yet, it was as good a start as any.

Bradon's gaze cut to her a moment before he lifted a finger, silently telling her to wait. She didn't mind waiting for him to finish his phone call—it gave her a chance to glance over the documents on his desk.

In their attempt to prevent her from seeing one thing, people had a tendency to forget everything else.

Very carefully, she pulled her phone from her pocket, making sure the flash was turned off before she snapped a couple of pictures of his desk, figuring she would sort through it later.

"Yeah, all right. I'll call you back for an update later." He hung up the phone before moving to his feet and extending his hand. "Karina Ashworth, right?"

She shook his hand. "That's right."

"Pinkerton says you're one of the good ones."

Karina shrugged. "I do what I can."

He nodded before gesturing to one of the hardback chairs with a stained cushion. "What can I do for you?"

"I was looking for information on the case you're working. Victim's name is Miranda Abernathy."

Bradon shuffled through the folders on his desk until he found the one he was looking for. "This was the—this is off the record, right?"

They always remembered too soon. "Of course."

He blinked pointedly.

She pulled her phone out with a sigh, setting it and her tape recorder on his desk. "Off the record."

"Ran her prints through the system and got a hit for a DUI. Besides that, she was clean. Dumped her phone and found next of kin who came out to identify the body. Nothing else of value really."

He stated the facts as if he was reading from a textbook rather than the case folder of a woman who'd died in her twenties in his hands.

Blunt, Karina remembered. "Anything else?"

He shrugged as if the fact they *hadn't* found anything else was odd. "Hell, the only thing interesting about it is that it happened two weeks before Paxton's merger."

That was why she had remembered his name.

She'd caught it at the end of a news program one day after work, though she had only been half listening at the time. Now, it all came rushing back, filling in some of the blanks she had about William Paxton.

His company was merging with some other conglomerate in the city. A big deal in the tech world, she thought, though she didn't remember the particulars.

"Could be one of his competitors?" she blurted out, hoping to see whether he had considered the same.

"Don't know," Bradon said with a shrug. "Far's we can tell, it had nothing to do with no one."

"Then why was she there?" Karina asked, as much of a question to herself as it was to him.

"Why does anyone go anywhere when they ..." He waved his hand as if to encompass everything he had seen.

"Still personal," she said.

At the very least, whether something *had* happened to her or if she had done it herself, the building—or the man who owned it—had something to do with it.

"If that's all there is, I'll be on my way. Other cases."

Right.

His attention had to be split—hers didn't.

Bradon inclined his head as he stood, grabbing his suit jacket before striding away as if they had never talked.

Blunt, she remembered.

But she had gotten everything that she could possibly get at this stage. If there was anything left to find, Bradon wasn't the one she needed to get those answers from.

There was one last person she needed to pay a visit to.

MAKING HER WAY DOWN TO THE PRECINCT'S MORGUE WAS surprisingly easy considering she wasn't permitted to be down here, but she had always been rather good at moving without being noticed.

The temperature decreased drastically once she stepped off the elevator.

She wasn't a stranger to death, by any means. Beyond the man in the snow who'd died from a gunshot wound to the face, there had been her great-grandmother's funeral—though she hadn't had to actually *see* her since the casket had been closed. Even the funeral for the first man her mother had loved and lost.

No, she was quite familiar with death.

But that didn't make being down here in a hallway that seemed to smell of death any easier.

She still felt the same level of discomfort as she had otherwise. Like the way her stomach seemed to twist itself into knots.

She purposely averted her gaze from the clear windows that showed a wall of freezer drawers as well as an exam table that she didn't want to think about. The sooner she finished, the sooner she could leave.

Down the lengthy hallway, she scanned over the names on the doors until she found the one she was looking for. It was already cracked open, so that allowed her a chance to glance in at the man she had come down to see.

The same one who had been at the crime scene earlier.

He was tucked behind an old but tidy oak desk with a pair of thick oval frames perched on the end of his nose. Whatever he was reading formed a pinch of frustration between his brows and had him tapping his thumb against the papers.

"Mr. Paul?" she called with a sharp knock on his door. "I'm Karina Ashworth."

"Nice to meet you, Karina," he said politely, albeit hesitantly, his gaze skirting past her as if he expected someone to come in after her.

"I was hoping I could ask you a couple of questions," she said even as she helped herself to a vacant chair before he could tell her otherwise, "about Miranda Abernathy."

Any other coroner, she reasoned, would have at least appeared momentarily perplexed, or maybe might have taken a moment to look up the name, but Lincoln Paul did neither.

Instead, he cleared his throat rather harshly, training his gaze on her face without flinching.

The first tell of a lie.

Most assumed if a person refused to make eye contact, or if they appeared nervous in any way, that meant they were lying, but in Karina's experience, it had always been the ones who were most careful about the way they held themselves that weren't being entirely truthful.

He was concentrating too much.

"As you're probably aware," he said with a pointed nod at the lanyard around her neck, "I'm not permitted to discuss open cases. Especially with members of the press. If you would—"

He trailed off when she made no move to stand as if he'd fully expected her to leave on her own.

He was an older man with white hair clipped low on the sides and completely bald on top. Bombarding him with questions would only make him hunker down. She needed to be patient.

Because something was niggling at the back of her mind—something that reminded her too much of the last time she had been stumped on a story she was working.

Just like in that one, the details hadn't all made sense, and she had wondered if that had been done on purpose.

Whether there was someone out there who excelled at formulating misleading information.

"Miss Ashworth—"

"Karina, please. We're on the same side here, I promise," she said with an acquiescing nod. "We both want justice for the young woman who lost her life too soon … if it's warranted, of course."

It's always about applying just the right amount of pressure.

She could almost hear her mother's voice as those words flitted through her mind.

"Of course," he responded glibly. "It just happens that in this particular case, an autopsy wasn't—"

Distract him. "I'm sorry. I couldn't hear you very well," she said, making it a point to shift forward in her chair. "What were you saying about an autopsy?"

"There was no …" He cleared his throat, red suffusing his cheeks. "An autopsy wasn't needed."

"Is that common?"

"Sorry?"

She smiled. Still calm. Still pleasant. Playing the part. "Is it common practice for a medical examiner not to perform an autopsy on a woman who allegedly jumped from a building that she had no prior connection to when the building beside it was of a greater height?"

The question silenced him. His throat worked as he attempted to swallow, his gaze darting past her for the first time since she sat down.

"But perhaps that's for the detectives to determine. Have you made your final ruling?"

"I—"

"Has the case been closed?" she asked before he could answer.

"I-I don't … why are you asking?"

"If you've determined without any evidence that Miranda committed suicide, shouldn't the case be closed by now?"

She saw it then, like a light flickering on and off in his eyes.

That flicker that said he knew more than he was telling.

"Well, I haven't made a final decision."

"Why not?"

"I do have other cases, Miss Ashworth. The woman in question—"

"But you told me she committed suicide as soon as I said her name."

His mouth opened and closed as he stumbled for an answer. "I haven't had—"

"Or is there another reason you haven't made a final decision?" she inquired, her tone curious.

"I wouldn't know what you mean."

"No one has asked that you hold off, have they?"

The detectives might have if either of them thought something had happened to her and they didn't want a suicide ruling to jeopardize their investigation so early on, but that flash of guilt on his face was too strong for it to have been either of them.

"*Anyone?*" she stressed.

His face paled as he pulled at the collar of his shirt. "I think it's time you leave, Miss Ashworth. As I said, I can't discuss open cases."

"Thank you so much for your time," she said as she stood, having everything she needed. "This has been a very enlightening meeting."

More so than he might have realized.

"I haven't said anything," he said as he stood after her as though he wanted to stop her from leaving but wanting her gone as quickly as possible.

"You didn't," she agreed with a nod, "but what you didn't say was enough."

❧ 4 ❧
DECISIONS

SAMANTHA SAT BACK, FOLDING HER ARMS ACROSS HER CHEST AS she looked at her expectantly. "What's on your mind?"

Tossing her pen on the desk, Karina considered her next words carefully because even though she had been running through the possibilities in her head all afternoon, she still wasn't sure why she still felt so unsettled.

A feeling that had yet to go away even though it has been a couple of days since her visit to the medical examiner.

It was almost as if the answer was dangling right there in front of her, but no matter how she reached for it, she couldn't quite grasp what she was looking for.

She needed a new theory.

"They believe she was an escort. A high-end one, considering her clothes."

After a more thorough look at the police file, she'd learned that not only had the girl had expensive taste in lingerie, but she also liked to shop at a high-end boutique in Chelsea that specialized in cocktail dresses. One phone call and thirty minutes later, she had learned that this particular boutique was a favorite for one of Manhattan's elite madams.

The girl she had been speaking to, who'd spoken in a hushed but excited tone, had been all too keen to share what made their boutique interesting, though she hadn't known she was spilling the store's secrets to a journalist rather than a potential customer.

"I haven't gotten confirmation on that just yet, though," she continued, pulling the tie from her hair and running her fingers through the strands until the tension eased at her scalp. "But it would make sense all the same."

It wouldn't be the first time a dead escort showed up in the early hours of the morning. Par for the course, she imagined.

But it *was* the first time she was the one looking into it.

"Okay ... what makes her interesting to you?" she asked.

Sometimes, there was no story to tell—no elaborate puzzle that needed to be pieced together and solved. Sometimes, people just killed people for any number of reasons.

But this didn't feel like one of those times.

"Besides the fact that she was found outside William Paxton's office? At the very least, that's saying something, especially since there's no known connection between her and that building."

Everyone checked out, apparently.

From the maintenance workers to the men who made up the top offices, *everyone* was ridiculously squeaky clean.

Karina still wasn't buying it.

"So if we're going with the argument that she didn't commit suicide, though that hasn't been ruled out yet," she added pointedly, always willing to play the devil's advocate. "Why there? Why Paxton's building?"

"Could have been a competitor upset about the upcoming merger."

"That's a bit extreme, isn't it? I doubt corporate heads are murdering people just to mess up a merger."

Samantha shrugged. "That's where I'd look anyway."

Because it was the most probable choice.

If not the workings of someone in the building, it had to have been someone with a grudge against Paxton. Someone who wanted to hurt him badly enough to tarnish his reputation by proxy. In this particular business, bad press wasn't still good press.

Bad press could ruin a person, and with the news channels all reporting on the death, along with a bright clear image of Paxton's building, Paxton was getting a lot of it.

Or ... was that what it was meant to look like?

Was it *supposed* to look as if someone was framing Paxton?

And what were the odds, she wondered, that Paxton would find the body himself before anyone else?

There were groundskeepers. Security who monitored video footage. And just other people in general.

Anyone could have found her, yet he had.

Unless ... it had always been meant for him to find the body.

Because maybe Miranda had been more than an escort, she thought.

Maybe she was a message.

One that came from someone capable of manipulating appearances. Of paying off officials who had taken an oath.

Someone whose name she still didn't know ...

The thought hit her so suddenly, Karina dropped her chair back down to the ground, the jolt only making her heart beat faster.

"What?" Samantha asked, her brows shooting up. "What are you thinking?"

"Nothing," she said quickly. "Yet. I think I'll go talk to Miranda's mother and see if I can learn more about her."

"I don't know if this one is worth all the trouble," Samantha added with a slight shake of her head, turning back to her computer screen.

Fortunately, it didn't matter whether anyone else thought it was worth it for now.

Because she did.

And if she was right, this could be her chance to face the man without a name ...

MIRANDA'S MOTHER'S HOME WAS A MODEST, ALL BRICK AFFAIR, complete with a red painted door and a broken white picket fence.

Karina glanced down at the dangling clasp that should have held the gate closed before slipping past it and walking up the front steps to the door. She pressed her finger to the doorbell, hearing the soft chime echo inside before she heard the excited bark of what sounded like a *really* big dog.

Before the door even came open, she was smiling.

As a girl, she hadn't had the chance to have a pet. Though she had always promised her mother she would look after her companion without help from anyone, "animals in the house" was something Katherine wouldn't bend on.

And after moving out on her own, with all the time she spent working, there just hadn't been any reason when she wouldn't be able to take care of them properly.

Karina didn't have to wait long before she heard shuffling footsteps, then a lock coming undone, and as the wooden door creaked open, it revealed a woman with graying blond hair with a black Lab excitedly trying to get out.

"Macy, move over," the woman said in an exasperated tone that said she did this often.

But Macy merely tried to squeeze her way through with a toy bone in her mouth, looking up with eyes that said she had never been petted a day in her life.

"I'm sorry about her," Miranda's mother, Nicole, said apologetically. "She gets excited for guests."

"Oh, it's no problem at all," Karina replied, and while her attention should have been on her, she was too busy reaching to pat Macy's head to pay her very much attention.

Though she rubbed the top of her head and scratched a bit behind her ears, it didn't quell the heavy thump of her tail against the back of the door.

"Come on in."

Nicole stepped to the side, pulling on Macy's collar just enough to give Karina room to actually walk into the house.

While it was certainly small inside, no more than three bedrooms and one bathroom that she could see, she rather liked it all the same. It had a warm sort of feeling. *Inviting*.

Cozy, rather than cramped.

Hardwood floors drifted throughout the house, an area rug separating the living room from the dining. Pictures of Miranda over the years lined the mantel above the fireplace while trophies from various sporting events, and awards, lined the bookshelf opposite it.

"You can make yourself right at home. I'll grab some tea."

As Karina moved over to sit on one of the armchairs facing the couch, the woman disappeared into the kitchen, Macy dutifully trotting along behind her.

Not for the first time, Karina wondered about the life Miranda had led before she wound up in that field of poppies.

She wondered about the story rather than the tragedy.

She knew all too well how looks could be deceiving. That everything she was seeing now (a home of a girl who was well loved and appreciated), could just be a façade. This could have all been manufactured to make her think one thing, but when she thought of the woman who had greeted her at the door—her eyes a little sad, and her clothes a touch bigger as if she hadn't been eating properly—she couldn't help but think she wasn't that sort of person.

"Here we are," Nicole announced as she came back in the room carrying a tray.

Karina, having heard "tea," expected to see a teapot resting on the tray with a couple of mugs and saucers, but instead was greeted to the sight of a pitcher and tall glasses, each filled with an abundance of ice and a lemon slice in each.

Georgia, she remembered from Miranda's driver's license. She had been from Georgia.

Maybe understanding where her thoughts had gone, or perhaps she was just attempting to fill the silence, Nicole said, "We moved from the South five years ago when Miranda's father got offered a new position at the company he works for."

"New York must have seemed so different," Karina said, remembering the day she herself had stepped off the plane from Heathrow into the cool, busy JFK airport. It still felt like yesterday that she'd stared out the window of her taxi at the towering buildings and bustling streets wondering whether this was really her life.

"Felt like a completely different world," she answered wistfully.

Times, Karina could imagine, were certainly different back then.

As she picked up her glass, happily accepting the drink the woman poured, she said, "I just want to say thank you for meeting with me. I know this must be incredibly difficult."

Her daughter's face was plastered on dozens of newspapers, featured in numerous news reports, and she could only imagine where else, considering the way Miranda had died. And as it had unfortunately happened outside of William Paxton's building, that had only made it bigger news.

"It's ... well, it has ... yes," she finally settled on saying, her tone a little sad. "It's been very difficult. Sometimes I wake up and wish it were all a dream, but then I'll leave my room and look out the window, and there'll be a reporter standing out there. It always comes back to me then."

Her expression fell a little as she sat, holding her own glass between her hands. Her gaze was distant as she continued. "You're the only person who called her by her name. Fifty calls in three days and you were the *only* one who actually said her name. As if she were a person," she finished bitterly, "and not just a title on a screen."

Journalists could be relentless in their hunt for a story. And in their quest for notoriety, they could also forget what they were writing about in the first place.

People.

"That's why I'm here," Karina said. "I want to learn more about Miranda. What was she like?"

Nicole's gaze grew reminiscent. "She's always been such a sweet girl. Never gave her father or me any trouble."

She told her about their life in Georgia, the small town they had lived in before their big move. It sounded, at least to her, as if things had been different when they lived in the southern United States.

New York, Karina knew, was a different sort of animal.

She didn't dare interrupt as Nicole weaved her tale, telling her about the girl Miranda had been and comparing her to the woman she was at the time of her death.

One thing that also became abundantly clear over the course of their conversation was that Nicole didn't know what her daughter had done for a living when she was still alive. She didn't know about the websites or the dates, or even the expensive dresses and baubles she had earned over the years.

Karina wouldn't be the one to tell her.

And if it had been up to her, Miranda's occupation wouldn't have been mentioned at all. It wasn't important.

It didn't *matter* in the end.

At least not to her.

As far as Karina could see, it had nothing to do with the way she died.

"She was seeing someone," Nicole said after sipping her drink. "She never told me his name—she'd always been cagey about him—but she said she'd tell me everything soon ... a couple of days before she ..."

She trailed off. Karina didn't blame her.

"I'll do everything I can," she promised.

Karina wanted to stay longer and talk more, but the first article on the mysterious woman who was found dead outside of Paxton's building was due for publication. She still needed to go over it one last time before she submitted it.

Nicole caught her hand as she turned to leave, her expression falling a little. "I just want the truth," she said, tears flooding her eyes. "I just want to know what happened to my little girl."

The least she could do was try.

────────────

TIME SLIPPED BY WITHOUT HER NOTICING AS KARINA SAT CROSS-legged on her couch, her laptop resting on her thighs as she typed.

From the moment she'd made it back home after talking with Miranda's mother, she'd sat in this very spot and opened up a Word document, watching the blinking cursor a moment before she set in, her fingers flying over the keys.

The first lines were always the most difficult. Trying to find the right words to convey exactly what she wanted the reader to feel. To make sure they paid attention for longer than a few seconds.

She wasn't sure how long she had been working—something that tended to happen often when she was too absorbed in her work to pay attention to anything else—but as she blinked, coming back to reality for a moment, she realized the sun had long since gone down, and she could see the glint of moonlight reflecting off the glass coffee table in front of her.

A break wouldn't hurt.

But even as she wanted to stand and stretch her legs to get the blood running back through her limbs, she could still hear Nicole's voice in her head. The soft, wistful tone of it. A woman bogged down by grief, though she was making a valiant effort to keep up a good front.

Not for the first time that night, Karina wished she could do more. Or at least ease her pain in some way.

She might not have known what it was like to lose a child, but she *did* know loss. She knew how quickly it could suffocate you until it was the only thing you could think about.

She knew what it was like to want to make that pain go away by any means necessary and to want the person responsible to pay for what they did.

It was for *that* reason that, no matter how tired she was, or how she longed to take a break and just unwind for a moment, she couldn't rest just yet.

There was too much work to be done.

If he was responsible, I want him to pay, Nicole had said with all the conviction in the world. A mother balancing on the edge of her sanity. Wanting someone, *anyone*, to help her get justice for her family.

And as it stood, Karina was the only one willing to challenge the narrative. She was the only one willing to do the dirty work.

It was only a matter of being willing to accuse a powerful man of something horrendous, while another—one she still wasn't quite so sure existed or not—waited in the shadows.

Because there was too much that was *missing* for someone like Paxton to have done on his own if he was the one involved. And by the end of the day when her article was published, she *would* know whether he had played any part in this.

She welcomed the challenge and danger that came with it.

She didn't care.

She *had* to do this. Not for herself or because it would start a firestorm she wouldn't be able to put out right away.

But for Miranda and her mother.

Because Miranda's story deserved to be told.

5

COMPLICATIONS

"OUTSIDE MY *GODDAMN* BUILDING?" PAXTON DEMANDED THE moment Uilleam came into view, his already ruddy face taking on a deeper, more alarming shade of red as he slapped down the newspaper he was holding onto his desk. "What the hell was the point in hiring you?"

"If I thought you would understand the complexities of what I did, I would actually waste my breath and explain." It took a moment for him to realize Uilleam was insulting him, but before he could go on shouting about that, Uilleam carried on. "But if you're asking *why* your building, it was all by design, I assure you."

Paxton looked as if he wanted to argue further as though he wasn't ready to accept that explanation.

Uilleam was starting to find that he didn't particularly *like* Paxton … or his face. The more he saw him, the more *annoyed* he felt. It wasn't often that he judged a man by his appearance, but there was something about the man that made him want to duct tape his mouth shut just to see how he would respond

"What the hell kind of design is it? You're doing the opposite of what I hired you for!"

"How could that possibly be true if you're the last person the police are questioning?" he asked dryly.

That, at least momentarily, shut him up.

A *blessing.*

Though he had taken great joy at the thought of Paxton's reaction once he'd learned what he had done—and this hadn't disappointed—there also *had* been a method to his madness. The reality he had created had such an open ending, it would be easy to manipulate it however he saw fit.

"Then what the hell are you going to do about this!" he demanded, tossing the paper he was holding across the table.

He should be glad that it managed to slide to a stop at the edge of the table instead of hitting the floor because if it had, this meeting would have ended very differently.

Reluctantly, Uilleam leaned forward just far enough to grab the paper and unfold it, his gaze first taking in the name—*The Gazette Post.* Not the *New York Times* by any means, but it had a decent following—then to the article that had clearly aiding in putting Paxton in his mood.

The Gazette Post

MYSTERY WOMAN FALLS TO HER DEATH INTO A FIELD OF POPPIES. —KARINA A.

Early Monday morning, a woman in her early to mid-twenties
fell to her death from the roof of the Paxton building onto
a field of poppies more than fifty feet below. Police officials
are still investigating whether the woman committed
suicide, but sources closest to the investigation have not
ruled out foul play.
When asked about the cause of death, Police Commissioner
Mason offered no comment at this time.
Billionaire media mogul, William Paxton, was said not to
have been on the premises at the time of the woman's
death, but an inside source at the NYPD has alleged that
Paxton's company ID was used to access the rooftop where
the victim allegedly fell to her death.
More details to come as the case develops.

An update was printed below it with more details than the common reporter would—*should*—have had. Unlike the others, her update wasn't as straightforward. There was a hint of something else there. A mild suggestion that it might have been something more.

Uilleam was intrigued, to say the least.

He had been waiting for the inevitable questions.

Uilleam could feel William's eyes on him even before he set the paper aside and lifted his gaze from the article that had resulted in a panicked seven a.m. phone call and a meeting here at the Waldorf.

Had William not paid him seven figures to make his little problem go away, he might have ignored the call and gotten a few more hours of sleep, but he didn't have the luxury of ignoring phone calls from clients, not with what he was trying to accomplish.

For now, he had to play his part.

"I fail to see the problem."

"The *problem*," Paxton stressed, his eyes narrowed as he paced the spacious room in quick steps, "is that this ... this ... *reporter* shouldn't know any of this. What the hell am I paying you for?"

Though Uilleam looked calm, he wasn't nearly as composed on the inside. Not when he didn't have an answer to explain *how* the woman had gotten her hands on that information. Not only was it not public knowledge—though she had now made it so—it hadn't been listed in any official police reports.

He'd *checked*.

So just *how* had she found the information?

And why was he only just now learning about it ...

"I believe I specifically asked you if anything would tie you to Miranda's death. You denied any connection."

"Because I didn't think it would matter," Paxton replied shortly, throwing his hands up in the air as if it was Uilleam who was being unreasonable. "It was never supposed to get out."

That was always the problem with secrets. They always came to light one way or the other, no matter who kept them.

Uilleam knew that fact very well. He even appreciated it, considering that was at the very core of what he did.

"Mr. Paxton, I assure you, you needn't worry yourself about this. This reporter is probably one of those overzealous women who look for a story in everything. You've entrusted me to take care of this, so I have, and I will. I just need you to trust me. Can you do that?"

Paxton drained his glass of scotch, seeming to rein in his anger. Now, he just looked apprehensive.

"Of course," he said, though his expression contradicted those words.

Uilleam did his best to actually care though it was a feeble attempt.

"If we're finished here," he said pointedly as he moved to stand, "there's work to be done."

In the span of time it took for Uilleam to get to his feet, Paxton seemed to recall he was the buyer and Uilleam the one agreeing to a service.

He set his drink aside, his chin going up a fraction as if Uilleam was beneath him. Years of living with a tyrant made him immune to the lofty treatment, but that didn't mean it made it any easier for him to curb his natural reaction and show the man just who he was fucking with.

"Don't forget who's paying you, Runehart. If you fail, I'll make sure no one remembers your goddamn *name*."

"FAR BE IT FOR ME TO STATE THE OBVIOUS, BUT YOU CAN'T KILL your clients."

As he donned a pair of opaque sunglasses, Uilleam cast a scowl in his Skorpion's direction. "Says who?"

Of all the men who he had come to work with over the past three years, Keanu Hamari—Skorpion, to most—had not only lasted the longest, but he was also far less annoying than the previous men who had held his position.

Beyond the skills he possessed, Skorpion *looked* like a threat, all six and a half feet of him plus the solid two hundred pounds of muscle he had to weigh. Uilleam wasn't a small man by any stretch of the imagination, but Skorpion could make anyone seem tiny in comparison.

"Perhaps if he wasn't being a cunt, I wouldn't be considering it,"

Uilleam replied as he slipped into the back of the truck, his mood only darkening further after his meeting with Paxton.

"Cunt or not, you still have a job to do."

Perhaps this was also why he kept Skorpion around, though he'd never admit as much out loud. He tended to be the voice of reason when Uilleam was being unreasonable.

"The better question is, what are you going to do about that article?"

The million dollar question.

Though he had only been in the business of fixing others' problems and concealing their dirty little secrets for a couple of years now, he had never run into a problem quite like this one before. He'd expected this job to be over and done with by now.

He'd covered all the bases.

Ensured the woman's death looked like a suicide.

Destroyed evidence to the contrary and made sure nothing could be linked back to his client.

He'd even gone as far as erasing any digital evidence of Paxton's involvement with the woman off multiple servers, which hadn't come cheap.

Yet this *journalist* who he had never even heard of had managed to find the one piece of evidence he'd overlooked.

Uilleam might have been impressed if he hadn't needed this job to go as smoothly as possible.

"I need everything there is to know about this *Karina*," he said, recalling the woman's name.

Starting with her last name.

ENTERING THE PENTHOUSE APARTMENT ON FIFTH AVENUE, Uilleam shed his suit jacket and tossed it aside as he went in search of the bar cart. It didn't matter that it wasn't even ten in the morning yet—he was in desperate need of a drink.

Something strong that would calm the storm brewing inside him and help him center his thoughts so he could focus on what had caused him to make a mistake.

Uilleam never made mistakes.

It was, by far, one of his more admirable traits.

It had never been trial and error with him—no learning from past digressions. He learned from the mistakes of others.

He remembered his father's unforgiving hand—the way his brother had suffered for the slightest of offenses. He learned to do better—*be* better. He shaped his reality into what others needed it to be.

And the more years he spent perfecting his trade, the better he got at not committing a single misstep.

Until now.

Grabbing a glass, he poured a fifth of whiskey, then sipped it slowly as he forced himself to cross the room to the sitting area where the day's paper was already waiting for him. The staff who delivered it couldn't have known he had already seen it and read it nearly cover to cover, but that didn't make him any less annoyed that it was sitting there.

Taunting him.

He couldn't help himself.

He snatched the newspaper off the table and unfolded it, his gaze scanning over the front page.

The Gazette Post didn't have the same prestige as the *New York Times* by any stretch of the imagination. Not even close.

Yet the story they had printed was already gaining so much traction that it had been delivered alongside the others he had actually requested.

Uilleam had only been sitting for a short time when the elevator chimed and the doors slid open, heavy boots on the floor announcing Skorpion's presence as he came around the corner.

Considering this hotel ran for five thousand dollars a night, one would think the man would take pride in his appearance, but the day he convinced his security to wear a suit would be the day he was lowered into the ground.

For the time being, he was in black jeans, a silver chain looped from front to back, and an AC/DC T-shirt that was probably every bit as old as the band. His dark, wavy hair hung in disarray past his shoulders, and if not for the sheer size of him, no one would ever think the two of them were connected.

Or that Skorpion was capable of things that would make any one of his enemies sleep with one eye open.

"What have you found?"

"Not much to find," he answered, eyeing the glass in Uilleam's hand before he collapsed onto a chair and stretched his legs out. "She's a junior reporter. Fluff pieces, mostly. A few others that were actually noteworthy."

"And those were?"

Skorpion handed over a number of photocopied articles, allowing Uilleam to read for himself. "A doctor facing malpractice. A partner over at Donelley, Smith, & Associates during an ugly custody battle where there was rumored domestic abuse. Oh, and the financial analyst who had a thing for hookers and chat rooms."

"Crimes against women," Uilleam said absently, only marginally focused on what Skorpion was saying.

The first article on the doctor was very much like the one Karina had written on his client. A simple statement of the facts with a touch of insider information she shouldn't have had. And he realized, as he read over it for a second time, it wasn't just an interesting article.

It also piqued his curiosity, making *him* want to look into the man more.

Which was how he found himself sitting there in silence as he read each one, familiarizing himself with the details long before he turned on his laptop and searched for her.

Not *her*, rather, but the men she had been looking into. He learned the truth about what they had done, including the doctor whose malpractice involved sexual harassment of his co-workers and a sexual assault that resulted in the loss of not just his job but his freedom as well.

The defense attorney had tried to use his position and authority to bully his wife into not only a divorce but also a custody agreement of his choosing.

These articles all involved powerful men who used their authority to take what they wanted without consequence.

Did she intend to be the voice of the voiceless?

It would explain her sudden interest in this particular case, considering he had made sure nothing about the woman's death could be traced back to his client.

Or, at least, he thought he had.

Except now she had found something, and it didn't matter that she was a lowly journalist. It only took the smallest ripple in the water to disrupt the current.

And most surprising of all was an article that hadn't gotten as much traction, but one he knew the intimate details of because *he'd* been the reason for it.

Several months ago, a new client had come to him asking to make a deal. In her article, she wrote about a woman who had died from ingesting the poison belladonna, but there had been no evidence as to how she had gotten her hands on it.

By Uilleam's design.

And now, she was looking into this ...

He needed to end this before it could go any further.

"Go back further," he said, finally dragging his attention away from the screen to focus on Skorpion again. "I wanted six months, but now give me everything there is on Karina Ashworth from the moment she was born."

He nodded once. "Will do."

His mobile rang loudly, the obnoxious sound cutting out once Skorpion answered and put the phone to his ear. "Yeah?"

He listened for a moment before passing the phone over, and while the last thing he was in the mood for right now was to speak to anyone, Uilleam took it.

"How can I be of assistance?"

"You said no one would find *out*!" a voice hissed on the other line.

Uilleam took a moment to place it before his tone reflected the way he felt at being interrupted. "I can't say I understand what you mean, Mr Paul."

"A woman—a *reporter*—stopped by and was asking me about the girl."

His fingers flexed around the electronic device in his hand that felt all too breakable at the moment. "And?"

"I didn't tell her anything," he rushed to say as if he was only just now realizing who he had called. "But I don't think she's done."

No, Uilleam suspected she wasn't.

6

CEASE & DESIST

"WE SHOULD GO OUT," SAMANTHA SAID WITH A SIGH, DROPPING down into her chair without spilling any of the steaming coffee in her mug.

Karina was thankful for the interruption because she had spent the past twenty minutes staring at a computer screen without getting any new information she didn't already have. Some days, she was sure she was on to something—that her search for the truth wouldn't be in vain, but then there were other days like today when she just wasn't sure.

It didn't matter that she had already managed to have two articles printed about Miranda. She still didn't feel as if she had done enough.

"I haven't done anything but work since I was given the Landers story," Samantha continued with a sigh before taking a sip of her coffee. "Which means a day off has been earned."

"What do you mean?" Karina asked with a laugh. "We had dinner last week."

Samantha rolled her eyes. "Yeah, after *work*. We haven't actually *done* anything, though. Let's go to a club or something. You know, *drinks*."

"I'm not much of a drinker," she answered absently, though even she wasn't quite so sure that was true.

Considering what little time she spent outside of work usually involved takeout, her couch, and whatever was playing on TV, Karina didn't *do* very much else, but this was what she knew. Her life had always been sheltered.

After boarding schools, etiquette classes, and learning from her mother, she hadn't had time to discover what else she might have liked outside of those things. The life Samantha was talking about, where she went out for drinks, to clubs, or parties in general, seemed like an entirely different world.

"Sometimes, Karina, it feels like you're twenty-one going on fifty. You have to get out more."

She thought of laughing the remark off or making up an excuse for why she couldn't—her mother would have expected her to since her attention and focus should have been on one thing only—but when she opened her mouth, ready to do just that, the opposite came out.

"All right, fine. Where do you want to go?"

Samantha prattled on about a club's grand opening that was coming up, one that would give Karina plenty of time to make sure she was able to attend without backing out, but while they were discussing what time they'd meet and where, the elevator chimed its arrival. When the doors slid open, four men in impeccable suits walked out, heading straight for Camilla's office.

She wished she could pretend she didn't notice, but from the second they arrived, barely passing the lot of them a glance, they were the only thing she could focus on.

"It'll be great," Samantha went on, oblivious to Karina's lack of focus.

"Yeah, I think—"

"Karina!"

They both turned at the sound of Camilla's voice, but unlike the last time, there was no question that Camilla wasn't pleased with her. And considering the men waiting in her office, it was worse than she was thought.

Even as she tried to trace back something she might have done—

because they couldn't have possibly found a connection between her and her family—Karina walked over, trying not to show the nerves she felt.

Being anxious wouldn't help her.

She needed to keep a level head.

The door to Camilla's office had barely closed behind them before she was speaking.

"Karina, these gentlemen are—"

"Lester Holt and Arnold Torrence from Holt, Gomer, and Torrence."

"The law firm?" she asked, keeping her expression neutral though she found it amusing that the men looked surprised she would know who they were.

While she didn't make it a point to know all the defense attorneys in the city, there was a file on this particular firm back at Ashworth Hall that she'd perused once or twice. She didn't know what their angle was, exactly, or why Katherine had kept a file on them, but it came in handy now.

Holt spoke again. "We represent William Paxton."

She knew what they were about to say before the words even left their mouth.

And as they spoke, she hardly heard a word they said, even as she watched their lips move. Pressing her thumbnail into the palm of her hand, it was all she could do not to react to the condescending tones and patronizing stares.

Oh, how badly she wanted to tell them all that she could ruin them, and maybe in the future she would. She wanted to be there the day those smirks were wiped off their faces. When everything they held near and dear was taken away without care or remorse.

She wouldn't forget.

Not ever.

"Should any other slanderous article bearing our client's name be published, we *will* sue for defamation and damages. Is that understood?"

The room finally fell silent as all eyes turned to Karina.

It took every last bit of her to nod even once.

Satisfied with her compliance, the men turned and left just as quickly as they had come in, though not a single one offered a farewell.

It was only once she saw them board the elevator that she spoke. "They don't—"

"Karina."

"But—"

"*Listen* to me," Camilla said in a tone that brokered no further argument. "Leave it alone. If you continue to pursue this, they will ruin you. I've seen others lose their livelihoods for less. Do yourself a favor, okay? Let this one go."

If this were anything else, she might have been able to walk away and leave it as it were. If she had never *known* about the woman or done any research into Paxton himself, she might have been able to cast it from her mind entirely.

But as she stood there, even nodding her assent, Karina wasn't done.

Not by a long shot.

Walk away.

The words resonated in her head even after Karina arrived home. They echoed in the chambers of her mind until they looped.

It wasn't until she walked out of her office building entirely that she remembered she shouldn't be upset about what had happened at all.

Because William Paxton had shown his hand.

To anyone else, her articles might have just been something to gloss over before moving on to something more interesting—especially since more than a week had passed—yet he had sent his lawyers all the same.

Guilty men couldn't ignore even an implication.

She had known the risks when she wrote the article, but she also knew the rewards.

The rage she had felt at the way the lawyers had spoken to her churned back to life as she entered her apartment and slammed the door. She barely glanced at where she tossed her purse before heading into the kitchen for one of her favorite long-stemmed wine glasses and the special bottle of rosé she kept in the refrigerator.

For now, this anger was her friend.

It was the only emotion she allowed herself to feel as she grabbed her laptop to start working again.

Somewhere, among the many threads of Miranda's death and Paxton's life, she would find the knot that tied them together.

BEFORE THE EARLY MORNING RAYS STREAKED ACROSS THE BRIGHT blue sky, Karina was already up and showered, padding through her apartment in a towel with her wet hair tied up out of her face.

Thankfully, she had gotten too lost in the work she was doing last night to drink more than one glass of wine, which meant she hadn't woken up with a headache.

It also meant that the breakfast meeting she had set up in the wee hours of the morning didn't seem quite so awful.

Besides, the quiet of the early hours was helping her think.

Yesterday, she had been too surprised by the sight of the attorneys to speak properly. If she had, she would have asked them why they were there, considering she hadn't written on their client in days.

She would have also asked why they didn't actually represent the Paxton company as a whole, rather just the man himself. And curiously enough, his head of security. The firm had only just been hired within twenty-four hours of her meeting them.

That tidbit of information had come as another result from her late-night phone call to a man she had promised to only call for emergencies. It wasn't safe, she imagined, to willingly give information about the people he worked with to journalists, but as long as she was careful about what she did with what he told her, he didn't mind divulging.

And last night when she had called, he had promised to tell her everything she wanted to know over breakfast.

The diner where she arrived at as the clock struck nine was small, located in the heart of Brooklyn between a dry cleaners and a check cashing place. It had that old-school appeal despite its surroundings—chrome detailing, neon lights that came to life at night, and the aroma of pancakes wafting out every time the front door opened and shut.

Karina slid the light scarf from around her neck as she stepped inside. The tiny bell above the door jingled softly, as the woman behind the counter greeted her warmly.

The scent of breakfast made her mouth water, but even as she thought about what she intended to order—deciding to forget all about the diet she hadn't been sticking to anyway—her gaze traveled over the warmly lit interior of the diner and found the man she was looking for.

He was hard to miss with all that dark hair and the deep auburn of his beard.

He was known by many different aliases, most of which she still wasn't sure of. But from the very beginning, she had only ever known him by one name.

Orion.

With a lean build and standing an entire foot taller than her, he was unmistakable even seated, but he also had the sort of pleasant symmetrical features that made it surprisingly easy to blend into crowds when he didn't want to be seen.

Before she'd entered, Karina had thought he was the one she saw stretched out across one of the benches that lined the front of the diner, but the steam billowing up from the sewer drain outside had prevented her from seeing him clearly.

A smile curled the edges of his mouth as she walked over and joined him, his gray eyes flickering down the length of her body as she sat.

"Been a while since you had to call on me, hasn't it?" he asked in that lazy way of his, his tone mild but curious. "I was starting to think you didn't care about me."

One other thing about Orion—something most people would learn within minutes of meeting him—he was a notorious flirt and didn't care very much who he offered his affections to. It was just the way he was.

She didn't mind it so much, though she had never taken him up on the offer that had never been explicitly spoken. "Work's kept me busy," she said, resting her hands on the laminate-topped table between them. "You know how that goes."

"No sleep for you ever, is there?"

A question he had been asking since the day they met behind a bowling alley in Hell's Kitchen. She'd been in the middle of researching a case, and he'd been taking bets for a man whose name she still didn't know. The meeting happened completely by chance, but the ones that followed weren't coincidental by any means.

"Not when there are bad people out there."

"Fair enough. I took the liberty of ordering for you," he said as a waitress walked over with four steaming plates.

One, in particular, was stacked high with pancakes, a pat of butter melting down the sides.

Orion knew her well.

"Enjoy," the woman called over her shoulder before leaving them alone again.

"So who's the unlucky bastard that wound up on the wrong end of your pen?"

"You've heard about the woman who was found outside William Paxton's office building, right?"

"Of course," he said cutting into a sausage link. "Who hasn't?"

"That's what I've been looking into."

She shared her suspicions about Paxton possibly being involved in Miranda's death as well as the visit from the lawyers. When she got to them, he paused in his chewing, his expression growing terribly serious before smoothing away once she told him they had left right after.

"Sounds like he's worth looking into at the least," Orion said with a shrug. "What do you need me for?"

"I had a thought, and I know it's going to sound crazy but hear me out."

"Hit me."

"Have you ever heard of someone who … *fixes* a situation. Like they make one thing look like something else."

Orion froze for about a millisecond before he resumed eating as if she hadn't noticed him hesitate.

But when she did, she leaned in closer to him. "Probably charges a lot of money if I'm right about what they do. Discreet, I would think." Considering the length of time that had passed between the first story she had she stumbled on and this one.

But perhaps these were the only two where she had actually *noticed* something. There could be more. Many more.

Orion made a low sound in the back of his throat, though he had yet to speak a word.

He didn't seem to realize that was as telling as an actual answer. "Maybe you've heard of him? *Her*?"

"Why're you asking about him?"

So it *was* a him. "What can you tell me about him?"

"Negative. Answer my question first."

"I think, whoever he is, might be involved in this."

"What makes you think that?"

If she had an answer to *that* question, she wouldn't have felt the need to sit in front of him now. She didn't know *why* she thought it. It wasn't nearly as simple as it she made it sound, but she just did.

"It's hard to explain," she settled on saying, knowing that answer wouldn't be good enough, but before he could say as much, she continued. "But I wouldn't be asking if I didn't think it was important, I promise."

He scoffed, calling her bluff. "You'd ask just for your own curiosity, and we both know that."

Yes, they certainly did. "Spill."

Orion might have lived his life as an outlaw and had a number of questionable traits, but he also had a tendency to treat her with kid gloves. He called it *looking out for her best interests even when she wasn't*, but she called it a bit overprotective, considering what they both did for a living.

"Is there a reason you don't want to talk about him?"

"Because you need to stay the fuck away from that one."

"Because he's a killer?" she asked, remembering the last time she had come to him for a similar reason, and that had been his answer.

"Killers are a dime a dozen," he said with an absent wave of his hand—a gesture that made sense, considering *he* was one too, though he had never admitted as much to her. "He's something … else."

"I don't understand."

"Death is quick. Finite. There's only momentary glory when you take the life of a man who's crossed you. Uilleam ... he doesn't kill, he *ruins*. He'll take everything you hold close and turn it to ash. He'll make you wish you had never uttered his name."

Despite herself, Karina felt a chill slide down her spine.

Seeing Orion's reaction and how uncomfortable he seemed even mentioning this *Uilleam* gave her pause. There was a new set of nerves springing to life, but she wouldn't say she was *nervous*.

Cautious, more like.

"Then it's true?" she asked, her voice softer now. "He can make problems disappear."

"Listen, babe," he said, placing his knife and fork on his nearly finished plate. "If you've got a situation, let me take care of that. Stay away from him."

"It's not for me." None of this was about *her*.

He looked resigned. "You really think the two are involved?"

"It's certainly possible."

"Jesus, you're turning into a pain in my ass."

"If it makes you feel better, I'm not after Uilleam—is that what you said his name was." *Yet.* "I'm merely trying to figure out how deep this goes."

"Why do you think there's a connection anyway? I thought the girl jumped."

She told him about her meeting with the medical examiner and how fidgety the man was acting, then she finished with the meeting with the attorneys and how she had practically been banned from ever mentioning the Paxton name.

Orion still didn't look convinced, but he nodded all the same. "I'll see what I can find, but you've gotta do something for me."

"Name it."

"Stay away from Uilleam, yeah? I don't want you to have *that* sort of problem."

She smiled. "You won't have to worry about that."

Not because she didn't intend to continue forward to get close to him.

She just had no intentions of lying about it.

7

THE STUPIDITY OF MAN

UILLEAM TRIED TO REMIND HIMSELF THAT NOT ALL MEN WERE AS inherently idiotic as Paxton was proving to be. Because the fact he had made it to the top position of CEO at all was a hard concept to believe considering what he had done.

"Let me see if I understand," Uilleam said, rubbing at the migraine starting to throb behind his eyes, already thinking of how best he could spin this if there was a need. And if the woman who had managed to rattle the man was anything like he thought, she wouldn't be particularly quiet about this. "Your reason for sending lawyers to that paper was …?"

The worst part about it all was the look of smug defiance on the man's face. As if he saw no flaw in his logic, and while it might have infuriated Uilleam a few years ago—when he'd been more prone to losing his temper—now he just wondered how it was possible to be that incredibly dense.

"You apparently won't take my suggestion to just get rid of her," Paxton stated as if all the blame should be on him, "so I made sure she can't print anything else about me."

"And what—" Uilleam caught himself before that flare of anger could turn into something else—like his burning this building to the ground and not giving a fuck who it harmed in the process. "And

60

what, exactly, was wrong with what was written? She made no accusations."

"Then apparently we weren't reading the same articles because she all but accused me of *murder*."

"All but," Uilleam said with a glare at the man.

Maybe it was Uilleam's tone of his voice—he couldn't keep all the ire out despite how much he tried—but Paxton finally caught on that they weren't on the same side on this. That Uilleam hadn't come to congratulate him on anything.

"What?"

"You said she 'all but' accused you of murder. That's an important distinction. If someone were to call me a murderer," Uilleam said slowly, even as the man's face turned an interesting shade of crimson, "though factual, they would have no evidence to support the claim. So why would I care? That journalist dangled a bit of bait, and like a guilty man, you took it without considering the consequences of your actions."

"And what consequences would those be?" Paxton asked, sounding nearly as irate as Uilleam felt. "I was within my rights."

"If she didn't think you were guilty before, she definitely does now."

There was no doubt in his mind that the journalist was already working on something else—something he wouldn't be able to refute as quickly.

Yet the thought wasn't necessarily an unwelcome one.

"Then *what* would you have had me do?" Paxton exclaimed, throwing his hands up in the air.

The diplomatic thing to say would have been to, 'Focus on the merger,' or even, 'Let me handle this,' but instead, the first thing out of Uilleam's mouth was, "Sit down and shut up."

"You can't fucking speak to me like that."

One of his paid help stirred in the corner, but only for so long as it took him to remember Uilleam hadn't entered this room alone. It only took a glance at Skorpion to remind him that a fight of any sort was not what he wanted.

"Would you rather I coddle you? If I wanted to deal with children, I'd have one of my own."

"Gaspard said—"

"If you would prefer to spend the next ten to fifteen years in prison, then, by all means, regale me with what *Gaspard said*."

Paxton made it far too much fun to get under his skin, but Uilleam's continued presence here was anything but laughable. If he wasn't careful, Paxton's irresponsibility could blow back on him. Not that someone would suspect his involvement, but rather that all his hard work was in jeopardy.

He hadn't spent the past three years building his empire to watch it crumble because of a man like *him*.

His business was his name.

And the moment anyone thought he wasn't capable of doing his job was when he would lose everything.

"I think you're forgetting something here," Paxton said walking around his desk, getting as close as he possibly could before Skorpion cleared his throat—a silent warning that if he took another step, he would regret it. "Without me—"

"*Careful,*" Uilleam said, the only warning he would ever give.

"Without *me*," Paxton continued recklessly, "you'll get *nothing*. Gaspard wouldn't look your way twice if I hadn't called on him."

That's where he was wrong, but Uilleam didn't bother to correct him. He let the man believe what he wanted even though he knew the truth.

That Paxton was an audition of sorts.

One that would determine how Uilleam would end this year.

No, he didn't say a word, merely smiled at the man as he came to a decision in his head.

Paxton's first strike had been their first meeting together after he'd accepted the job. Par for the course, he had suspected he wouldn't get along with the man simply because of the way he'd summoned him—leveraging his business relationship with a man to try to manipulate him.

This was his second.

Uilleam doubted very much he would get a third.

8

FIRST ENCOUNTERS

THE QUIET HUM OF HER PHONE MADE KARINA GROAN AS SHE woke slowly, the pillow resting over her face blocking out much of the noise, but as much as she wanted to ignore the call and drift back off to sleep, it was the second time it had rang in as many minutes, and she knew the caller wouldn't be giving up anytime soon. After a moment of silent contemplation, she blindly reached out, shifting keys, a glass of water, and other bits on her dresser until she finally grasped the phone and connected the call.

"Hello?"

"Is this what you sound like when you fuck because if it is, I'll try a little harder to get you in my bed."

Grumbling out a curse, she considered whether it would be in her best interest to end the call now before Orion could annoy her any further. "What do you *want* at" — she squinted as she pulled her phone away to glance at the too bright screen — "four in the damn morning?"

"Doing what I said I wouldn't."

"Leave me in peace to sleep?"

"Help you get close to Uilleam Runehart," he replied dryly.

The name instantly sent adrenaline racing through her, and any chance of falling back asleep went right out the window as she sat up and shoved the tangled strands of her hair back out of her face. "*How?*"

"Seems I've got your attention now."

She rolled her eyes, not caring that he wouldn't be able to see it. "You knew you would. Now answer my question."

Maybe it was urgency in her voice or his own fascination with the man, but he stopped joking around. "Calm down. It's not going to be what you think."

Whatever it was, it wouldn't matter if he could do what he was suggesting. "What did you do, Orion?"

"There's a dinner in a couple of weeks–a fundraiser for whoever the fuck. Anyway, the guest list is full of your usual deep pockets, but they also invited a few people who I know for sure have been on Uilleam's client list a time or two and a few more trying to make their way onto it. If they're going to be there, I figure he will be too."

Two weeks.

She didn't doubt that what Orion told her was the truth. She knew him well enough to know that he wouldn't joke about something like this. Especially something he knew was important to her.

He didn't waste time with lies and misdirection.

"Invitations are going to be impossible," she muttered out loud, already considering the possibilities and the number of favors she would need to call in.

And even that was a long shot.

"Why do you think I'm calling, babe?"

She smiled, even before she meant to. "Should I even ask how you managed this?"

"Friend of a friend of an enemy. Small circles, ya know."

Sometimes, it felt that way, but she was often reminded that while everyone seemed to know the next criminal, no one knew everyone. She was counting on that.

"So I've got an invitation and need a plus one. Know anyone available for me?"

Now was her chance. "Pick me up at seven."

SHE MIGHT HAVE BEEN QUICK TO AGREE TO ATTEND THE DINNER, but the event had quickly slipped Karina's mind as she continued working and doing everything she could to further her investigation into Paxton.

Between trying to get back into the good graces of her boss—who was slowly coming around and giving her less grunt work—she wasn't at all prepared for a night out with people who would be dressed as if they were walking a red carpet.

Her wardrobe consisted mainly of jeans and blouses, even a few blazers here and there—nothing at all that would be appropriate for a night like this.

At first, she considered wearing the little black dress that hung in her closet ever since the paper's 4th of July party, but after reviewing the guest list Orion had texted her a picture of, she knew the simple outfit would make her stand out in a bad way.

And while she might have been living in NYC for nearly a year, she still wasn't at all familiar with the numerous boutiques. But, she did know *one* person she could call, and while they were currently busy in Berlin, she knew they knew the city like the back of their hand.

"As happy as I am to hear from you, you do realize it's creeping up on midnight here," Isla said, her voice carrying only the slightest traces of sleep.

It didn't matter that it was late where she was in the world, or that she probably had endless things to do the next day—because she always stayed busy—there was never a time when Karina called that she didn't answer the phone.

"I have a problem you can help me with," Karina said, smiling as she listened to her sister's voice.

This wasn't the first time they had gone more than a couple of months without speaking, caught up in their own lives, but just as she had before, that feeling of homesickness weighed heavy on her.

Isla, if no one, else was what she missed most about being home.

The pale pink cherry blossom trees that bloomed so prettily in the spring were a distant second.

"Anything for you," came her quick reply.

As she had expected it to be. "I need a dress. Something formal, but easy-going. Nothing too ostentatious, but enough that the right person would notice."

One person in particular, but she didn't bother to mention that to Isla.

It wasn't quite time for that yet.

"What's the occasion?"

"It's a fundraiser dinner."

Isla made a humming sound in the back of her throat. "The city's elite, I imagine."

"From the more popular families, yes."

The ones with more money than they could ever spend in a lifetime.

And after doing a little research, they were also some of the ones who liked to dip their toes in illegal activities, though it had yet to be proven.

"Go to Shauney's on 15th and tell Donna I sent you. She'll make sure you're taken care of."

"Thank you."

"Of course." She paused for a moment. "When was the last time you talked to Mother?"

Karina grimaced as she stepped up to the edge of the sidewalk, raising her hand to flag down a cab. This was the one question she'd been attempting to avoid. "Not recently."

"Karina." She managed to sound both admonishing and amused. "You know she requires check-ins … or would you just prefer she show her face? She's not above that, you know."

Unfortunately, she *did* know. and while she hoped the latter wouldn't happen, she still wasn't ready to take her phone call.

"Couldn't you stall her for a bit?" Karina asked, breathing out a sigh as a taxi quickly switched lanes and pulled to the side for her. "I'm working on … something, and —"

"Something interesting?" Isla asked, sounding more awake now.

Karina slipped into the back of the cab, quickly giving the address to the man behind the wheel, but as she readied to explain everything that had happened over the past few weeks — months, really, considering how long she had been looking for Uilleam, though she hadn't known it at the time — nothing came out. The mystery behind him had been such a well-kept secret of hers that she didn't even work on what little she could gather about him until the wee hours of the morning though there was never anyone around to see what she was doing.

He was also a man who she didn't enjoy the thought of sharing with anyone just yet. It had become imperative for Orion to know, considering she had needed his aid directly, but she couldn't imagine sharing anything with anyone else.

Not until she had more.

This was something she needed to sort through herself.

"Not your sort of interesting, Iz," she said quickly, hoping she wouldn't push further. "Just a few bits at work."

"Careful," Isla said oddly. "Your accent slipped a bit there."

Karina played back her words in her mind, thinking of what she'd said and realized the mistake she'd made. Anyone else might not have noticed her misstep, or at the very least, they would have thought she was watching a lot of BBC America television shows — which was accurate, all the same — but only Isla would pick up on something so minuscule.

It was what she was taught to do.

Both of them, really, though Isla had always been better at this sort of thing.

From the moment she had arrived in New York and began a new life where no one knew her name or where she had come from, she had quickly adopted the accent around her.

She blended in.

It made starting a routine and slipping into everyday life rather easy, considering no one would ask about the accent she hid or why she had moved to the States at all.

That would undoubtedly be the first question, and while innocent in nature, it was quite easily the most complicated one of all.

"It's because I'm talking to you," Karina reminded her, staring out at the city around her as she ventured farther into the city. "And honestly, Iz, it's been a year. You don't expect me to lose it completely, do you?"

"You'd do well to, but that's neither here nor there. The one you're using now works just as fine."

A noise sounded in the background, then a hushed, highly masculine voice spoke, and Isla murmured her reply. Karina didn't interrupt, not when she didn't know who Isla was in the room with.

It might have been a boyfriend that she didn't know about ... or a leader of a foreign government.

There was no telling with her.

While she waited for her return, Karina paid the cabbie before climbing out and crossing the street toward the boutique with the minimalist sign hanging above the doors.

"Sorry," Isla said, returning to their conversation. "What were you saying?"

"You were lecturing me about my use of a noun."

"I wouldn't have to lecture you if you actually followed Mother's rules instead of trying to rebel against them. The constant battle must be tedious by now."

Karina thought of responding and telling her that it wasn't necessarily the rules she was refusing to live by—rules Isla followed nearly to a fault. It wasn't tedious either, constantly seeing the differences between her and her family.

While Mother worked steadily toward her goal of becoming a formidable opponent against men in her field, with Isla quickly following on her heels, Karina was content *not* to be a part of the family business.

It wasn't that she couldn't do it, or even that she didn't find the work interesting, but she didn't feel the same calling to it as they did.

A conundrum, considering what she did for a living.

But it was one thing to learn all the bad things people did for the sake of money or power. It was something else entirely when she was the one actively participating.

For now, however, it wasn't something she needed to think about.

"As much as I'd love to get into a discussion about that, I'm already running late."

Not to mention, she still needed to get home, shower, and do her hair and makeup. The longer she idled—or rather, avoided the topic of conversation entirely—the more time she was wasting.

"Evasion won't save you forever," Isla warned. "You know she's going to try to get you to change your mind."

Which was the exact reason Karina was avoiding her calls for the time being because she still hadn't made a decision yet.

"A dress, Iz. I need one."

Avoidance would only work for so long, but for now, it would do.

AT THREE MINUTES TO SEVEN, A HEAVY KNOCK SOUNDED ON THE front door.

Though she had already been ready for a half an hour, Karina still double-checked her appearance in the full-length mirror resting against the wall next to the front door, making sure her makeup was impeccable and the wisps of hair that had fallen free of the loose bun she had twisted it into still looked nice.

She was as ready as she would ever get.

Taking a breath, she opened the front door to find Orion waiting for her.

He might have been most comfortable in a pair of jeans and a leather jacket, but tonight he made quite the sight in an Armani suit with his dark hair combed and gelled into place. The dark auburn of the scruff covering his square jaw only added to his overall package.

"You clean up nice," she remarked with a smile, stepping out of her apartment and pulling the door closed behind her.

"Yeah, maybe," he agreed with a shameless shrug, but it was nothing compared to the way he shamelessly ogled her. "But compared to you ..."

No one could say Orion wasn't charming—he was definitely that—but she was immune to his flirtations. Not to mention, a romantic affair was the last thing on her mind.

Tonight was about work even as she was in a four-figure dress and similarly priced heels. It might have been the opposite of her usual casual attire when she went into work at the paper, but she still felt like the same girl.

Once she had her door locked, Orion placed a calloused hand on the small of her back. Ever the gentleman as he led her down the flight of stairs to the first floor.

Outside, a Rolls Royce idled at the curb, jet black with black rims and tinted windows. A boy who couldn't be more than twelve years old stood next to the expensive car with his hands tucked into his pockets, his expression stern as if he dared anyone to approach the car.

Spotting Orion, the look cleared as he straightened and gestured to the car. "Not a scratch on it, just like you said."

"Thanks for looking out," Orion replied with a smile before he pulled a wad of bills out of his pocket and handed them over. "Spend it wisely."

The boy looked alarmed and seemed ready to shake his head and refuse the payment, but he never got the chance before Orion practically shoved the money at him and sent him on his way.

As he opened the passenger door—that opened from the opposite side as opposed to a regular car—he met her gaze. "What?"

"That was nice of you."

He shrugged, as if giving away more than a thousand dollars to a kid he didn't know was no big deal. "Someone's gotta look out for them."

Them.

A street kid, she knew.

Same as Orion had been once upon a time.

She still remembered a story he had told her during one of their early lunches together. About how he had grown up as an orphan in the Bronx, bouncing from foster home to foster home before finally wagering he'd be better able to make it on his own than under the care of people who, "didn't give a shit whether he made something of himself or not," as he'd put it.

Two types of criminals littered the world.

Those like Paxton, who used their money and influence to take what they wanted without care of who they harmed in the process.

Then there were those like Orion … doing what was necessary to survive, and while they might have caused some harm, they still tried to make up for it in some way.

Slipping into the passenger seat, she inhaled the scent of leather and cologne as Orion hustled around to the other side and sat behind the wheel.

As she reached for the door handle, Orion stopped her. "I got it."

Was he going to get back out and—

With one press of a button, the door closed on its own.

"Should I even ask where you got this car from."

He smirked. "You already know the answer to that."

Right.

A friend of a friend of an enemy.

Checking his side mirror, he pulled out. Resting his hand idly on the gearshift, he kept his gaze straight ahead.

"I'd say we have solid thirty minutes with this traffic before we get to the venue."

"Is this the part where you tell me I need to be on my best behavior?" she asked, glancing over at him.

"If you already know, I shouldn't have to tell you."

"Don't worry," she told him. "I'll be on my best behavior."

He made a low sound in the back of his throat. "Why don't I believe that?"

Because he knew her far too well.

***

THE EVENT HALL WAS LAVISH, THE FLORAL FRAGRANCE OF THE flower arrangements in sitting pots lining the marble stairs just as beautiful as the room itself. The grand chandelier that hung over the main room cast arcs of rainbows against the glittering crystals, offset by the white décor and expensive paintings hung along the walls.

Hired staff in waistcoats circled the room, distributing drinks and directing others to their tables. As one passed, Orion grabbed a flute of champagne for them both.

"I'm curious," Karina said, her gaze dancing over the crowd of people before turning over to Orion. "Is your boss here?"

He might have told her anything she wanted to know, *within reason*, and had even shared personal bits about his past and the former family he had once belonged to—the only one he made a point to visit whenever he could—but he had never told her a single thing about the man he worked for.

The only thing she could say for certain was that the man was Russian, and the only reason she knew that was because she had briefly overheard a conversation between them and recognized the language Orion spoke in hushed tones.

She wasn't sure whether it was because he didn't want her looking into him, or because the man wouldn't look kindly on his association with someone in her field, but either way, it had left her curious all the same.

Especially since she still wasn't sure *what* he did exactly.

"Even if he was," Orion said with a hint of a smile, "I wouldn't tell you."

"Why not?"

"Because you're my date, and you don't mix that shit."

A light laugh left her. "Did you forget *why* you brought me here in the first place?"

"Unfortunately not, but he's not the one I gave an oath to."

Who *had* he made an oath to?

Before she could ask him just that, he cleared his throat, bringing her attention back to him, but instead of looking at *her*, he was staring straight ahead at a man coming down the same marble stairs they had ventured from some minutes ago, dressed in all black.

She knew, without Orion having to say a word, who he was.

It shone in the way he carried himself.

No mental image she could have come up with compared to the man in front of her.

It didn't show the wide breadth of his shoulders or the way he filled out that black-on-black three-piece suit he wore so well. The gleam of his hair and cut of his jaw.

It was as if his very presence had caused the room to become electric. They weren't the only ones focused on him.

For once in her life, Karina found herself speechless as she regarded the man she had only recently heard so much about.

"That's him," Orion said after a moment, his voice low even though the nearest person to them was several feet away.

They, too, were staring at him as cleared the stairs and entered the room fully, a charming half-smile lighting up his features as he shook hands with the man waiting at the base of the stairs for him. But that smile, Karina noted, didn't reach his eyes.

Not even close.

"Shit."

Orion's curse managed to break her concentration, drawing her gaze in his direction. "What?"

"You've got that look," he muttered before draining his own glass, already looking for another.

A smile crept its way onto her face. "What look would that be?"

"The one when you're about to do some reckless shit."

That startled a real laugh out of her, and despite his serious expression, his lips quirked at the corners.

"Am I that easy to read?"

He shrugged. "Nah. I just pay attention."

As quickly as Uilleam had seemed to become the center of her universe—or the way the room had seemed to freeze at his arrival—she looked away from him.

Probably best not to court his attention so soon.

Orion, glad to have her focus back on him, walked around the room with her, making small talk with two senators, a Fortune 500 CEO, and a few other notable figures, yet not one of them turned their noses up at him. Instead, they seemed almost eager to talk.

They only spared her the barest of glances, probably believing she was merely a pretty face on his arm for the night, and she didn't bother to correct them on the assumption.

Instead, she sipped her champagne and listened, observing everything and cataloging details that might prove worthy later on.

Though she still wasn't entirely sure how Orion had managed to score tickets to the event, she was grateful all the same.

Especially once they arrived at their table and she found she had a direct view of Paxton's table from where she sat. His wife was already seated as he made his way around the table, shaking hands with every man there and kissing their wives on the cheek. Now, just like in his pictures, he had a politician's easy grace.

The ability to be comfortable around anyone, all while charming them to the point that they didn't know they were being deceived.

Karina wasn't so gullible.

She stared across the distance at him from the time it took him to circle the table and stand behind his chair to the moment when his gaze lazily drifted over the crowd of people moving to their seats and double-backed to her.

She didn't even try to fight the satisfaction she felt as she watched rage burn like fire in his eyes. She was the last person he was expecting to see, no doubt, especially not so close with no one seeming the wiser.

But even as satisfaction filled her, her own gaze didn't linger on him for very long before she was scanning the crowd again, looking ... looking ...

"Looking for me?"

The low, delightfully accented voice made her freeze where she sat, and out the corner of her eye, it was impossible not to notice the way Orion stiffened too.

The rumors she had heard didn't at all do the man justice. She had thought him beautiful when he'd stood across the room, oblivious to her perusal of him, but the man in front of her was more than that.

So much more.

This wasn't the first time she had been around handsome men— Orion could hold his own beside him—yet she couldn't mistake the sudden awareness that crept through her now that he was so close.

There was just something about *him* that made her heart stutter.

She considered, for a moment, pretending as if she had no idea what he was talking about—to pretend she had no idea *who* he was— but she thought better of it before she opened her mouth.

"It's nice to finally put a face to the name I've heard so much about." At least her voice was steady despite the rest of her. "I thought you would be older."

Contrary to what she had believed, if she had to guess, he was only a few years older than her.

His cool expression warmed as he regarded her, cracking some of the ice around his eyes, and despite herself, she could feel the flush rising in her cheeks.

How utterly affected she was just around him ...

It didn't make any sense.

"I thought you would be less beautiful," he returned, his eyes dipping down her front, his gaze lingering in all the places that were far too intimate for a first encounter before he lifted his gaze back up again. "Seems we were both mistaken."

The compliment was unexpected, and had it come from anyone else, she might have been able to let it drift into one ear and out the other, but *his* words lingered.

And for a moment, they repeated themselves over and over in her head.

"Are you always so forthcoming with your thoughts?"

"Depends on who's listening."

He helped himself to the seat opposite her, blatantly ignoring Orion altogether as he gave her his full, undivided attention.

This close, she could *just* see the golden flecks in his eyes.

"You obviously know who I am," she said when she regained the ability to speak, "then you have to know what I do."

"Which is why I had security retrieve all potential recording devices from everyone before they entered this room."

"Clever," she admitted grudgingly. She *had* wondered why they had asked for them when they had arrived, but had dismissed it thinking the guests in attendance hadn't wanted their pictures taken for any reason.

He inclined his head. "So I've been told."

"Clever or not," she said, holding her head up straight, "that's not going to change what I'm doing here."

If anything, that managed to make his smile tip up a little further as he extended his hand palm up. "Dance with me and tell me all about it."

She could only imagine the surprise reflected on her face at his suggestion. At most, she had been expecting a thinly veiled threat or at least a warning that she needed to stay away from Paxton and the death she was looking into.

But perhaps that had been what the lawyers were for. A test, of some sort. Meant to see whether she would back down at the slightest provocation, or if she would continue as if their warning hadn't been enough.

The fact that she was here at this event was an unspoken acknowledgment that she wasn't leaving this alone just yet.

"I don't dance with strange men with unclear motives."

"I want to see what secrets spill from those lips of yours. There's nothing unclear about that, Miss Ashworth."

Karina didn't realize she was reaching toward him until she felt his fingers close around her hand, his hold gentle but firm. Her legs carried her out onto the dance floor behind him through no thought of her own, but her heart was beating so fast in her chest that she could only focus on the echoing thump and the blood rushing in her ears.

This was the moment she had been waiting for—the moment that would trigger the beginning of the end.

Before she could get lost in her own head, she blinked back to reality when she felt Uilleam's arm slide around her waist, the palm of his hand pressing against the small of her back.

It was almost too easy to slip her hand into his, pressing just close enough that she could feel the lean muscle through the fine fabric of his suit.

He was *beautiful*. Without a doubt.

Everything about him felt designed to draw her in.

But as quickly as she had been focused on him, she glanced beyond his shoulder where a couple wearing matching purple whispered to each other as they watched them.

"People are staring."

Uilleam didn't turn. If anything, his grip on her grew a little tighter. "Everyone likes to study beautiful things. Of course they'd be looking at you."

"Is that how you do it?" she asked, trying desperately not to be flattered. "You charm your way into getting what you want?"

"Charm only gets you so far."

He spun them, moving them deeper into the center of the room, as sure on his feet as he was with his words.

Those mornings spent in the ballroom learning how to dance were worth every second now as she easily kept up with his sure movements.

"The rest is what you know, but I'm getting ahead of myself, aren't I? You still haven't told me what it is you think I do."

He spun her, as smoothly as if he had been dancing all his life … or had taken lessons. She vividly remembered the sheer number of them she had been forced to take from the time she was five until just after her seventeenth birthday.

Had his parents forced the same on him? Or had he learned at a prestigious boarding school where that was a standard?

Uilleam certainly had the demeanor and manners that said he might have attended one. Not to mention, the careful way he enunciated his words, his accent a touch more posh.

Did it really matter considering what she knew about him?

Why was it even a thought?

"Would you tell me?" she asked curiously. "If I were to guess correctly, I mean. Would you tell me if I was right?"

His smile was a touch more rueful. "I'll certainly tell you where you're wrong."

"You broker deals," she started, thinking back on the board she had created in his honor. Remembering the various bullet points and question marks that had rested beside each written out assumption.

"Not in the way you think, I'd imagine."

"Are you going to elaborate on that?"

"You're a journalist," he said, pulling her in close. "Phrase your wording better."

"You make desperate people offers they're too stupid to decline."

When Uilleam was amused, she was beginning to see, only one corner of his mouth tilted up in an infuriatingly sexy smirk, but when he was impressed ... his smile took over his face, lips splitting to reveal perfectly straight white teeth. It would have been impossible not to get lost in his smile for a little.

No one could possibly ignore it.

She couldn't be blamed for the way she stared.

"On their own merits, they all believe they're the smartest men in the world."

"Is that what you are?" she asked. "You believe you're the smartest man in the world?"

"Decidedly not. But I know enough about people that it all becomes rather predictable."

"How do you pick them?" she asked, trying very hard to ignore the way his fingers flexed against the small of her back.

"So certain that people don't merely request my services and I see it done?"

"They might come to you, but it's ultimately your choice," she said. "Otherwise, we'd have had this little meeting sooner."

Because he would have worked for anyone if the price was right, and the more people he worked for, the likelier it would be that someone like her caught on to what he was doing.

While she didn't doubt that he had probably worked on a number of other jobs before she caught wind of the first she'd stumbled onto, she doubted there would be more than a dozen more.

Mere minutes in his presence made her think he was more selective, leaning toward cautious. She still vividly remembered the way Orion had reacted to her describing him, and how he had seemed so reluctant to talk about him. Not to mention that when she had casually mentioned Uilleam's name to others, they either had no idea who he was, or changed the subject entirely

It was odd the effect he had on people, but instead of scaring her off, it made her more curious.

"So sure about that?" he asked a question of his own, pulling her to a gentle stop.

"Quite certain."

"And why is that?"

"Because you're standing here with me right now. I don't imagine you make it a point to get close to anyone, let alone a journalist who's trying to unravel your secrets."

He stared down at her with unreadable eyes, though in this position, she could see the darker ring of brown that outlined his irises. "No," he said. "I don't."

But something about her was different.

She could almost hear the thought running through his head. And the last thing she should have been was happy about that thought.

"Our paths would have crossed eventually."

He looked as if he was readying to speak, but something snared his attention to the left of them. "The man you came with, who is he?"

The sudden turn in conversation momentarily made her blink in confusion before her brain caught up with what he was asking. She turned to where his gaze had gone, spotting Orion lingering at the edge of the crowd of onlookers, his expression anxious.

Curious how she had forgotten all about him the moment Uilleam's attention fell on her.

"A friend," was all she was willing to say. "But whatever problem you have with me, you shouldn't take it up with any but me."

"My motives are a touch more singular."

Uilleam didn't seem like the sort of man to flirt for flirtation's sake, and his expression all but confirmed that.

His gaze was steady and unflinching, no denying the question behind those words.

"Have you always been this arrogant?" she asked, genuinely curious while also guessing he had.

With a face like his, it had probably been all too easy for him.

"I was being genuine when I said I'd hoped you would show up here tonight. You've already been warned about staying away from Paxton, yet here you are."

"If I didn't, who would?" she asked, believing those words now more than ever.

Everyone else had backed off the story—had accepted it at face value and allowed a man like Paxton to continue with his life as if he hadn't prematurely ended the life of another like she thought.

"But what does that have to do with my question?" she asked next.

"Not many are as bold as you. Daring, even. I find that … refreshing."

Did that really make her so different?

"You won't for long," she warned him. "I'm not going to stop this story just because you look good in a suit. Paxton deserves to pay for what he did."

"Perhaps."

Karina waited, expecting him to continue, but he just stopped.

One word.

Perhaps.

What the hell?

"If you stand in my way, Uilleam, I will go through you."

"I look forward to your attempts."

"I guess we'll see."

"Excuse me, miss."

Karina turned at the sound of a new voice, only to find two men in security uniforms staring back at her.

It seemed Paxton was finally ready to do something about her presence here. Unless Uilleam was far more good at subtle cues than she had thought.

What was almost comical, though, was the size of the two men he had sent over to escort her out of the dinner. She was only five-five, if an inch, and couldn't have weighed more than one hundred and twenty pounds, yet they were both nearly a foot taller that her and looked as if they hadn't missed a meal since the moment they were born.

"It's time for you to leave," the one on the right said, his eyes narrowed even as he reached to grasp her upper arm.

Karina was all but ready to snatch her arm out of his hold and move out of reach, but Uilleam's hand was suddenly on the man's wrist, applying enough pressure that the man grunted.

"Remove your hand or lose it."

The words were spoken carefully, though even she could hear the thick layer of steel surrounding the command. And despite his casual tone, the room seemed to fall silent around them.

As if his threat had been heard by them all.

The youngest man in the room ... yet he held the most power.

Uilleam Runehart was a different breed of animal.

Though it was clear the man, who had quickly let her go, was employed by Paxton—his company's logo was stitched on the pocket of his suit jacket—Uilleam didn't seem to care one way or the other.

But the man didn't, not even for a second, take his eyes off Uilleam.

"I'm just following—"

"Move," Uilleam said, this threat more clear. "Or I'll have you moved."

Without another word, the security guard took a step back, his companion right beside him—who still had yet to speak a single word.

"I don't believe you understand the magnitude of this game you seem intent on playing with me, Karina Ashworth," Uilleam said after a moment, turning his eyes back to her.

"All the same," she said in return, taking her own step back, feeling as if the rest of the world was finally filtering back in now that his hands had fallen off of her. "I look forward to playing it with you."

And as she risked one last glance back in his direction, she saw it.

The thrill.

Excitement.

He was looking forward to it too.

✻ 9 ✻

CURIOUSER & CURIOUSER

IF ANYONE ASKED WHY UILLEAM WAS THERE, HE WOULD BLAME IT
on Paxton.

Research, he would say.

But *he* knew it wasn't nearly as simple as that.

Because Karina Ashworth was proving to be a puzzle wrapped in
mystery with a smile he wasn't sure he would ever be able to erase
from his mind.

He saw that smile when he closed his eyes at night, haunting the
few hours of sleep he was able to get.

He saw it when he should have been working or at least focusing
on other important matters—like the fact she seemed quite determined to become a thorn in his side.

It didn't matter that almost all of New York had moved on from
the woman's death and Paxton's merger had finally been completed
successfully.

She was still *there*.

Waiting.

Lingering.

Remaining inconspicuous while also digging for as much of the
truth as she could get.

Something had told him, that night at the party, she hadn't come solely for Paxton. He saw it in the way her gaze had skirted over him more than a few times, and beyond a look of disdain, she didn't seem affected by his presence at all.

No, she had been searching for someone.

Him, he'd come to realize.

The part of him that his father had stoked with fire and hatred had been screaming for him to remain in the shadows—to observe her from afar and use whatever he gleaned against her.

But the *man* in him had had other ideas.

Because beyond the grainy image used on her profile for the paper, he hadn't expected to see someone that looked like *her*.

Even on the screens in the back control room at the fundraiser, he had only caught glimpses of her on the camera. She eased her way around the room, managing to blend in with the others around her while still standing out.

He'd noticed her immediately.

All because of the white dress she wore, the color of freshly fallen snow, clinging to generous curves that had had his hands curling into fists.

But while she might have been all but invisible to the others, she was a keen observer. He had watched her gaze skim over everyone in the room. As he had done on dozens of occasions.

He'd found himself wanting to delve into her mind in that moment.

To see how she saw the world.

Would it look like his?

How had the sheep below not noticed a wolf among them?

And when he did finally decide to sate his curiosity and see if the woman was as interesting as the idea he had of her, he certainly hadn't anticipated what happened next.

The way her dark hair was swept back into a charming bun, wisps of it framing a heart-shaped face, and eyes had pierced right through him. When she'd finally looked up at him, it wasn't with surprise. There had been a knowing gleam to those dark brown eyes of her—as if she knew him already.

She had smiled when she saw him.

Not afraid.

Not nervous.

She'd been *expecting* him.

Karina Ashworth, who was turning out to be his not so innocent journalist.

A woman who was quickly becoming a delightful problem.

She wasn't doing what he expected of her.

She wasn't backing off because of Paxton or the lawyers. She hadn't walked away, though he had wanted her to.

She *couldn't* stop. Like him

She was too stubborn. Foolish.

Fucking *enthralling*.

That had only made the desire to learn more about her all the more pressing.

Which was how he found himself in the back of the black Suburban, peering out at the brick building that housed her apartment.

For a woman on her salary, he thought she would try to move as close to Manhattan as possible or at least live where there was a proper doorman.

This building was a bit run-down, built decades ago—which was also the last time the exterior had been properly cleaned, he imagined. Though, he shouldn't have had an opinion on anything to do with her.

His work here in New York was all but finished, yet he found himself lingering—paying for another month at his hotel. Even retaining Skorpion's services for a while longer, though there was really no need.

For once in his life, he was a man obsessed.

For days, he had watched her—or maybe it had been longer now?—learning everything he could.

He wanted to understand her interest in this—why she refused to give up despite being given ample reason to. She had written a number of articles for him to read, some fluff pieces that seemed to signal the start of her career at *The Gazette Post*.

But as time went on, not only did the subject change, but also her style of writing. The elegant prose, the inquisitiveness of her tone through her words that made even *him* question whether what he knew was the truth or if it was what someone wanted him to think.

It also made sense why Paxton had thought to shut her up with lawyers. It was better to silence a voice like hers before too much power got behind it.

She wrote about the victims.

Sure, she took a moment to name the guilty and place her scorn on them, but she always talked more about the person who was hurt. About their lives and hopes and dreams. She made them *human* again.

Especially the victims of powerful men.

He wondered whether she had suffered at the hands of one, and if she had, where were they now?

All the same, he could have sent Skorpion in his place —he quite imagined she would be looking for him rather than his mercenary — and should have. He had opened his mouth, all but ready to do it, then he hesitated.

Hesitated because he wanted to make his own observations.

Learn about her himself.

On the first day, he'd trailed her for hours, taking note of the places she went—stowing it all away with the other bits he knew. The food she liked to eat. Her favorite shops, though he rarely saw her buy anything when she did go in them.

Now, he could see her in her living room through the window. In the kitchen, though, he could only see brief passes of her from his vantage point.

For quite a long while, he remained there, watching as she made dinner before lounging on her couch. Stared as she sat on the lone couch in the apartment and turned on the television.

He remained until he saw her fall asleep right there before finally driving back to his hotel.

One day had turned into two, and now he wasn't sure where he was.

"She's like a fucking saint for the innocent," Skorpion had muttered the first day he'd driven him around after reading over her articles as he had.

Uilleam agreed, though he didn't say as much.

"What's your interest in her anyway?" Skorpion rightly asked, glancing at the time on the dashboard of the SUV.

He had no business making repeated trips out here, risking anyone catching him unaware or *her* noticing a strange vehicle following her home, but he dismissed the idea just as quickly.

If she was anything like he thought she was, she wouldn't mind his light stalking. She would try to use it against him.

He waved for Skorpion to pull off, but not before he forced himself to answer his question with the only answer he could give. "I don't know."

10

THE GAMES BEGIN

NOTHING.

Not a single message of any sort despite the moment they had shared at the fundraiser. It was as if he had disappeared off the face of the earth again, and she didn't even know where to begin to search for him.

Which was another reminder that he was still a walking mystery. Sure, she had seen more of him in the past few weeks than in the numerous months she had spent trying to figure out who he was and what he did, yet she still didn't know how to *find* him.

Not that she should, despite the desire she felt. What did it matter if she hadn't spoken to him? It didn't change what needed to be done—and even if it did, it should have been fine just knowing he was out there somewhere.

She had spent twenty-odd years never even knowing he existed. Surely, it couldn't be hard to forget a man she didn't actually know.

At least, that was what she kept telling herself.

Hopefully, one day she would get back to a life when she wasn't constantly thinking about him. About his smile and the way it lit up his face. Or the careful, deliberate way he moved that had made her want to follow him with her gaze.

She was eager for the time when he wasn't such a mystery and she didn't feel the spark that had yet to dissipate.

Though she had thought their moment together would spark another run in, she was mistaken.

One day quickly turned into six, and six turned into ten, and when she woke up this morning, Karina had finally settled on the fact that that night would be the only time she crossed paths with him.

It didn't helped that Orion had told her just how rare it was for Uilleam to spend more than a handful of minutes with any one person when he was in a crowd—a way to ensure no one thought they held his favor. A fact that made her ask just how much *did* he know about the man and why wasn't he sharing more with her?

If anything, their brief encounter had only made her curiosity more rampant. And no matter that she knew it was a bad idea—especially one Orion wouldn't approve of—she found herself asking questions, digging into secrets and more rumors than was probably safe.

But some part of her had let go of that careful caution she usually implemented when she was on assignment.

Figuring she just needed a change of scenery, she pushed her laptop aside and shoved the covers off her legs, stripping out of her clothes once she reached her closet. Though she spent the majority of her time inside this apartment writing, and she rather liked it this way, sometimes she needed to get out of her own head.

Experience and soak in everything around her.

So she dressed quickly in jeans and a tank, then grabbed her favorite jacket and left her apartment in search of a coffee shop.

Two birds, one stone.

The quickest and easiest way to both get her mind off the ever revolving circle she found herself in, as well as a chance to recharge with a nice cup of coffee.

Coffee, then work again and finally, a night off where she and Samantha would finally hang out.

A night to herself..

She deserved it.

Even before they stepped onto the curb, Karina was sure she could feel the vibrations from the bass bleeding through the brick building to her left.

She had never heard of this particular place when Samantha suggested it—this would be her first time going to a club whatsoever, though she didn't bother to mention that—a couple of weeks ago, but she seemed to be the only one.

The line extended past the double frosted doors at the entrance and wrapped itself around the side of the building. A wide variety of people stood waiting to get in: women in glittery, short dresses and heels to match; some men in suits, others in casual wear, and everything in between.

Karina was ready to walk to the back of the line before Samantha snagged her hand and tugged her toward the front where a man with a clipboard stood with a coiled wire earpiece tucked behind his ear.

"Johnny owed me a favor," she explained with a smile that explained all too well that Karina probably didn't need to ask why he owed her a favor.

It felt like seconds between their standing outside and having their IDs checked after making sure their names were on the list to being inside the long hallway that pulsed with red light as music played, but it wasn't until they reached the open balcony and she got her first glimpse of what the club had to offer did she finally pause and absorb everything around her.

Bottle girls in tailored pants and heels drifted through the crowds of writhing bodies, carting champagne bottles with sparklers shooting out the top. The atmosphere almost felt electric with energy.

For once in her life, Karina felt her age.

From the time she was a little girl, her mother had taught her about being responsible. How never to step outside of the lines or deviate from the correct path because they would result in failure.

And failure was *not* an option.

Her mother would consider her time spent here as a frivolous pastime that served as nothing more than a hindrance from work.

Karina saw … freedom.

Ease.

A distraction.

Something she had never allowed herself to think about before now.

The most she had ever stepped outside of her mother's lines and what she wanted for her was asking if she could come *here*, to New York, and live as someone —*anyone.*

How else, she had argued, would she learn what she really wanted if she immediately joined the family business without experiencing anything.

She wanted to see what she was made of outside her family.

And for more than a year now, she had been doing just that, so she deserved this.

She'd earned it.

Following Samantha down the winding stairs, she tucked her hair behind her ears, feeling more nervous than she should.

It was almost funny how she was comfortable in the office or questioning people to learn their secrets, but something as simple as walking through a crowded dance floor made her anxious.

After a bit of careful shuffling and quiet apologies, Karina finally made it to the bar in the center of the floor, the wall of liquor backlit in neon blue. She had only just started reading the night's drink specials when Samantha appeared beside her and raised her hand to get the bartender's attention.

"Four shots of tequila, please!" She looked at Karina then. "You drink tequila, right?"

She couldn't help but laugh. "I've never had it."

Samantha made a funny face as if she couldn't fathom how Karina had made it this long without drinking that.

She didn't want to explain that Katherine Ashworth was a wine drinker and refused anything else, and she expected her daughters to do the same.

But tonight wasn't about her mother or her expectations.

Four shot glasses were set in front of them, all polished to a gleam, then the bartender filled them to the brim with clear liquor.

Samantha was all too excited to grab her first with one hand and a slice of lime with the other. Karina followed suit, though briefly wondering how, exactly, she was supposed to swallow it all down in one go.

"Cheers to another week," she said over the pounding music, tossing her drink back and swallowing it down before sucking on the lime.

Karina followed suit, though she was a touch more clumsy as she tasted the alcohol and nearly gagged. It was like swallowing gasoline that burned all the way down her throat before settling heavily in her stomach.

The taste of the lime was only mildly better, but that didn't stop her from reaching for the next glass and drinking that one too.

Before she knew it, she was smiling, the rush of adrenaline and tequila making everything fuzzy around the edges.

So this was what it was like to feel buzzed. For everything to be slightly off-kilter and a little brighter and a little louder.

It was easy, she thought, a little tipsy, to get lost in this life—to be … normal.

No expectations.

No doubts.

Just living everyday in the moment.

The next time she had a drink in her hand, this one in a taller glass with sugared fruit and a straw inside, she took her time drinking it, already guessing that her limit for alcohol was much less than Samantha's.

Already she could feel herself swaying to the music, her eyes briefly sliding shut as she drifted into her own world and got lost.

Later, she wouldn't recall what it was that made her open her eyes and look toward the shift of shadows on the roped-off balcony above her on the other side of the room. From where she stood, it was hard to make out much beyond the furniture and bodies blocking whatever was on the other side, but then she caught a glimpse.

Of someone, she thought.

The cut of a man's jaw.

The sharp lines of his suit.

The glint of hair whenever the lights dipped to red.

If she hadn't been standing there oblivious to everything around her as she continued to stare unabashed, she wouldn't have believed he was *here*, of all places.

He was an international criminal from what Orion had told her, and one that now seemed intent on ruining her, but men like him didn't have time for nights out like this.

Had she not been sure that was him sitting there, she would have wagered he was off somewhere, plotting more of her downfall with Paxton and not giving her more thought than that.

But there he sat.

Watching her.

She should have turned away, pretended as if she hadn't noticed him and gone on about her night because if he was here, then it was quite clear he had come for *her*.

Instead, she felt frozen in place, watching him watch her.

At least until he flicked two fingers at her in a salute of sorts. Even as her face flushed, she shook her head once and finally forced herself to turn away, breaking the spell he had her under.

Tapping Samantha's shoulder, she pointed in the direction of the restrooms and hurried off that way before she could ask any questions.

She just needed a second to wrap her mind around the fact that Uilleam was here, and she was a little more than tipsy. She was off her game.

This was supposed to be her night off—one where she didn't have to think about why she was here and the responsibility she had at work.

She needed to sober up.

Her brain was foggy with alcohol, and by the time she made it into the restroom and stood in front of the mirror, it almost felt as if she was coming down.

Yet when she actually looked at her reflection, she didn't look like herself.

Her hair wasn't tamed with every strand combed into place.

Her makeup was a touch heavier than she would have worn around the office.

This version of her was practically a stranger.

Dragging in a sobering breath, she tried to right her appearance as best as she could with the other girls bustling around her.

The door opened suddenly, a huddle of women walking in, the restroom becoming quite full quite quickly.

Karina stepped away from the mirror to give another girl her spot, moving toward the door when she brushed by a girl on accident. "Oh, pardon me."

"Oh my God, are you from London?" the girl asked with genuine excitement, though the slight slur of her words gave away her level of intoxication.

Her first thought was to correct her.

Burford, she would say. A small little English town that very few people knew about. But right as it was on the tip of her tongue, she remembered who she was—who she was supposed to *be*.

And Karina Ashworth, the journalist at *The Gazette Post*, was no one from nowhere, United States.

And *that* Karina wasn't supposed to have an accent.

Accents were something a person remembered.

"There's a boy in my class who transferred from Oxford," another girl said. "I could literally listen to him talk all day."

As the conversation dissolved into who the mysterious boy was, Karina slipped away, thankful she had got out of answering, remembering to keep a firmer check on the way she spoke.

But she came up short when she saw the man waiting in the wings.

The same one who had been at the gala with Uilleam. Except tonight, he wasn't in a suit. If anything, his already massive frame looked bigger, more imposing somehow, in the dark jeans he wore and the scuffed boots on his feet.

It wasn't until her heels clicked against the concrete floors did he finally look up and directly at her, making it clear she was the one he had come for.

"You work for him, don't you?" she asked, keeping her voice level.

He shrugged. "Depends on the day."

That made no sense at all to her. "And today?"

"I do."

"What does he want?" Karina asked, figuring there was a reason he had sent this man to seek her out, but as that thought hit her, she realized she already knew the answer.

Her.

He wanted her.

"Who are *you*?"

He seemed to consider the question a moment. "Call me Skorpion."

"Do you have an *actual* name?"

"Not one I'll be giving a journalist."

Fair enough.

"Fine, take me to him."

THE LAST THING ON HER MIND WAS THE JOB.

Every step she took behind Uilleam's guard wasn't because she was going along with this so that she could glean new information that might help her investigation. Rather, she wanted to give in to her own curiosity.

And since a part of her was drunk enough not to consider whether this was a bad idea or not, she hadn't hesitated in going along with the man when he'd pushed off the wall and steered her through the club.

The bouncer standing at the rope that sectioned off the private stairwell from the rest of the dance floor took one look at Skorpion walking in front of her and stepped aside, not asking a single question about her sudden presence there.

At first, all she saw was the strobe lights that grew bigger and brighter as she climbed the stairs until she reached the second level, but as the song changed to something darker, the lights all changed to one color—red.

Just as it had been when she had walked in earlier.

It was hard to ignore the rapid beat of her heart, or how she felt out of breath the moment she saw him. His guard had stopped just ahead, gesturing for where she needed to go as if the action was necessary. Her gaze immediately sought out Uilleam the moment she was up here.

He was hard to miss.

His suit jacket was missing, but his waistcoat was still present, the sleeves of the sky blue shirt he wore beneath rolled up to his elbows. One arm was draped across the back of the sectional he sat on—as if he were a king on his throne observing his subjects.

It almost felt as if he was in control of everything and everyone around him.

As if they, her included, were all here to serve at his leisure.

The arrogance of it all shouldn't have been appealing.

It shouldn't have made her want to draw closer just to see what would happen.

The thought was tempting—a temptation she never thought she would feel.

This was the last thing she should have been feeling considering everything, including her temporary demotion at her job that had grown to mean more to her than she thought possible.

But as if her feet had a mind of their own, she found herself drawn to him anyway.

"Did you follow me here?" she called over the music, stopping several feet in front of him, knowing the distance would help her think more clearly.

"Perhaps you followed me here, and I'm merely taking advantage," he said back, his smile easy. "You *have* been asking questions about me, yes?"

"What makes you think that?" she asked, keeping her voice neutral.

"Your date from the other night. I thought he looked familiar."

"That's the second time you've mentioned him," she said with a cant of her head. "Jealous?"

"Curious," he corrected, then amended, "but the two often go hand in hand."

He crooked his finger at her, beckoning her to come closer.

Tempting.

So very, very tempting.

"I'm good where I am."

"Why's that?" he asked.

"Because I don't trust you."

He laughed even as he shrugged, shifting to stand in a move far too fluid for a man to have pulled off. He walked over to her, and it was as if he had his own force field the way others seemed to move out of his way without being prompted.

Instead of backing away, Karina planted her feet and crossed her arms in front of her, though it made very little defense against him when he got close.

His hair was messier tonight, and even the scruff along his jaw was more prominent—it was a shame that both only managed to make him more attractive.

Maybe she wouldn't have felt this unexplainable draw if he'd been the opposite.

He waited until he was close enough that she couldn't miss the smile on his face as he said, "Trust is overrated."

She wouldn't dignify that with a response. "You obviously wanted to see me," she said with a pointed glance over at his associate. "What do you want?"

His smile tipped a little higher, but instead of answering her question, he extended his hand between them, palm up. He didn't tell her to take it or even take her hand himself.

The choice was hers.

She took it.

And God, the decision shouldn't have been an easy one.

It was the alcohol, she reasoned. Tequila could make anyone pliable if they drank enough of it.

It surely wasn't because *she* felt drawn to him.

It couldn't be because she was already anticipating the moment his fingers closed around hers.

But it *was*, even as she lied to herself that it wasn't.

With the gentlest of pressure, he drew her closer to him, and with each step she took forward, he took one back until she was where he originally wanted her, but instead of sitting, he turned them so her back was against the wall near the sectional and he was all she could see.

The music pulsed through the wall, vibrating against her back, sending her nerve endings racing with sensation. For all she paid attention to the rest of the room, they might as well have been the only ones there.

Resting one hand on the wall beside her head, Uilleam leaned in close, his lips nearly brushing her ear. She couldn't bring herself to care that he had probably felt her shiver.

"You're becoming a problem for me, Karina Ashworth."

The logical side of her knew those words were meant as a threat just as much as an observation. That if she didn't back down from this, he would make her regret it, but he didn't sound upset at the idea of her interference with his business.

Quite the opposite.

Swallowing, she tried to ignore the way his cologne invaded her senses. "I'm trying to do my job."

His shoulders shook with silent laughter, the sound dark in her ear. "I could say the same."

"Except I'm trying to help the innocent."

"No one is ever truly innocent, Karina. You'd do well to remember that."

He was right.

Especially when it came to *him*.

But while everyone had a gray moral line, there was no line with him, so she had heard.

Uilleam leaned back just far enough that he could meet her gaze, searching her expression as if he might find the answers he was looking for within it.

"How much would it take for you to walk away?" he asked, his gaze dropping to her mouth when she drew in a breath.

If she were a betting woman, she would have guessed he wanted to kiss her.

And a part of her wanted him to.

Desperately.

Even as the urge made zero sense.

The longer she stood there, the more she really, *really* wanted him to.

He was a man who had done awful things for worse reasons, yet she was drawn to him all the same.

"Nothing," she told him and meant it. "No amount of money in the world."

He sighed with a slight shake of his head, though she was sure the answer she gave was exactly what he'd anticipated. "You're stubborn."

"You don't intimidate me, Uilleam."

"I haven't begun to try," he answered, voice still pleasant.

She lifted her hands and placed them against his chest, prepared to push him away just to give herself some room to think, but it was the wrong move to make because as she was touching him, that gave him unspoken permission to touch her in return.

He caught her hands before she could push him away, holding her wrists in one hand as he dragged them down his chest until they were firmly held between their bodies.

It was impossible not to feel the wall of muscle that was his chest or even the dips and contours of his abdomen that were far too distinct.

This time, it wasn't the tequila that brought a flush to her cheeks.

When she attempted to move away from him, he held fast, keeping her in place, giving her no choice but to remain there.

"Be careful," he warned her.

She arched a brow. "Or?"

"Is this truly the hill you want to die on?"

"I could ask you the same question. Would you really prefer I out you and whatever it is you do for a man like William Paxton? Is he worth all that to you?"

"You would never get the opportunity, poppet."

"Yet, I've made it this far." Now, it was her turn to lean into him, tilting her head back to look up at his face. "If you're really the man you claim to be, what's stopping you?"

He caught her face in his free hand, holding her still and facing him.

The fire sparked in his eyes, molten and hot. Pinning her there.

The chill that had swept through her before now burned something hotter and pooled between her thighs. His closeness only ratcheted the feeling up further.

"Let's hope your allure doesn't wear off then, shall we?"

With that parting remark, he finally retreated, giving her room to take a proper breath without feeling as if she was drowning in him.

The heartbeat's time that passed seemed to stretch on as they stared at one another, oblivious and uncaring about anything happening around them.

Did he feel it?

That inexplicable yet undeniable draw she felt?

Curiosity that certainly didn't feel healthy, and not at all to do with Paxton?

She wanted to believe it had nothing to do with the fact she found him interesting.

The *tequila*, she told herself again. Because that was all it was.

That was all it could ever be.

She now had every opportunity to leave, but she stood there. Watching as he crossed the room and sank back onto his temporary throne. She also knew that if she turned to leave at that moment, he wouldn't stop her.

Watch her leave, perhaps. Maybe even have his associate follow her out. But he had no intentions of moving again.

He'd made his point.

But that didn't mean he wanted her to go, not with the way his left fist kept flexing as if he had to make a concentrated effort to keep his distance.

And that realization sparked an epiphany in her head.

"It's not all about the story for you, though, is it?" she asked, tilting her head to the side as he had done, not backing down from the fierceness of his stare but rather feeling emboldened by it.

"This is the second time you've sought me out in person. Can others say the same, or am I special?"

"I usually don't play with my food, but"—he shrugged, a lazy smile forming—"it's entertaining, to say the least."

"Everyone's afraid of you," she said, thinking of the way the others had responded to his presence at the dinner or even Orion's hushed tones when no one was even around to hear him. "But I'm not."

"You'll learn to be."

She voluntarily walked closer to him, feeling the weight of his gaze as it dropped to her legs. "No, I don't think that's what you want at all."

Instead of going to him, she kept moving forward around the sectional, now making him come to her, and oh, there were no words to describe the satisfaction that thrummed through her when he did just that.

He wasn't the only one who held power in this room.

"It's why you came here tonight, isn't it? Because you wanted to see if you had managed to scare me off yet. Are people really that easily subdued by you?"

In her quest to get answers out of him, she hadn't realized she had been backing herself into a corner, but *he* did. He crowded her until they were in the same position as earlier.

"Yes."

"To which question?"

He seemed to think about it a moment. "Both."

"Does Paxton know?"

He arched a brow.

"Does he know the game you're playing with his life?"

He didn't seem to be paying attention to her question, rather his eyes had dropped to her mouth and lingered there. This time, she didn't have to wonder what he would do next.

He kissed her as if it was the first and last thing he wanted to do.

As if he *had* to.

Her surprise melted away as quickly as it took her hands to fist in the front of his waistcoat. She should have been pushing him away and putting more distance between them—she needed to remember who she was and what was at stake.

At the very least, remember who *he* was.

Yet it wasn't enough to stop her from kissing him back—to breathe him in as much as she possibly could before this moment ended. But Uilleam seemed content to drink his fill, pressing in tight against her, his tongue stroking over hers, then pulling her bottom lip between his teeth.

Never in her life had she been kissed quite like this before.

Like the world began and ended where their lips met.

Time was a construct. One second, she was fighting to get closer to him, and in the next, he was squeezing her ass as she wrapped her legs around his waist, the skirt of her dress quickly creeping up her thighs.

But she *still* couldn't bring herself to care.

Not when everything she knew was wrong felt like this.

And then for one, perfect second, they were flush, and she could feel the hard, heavy length of his erection pressed right up against her core.

A breathless gasp escaped her as the throb between her legs only grew worse. She knew the moment Uilleam felt it too because the sound he made wasn't nearly so breathless.

It was nothing short of a growl—a low, guttural sound that had her thinking if he wanted to just rip her panties off right then and there, she wouldn't hesitate to let him.

But before the moment could get away from her, someone cleared their throat loud enough to pierce the haze of lust she had fallen under.

Karina jolted, but Uilleam remained at ease, a heavy sigh escaping his mouth as he turned to look over his shoulder.

Skorpion.

If the man had any thoughts about seeing the two of them together like this, he kept them to himself. Even his expression didn't betray him.

"Five minutes," Uilleam said.

Karina busied untangling herself from him and righting her dress, though there was very little she could do for the rest of herself. She didn't wait to hear Skorpion's response, already slipping around Uilleam, but his voice paused her in her tracks.

"If Paxton knew the game I was playing, you wouldn't be here."

There were two ways he could have meant that remark.

Except she didn't want to know which.

II

HER

UILLEAM BREATHED OUT A SIGH AS HE STRETCHED HIS ARMS OUT, shutting his eyes against the world around him.

There was no place for anger in business—for pettiness, as his brother would describe it—but Kit had always been better at containing his emotions. He, on the other hand, tended to react first without carefully considering what it might cause.

Perhaps if Paxton had chosen to work with his brother instead, his downfall wouldn't be imminent.

If Uilleam were a better man, perhaps he wouldn't be unraveling every contingency the man had in place to bring him back down to where he had been before Uilleam stepped in and cleaned up after him.

He wished he could say it was because he wanted justice for the dead woman or even closure for the grieving mother whose interviews were still being played occasionally. But it was neither.

Paxton had brought this upon himself.

His fucking hubris.

He seemed to have forgotten that his disrespect or even perceived slight wouldn't be tolerated in any form.

Because if there was one thing to be said about the way he

worked, Uilleam worked twice as hard against his enemies than those who sought his aid.

Now, he had a decision to make.

One he had been stewing over the past couple of days since he'd last seen Karina. Since he'd last seen the raw emotion on her face, once when she told him she was never backing down and then again after he kissed her.

If he were honest, he'd known then that he would give her what she wanted, if only because she made him hunger in a way he had never felt before. Like every emotion coming to life inside him was for the first time.

Even he didn't understand the animal desire that seemed to be rushing through his veins.

Footsteps made his eyes pop back open, his gaze landing on Skorpion as he entered the suite, carrying two boxes of chicken that were undoubtedly meant only for him. Uilleam was sure the man consumed at least four thousand calories a day.

"You've got that look," Skorpion commented dryly before he took a seat on the sofa opposite Uilleam, better facing the television he had muted minutes before.

"Which one is that?"

"That you let a man think he had a winning hand only to have reveal an ace up your sleeve."

"I'm benevolent to a fault. I give and take whatever I see fit. He should have remembered that before trying to act against me." His arrogance would cost him. "Besides, I want to ensure Gaspard has a very clear understanding of what I'm capable of."

"And you wanna use the journalist for that?" Skorpion asked, popping open the first box. "Doesn't sound like your usual MO."

"That's because you know I fancy her," Uilleam returned dryly. "Otherwise, you would think it was ingenious."

If Karina was any other woman, it would be as if he was working two jobs at once. Eliminating his Paxton problem while ensuring a journalist was indebted to him who would give anything to advance their career.

It was brilliant.

But even he could see the difference in how this was and how it would usually be.

The field before him wasn't quite as transparent as he'd like it to be.

"If anything goes wrong, she'd have to be eliminated. Or are you forgetting that?"

"I'm not worried about that."

He had no reason to.

She was too curious about him, as he was about her, to reveal his presence or involvement to anyone. And it was also for that reason that he wondered whether her interest in him was purely because of what he did for a living ... or if she was interested in *him*.

The former, he knew, she understood very little about, but he'd shown her more bits of himself than he had any other person in a long time.

"Women are fickle creatures but don't underestimate them."

"Though I doubt it, I've prepared for that contingency as well."

He trusted he'd read her correctly, but he knew that trust could be a blind thing at times. He needed to ensure his own safety no matter what happened.

"Besides," Uilleam said, "I thought we'd pay her a little visit today to make a final decision."

"Really?" he asked, looking up from the box on his lap. Over the span of their conversation, he'd managed to inhale a breast, both drumsticks, and a wing.

Remarkable, really. "Of course we can wait until you're finished with ... all that."

"At least there's that."

Uilleam canted his head to one side. "Eating for two, are we?"

"Fuck off."

BEFORE HE SLID INTO THE PASSENGER SEAT OF HIS TRUCK, Uilleam had to ensure one important detail before he went any further.

Though he was more than eager to put Paxton in his place and remind him just who he was up against, there were bigger and far more important deals to be had that were contingent on the way this played out.

Even now, the conversation he'd had with Gaspard after striking the deal with Paxton.

"*I want to be impressed,*" Gaspard said during the early morning phone call Uilleam had taken while he watched his cleaners get rid of every shred of evidence inside the office.

He hadn't mentioned *how* he wanted to be impressed—which could present a myriad of problems, but it was an issue for another time.

Which meant, however he proceeded was entirely up to him.

And since Paxton was making it a point to get on his very last nerve, his method of impressing Gaspard wouldn't be in the other man's favor.

"I can handle her apartment alone," Uilleam said before Skorpion could step out of the car after him.

He didn't mention that some part of him—a part that didn't entirely sense to him either—wanted to learn more about Karina without anyone else being involved.

It was one thing to have him research her and report back with his findings. Her apartment was different.

More intimate.

A true reflection of the woman he was curious about.

And while he wasn't quite sure why yet, he wanted this for himself.

Skorpion passed him a look of censure but stayed put, turning back to stare out the windshield at the crowded street ahead.

It was easy enough to slip into Karina's building behind a woman carrying groceries who was oblivious to who held the door open for her. She merely called back a quick thanks and continued until she reached an apartment down the hall on the first floor without ever looking back.

Uilleam couldn't help but survey the building—the peeling paint on the walls and the stairs leading up to the next level that could benefit from a good scrub.

It was as if he had stepped into a different world.

Money had never been a thing he needed to worry about, not with his family's fortune. A fortune that spanned generations and the benefits of Alexander's criminal enterprises would ensure that even Uilleam's grandchildren would be born into a life of privilege.

On the fourth floor, he glanced up at the light bulb that flickered, briefly illuminating the long hallway before shrouding it in darkness once more.

He stopped in front of Karina's apartment, the number 3 staring back at him. First, he checked underneath the welcome mat for a spare key, then along the doorframe, brushing the dust from his fingers off along his trouser leg once he came up empty.

While Uilleam didn't make a habit of breaking into residences — he had men for that, after all — he still knew *how*, courtesy of the brother he hadn't seen in many years. Kit might not have been around much, but he had shared valuable knowledge that had aided him well over the years.

Pulling out the pick from his pocket, he carefully inserted it into the lock, counting down the seconds until an audible click sounded and the door sprung open.

Thirty-two seconds.

He was a little rusty.

With one last glance to make sure no one was around to see, Uilleam slipped into the apartment and closed the door behind him.

Lavender, he thought as he took in the space. That smell had lingered for days after the last time he had been in her presence. He hadn't been able to place the fragrance the first time they met, nor the second, but now that he was surrounded by her things, he was finally able to pinpoint what it was.

The apartment was modest — a tan-colored sofa with a plush, muted white throw blanket tossed across the back of it, resting on the edge of an area rug that was as wide as it was long.

There was no television that he could see, at least not out here in the living room, and if he had to guess from the sheer number of books and papers and assorted things, this was where she spent the majority of her time.

As Uilleam drank in everything around him, reading book titles and studying the few abstract paintings from department stores hanging on the walls, he tried to get a sense of who Karina was.

He knew of the tenacious journalist she was—one who would much rather test boundaries than back off from a story she was following—but now, he was curious about the woman.

And for the life of him, he couldn't figure out *why* he was so interested.

The woman had proven to be a thorn in his side and had yet to back down even though he had threatened her in no uncertain terms. Yet here he stood.

He couldn't remember the last time he had been curious about someone enough to warrant this sort of reaction.

His life had been spent studying others, trying to predict what moves a person would make before the thought ever crossed their mind. He saw what others didn't want him to see.

Yet with Karina, it was as if he was staring at a blank canvas, and the image refused to paint itself. This had never happened to him before, and he refused to believe that a junior reporter could prove more of an adversary than some of the men he had crossed paths with over the years.

Shaking the thought from his mind, Uilleam focused on the task at hand, bypassing the kitchen as he left the living room entirely and found his way into her bedroom.

Here, the floral scent was stronger.

In here, it felt as if he was seeing a reflection of the woman who plagued his thoughts.

White bedding stretched across a queen-size mattress, the duvet tucked in place. The pillows all fluffed and neatly placed. He thought of his own bed in the hotel where he was staying and how the sheets were twisted, the comforter rumpled.

His mother had always told him that a disorderly bed spoke of a disordered mind, and perhaps she wasn't wrong in that regard. Because while he was able to do his job without complaint, when he climbed into bed at whatever hour his work finished, he could never get his brain to shut off for very long.

Thoughts of what came next—whether another client, another deal, or just what he would need to accomplish the following day—

plagued him constantly. He'd yet to find anything that calmed him enough to allow him a good night's sleep in years.

But at least he now had something that was proving a worthy distraction.

His mobile chimed with an alert. A text from Skorpion.

She's coming up.

Uilleam checked the time, surprised to find she would be home this early in the day, but even knowing that she was almost upon him, he didn't rush to leave her apartment. He merely set the picture frame back in place before he walked out of her bedroom.

He was nearly back in front of the couch when the front door swung open, and there she stood, a vision in a navy blue skirt that fluttered at her knees and a sheer blouse with white polka dots.

Elegant was always the word that came to mind when he thought of her. Everything about her was unlike any woman he had met in all his years.

And more curious was the fact that she didn't appear alarmed at the sight of him standing in her apartment.

"I thought you'd send the other one instead of coming yourself," she said, pushing the door closed but not moving deeper into the apartment. As if she were giving him the semblance that she wasn't afraid of him but had a way out should she need it.

"The other one?" he parroted, walking over and sitting in the armchair opposite the window.

"Your associate? Bodyguard? I'm not quite sure what he is to you."

Skorpion, she meant. "How did you know I was here?"

A smile curled the left edge of her mouth before she tucked dark strands of hair behind her ear, then pointed at her laptop across the room. A detail he *had* noticed when he came in but dismissed just as quickly, but now that she pointed it out to him, he saw the red light blinking every few seconds.

A poor man's security camera.

"I answered your question," she said with a slight cant of her head. "If you'd answer mine ..."

"Please," he offered with a gesture of his hand for her to sit.

She only hesitated a moment—and he would have paid a fortune to know what she was thinking in that pretty little head of hers—before she crossed the floor and sat, crossing one ankle over the other and folding her hands in her lap.

Graceful in a way that wasn't forced.

"Why are you here?"

"D'you truly wish to waste time asking questions you already know the answer to? Ask what you *don't* know, not what you do."

His attempt to get a rise out of her, just to see how she would respond, didn't work. If anything, while there seemed to be a cutting edge to her gaze now, her smile only grew a little wider.

"What really happened to Miranda Abernathy?"

"You believe I harmed that woman?"

She shook her head. "I believe you know who did."

"Interesting. Would you be a dear and turn that off?" he asked with a nod of his head in the direction of her laptop.

She might have been distracting—from her delicate features, down the hollow of her throat where a pendant rested, and even farther down the long length of her legs—but he wasn't so distracted to know that he wasn't still being recorded.

Something he would need to get rid of in the near future.

And if she were smart, as he imagined she was, it wasn't the only thing she was using either.

"Sure." She walked over and closed the screen, the scent of her perfume lingering even after she returned to her seat.

And when she moved to speak again, he cut her off. "And the other, if you'd please."

For a moment, he wasn't sure whether she would deny the existence of the other, but instead of denying his words, she simply reached into the bag at her hip and pulled out a silver tape recorder, making a show of clicking the side button to turn it off and set it on the table between them.

"Now that it's just you and me, care to answer?"

"Again," he said, tapping his thumb against the armrest. "There's no point in me answering questions you already know the answers to. It's terribly boring."

"It's not always about what you know, Mr. Runehart. It's about what you can prove, but you already know that, don't you? Otherwise, evidence to Paxton's involvement in her death would have surfaced by now."

She didn't break eye contact nor fidget when she spoke. She was calm, collected, and seemingly ready to catch him in a lie.

But she wasn't afraid.

Not even a little.

"What is it that you suspect I do, Karina?"

She blinked when he said her name, a momentary break in her careful expression. She appeared caught off guard, as if now, for the first time, she suspected he *saw* her.

"Helping murderers get away with their transgressions, I imagine."

He laughed, the sound light and surprised. "You think so little of me."

"Correct me where I'm wrong then."

He would love to, but there was no fun in telling her everything all at once.

Not to mention, what she was describing was the very least of what he wanted to be.

There was still much work left to be done.

"Nothing is ever so black and white."

She shook her head. "It can be."

Tapping his thumb against the side of the chair he was sitting in, he rose to his feet and crossed to her, watching the wariness that entered her dark eyes before she dutifully tilted her chin up, refusing to show any fear.

Was *that* what he liked about her?

Her defiance?

Her ability to stand up to him though she already thought he was capable of monstrous things?

When he got too close, however, she stood. Not backing down. Not flinching.

He *wanted* her.

He took her face in his hands, his thumb stroking over the softness of her cheek, the curve of her lips, all but feeling the way they parted as she inhaled.

She was very good at pretending, one of the best he'd seen, but she couldn't hide the way he affected her.

Not when her breath stuttered, or the way her pupils ate up every last bit of the beautiful brown of her eyes when he got close.

No, it wasn't all fear that kept her entertaining him.

"You don't fear me, but you should," he whispered, holding her gaze. "I would eat you alive."

Her smile was too gentle, too soft compared to the heat in her eyes. "You don't fear monsters. You make monsters fear you."

He had the ridiculous urge to kiss her just to see what her mouth tasted like. Would it be as good as he remembered? *Better*? "Is *that* what you think?"

"Isn't that why you're here?" she asked with a little tilt of her head. "To intimidate me into silence?"

"You think so little of me," he repeated for the second time.

"I don't know *what* to think of you," she returned, sounding remarkably earnest.

As if she *were* curious, even beyond the reason they had crossed paths in the first place.

It was no secret to him that she had heard rumors about him. Some were, undoubtedly, true, others just a part of the lore that came with being a man in his position. Not once had he ever considered correcting someone's assumptions about him.

He neither had the time nor patience to do so in the past, but he wanted to for her.

Because she fascinated him and was nothing at all like he had expected.

She made him *curious*, and that was, by far, one of the few emotions he hadn't felt in ages. And instead of being annoyed by that fact, it only drew him to her further.

Which was why, for the first time in a long time, he was going to do things differently. Change the narrative after he had already crafted it.

He didn't give a shit about Paxton or what came of the man, so long as it served his endgame, and if he was able to accomplish it, he would have exactly what he wanted.

And her.

He would have *her*.

12

MIDNIGHT MEETINGS

As night fell over the city, pale blue shifting to a dark navy, brisk winds picked up fallen leaves and swept them down the street.

Karina stood on the corner of 10th Street at the very edge of Clifton Park, waiting for any sign of the man she had come to see.

She wasn't sure how long she'd been standing there, her coat wrapped tight around her against the cold weather, but even as time seemed to creep by without any trace of the man she was waiting for, she couldn't bring herself to leave just yet.

Instead, she waited.

And waited some more.

Anticipating the moment when Uilleam would show his face.

If he would show his face, rather, considering the sort of man she was starting to realize he was. Considering her last few interactions with him—including his impromptu visit to her apartment—she had no guarantee he would actually do as she thought he would.

He was proving unpredictable that way.

But she hadn't cared about that after receiving a text from the anonymous number some hours ago with a time and location. She knew it was him, even without it saying as much. And though she knew she should be cautious, even set the terms herself, dreaded curiosity had made the decision for her.

Taking one last look around, she was ready to accept that Uilleam had stood her up, but just as she was about to turn and signal the upcoming taxi driving in her direction, she saw the big man emerge from behind the shadow of a tree.

She conjured his name from the recesses of her mind, ready to greet him properly once she darted over to him, figuring Uilleam couldn't be far behind if he was here now, but when she attempted to step around him, he remained in her path, his gaze expectant.

He couldn't be serious … "Seriously?"

"It's not personal," Skorpion said with a shrug. "I don't trust anyone."

A trait that had probably kept him alive this long.

In their line of business, those they trusted the most held the most secrets.

"Fine," she replied, holding her arms out on either side of her, the straps of her bag clutched in her hand. "Do you need to search me?"

Skorpion didn't respond, not when his actions did all the talking for him. He started at her wrists and worked his way in, brief passes of his hands over her frame and all the optimal places she could conceal a weapon. When he was satisfied, he took a step back.

"He's waiting for you."

She nodded, already moving around him before the last word was out of his mouth. The admission would never leave her lips, but Karina was eager to see him, wondering whether she would get a glimpse of the charming man who had swept her across the dance floor with her hand tucked in his and his other resting firmly on the small of her back, or if she would see a hint of the man who had warned her to walk away with a darkness in his eyes that she could still see when she closed her own.

Walking deeper into the park, her heels clicking on the cement, she couldn't help but notice *him* sitting alone on the bench a few feet away.

He couldn't be missed.

It didn't matter that his dark suit blended with the night around him, or that he was tucked away *just* enough that one's gaze might have skipped over him if they weren't paying attention.

But Karina saw him.

She feared she always would.

Uilleam sat so casually, his foot hooked over his knee, his arm stretched out across the back of the metal bench, the platinum watch on his wrist glinting as his jacket and shirt sleeve shifted back a touch.

He stared out at the water, and she was almost sure he was oblivious to everything around him until his mouth opened once she got close.

"A pleasure to see you again, Karina."

Such simple words, yet they affected her so greatly.

There was something about the way he said her name … 'Miss Ashworth,' was always said in a slightly sardonic tone, but when he said her *name,* as if he liked the way it sounded himself, it made her pay attention. She'd heard dozens of people say it before, yet it had never sounded quite so … intimate.

"I didn't realize we were on a first-name basis, Uilleam?"

"I quite think we're beyond formalities, no?" A flash of white teeth as he smiled. "Please. Sit with me."

It was the middle of the night—or the wee hours of the morning, depending on who was asked—and while the majority of him was cast in shadow, she could still *feel* his presence. She was too acutely *aware* of him sitting beside her, even with the distance between them as she sank down onto the bench.

It was proving nearly impossible to stare out at the water or the trees or *anything* other than his profile.

The cut of his jaw and the slight scruff there. The little tease of a smile that had yet to fail in making her heart thump a little bit harder in her chest.

Clearing her throat to force those thoughts out of her head, she finally spoke. "You asked me here. What can I do for you?"

"I've come to proposition you."

Perhaps it was the way he worded that remark or even that she could *hear* the smirk in his voice, but whatever the reason, she finally looked at him. "I'm *sorry?*"

"Was there something about the question that wasn't clear?"

"What are you propositioning me for … exactly?"

Now she could see the smirk on his face as he turned to look at her. "Which would you prefer?"

"I … well …" Why was she struggling to answer such a basic question? "You asked me here about Paxton, didn't you?"

He studied her a moment, his gaze flickering over her face. "For now."

Something very akin to disappointment flitted through her before she dismissed the feeling altogether. "Then you want to offer me a deal like you have others?"

"Of a similar sort, yes."

"And what exactly do you expect in return?"

"A favor to be called in at a later date."

"That leaves too much room for misunderstandings."

"Yet it's what I'm offering all the same."

He had her backed into a corner, and she would bet everything she owned that had been his intention all along.

It wasn't as if she could refuse him, not when he was the sole individual who would help her get what she needed against Paxton.

He held all the power, and he knew it.

"I won't hurt anyone for you."

His laugh was light, though so distinctly masculine it made her blush. "I'm fully capable of handling that on my own."

"I won't help you cover up a crime either …"

"I think we can both agree I don't need any aid in that area either."

Unfortunately, she did. She knew that quite well.

So what did he want?

Even as the question repeated on a loop inside her head, she knew that she wouldn't be getting an answer tonight. "How can I trust that you'll deliver whatever it is you're offering?"

"You can't."

She glanced up at him sharply. "What?"

Uilleam angled his body toward hers, leaning in her direction. So close now that she could see the golden flecks in his brown eyes. "Criminals, by nature, are unreliable. Nor do we deserve anyone's trust. I'm not telling you to trust me, but the decision is yours to make, all the same."

Which meant, she didn't really *have* a choice in the matter. Not if she wanted the truth and he was the only thing left standing in her way.

"Fine."

"Not nearly good enough, poppet," he whispered, though the words sounded impossibly loud with the way she was so focused on him. "I need to hear you say it."

Tucking the loose strands of hair behind her ear—a nervous gesture she needed to give up—she forced herself to say the words she knew he wanted to hear. "You have a deal."

He smiled. "Everything you need to give justice to the woman will be at the address I send you. Wait for my text."

"I was under the impression that if there was any evidence connecting him to her death, you would have destroyed it."

"I might work for my clients, but I *always* do what's in my own best interests first."

More like he was keeping collateral, she thought.

It was smart, she grudgingly admitted to herself. Especially considering the risk he was taking himself. It was only appropriate to take measures to ensure he was protected as well.

And now she was making excuses for him ...

"I'm curious."

"Hmm?"

"Do your clients know you keep dirt on them?"

"Those that know better, I imagine."

That startled a laugh out of her. "People really don't understand the gravity of what it means to call on your services, do they?"

Another smile from him. "They overestimate their own abilities while underestimating mine. Considering things usually work out in my favor, I don't mind it so much."

She was impressed, more than she probably should have been, all things considered, but while she could admire the clear power he seemed to wield, it also brought another thought to mind.

"Do you even know her name?"

"Who?"

"The woman your client killed. Do you know her *name*? Did he?"

His brow furrowed. "How is it relevant?"

Another simple question, yet it held such a complex answer.

An answer that made her frown as she regarded him.

Uilleam didn't appear ashamed, nor did he seemed bothered by the fact that he didn't seem to have an answer to her question. And while he might have been unnecessarily attractive with a keen mind, it didn't erase the fact that he also didn't seem to have any regard for anyone else.

A beautiful man with a black soul.

"I'll be waiting for your text," she told him before standing, leaving the conversation there. She was blurring the lines, and that had to stop.

She turned to leave, her thoughts on what she might find at the address he planned to send her.

Would it all be circumstantial?

Would it be exactly what she needed to give a grieving family peace?

She wished she knew.

"Karina."

She'd hardly made it a foot away before his voice had her turning to look back at him.

He stood as well, stepping forward far enough that he was no longer shrouded in darkness. Now, she could better see the strawberry blond hue of his tousled hair, as if he ran his fingers through it incessantly, and the expression on his face that she couldn't quite read.

"Miranda Abernathy was her name. An only child. She came from loving parents, but caught up with a man she shouldn't have trusted."

He rattled off more facts about her, some she knew, others she didn't. He knew more than she would have ever given him credit for.

She was too surprised to think of a response quick enough before he stood in front of her, his gaze trained on hers.

"Trust your instincts."

She looked at him. "What does that mean?"

"Your expression changed," he said with a shake of his head.

"For a split second there, you started to think better of me than I deserve. Before you came and disrupted my work, I *didn't* know what her name was nor did I care to find out." Now he was the one tucking her hair behind her ear, the feel of his touch lingering long after he pulled his hand away. "I'm a different sort of monster, Karina. Don't ever forget that."

Before she could respond, he turned and disappeared into the darkness.

13

TRUTH OR LIES

TWISTING HER HAIR UP INTO A TIGHT BUN, KARINA CHECKED HER reflection in the mirror.

This part was easy.

Changing her clothes from a skirt and heels to leggings and running shoes was almost second nature. She didn't have to think about what she was about to do while she dressed. She could pretend, almost, that she was doing something else.

Something as innocent as running a few blocks before jogging back home. Or even down to the corner store where she could pick up another carton of milk that she needed to do anyway.

Anything other than preparing to go off to the address Uilleam had given her, especially when she didn't know what was waiting for her once she got there.

The scrap of paper she had written the address on was practically burning a hole through the pocket of her jacket. A damning bit of information that was more of a siren's song than she had anticipated.

Though she had been curious enough to want to go to the address just to see what was there, Karina wasn't a complete idiot. While she could almost believe that Uilleam was willing to betray his own client, she also didn't doubt he was capable of anything.

And for that reason, before she had ever taken off her clothes to get ready to head back out, she opened her laptop and searched the address through Google.

A picture of a brownstone with light colored bricks stared back at her. A residential address on the Upper East Side.

She couldn't find any mention of the owner in the listings—nor did she find any connection to Paxton either— but she felt less nervous about it being someone's home rather than a remote location.

More interesting was the fact that he hadn't told her what, exactly, she would find there. It could have been a person—perhaps another mistress that he'd tucked away to make sure she couldn't be questioned—the place itself, which was a likely possibility, or something else within the brick walls.

She wouldn't know until she was there.

And *that* thought worried her the most.

Zipping up the front of her hoodie, Karina double-checked her reflection one last time before she grabbed her keys and tiny pocket-size bag from the top drawer of the side table near her front door and slipped out of her apartment.

Despite the hour, the city was still alive and crawling with people. Some on phones and oblivious to everything around them. Others taking pictures and lost in the world that was bright with lights. No one paid very much attention to her as she eased through the crowds and waited until she got well enough away from her apartment before hailing a taxi.

It was a short drive to the quiet neighborhood, the glow of the streetlights providing the only illumination on the street.

Karina lingered in front of her destination until the cabbie was well on down the street, his taillights fading as he disappeared around the corner.

Once she was sure he was gone, she hurried up the flight of stairs until she reached the front doors. Ducking down, she grabbed her pack from her pocket and unzipped it, staring at the number of tools strapped in place.

It had been ages since she'd needed to use them, but she imagined picking a lock was very much like riding a bike.

Muscle memory.

The minute her fingers closed around the tension wrench, she was taken back to when she had been ten years old and had locked herself out of her room. She had always liked to fiddle with the lock, though Katherine had always warned her to be careful or else she would make a mistake.

She had been quite sure she wouldn't turn the lock accidentally, but for whatever reason, that day she *had*.

While she had been afraid to tell her mother about what happened, she also knew there was no point in delaying the inevitable.

Katherine would find out soon enough.

Her mother hadn't been angry, however—at least not the sort that would result in her being punished for a few days—she had simply left the kitchen where she had been rolling out dough for a strawberry and rhubarb pie and led her into her office off the side of the kitchen.

Karina had stood there in silence, watching her every move, anticipating the moment when her calmness would turn to something else, but she had merely grabbed a small pack—very much like the one she held now—and showed her how to open a locked door.

It was here, she'd thought, that the lesson was that mistakes could be forgiven, especially for a first.

But instead of leaving the door open, Katherine had leaned in and twisted the lock once more before shutting the door again. She then handed over the tools without another word and left her to it.

For a moment, Karina had stood there, not knowing what to say or do, but after a while, it clicked that the only way she would be able to sleep in her own bed that night was if she was able to replicate what her mother had just done.

The *real* lesson in that had been whether or not she had been paying attention.

Even now she could remember the way her knees had ached, and how fatigue had made tears form in her eyes as she had sat there for hours, failing time and time again. But the struggle made it all the more worth it once she heard the lock click and she was finally able to twist the knob and collapse onto the floor in relief.

That familiar anxiety wormed its way through her as she started on this lock that was far more complex than the simple one that had been on her bedroom door all those years ago, but she didn't let it deter her.

Instead, she *embraced* the fear that she might fail.

She used it to make sure her hands held steady, and her focus didn't waver as she started the delicate process of picking the lock.

A benefit to this sort of neighborhood was that it was quiet, with only a lone vehicle passing through every few minutes. She went virtually unnoticed as she kneeled on the stoop and worked.

Her heart beat steady in her chest as she carefully turned the wrench, a breath of relief leaving her once she heard the lock click. A smile almost curled the edges of her lips as she quickly hurried inside and closed the door behind her, already scanning the entryway for the alarm system.

But when she found it and looked it over, expecting to need a password, it was unarmed.

Uilleam's doing, she imagined.

Standing in the middle of the floor, she pulled off her glove long enough to grab her phone and turn on the flashlight before pulling the glove back on and starting forward.

The brownstone was impeccably clean, though there was a lingering soft scent that said someone had been here recently.

Karina started in the living room since it was closest, checking the bookshelves and display pictures. She looked for anything out of place or a hidden safe but came up empty. Five minutes later, she found that the entire ground level was empty of anything she thought might be of interest.

Slowly, she made her way upstairs, pausing when she spotted the line of photographs hung up on the white walls.

Though it wasn't much of a surprise, she still paused over the portrait of Paxton and his wife, their smiles stiff, a glass of champagne in both of their hands.

It was easy enough to believe that Paxton had other properties besides the ones she or the police knew about, but she *was* surprised that Orion hadn't been able to find this one either.

Also Uilleam's doing?

He was very good at making things disappear, she was learning, but it was even more impressive that he could also hide things from other people who did what he did.

Karina headed for the master bedroom next once she reached the second landing, the wood groaning softly as she crossed the floor.

The bed was undone, a pair of men's pajamas left abandoned on the floor on the left side of it.

She thought she would have heard if Paxton had left the city, but with Uilleam monopolizing her attention for the past couple of weeks, she couldn't be so sure.

There was probably a lot she had missed, a thought that suddenly made her uncomfortable.

You'll find what you're looking for at the address I send you.

Those words played over and over in the back of her mind as she ventured around, careful not to touch anything as she moved from room to room, searching for anything that could be used to convict Paxton.

She didn't doubt that whatever it was would be obscure enough to mean nothing to someone else, but everything to Paxton. It was the only thing that made sense. Not only had she done her research on Paxton, but she had done the very same for Miranda, even going to her childhood home to learn more about her.

No doubt Uilleam knew about that.

He trusted that she could find whatever was left behind.

But just as she was sure whatever clue was here she was completely missing, she ventured back downstairs to the kitchen and found an office off to the side of it.

She pushed the door open with one hand and flipped the light switch up with the other.

And to her surprise, wrapped around a lamp sitting on the large desk was a gold necklace.

One with a very distinctive charm.

A necklace that had been around Miranda's neck the night she died. Something that Karina had only learned about later after a late night phone call with Nicole.

"She never takes it off," Nicole had said between tears. *"But it's missing and no one can find it."*

And now, here it was.

Would it have Paxton's prints on it?

Would it matter since it was found here, in his place?

Would he —

"Freeze and put your hands where I can see them."

Karina didn't immediately mean to follow the command, but at the sound of the voice behind her, she stopped where she stood, keeping her hands visible at her sides. The back door loomed just ahead of her, practically taunting her with escape.

And with the adrenaline rushing through her, she was almost positive that she would be able to reach it and get the door open within a few seconds.

But she fought that instinct and slowly turned to look over her shoulder.

A uniformed officer stood across the room, his gun firmly trained on her, his gaze unblinking, but even at her distance, she could still see the bead of sweat at his temple. The glow of red and blue lights broke out then, shining through the front windows, and she knew at that moment that she couldn't do anything to get out of this.

Whether she ran now wouldn't matter. She was caught.

And above all else, she also knew this was Uilleam's doing.

He had set her up.

Tricked her into believing pretty words that ultimately meant nothing.

And she had all too eagerly fallen for his bait.

Just as so many others had, she was sure. She'd been a fool to trust him.

As the officer crossed the room, more certain now that she wouldn't try to run, she thought of the phone call she could make. One phone call to one person who would make all this go away.

It would be as if it never happened at all.

But even as she felt cold metal wrap around her wrists, she remained silent.

TOBACCO AND SOME KIND OF CLEANING PRODUCT WERE ALL Karina could smell in the back of the black and white cruiser.

And even as her heart was in her throat, she still couldn't bring herself to speak, not even when they'd been reading her rights to her back at Paxton's other house.

She couldn't afford to incriminate herself, but her mind was racing, no matter how calm she appeared on the surface.

The drive to the station was over far more quickly than she expected. Even the walk upstairs to the bullpen proved rather uneventful.

The officer whose name tag read Jacobi took off her handcuffs and left her standing next to an empty desk, mumbling for her to stay put while he disappeared around the corner. She wasn't sure where his partner had taken off to.

Odd.

She had never been arrested before, nor had she ever actually seen anyone getting arrested, but she couldn't help but think this wasn't standard procedure. She doubted people who broke the law were just left alone without someone to ensure they didn't just walk out the way she was tempted to.

Yet no one was paying any attention to her.

She wasn't even sure if anyone had actually noticed their entrance.

For a while, Karina did as she was told, standing in the same spot where Jacobi had left her, shifting her weight on her feet, but after minutes of this, she finally sank into the chair next to her hip and waited.

And waited some more.

And waited even *longer*.

Before she knew it, nearly half an hour had passed, and neither Jacobi nor his partner came back.

What the hell was going on?

"You waiting on someone, miss?"

Karina turned, spotting the officer who was looking at her expectantly. For once in her life, she had no idea what to say.

The truth ... or a lie.

"Ma'am? He's already finished taking your statement, so you don't need to stick around. We have everything we need."

She blinked, not sure she was hearing him correctly. "Sorry?"

He smiled as if he dealt with people like her every day. "Once he took your statement, that's all that's needed. You don't have to stick around for the paperwork. The officer explained that to you, right?"

She hadn't the slightest idea what he was talking about, but she still found herself saying, "Yeah, he did."

"All right then," he said with a smile and a nod. "Have a good evening."

Maybe this was some sort of game they played with perpetrators, but as she slowly rose out of her chair, she was willing to play it.

But she did wait until he turned—once he realized she was actually moving—before she stepped away from the desk, unable to keep from glancing back to see if Jacobi was returning.

Still, no one attempted to stop her.

She kept her hands balled into tight fists, then folded her arms across her chest as she made her way out of the police station, taking a calming breath with every step she took.

Karina didn't relax until she was back in her apartment with the door shut and locked behind her before she slid to the floor.

Only then did she drag in a noisy breath and finally exhale.

❧ 14 ❧

EXAMPLES

GOD HELP HIM SHOULD HE EVER SEE THE INSIDE OF A PRISON cell, even if it was inside a facility as nice as this one — Uilleam would be prone to drastic things if he was ever confined.

Though he had lost his image ... and reputation ... and his company was currently selling stocks as quickly as they possibly could, Paxton could still afford some luxuries.

For now.

His lawyer, a man who was far more brilliant than Uilleam had originally pegged, had managed to get him housed in a white-collar prison as opposed to one where more violent criminals were held. Though when he thought about it, and a smile usually crept on his face when he did, he knew Paxton wouldn't survive a day inside one of those.

Here, at Gardsdale Prison, there were fewer guards — and those that *were* here were rather lax with the prisoners — as well as amenities men who had committed felonies shouldn't possess, but to a man like Paxton, who had always been able to get whatever he wanted at the snap of his fingers and was used to the finer things in life, this was his own personal hell.

It didn't take much effort at all for Uilleam to arrange a visit, to slip inside during the changing of the guards. When the video cameras froze within seconds of each other as he made his way through the various hallways until he found the designated meeting room he had requested.

It was an all-white affair with plain gray carpet. A desk bisected the floor, three bookcases on both the east and west walls, and two high back chairs that didn't seem to belong in such a place.

The warden's office.

A man who didn't care very much about the criminal justice system and the way it worked so long as he had prisoners occupying his cells—that was the way of private prisons. There was good money in it.

One carefully wrapped bundle of hundred-dollar bills had ensured that the man would be absent and there would be no mention or recording of Uilleam's visit here.

As he entered the man's office, he didn't bother sitting in one of the armchairs as if he were a guest but helped himself to the warden's desk chair—the position of power in the room.

After all, that was what he was and had always wanted to be.

The most powerful man in the room.

He glanced down at the *Ulysse Nardin* watch on his wrist, counting the seconds ticking by as he waited for his guest to join him.

Funny, how quickly the tables turned.

How it had been Paxton waiting on him not too long ago. When he'd been the man behind the desk.

The irony wasn't lost on him.

It wasn't long before he heard the thump of heavy footsteps outside the office door, then the unmistakable rattle of a doorknob being turned before two men were entering the office—one in a guard's uniform and the other in a white prison jumpsuit.

Paxton had looked expectant as he entered the office as if he had been anticipating someone else where Uilleam was sitting, but when he saw who sat before him, his face mottled with red, a telling sight, but he didn't utter a word.

Not until the guard handcuffed his wrist to the chair he sank into with a nod to Uilleam before leaving the room entirely. He wouldn't go far—not so long as they were alone together. While the warden might have been willing to accept a bribe in letting this meeting happen, he also had to ensure that everyone left the room alive.

More paperwork for him otherwise.

"Come now," he told the man, unable to help the smile forming on his face. "Why so glum?"

"As if I would ever have to explain that to you."

"Surely, you don't think I was the one who put you in here," Uilleam said, rearing back and going as far as to look astonished by the accusation. "I never lifted a finger against you, Paxton. That's a promise."

The man scoffed, not easily convinced. "You found a way around that fucking promise, didn't you? This was your doing—everyone fucking knows that. People see you for what you truly are."

"And what would that be, exactly, Mr. Paxton?"

"A two-headed snake."

Uilleam wagered he should have been offended by that. Paxton was clearly trying to get a rise out of him, but what the man failed to understand was that he had already won. The game was over. There was no need for him to feel any more emotional attachment to something that no longer meant anything.

He also didn't mind the imagery of the perceived insult.

"I'm going to make you pay for this."

"You never seem to understand when there's no dog left in the fight, do you?"

"Gaspard will hear about this."

"Who do you think came up with this little idea?"

Of course, Gaspard had never explicitly said as much, but it had all practically been spelled out for him since the beginning. He hadn't understood, at the time, what the man had been trying to get him to understand, but after putting Paxton in here with no blowback to himself, he understood what the man really meant.

It was too easy and uncomplicated to conceal a dead body and paint an image that could just as easily be explained away any problems with the painted theory. There was no mystery or finesse.

Anyone could do that.

But not everyone could reverse everything they had done while making sure there was no connection to themself, and then and make it seem as if the evidence had all been right there in the first place.

The thought made him smile.

Those that underestimated him usually learned to regret it.

"We had a deal."

"And you violated it the moment you went behind my back or had you thought I wouldn't find out what you had done?"

Truthfully, he had already had plans to forsake the deal he'd made with Paxton long before he had actually done so. But before he had requested Karina meet him, word had gotten back to him about a certain conversation Paxton had.

"I don't know what you're talking about?"

"No? You weren't attempting to have me blackballed?" Uilleam asked with an arch of his brow.

He wasn't necessarily upset that the man had tried—at least it proved that he had a set of bullocks on him—but that didn't mean he could let the slight go unanswered.

And simply because of the sheer unmitigated gall, he'd needed to make an example out of him, so here they were.

"It was a mis—"

"Let's not rehash history."

Some of the righteous fury in Paxton's eyes died down, his back pushing a little straighter as he adjusted in the chair. It was too late to try and defend his actions.

He was already in prison awaiting trial and Uilleam simply didn't care one way or the other.

That fact was probably written across his face.

The poor, foolish man.

"If it's any consolation, I don't blame you for your mistakes. We were all weak once—some of us just grew out of it."

"It wasn't—"

"Though I would delight in providing you with all the sordid details, there's just not enough time in my day for that, I'm afraid." He tapped his thumb against the the stack of papers sitting on the desk, considering his next words. "We all have a part to play in this world, Paxton. Yours was to fail."

Perhaps he finally recognized that there was no getting out of his current predicament. Not when Uilleam had placed him here and there was nothing he could do about it.

But his spirit wasn't beaten, not completely.

"You'll never be anything more than what you are right now. A maid cleaning up another's mess. You're *nothing*. Just a stupid boy who will die before you ever —"

Uilleam stood and planted his hands in the middle of the desk, leaning his weight forward. "If you finish that remark, I'll have you transferred to maximum security and you'll learn in the worst of ways what cleaning up someone's mess actually means."

Paxton wisely pressed his lips together.

Uilleam had come from a long line of great men.

Men who took without waiting for something to be given.

He would accomplish more than they had ever dreamed. And just because he hated the man, he would see Paxton transferred anyway.

An example for those that came after him.

15

ROYAL EVE

ACROSS THE CITY, JUST OUTSIDE OF BROOKLYN, THE ROYAL EVE Bistro sat on an unremarkable corner of 16th Street—the kind of place that blended in with the other buildings on either side of it so it might have been missed if one wasn't looking for it, but it was unmistakable with its pale blue trim and white painted wrought-iron furniture.

Karina couldn't remember how she had discovered the little restaurant or the delicious buttery croissants they made fresh each day, but once she had, she made it a point to dine here at least once every couple of weeks.

A treat for when she deserved one.

And there was no better time for sweets than when avoiding a jail sentence.

It wasn't the arrest, necessarily, that had bothered her the most over the past couple of weeks since it happened, but rather the fact that she still didn't know whether the police had caught her there by chance, or if it had been by design.

Either way, she wanted to see Uilleam.

She wanted to know whether it has been his doing—if he ever intended for her to get any evidence against Paxton or if he only wanted her out of the way. Had the police been there because it was a part of his plan all along?

She had so many questions and not enough answers.

But there was no way she could get anything when she couldn't actually find him.

Until then, she would just enjoy breakfast.

She followed the hostess through the restaurant and out the side door that led to a patio with more than a dozen of tables, the majority of them already taken. She found a vacant one just to the left of the middle, but as she took her seat, her phone chimed.

Camilla had already suggested—demanded, really—in that no-nonsense way of hers that Karina should take some time off after everything. It was left unspoken that Camilla thought she had gotten too close to this one, and she hadn't been able to admit as much until after Paxton was arrested and she felt like her work was done.

It was something she didn't want Karina to repeat again.

But Camilla didn't know that, in part, it was because of Uilleam that she had stayed on it so relentlessly. And though things had gotten a little muddled in the middle when she had been far too focused on one-upping Uilleam, in the end, it had still been about Paxton going to prison.

So if it wasn't work calling, then there was only one other person it could be.

The one phone call she *really* didn't want to answer.

She reached for it but changed her mind at the last moment. Katherine would just have to wait until she was in a better headspace to explain what all had happened.

The ringing tapered off, just long enough for the waiter to come and take her drink order before disappearing again.

The silence of her phone had her breathing a sigh of relief.

If only for a second.

Because not even a moment later, her phone was ringing again.

Once was forgiven, but she knew better than to ignore it a second time.

Karina plucked the phone from her bag and answered. "Hello, Mother."

Even though the rational side of her knew that the woman on the other end couldn't possibly see her since she was home more than three thousand miles away, she still sat up a little straighter and smoothed her hair back off her shoulders to make sure not a single strand was out of place.

Appearances are important, her mother would say.

"Karina, darling. It's been a spell, hasn't it?"

Only Katherine could load a seemingly innocent question with meaning. Her tone didn't have to change for Karina to know her mother was disappointed in their lack of contact.

She should have called her at least once over the past few months to keep her informed of the work she did here in New York or what she might have heard, considering Paxton's very public arrest.

That quickly, she didn't feel like an adult working and in control of her own life, but rather the same little girl she had once been.

For a moment, she was back at Ashworth Hall, her head tucked forward in shame, too afraid to meet her mother's stare, but she also hadn't wanted to see the looks the other girls would give her.

One of her greatest weaknesses—she cared too much what others thought of her.

"The paper has kept me busy," she answered simply with as much of the truth as she was willing to admit to at the moment.

Because while she thought she might have garnered some strength and power during her interactions with Uilleam, one conversation with Katherine would have her believing she had not only made a complete fool of herself, but she had gained nothing in return.

Worse, she knew she wouldn't be completely wrong.

"Too busy to let your poor mother know how you are?" she asked, and though Karina wasn't in front of her, she could almost imagine the quirk of her brow as the question hung between them.

"I've spoken to Isla," she returned softly, her gaze scanning the immediate area, wishing the waiter would return to give her an excuse to end the phone call.

Though Katherine enjoyed her lectures and would much rather hold her here until she answered all her questions, she would frown upon anyone on the phone in a restaurant.

Manners were most important her.

"I'm aware," Katherine said, to her surprise. "*She* keeps me updated."

While she might have attempted for that to be used as a slight, the admission came begrudgingly. Isla might have called her, and had probably mentioned her and Karina speaking, but she had her own reasons for keeping their mother updated with all the sordid, seedy details of her life.

If only because she knew it got a rise out of her.

"I promise to call when there's something worth calling about," she said, though she wasn't sure when this moment would be exactly.

She had thought that call would center around Uilleam and everything she had found out about him, but he had managed to slip through her fingers much too quickly.

"I'll be expecting it in two weeks' time. Otherwise, I might have another business venture I want to put you on."

Karina couldn't dignify that with a response.

At least not one that wouldn't get her into trouble.

Forcing a smile, Karina nodded to herself. "I'll call you, Mother."

"Looking forward to it, dear."

She was so focused on ending the call that she hadn't noticed the shadow that fell over her table until the seat across from her was pulled back and a man wearing an impeccable suit and opaque sunglasses sank down in the chair across from her.

It was all she could do not to look surprised by *his* sudden presence. As if the mere thought of had conjured him. Worse, she had been so distracted with Katherine that she had stopped paying attention to her surroundings, which even allowed him to get so close in the first place.

A mistake she couldn't make again in the future.

"Radiant as always, poppet."

God, that *pet name*. "What do you want?"

Her eyes dropped to his mouth before the question fully left her mouth.

The troubling thing about Uilleam was that he had a beautiful smile. One that radiated warmth and genuine amusement, and every mischievous thought in his head.

Even as was impossible for her not to feel *something* when she saw him, she at least wanted that feeling to be anger. Because while she might not have been forced to stay in jail, she had still been arrested and left to sit at a desk for nearly an hour.

"I thought you would be happier to see me," he commented thoughtfully with a casual tilt of his head.

"Do the tormented ever feel joy when they're faced with their tormentor?"

"Is that what you think this is?" he asked, his movements far too graceful for a man like him. From the way he unbuttoned his suit jacket as he sat to the way he rested his hand on the table, offering her a clear view of the antique-looking silver ring on his finger with an engraved *R* in the center of it. "*Torment*?"

"Does it matter?"

"I don't ask about things I don't care about," he answered back bluntly. "It's a waste of time."

She shrugged, fully content with not giving him an answer at all.

But he didn't seem to like that very much. "I thought it was clear by now that everything where you're concerned matters to me."

That … was not the answer she was expecting from him. "You had me *arrested*," she reminded him as if he even needed it.

He nodded in understanding. "Ah, is that what you're upset about?"

Did she really need another reason? "Do I really need another reason?"

"I considered that a choice, poppet. I didn't make you do anything you didn't want. It would completely defeat the purpose of the deals I make."

"Pet names aren't going to win you any points with me, Uilleam. And the way I see it, you didn't make a deal with *me*."

"Yet this one made you smile all the same," he responded just as quickly, only addressing the first part of her statement.

Was this what it felt like to be annoyed yet utterly charmed by someone? She couldn't say whether she liked it or not.

"You had me *arrested*," she repeated dryly.

"Were you?"

"It's something I don't think I'll forget."

His smirk was still firmly in place as he looked just past her, lifting his hand ever so slightly before giving a nod of his head. She only managed a couple of seconds of regarding him before she turned to look over her shoulder, curious who he was gesturing to.

Her answer came in the form of a rolling trolley carrying a number of dishes, all of which she was pretty sure she hadn't ordered. It was only after her waiter returned with both a drink for Uilleam and the bottle she had requested did she finally gather that he was the reason the waiter came back so late.

Of course, he wouldn't find anything wrong with his actions.

"Just how long have you been here?"

"Long enough."

She glanced past him, looking for any sign of Skorpion. "Have you been following me?"

He picked up his glass and took a sip, the muscles in his throat working as he swallowed. "I suspect you and I both know the answer to that, don't we?"

Of course, but what bothered her most was that she hadn't known he was there.

She was sure she'd recognize a face like his even in the midst of a crowd. Yet she hadn't seen him until he was ready to make his presence known.

"Yet you still haven't told me what you wanted."

He merely arched a brow, his silence speaking for him.

He wanted *her*—his presence here confirmed that.

"I've come to make you an offer."

"Yeah, right ... After what you just pulled?"

He gave a slight wave of his hand. "I gave you what you wanted, no? Your article has been featured everywhere, and Paxton has been arrested."

"You had *me* arrested!" she hissed at him, careful to keep her voice low.

"Were you really, or had you just appeared to be detained?"

That ... made her pause

So it *had* all been by design.

A product of his own making.

Some part of him had known they would end up here.

"You don't think you should have clued me in to that fact beforehand?"

Instead of responding, he gave her another of those shrugs. He was *impossible*.

They were interrupted by the waiter returning one last time, now setting a tray of warm croissants in the center of the table before disappearing again.

"I want you to go out with me."

Karina sort of froze where she sat, staring across at him. She *almost* believed she hadn't heard correctly. "You're not serious."

Maybe this was just another part of his game ...

"Why wouldn't I be interested in you?" he asked with a little tilt of his head as if the answer evaded him.

That shouldn't have made her feel as good as it did.

"We're opposites, for one. You help people break the law—I make sure they get what they deserve. Those two sorts of people don't mix."

"Yet we've been getting on quite well. Don't tell me you haven't enjoyed this back and forth between us."

She wanted to say there *was* nothing between them, but as she hesitated over her answer, she realized that wouldn't be quite true.

Whether she was ready to admit it to herself now or not, there *was* something between them.

Something that had made him turn against his own client.

Something that had him helping her when he had absolutely no reason to do so. In reality, the decision would have harmed him had she been someone else.

Something that had *her* doing things she never thought she would.

And maybe that was it.

Had either of them been someone they weren't, she doubted the pair of them would be here now.

"So tell me," he said a moment later, raising his drink to his lips. "Where would you like to go?"

"Not anywhere with you."

"Without me," he returned easily.

He wouldn't be so easily deterred.

Karina could think of almost a dozen different restaurants off the top of her head that she had wanted to try, but she wanted to save those though she couldn't put a reason to why just yet.

Instead, she blurted out the first outlandish place she could think of. "Paris," she said a moment later. "If, for whatever reason, I was going out with you, I'd want to go to Paris." She paused, long enough to watch that answer sink into his mind.

"A beautiful city," he agreed with a nod.

"And blue roses."

"Sorry?"

She rested her elbows on the table in front of her, leaning forward, smiling a bit at the way his gaze dipped down her front as if he couldn't help himself.

"Blue roses," she repeated. "If you've ever seen them in person, you'll know how beautiful they are. Unique. And only certain florists get the dye *just* right so they look natural."

She wasn't sure when her obsession with the flower had started, but from then on, they had become her favorite.

He smiled as if he were charmed by her. She liked the softness of his expression, and the way it made him look younger.

She'd suspected he was young already—certainly younger than she'd originally thought before she'd put a face to the name—but when he smiled like that, showing off the dimple in his right cheek, she thought he was closer to his early to mid-twenties than older.

"Duly noted."

"So, you see—"

"Paris can be arranged."

Karina practically choked on her drink. "Sorry, what?"

"When would you like to leave?"

He said it as if it had all been decided already.

"*Paris?*" she asked, unable to hide her disbelief, still holding the breadstick suspended in the air. "It was just a suggestion."

Of all the things in the world he could have said, that didn't even factor on the list. Sure, some part of her had thought—*wondered*—whether he would ask her out, whether he had that type of interest in her.

An interest he'd been all too willing to show her that night in the club.

But beyond that, he hadn't made any other advance toward her. It had all been rather ... businesslike between them.

"And I want to make it a reality. It's beautiful this time of year," he said, sounding as calm as she was astonished.

He didn't seem to think anything of the offer either. As if it was nothing for him.

"I ... I can't just go off to Paris with you."

"Why not?"

"Even if I ignored what I *do* know about you, there's a lot that I don't."

"Let's see about changing your mind where I'm concerned."

That shouldn't have thrilled her at all.

Not even a little.

16

PROMISES ARE PROMISES

HER MIND WAS A POWERFUL THING EVEN WHEN SHE WASN'T conscious.

Because deep in the throes of her slumber, she dreamed of him. Saw the sardonic curve to his lips. Could almost even feel his fingertips when he'd skimmed them over her jaw.

The promise of darkness in his eyes was an aphrodisiac she didn't just want to see. She wanted to taste it. *Feel* it.

In her dreams, it was always offered as a choice.

He extended a hand and waited, daring her to accept everything she didn't know and more still.

She needed to embrace the black world he lived in.

The only thing she had to do was take his hand …

Karina woke with a start, lurching up, her heart in her throat, the pounding force she felt in her chest echoing through the rest of her. Waking up nerve endings she hadn't felt in a long time.

She blew out a heavy breath, shoving the slightly damp strands of her hair back out of her face while trying to get herself under control.

The last threads of the dream finally loosened their hold on her and slipped away. She was alone in her apartment, and everything was as it had been the day before and the three that came before it.

Uilleam had disappeared, as he was prone to do, and despite his surprising presence at the bistro, she hadn't heard from him since.

Something akin to regret swept through her as it had the moment she'd declined his offer. She hadn't known that would be the last time she'd see him. If she had, maybe she would have answered differently.

She didn't like admitting to herself that she was a bit too enthralled by him. Too curious. Too eager.

Especially now that it was all over.

She put it to the back of her mind as she got ready and headed to work, resisting the urge to check her phone every few minutes.

But standing in the back of the elevator, watching the numbers tick by on the monitor in the upper right-hand corner, she wasn't sure how she would get any work done with this distraction she felt.

As the doors opened, she settled in for a long day ahead—for as long as it took her to notice the pop of blue resting on the corner of her desk.

A little voice niggled at the back of her mind, but she refused to listen to it as she ventured closer, his gaze focused solely on the vase of blue roses that were waiting for her next to her computer screen.

They almost didn't look real with the deep shade of blue that seemed impossible, but when she reached out to touch one, feeling the buttery softness of the petals, she knew they were real.

That the task she had thought would be entirely impossible was sitting right in front of her.

"Looks like someone has an admirer," Samantha called as she joined her, handing over a mug of coffee identical to the other one she carried.

Radio silence, then this.

Tucked among the blooming flowers was a single black card. She plucked it free and ran her fingers over the wax imprint on the back before turning it over to read the back.

Promises are promises. — U.

Some part of her had suspected that whatever she asked of him would go in one ear and out the other—that was, in part, why she had asked for something so obscure. She hadn't expected him to take it seriously.

Let alone deliver on it.

But with this arrival came the knowledge that this was only the beginning.

Uilleam would be paying her a visit very soon.

SEVEN DAYS.

Seven bouquets.

Seven tiny notes tucked away for her to find with his stamp across the back of them.

If he was trying to make sure he was at the forefront of her thoughts at all times, he'd accomplished that and more.

Every morning when she came in to sit at her desk and every afternoon when she traveled home after work, carrying a fresh bouquet, fighting the ridiculous smile that had yet to wane.

Today was no different.

She could practically smell the fragrant scent of roses from the moment she boarded the elevator upstairs. It was becoming the high-light of her morning, but she did wonder how long he would keep this up.

Noon came around far too quickly.

Most of her morning had been spent taking various phone calls, entranced by the flowers she couldn't look away from. Others on the floor came by to inquire about them—it wasn't as if in the entire year she had worked here, a man had ever sent her flowers—but she had merely smiled and didn't say a word.

Back from lunch, she was ready to get back to work until she saw him. Sitting beside her desk, as if conjured from the deep recesses of her mind,.

Had no one else noticed him? It wasn't as if she had male visitors every day. And something about him refused to blend in with the world around him. Yet, no one seem to pay him any mind.

He could have been doing anything—rifling through her drawers or even the files on her desk—but instead, he was just sitting there as if he had all the time in the world to wait.

For her.

The thought was welcoming even as it was baffling.

She waited until she was standing behind her chair before she spoke to him. "Is there something I can do for you?"

"Did you like the gift?" he asked with a tilt of his head at the flowers that were still sitting on her desk once she neared.

Saying she *liked* it was a bit of an understatement. It didn't matter that he had sent a bouquet every day after, or that those flowers littered her apartment. That very first batch of blue roses he sent were the ones she kept here at work.

She changed the water daily and made sure it was the perfect temperature before adding food to it.

Karina cleared her throat, trying not to show just how much they meant to her. "They're very lovely."

Now that she was here with him, he didn't mind reaching for the files on her desk, tipping one open to read the contents inside. She swatted his hand away, pulling the manila folders further away from him.

"I can guess you didn't come here about my work."

"No? That seems to be what connects us, isn't it?"

She dropped her elbow onto her desk, resting her chin on her palm as she looked him over, finding far too much enjoyment in seeing him there.

"I don't think that's true at all."

Uilleam had a way of looking so confident that for a moment, she thought she was going to give him what he wanted.

A part of her desperately wanted to.

"When would you like to leave? I'm flexible."

"Lovely flowers or not, my answer hasn't changed."

His smile was a little smug. "You like me."

"As all people like dangerous things. That doesn't mean I want to get bit by the wolf."

Her phone chose that moment to vibrate across her desk, Orion's name proudly displayed on the front of the screen.

An acknowledgment that she did, very well, entangle herself with bad men.

Just not with him.

"Him again," he said with a twitch of his lips. He didn't look particularly happy about the fact that Orion was calling her.

"Work is calling," she answered, opting for the truth instead of alluding to something more.

For whatever reason, she didn't want him to think it was anything other than what it was.

But he didn't seem to buy that.

Nor did he seem particularly fond of Orion at all.

17

FINAL WARNING

SHOWING HIS FACE MORE THAN ABSOLUTELY NECESSARY WAS THE last thing Uilleam needed at the moment, considering how vital it was for him to stay under the radar, but for tonight, he was to making an exception to that rule.

"So at what point do I get to say you're becoming a pain in my ass?" Skorpion asked as he shoved the car door open and stepped out, managing to both look bored and menacing.

"Tonight should be easy," Uilleam said with a shrug, trailing him.

"Right ... because you didn't come here to fuck with the dude dating your obsession?"

Annoyance flared to life inside of him, so swift and sure that he wanted to affirm the man's words—that he wasn't here because of Karina—but as quickly as the emotion clogged his every thought, it faded.

He was too involved.

Too utterly affected by a woman he hardly knew.

He wasn't even thinking clearly ... yet that thought wasn't the one that bothered him most.

If anything, she was the reason he felt alive again.

And if for only that selfish reason, he wanted to keep her to himself until he found a way to scratch her presence out from beneath his skin. The easiest way to ensure that was to eliminate any distractions not of his own making.

Including her *Orion.*

Unfortunately, his spies hadn't been able to give him much in the way of information about the man. He kept too low of a profile, and besides a few burner phones he kept on his person, there was no other way of getting in contact with him.

No social media.

No work history that Uilleam could find anywhere over the past several years.

The man didn't even have a bloody email.

So for lack of any better options, he'd asked around until he had gotten a name and location so he could attend to this problem in person.

"I don't think I've been obsessed with anything since I was a boy."

In those days, he'd had a fondness for sweets and pastries.

This feeling he had now … it was something else entirely.

It was something dangerous and foreign, and though he knew it was in his best interest to leave her be, he wanted her.

He had hardly cleared the entryway onto the warehouse's main floor when he spotted Sergei Yurinoff standing in front of a row of tables, each one holding identical M-5 assault rifles, all polished to a shine and awaiting inspection.

It was hard to miss a man like Sergei, just from the sheer size of him, not to mention the dark tattoo stamped on the side of his neck in black ink. Despite its bold and rather prominent placement, the man had no other visible tattoos.

Turning ever so slightly, Sergei speared him with a glance, his chin tipping up in greeting before he placed the assault rifle he was holding back in line with the others, wiping his hands across the front of his jeans.

"I didn't expect to see you back here so soon," he said by way of greeting, his accent thick and his stare flat as he watched Uilleam cross the floor toward him.

He hardly spared Skorpion a glance, though his mercenary had more than seventy-five pounds on every man in the room. But Sergei had never been one to show fear.

It wasn't the Russian way, as he would say.

"Fortunately for you, Sergei, you're not who I came to see."

He cocked a dark brow, wordlessly waiting for an explanation.

"There's a man who works for you—Orion. I need to speak with him."

This wasn't the first time Uilleam had made such a request, and judging from the way Sergei's eyes narrowed ever so slightly, he was also remembering the last time he had come seeking one of his employees.

"Kanoff was a shit and caused more trouble than he was worth, but Orion does good business."

"This won't be one of those conversations," Uilleam assured him.

While he liked putting an end to his problems on a more permanent basis, Uilleam also knew with some certainty that he wasn't ready to get rid of Orion just yet. Not because he feared any backlash from Sergei—he could find him a dozen good men if needed—but because he wasn't sure how Karina would take the news of his death.

She would suspect him first without question, and while he manipulated the truth to fit his own needs more often than not, he never outright lied.

And should she ever ask, he would tell her what he had done.

Best to avoid that scenario entirely.

"He's back in the stacks," Sergei said with a nod of his head in the right direction.

Uilleam nodded before turning to leave, mindful of the way he had become the subject of attention as the other men gazed on.

While most people in his line of work had their own sort of war room—the place in which most of their business was conducted—Sergei only had a place he affectionately dubbed "the stacks" due to the sheer number of wrapped bundles left inside.

Though weapons accounted for more than seventy percent of his operation, the other thirty came from four different hair salons across the city, all of which he used to launder his illegitimate gains.

One side of the room had already been processed, each ten-thousand-dollar bundle of cash neatly stacked. The other had a number of duffel bags, buckets, or whatever else was handy, all filled with loose bills. Some crumpled, some not.

There were even a number of which covered in what appeared to be blood or some other substance Uilleam really didn't want to think about.

Orion sat behind a table wearing latex gloves, alternating between the trio of machines cycling through the cash he stacked in them.

Even without the warning, he had heard in Sergei's voice earlier, it was clear the man trusted Orion implicitly. The other man Uilleam had seen in this room had been stripped down to nothing but the watch on his wrist.

Orion still wore dark jeans, boots, and a cotton gray T-shirt. A testament to how much he was trusted.

He briefly glanced up when Uilleam entered the room, doing a double take once he realized just who was standing before him.

His reputation preceded him.

"Evening. I thought I'd find you here."

"Yeah?" he asked, pausing momentarily to wrap a rubber band around the bundle of bills in his hand. "What can I do for you?"

"What's your interest in Karina Ashworth?"

His response was immediate and guarded. "What's it to you?"

"My reasons are my own."

Orion made a low sound in the back of his throat before he stood, walking around the table. If nothing else, Uilleam admired his fearlessness.

"Perhaps it would be in *your* best interest to stay away from her."

Had he merely been a lowly soldier and not someone who held Karina's interest, Uilleam might have admired the completely emotionless mask on the man's face. As if he didn't know the danger he was courting the longer he stood there defiant.

"Yeah? And what are you going to do if I don't?"

If he thought the man would walk away if he paid him, Uilleam might have offered him an obscene amount of money to make sure he never showed his face again. But he could see in a glance that that wouldn't be enough.

Interesting.

He'd always liked a challenge.

"Consider this your warning."

Finished with him, Uilleam turned to leave, not caring for the man's response. He'd said what he had come to say, and now he was done.

There was nothing else to be discussed.

But his light chuckle was enough to make him pause for a fraction of a second, his hand on the doorknob.

"You might want to be careful."

Uilleam turned to glance over his shoulder at him, more curious than he was willing to admit. "Sorry?"

"What do you think, she's just a conquest or some shit?" His smile was mocking even as he gave a light chuckle. "You've no idea who she is or what she's capable of. Should be me giving you the warning."

Orion moved to his feet, boldly staring him down as if they were of equal footing. "Everyone else might fear you, Runehart, but I don't. Don't ever fucking threaten me."

It was the little things that could dig their way beneath his skin. That resonated within his bones and inspired him to react.

Violently.

He would make Orion regret those words.

Yes, he fucking would.

❦ 18 ❦

EDGE

ONE WEEK PASSED IN THE BLINK OF AN EYE.

A week since she had last seen Uilleam and he'd made her an offer she was finding hard to forget. It didn't matter that she had declined and had every intention of sticking with that answer, she still found herself thinking about him when she shouldn't.

Everything about him was a bad idea, she knew, but that didn't stop her curiosity from running rampant. It didn't stop her from imagining just what a date with Uilleam would be like.

Because while one part of him seemed the perfect gentleman—opening doors for her, sending flowers, and saying all the right things when he wanted to—there was the other side of him. A darker side she had only gotten a few glimpses of.

Which part was pursuing her?

She understood the allure of what could have been—it was impossible not to feel it. That animal desire to get close to the predator that was both beautiful and dangerous.

The need to see just how far over the precipice she would lean before she fell.

It was ridiculous, especially considering how she had even learned of his existence these past several months, but she just couldn't bring herself to care.

He was quickly turning into a drug.

Shutting her laptop screen for the seventh time that night, Karina rubbed her tired eyes, wondering why she was even bothering to try to get any work done when there was only one thing that occupied her thoughts—one *person*.

Isla would have called her a hopeless romantic, too blinded by matters of the heart to see reason. And while she might have clucked her tongue at the very idea of falling in love with a man because she didn't think she was capable of it, she wouldn't have dismissed Karina's feelings outright.

Rather, she would ask why.

What could she possibly see in a man like Uilleam Runehart? Someone who possessed the very traits she condemned others for.

It wasn't because he was attractive—there were more than a few attractive criminals out there to pick from—though that was part of it, there was something *else*.

Figuring there was no better time to grab dinner since it was already late, Karina slid off her bed and headed for the kitchen, hunting through the drawer for the number of menus inside. She had almost settled on one when her phone's soft chimes echoed back in her bedroom.

The number wasn't already saved in her phone, but it looked oddly familiar.

"Hello?"

"You have a collect call from—" the automated voice cut off as a gruff and *very* familiar voice came over the line and grunted a name before the robotic voice started back up again, asking whether she was willing to accept the charges.

She didn't even give it a second thought. It only took a few seconds of drumming her nails against her comforter before the call connected.

"Glad you—"

"*Orion*? What the hell are you doing calling me from—"

"I'll explain later," he said quickly, cutting her off before she could ask the most important question. "I need a favor."

"Anything."

And she would, in fact, give him anything he asked of her. Whenever she had needed someone or help with a particularly difficult assignment, he had always offered his services. Without hesitation and without fear of what might happen to him if anything went wrong.

She listened, without interruption, to what he needed from her, memorizing the list of tasks before ending the call and walking into her closet to get dressed before leaving her apartment.

Her first stop was to a drop box on the other side of the city, located inside one of those places that didn't ask any questions about its renters so long as the monthly fee was paid on time. Inside, she found a small bag filled with fifty-dollar bills.

More than a few thousand, for sure.

Her second stop was to a bail bondsman. The process was pretty straightforward, the actual filling out of the paperwork and waiting in the cramped space made it all feel tedious.

But three hours later, as she waited at the corner for Orion to step out of the building across the street, she didn't care how long it took for it to happen—she was glad he was out.

He was still sorting through the plastic bag of his personal effects when the door was opened by a guard, and he walked out. She wasn't even sure he saw her coming before she was in front of him, throwing her arms around his shoulders.

"Ready to tell me what you did?"

"Your new stalker."

"I'm sorry?"

He fished out a pack of cigarettes, practically ripping one in half as he placed the stick between his lips. "Sorry, your *admirer*—the jealous motherfucker."

The last bit was said through a cloud of smoke, and while his shoulders sagged the farther away from the jail they walked, he was still utterly and undeniably pissed off.

"Uilleam?" she asked, unable to keep the surprise out of her voice. Not just because she was in disbelief, but because this was about *Uilleam*. "He had you thrown in jail?"

"I was in the middle of making a drop," he explained with a

shrug, though he didn't expand on just what he had been doing. He never did. "I'd barely made it down the block when I was stopped and picked up."

And she knew far too well the sort of ties Uilleam had within the NYPD. She had also been in the unfortunate position of being grabbed by officers who were in his pocket.

She also remembered the look on his face when he had asked her about Orion—how he had seemed annoyed that she had chosen to take his phone call instead of entertaining his invitation.

She hadn't thought he would go this far though.

But if he wanted her attention, he had it now.

And he wasn't going to like the way she responded.

———

KARINA COULD COUNT ON ONE HAND THE NUMBER OF TIMES SHE had ever visited the Waldorf Astoria in Manhattan. Not only because her job at the paper meant she absolutely could *not* afford it, but she had always thought the building, as beautiful as it might have been, wasn't to her taste.

Smiling at the doorman as he opened the door and allowed her in, she didn't bother stopping by the reception desk to find out Uilleam's room number.

She could guess what floor he would be on.

As the doors to the elevator slid open, the concierge inside stood a little straighter as he asked for her floor.

"The penthouse, please," she said with all the confidence that her order would be heeded. "He's expecting me."

He only hesitated a moment before obliging, inserting a key and giving it a twist to the left before pressing the silver button next to the engraving of a star.

The floors ticked by, the glowing numbers making her heart skip a beat. This wasn't like before when she'd had time to prepare herself. When she was walking into a familiar place and wasn't completely on his turf.

But if she hadn't allowed him to walk all over her when it was about an article she was writing and the man at the very center of it, she certainly wouldn't do it when it came to the people she cared about.

The doors opened to a white marble foyer, an orchid in a black vase sitting on a pretty table to her left. Sure, she had anticipated how beautiful the penthouse suite would be, but she was still just as fascinated by all the luxury all the same.

But the feeling only lasted for as long as it took for her to hear quiet voices and the clinking of ice hitting crystal.

Uilleam might have been one of the most powerful and dangerous men she had ever crossed paths with, but that didn't stop her from rounding the corner with her head held high, more than willing to stand toe to toe with him.

He might have made her feel a lot of things, but fear wasn't one of them.

She had only just rounded the corner when she caught sight of him, looking far too good in his relaxed attire. His tie had been abandoned somewhere, the top few buttons on his shirt left undone, and the sleeves rolled up to his elbows.

He looked as if he had just come home, and she could only imagine the kind of things he got up to in a day.

Like throwing innocent—relatively speaking—men in prison just because he had a complex.

Uilleam wasn't alone, however. Skorpion was stretched out on the couch that seemed far too small under his impressive height and weight, one booted foot kicked up on the table. As if he didn't aspire to grace and didn't care if anyone else noticed either.

But as their gazes turned to her, his in relative surprise—from the way his brow arched up at her entrance—Uilleam didn't look surprised at all to find her standing in his suite with her arms folded across her chest.

He looked expectant.

"Give us the room," he said without taking his gaze from her, "if you would."

Even as she wanted to lay into him, to tell him exactly how furious she was at what he had done, she waited until the elevator sounded as the concierge disappeared and Skorpion turned to follow him, his fading footsteps the only thing that told her he wasn't sticking around to listen.

"Karina," Uilleam began with a smile. "You look radiant as always. Care for a drink?"

"Would you *care* to tell me what it is you think you're doing?"

With a downward tilt of his mouth, he looked from the glass of whiskey in his hand back to her. "Having a drink?"

His sarcasm grated on her last nerve. "I know about Orion."

He didn't even blink. "As you were intended to."

"*Why?*" she suddenly snapped. "Why would you do that? And don't say it's because he made a deal with you."

He tossed back his drink, his expression becoming less indifferent. "In case it might have escaped your notice, I don't like to share."

She glared at him even as he crossed the distance between them. "I'm not *yours*."

"Aren't you?" he asked before he caught her face in his hand, gripping her jaw and forcing her to look up at him. "I don't think you would be here if you weren't."

"Mighty full of yourself," she said through gritted teeth, more annoyed with herself that she was reacting to his *words* as much as she was reacting to him.

"Go on then and deny it."

"I'm *not*—"

He took her lips before she could get another word out.

She wished she could say it was a surprise, but she'd watched the moment his gaze flickered down to her mouth, even the slight knowing grin on his face, before she couldn't *see* anything.

But she felt him just fine.

The softness of his collared shirt.

Smooth but hard forearms.

The line of his body pressed against hers.

He robbed her of rational thought. Made her forget every reason she was furious with him.

All she could focus on was how good it felt to be kissed by him.

She could taste the whiskey on his tongue, the bite of alcohol sparking every nerve ending inside her.

But as quickly as she was lost in the feel of his mouth, he pulled away, his smile growing a touch at the way she was still leaned up toward him. His free hand trailed down to the curve of her thigh beneath the dress she wore.

It was hard to ignore the way he he held her face—or even the grip he had on her thigh—and the way the sensation had heat racing down her spine.

She could deny what she felt when it was just words, but she couldn't help the reaction her body gave when he had his hands on her.

"If I got my hand between these legs of yours, would I find you wet for me, Karina?"

She hated the smugness so clear in his voice—the surety.

She hated *more* that if he shifted his fingers just the slightest bit, he *would* find her wet. That there would be no denying the way she wanted him.

And God, what did that say about her that she was already aching for his touch when she should have been furious with him. When she'd had every intention of coming here and telling him off, yet the second he got his hands on her, all the fight fled and her anger turned to something else.

She was weak where he was concerned.

"It's okay," he whispered against her mouth a moment later, his own lips curling up in satisfaction. "It can be our little secret."

She should have said no.

She should have retained her power by denying him what he so clearly wanted.

No should have been the one she was chanting inside her head, but her brain and body were on different wavelengths.

She had never been so close so quickly, and with so very little work on his part.

"Ask me to make you come, and I will." He added just a bit of pressure with his thumb right in the spot where thigh curved into hip, and if he moved the barest amount, he could be right beneath the lace. "I'd give you anything if you ask for it."

The question—the *plea*—was right there on the tip of her tongue, and she knew the moment the words were hanging there between them that he would give her what his eyes were promising.

"Uilleam, make me—"

His phone vibrated so loudly against the glass table it rested on that she jolted, her heart racing again for entirely different reasons this time.

As quickly as she had been drowning in him, more than happy to lose herself in this bliss, she snapped out of it.

Shit.

Shit.

Uilleam sighed as he slid his hand from between her legs.

As he moved over to the table to answer it, she didn't miss the hard outline of his cock through his trousers.

It had been one thing to feel it pressed against her, but now seeing the impressive length of it—and how he seemed as utterly affected as she did—she knew she had to go.

Before she did something incredibly stupid.

"Don't misunderstand me," he said before she could take a step after tossing the phone back down, his gaze drifting over her face. "The only reason he didn't suffer worse was because I was sure you'd be cross with me."

"You want to have a go at me, Uilleam, feel free. But the people I care about are off-limits to you."

That cocky smile of his was back. "And if I ignore that directive?"

"I'll make you regret it," she vowed, meaning every word.

"I can tell you truly believe that."

She could tell, just from the way his lips twitched, he was fighting a smile. He wasn't worried about what she might do, or even *if* she would do anything at all.

He thought he was untouchable.

Now he was the one underestimating her.

Then it was decided.

If he wanted attention so bad, she would give him *exactly* what he wanted.

FROM THE MOMENT SHE HAD WALKED AWAY FROM UILLEAM IN that penthouse, ignoring him calling her name, Karina hadn't allowed any time to go to waste. When she wasn't at the paper working on assignments, she was working on her *other* project. One she had put off for a while because she had finally met the man she had been researching.

Now, it was better.

Now, she knew enough, if not a lot, about him that she could use it to her advantage.

But it wasn't just Uilleam's attention that she wanted—she wanted a reaction.

She wanted to see his discomfort.

At first, her goals had been loftier, hoping to step in and ruin another of his deals, but she doubted he would be making the same mistakes in that regard when it came to her. No, he would see that coming.

And then it had hit her, out of nowhere, while she'd been lounging on the couch with the top of her pen between her teeth and a notebook open in her lap.

If nothing else, there was one thing, for certain, she was arguably good at.

Writing, even in school, had always been her strength. The one subject she excelled at even as she struggled in others before learning to apply herself more.

It would be explicit enough to make her threat to him abundantly clear but still subtle enough that others wouldn't directly connect it to the man she was up against.

Now, she just needed to dangle the bait and watch what he did with it.

"HAVE YOU LOST YOUR ENTIRE FUCKING MIND?"

Karina barely had the door open before Orion was shoving his way inside, his eyes narrowed with rage as he moved past her.

"By all means," she muttered dryly, waving after him though he had already disappeared past her. "Come on in."

She'd hardly had the door closed before he was speaking again.

"Have you never listened to a fucking word I've said?" he asked once she turned to face him, his hands gesturing wildly as he spoke.

"I like to think I listen to everything you've said." Even when he probably thought she wasn't.

"Don't bullshit me. You know what I'm talking about."

Uilleam.

Because at the moment, that was all they *could* talk about.

Which meant he knew what she had done, though she had been careful not to share that with him. It would definitely explain his irate appearance in her apartment this late at night.

The thing about criminals? They didn't always check the local news for information. They also sought out information that was only available via the black web. The chat rooms on those sorts of websites weren't readily available to the public, and considering the proprietary nature of the sites themselves, it was hard to trace who posted what and from where.

Karina had counted on that.

"All the shit I've been telling you for the last year wasn't so you could make an enemy out of Uilleam fucking Runehart. And you sure as shit shouldn't be on Red Rum."

There were more than a dozen websites on the dark web specifically for offering up information. On some you had to pay for access, but on Red Rum, one could post at any time from anywhere.

There was even a feature that allowed certain posters to curate followings—and the bigger their following, they more they could potentially earn for the information they provided.

It had been the perfect place to write an informative piece about a man everyone seemed to fear …

Though she could tell Orion was upset with her, she couldn't bring herself to regret her actions. "It's hard to avoid someone when they're seeking you out."

Orion blinked.

Actually blinked.

"You're not fucking serious."

"Orion—"

His glare told her everything she needed to know.

Not that she expected otherwise after what she'd done. She'd known it had only been a matter of time before he would read it too, but she hadn't expected it to reach him so quickly. At the very least, she thought he'd be busy recovering from whatever havoc Uilleam had wreaked on him.

Because while he might have been out of jail at the moment, he had still been caught with whatever he'd had on him at the time.

"You got some kind of death wish, babe? Because you're asking for a problem, and this ain't one I'm gonna be able to solve."

"I'm not worried —"

"You should be!" he shouted suddenly, so loud and forceful that her thoughts blanked entirely. "Have you any fucking idea what he's capable of?"

"Yes," she said with a swallow. "I know very well what he's capable of."

"Then what the hell are you doing?"

"Making it clear that he can't walk all over me."

Which was a point he seemed to be missing.

It went beyond the pettiness of the deed, and realistically, it wasn't about Orion at all.

It was about *her*.

That he didn't want to *share*, as if she were some sort of toy in his possession that he could put in a box when he wasn't in the mood.

Orion muttered a curse, stripping out of his jacket and tossing it on the couch before he helped himself to the bottle of vodka in her kitchen. He didn't even bother pouring the drink in a glass, but rather took the whole bottle for himself.

"Him having you pulled over wasn't about *you*, necessarily," she explained, though his expression said he didn't care one way or the other. "He was trying to send me a message."

"A message you're electing to ignore, looks like," he muttered before taking a healthy swig. Not even grimacing as he swallowed.

"What would you have me do?" she asked, coming over to sit across from him.

"He's a master manipulator ... do you get me? *This* type of shit is what he's good at—what he lives for. You're trying to compete in a game he's already winning." Orion dragged in a heavy breath, leaning back as he sighed. "What's he want with you anyway? And how the fuck do I factor into that?"

"He ... well ..."

This was a question she didn't think she would have ever had to answer—and even if she had, she didn't think this conversation would have happened with *him*, of all people.

Orion arched a brow, waiting for her to elaborate, but after a few awkward seconds of silence, he formed his own conclusion.

"You'd be a fool to even entertain that."

Oh, how she wished she could tell him that she wasn't thinking about it—that she had spent the last week focusing on anything *other* than his offer—but it would be a lie.

A big one.

Uilleam Runehart was all she could think about.

He plagued her every thought.

He was intriguing and different, and she wanted to see what he was like when he wasn't actively manipulating people around him.

This was a rabbit hole she wanted to willingly fall into.

Orion shook his head, knowing what her silence really said. He looked disappointed, but something else she couldn't put a name to darkened his expression.

"Whatever this is, however the fuck it ends, leave me out of it, yeah?"

He didn't give her a chance to respond before he was exiting her apartment, leaving the door wide open in his wake.

For a long time, she stood there staring after him, wondering whether this was all a mistake.

KARINA TUCKED HER NOTEBOOK BACK INTO HER PURSE, HER focus on her task rather than her surroundings. Had she been paying attention, she might have noticed that the elevator she was boarding wasn't, in fact, empty as she had first thought upon entering.

But it wasn't until the doors slid shut and the elevator started to ascend that the person cleared their throat and made her look up.

"For a journalist, you're extremely hard to get a hold of."

She was glad her heartbeat wasn't an audible sound considering the way it sped up when she heard Uilleam's voice. "That should tell you all you need to know, shouldn't it?"

"I don't like to deal in assumptions," he answered, pushing off the wall of the elevator, but instead of moving closer to her, he turned in the direction of the control panel and pressed the STOP button, grinding them to a halt.

The overhead light faded, the muted light making her heart skip a beat. She was reminded of their time together at the club when he had backed against the wall, and he was all she could focus on.

It was much easier confronting him when other people were around. Then, she was better able to focus on what she was *actually* meant to be doing.

Rather than what she'd rather do.

She wondered if he exuded this same level of charm and utterly captivating darkness when he dealt with other women. Did they feel the inexplicable draw? Did they want to throw themselves at his feet in supplication?

Only when she felt the cool brush of metal did she realize she had taken a step back once he turned to her, but there was nowhere for her to go. And the space between them seemed to be growing smaller by the second.

But she didn't allow the nerves she felt to be reflected on her face. Instead, she cleared her throat and asked, "Is there a reason you needed to see me?"

"The better question, I imagine, is how you were able to access that website where you posted a rather interesting article about me." He smiled coldly. "Though I must admit, *Kingmaker* does have a rather nice ring to it."

So he *had* read what she wrote on Red Rum

"Isn't that what you are?" she asked, genuinely curious whether he saw what she did. "Grant favors and make people into kings ... for a price. To some, you're even a little more than that."

"Yet that's not fear I'm seeing in your eyes right now, is it?"

How could his mere presence jumble her thoughts the way it did? As if she had never been around a man before, but then again, she *had* never been around a man quite like him before.

There was no doubt about that.

Ignoring his question, she asked one of her own. "Is there a reason you're cornering me in an elevator?"

"You wanted my attention, and now you have it." He tucked his hands into his pocket, canting his head to the side. "You had to know I would find it."

"I quite deliberately omitted your name."

"Yet here we are."

She ... didn't have a response to that. Not one that would be good enough.

Because she *had* wanted him to read it.

She wanted exactly what he was giving her.

From what she had gleaned about him from others and from the people she'd witnessed him with, he very clearly valued his privacy.

"If you wanted to finish what we started the other night, I'd be more than happy to acquiesce you." His smile was a touch too wide. Too rueful. "Or you could just say yes to Paris," he said, leaning into her. "Put us both out of our misery."

"You're just refusing to take no for an answer."

"Am I? Go on then," he said with a tilt of his head. "Tell me no."

She bit her lip, and the hesitation cost her. He knew exactly how she felt about him.

"Go on," he taunted. "Say it like you *really* mean it."

She refused to let him get the best of her. "Have you always been this arrogant?"

He chuckled, low and dark. "In most things."

At least she knew what she was dealing with.

He reached over and pressed the button to start the elevator back up again.

"Have you packed yet?"

"Sorry?"

"For Paris. You seem the planning sort."

Oh, he couldn't be ... "I never said I was going."

"No?" he asked as the doors slid open. "I'm the Kingmaker, poppet. I always get what I want, don't I?"

With that parting remark, he pressed the button that sent the elevator moving again, and then walked out onto the next floor as if he hadn't shaken up her world all over again.

19

WANT

EVERY TIME HIS THOUGHTS TURNED TO HER, A LITTLE SHOT OF adrenaline swept through him. Making him feel alive.

Making him *want*.

Uilleam couldn't think of anything he could possibly want more.

She was everything he had never known.

The confusing emotions he felt for her should have dulled after her little stunt with the post on Red Rum—she might not have posted his name, but she *had* added her own little moniker with with enough details about him that some would be able to make the connection—but it had only made the craving worse.

When he closed his eyes at night, he didn't have to worry about the nightmares that usually plagued him. Instead, he heard her voice when she was challenging him, or her soft panting breaths when he got close to her, and even the delightful moans that spilled out of her when he kissed her that ensured he hadn't been able to get any fucking peace until he had his hand wrapped around his cock.

And once wasn't enough. Not nearly. The need was relentless.

He was getting fucking restless.

Even now, as he rested his palms flat against the shower wall, he couldn't help but peer down at his rapidly hardening cock, wondering when he'd reverted to a teenage boy.

The lust was never-fucking-ending.

His eyes slid shut as he gripped himself. All he could see was the look of abandon on Karina's face when he'd been about to make her come.

It was *that* look in the back of his mind that got him off.

He groaned, resting his head against the cool subway tiles of the shower, letting the water streaming down from the trio of rainfall shower heads drench his hair and slide down his back.

It had helped, for a moment, to loosen the tight muscles in his shoulders—to relax him further, considering he had spent another night with little sleep.

But the shower was doing fuck all to calm the raging erection he had, and it was becoming something he couldn't ignore.

He didn't even *want* to ignore it.

Not when he could still taste her on his tongue.

It didn't matter that it had been twenty-four hours previous, or that he'd eaten and brushed his teeth and had drinks in the span of time between him being with her and his arrival back at his suite, but that didn't stop the memory from conjuring whenever his thoughts turned to her.

Whether it was for a mere few seconds—the edge of the newspaper sitting on the corner of his coffee table had been the leading reason he was in the shower now—as soon as he thought of her, his cock hardened, and the rest of him grew anxious.

She wasn't a complication as he had first deemed her so many weeks ago.

Karina was a fucking *virus*.

An infection down to the bone and threading through the marrow, but he still didn't bloody well know whether he *liked* the feeling or not.

UILLEAM HAD BEEN HOURS INTO HIS WORK DAY AS SEVEN A.M. rolled around while the rest of the world seemed to only now come awake. He considered retiring to his room for a while since he didn't have any meetings to attend for another few hours, but the thought was just as quickly abandoned when he considered what else he could be doing in that time besides attempting to sleep.

His work never ended.

As he grabbed his phone, sorting through the messages that had come in while he'd been busy working on other matters, the elevator chimed, the concierge rounding the corner a moment later. He rolled in a cart with a gold-domed dish, three different newspapers, and three bottled waters with sealed tops.

One could never be too careful.

"Morning, sir," he greeted as he always did before unveiling the platter of food the chef had personally prepared for him.

He only had a few moments to enjoy the peace and quiet before Skorpion joined him, his face twisted into a scowl.

"While I'm all for everyone doing whatever the fuck they want so long as they're not hurting anyone else, you clearly can't be fucking allowed."

Sometimes even he forgot he was the boss in their little arrangement rather than the other way around.

Uilleam wondered for the seventh time that day why he bothered to put up with Skorpion at all. He had a complete lack of respect for authority.

Became distracted by food more often than he didn't.

And there was never a single time when Uilleam didn't know the man's opinion on something because he wasn't one to hold back on that front.

The question played on a continuous loop as Uilleam sighed before finally giving the man the attention he had all but asked for. "I sincerely don't want to know what you're on about."

"Your latest obsession has been busy."

He considered, briefly, correcting the man—he didn't think he had ever been obsessed with anything in his entire life—but thought better of it as a newspaper was slapped down in front of him.

A cursory glance at the cover page told him the name of the paper—*The Gazette Post*—and the current date. Even if there hadn't been something curious lingering in the back of his throat as he spoke, Uilleam would have still been searching the paper, looking for a name he was all too familiar with.

He suspected that she would get back to work sooner or later now that Paxton was away and his story was finished, but as he turned the paper onto the fifth page where there was merely a small column of text to the left, he was surprised to find that her next story wasn't closer to the front.

That was usually the way of it when a journalist managed to earn notoriety from what they wrote. Their stories would become more closely followed.

They would become as interesting as the articles they wrote.

"If you're not careful," Skorpion continued, "she's going to cause more problems than she's worth."

Oh, he wasn't so sure about that.

He didn't doubt for a second that she could cause him problems. If he hadn't been willing to turn on Paxton, that situation would have turned out very differently, but at the same time, he couldn't bring himself to care.

Not even a little.

"You're not seeing the bigger picture," he answered, looking from the paper back to the mercenary. "She could be an untapped resource should I ever have the need." And he was always in need of people with various skill sets.

It was because of people like her that he had gotten to where he was now.

He just wasn't going to admit that wasn't the only reason he wanted her.

"Right ... so what the hell are you going to do about her?"

That was a question even he didn't have an answer to yet.

HE HAD A MYRIAD OF THINGS HE COULD BE DOING RIGHT NOW, but they all paled in comparison to what he actually *wanted* to be doing.

The only way to remedy that was to feed his compulsion.

Which was how he found himself back in Karina's apartment, helping himself to the tea he found in her cupboard—a blend he had always enjoyed when he lived in Wales.

And this time, he wasn't as concerned whether she knew he was here or not. He was hoping she did, actually.

He waited with his cup in hand, wishing he could ignore the soft vibrations of his phone. His work never ended, though it would probably be worth taking a day or two off at a time.

He was in the middle of sending a text confirmation that would have him a quarter of a million dollars within the hour when Karina finally returned.

She hadn't been at work, that much he could tell. Her hair was down instead of up. And she was in a pair of jeans with a rip in the left knee.

There was no reason he should have known the difference between her casual attire and business, but he did.

He knew the moment she spotted him because she gave a little jerk, her eyes widening partially before she rested her hand on her chest and sighed audibly.

He couldn't help but smile at the idea that she didn't fear him in the least, though he had given her every reason to.

"It's weird that this is the least concerning thing you've done since I met you."

"Lucky you." Others weren't always so fortunate.

"What have you come for this time?" she asked as she stepped out of her heels first, then slid off her jacket. "Have you found a new creative way to threaten me?"

"There's no need. Your post was a one-off."

"Is that what you think?"

He shrugged.

They both knew the answer to that.

"Has there ever been a time in your life when you weren't this arrogant?"

For just a second, Uilleam flashbacked to when he was a child, remembering the searing heat in his cheek whenever Alexander lost his temper at what he considered as his incompetence. He'd been unsure of everything back then, often wondering whether there was *anything* he was good at.

"I am who I am." It was as simple as that.

One finely arched brow rose, but there was something about her expression that made him think she knew he wasn't as at ease as he appeared. "Yeah, there's no doubt about that."

"A Kingmaker is what you called me, right?"

"It was a figure of speech."

Yet he could think of no better title that fit.

No better ideal.

He *could* make anyone into a king … for a price.

And he rather liked the sound of that.

"One that I thank you for." He set his tea aside and stood, crossing the floor until he was nearly in front of her. He watched the moment she anticipated him reaching for her, but he chose instead to gesture at the picture sitting on her dresser that he hadn't paid very much attention to the last time he was here. "Who's this?"

Her gaze skipped to the picture as if she didn't already know which one sat there. Something odd and unreadable passed over her face before her expression settled.

"My sister. Why are you here, if not to threaten me?" she asked, changing the subject back to him.

"I asked you a question before," he said turning to better face her. "Now, I'm ready for an answer."

She blinked once, confusion marring her features before it dissolved into understanding. "You seriously want me to go away with you?"

"I thought I made that rather clear."

"That doesn't mean I understand why."

"It doesn't make any sense," he admitted.

Even he didn't understand the compulsion—the *need* to get closer to her. Learn who she was and what she liked.

Figure out how he could get her to react.

Before, he thought he had all the time in the world to give her a chance to change her mind. He would have wooed her for as long as it took if only because he rather enjoyed the game they were playing.

And he liked, though it was proving quite frustrating, that she wasn't immediately giving in to whatever he wanted.

He would have quite happily persisted until she changed her mind, but now he just didn't have the time for it.

This opportunity was too good to pass up, and with the current state of things, he doubted another opportunity would present itself in the near future.

If he wanted a hearing about the empty seat, he would have to go now and hope that all he had done proved just how valuable he could be.

The only thing left now was the details.

"What would it take for you to say yes?"

"You have to give me something in return."

God, those words thrilled him. "Beyond what I'm already offering."

Her laughter was light and amused, the lyrical sound making him smile. "Yes, beyond even *you*."

"Name your price."

He loved the eagerness he saw in her face as she turned to better face him.

The way her eyes came to life when she thought she was getting what she wanted.

But more than anything, he wished he knew why he wanted to give her exactly what she wanted when she looked at him like that.

"Orion. You have to make those charges go away."

At the mention of *his* name, some of Uilleam's good mood fled. "Name something else."

"Are you *serious*?"

"Making a crime disappear takes time and effort, poppet. Not to mention money that I severely doubt you possess."

"Sure, Uilleam. Keep going and see how this ends for you."

For fuck's sake. "*Fine*. I'll make sure your pet is taken care of."

"Call him that again and this conversation ends."

"A lot of loyalty to someone you proclaim is not *yours*."

"He's my *friend*. There's nothing wrong with being loyal to people that are loyal to you. That's how it works."

Not for Uilleam. Even those that were meant to be the most loyal sometimes couldn't help themselves. He'd started to expect the worst from people.

"Consider it done then," he said begrudgingly.

"*And* I want to know how you did it," she said, resting her chin on her fist. "Give me that much at least."

"Did what exactly?"

"Paxton. All of it. I want to know how you did it."

Uilleam couldn't think of a single individual he had ever explained his process to. Skorpion knew of it, of course, but he didn't know the details behind his orders. He merely did what he was told. But he found he wanted to tell her.

"The men who pretended to arrest you owed me a favor."

While there were plenty of upstanding police officers in the world, there were also the few who forsook their badges and happily turned to the other side to make more money than the paltry amount they made from the department year after year.

He didn't begrudge them their greed, but he also wasn't above using their deceit against them.

These two hadn't actually done very bad things themselves. One had a nearly five-figure gambling debt, and the other was in the midst of an affair with his captain's wife.

But they were important enough for the men to want to pay any price to make sure their secrets were kept.

"So they were willing to just let me go?" she asked, an adorable little pinch between her brows forming.

"As far as they were aware, no crime had taken place."

"But I broke in."

"The door was unlocked when you got there," he said easily. "And you were concerned for whomever might be inside."

She didn't respond to his statement immediately. Instead, she studied him as if she were trying to put the pieces together herself. "And I hadn't actually stolen anything because I hadn't left the property."

He nodded once. "And taking your profession into account, I was fairly sure you wouldn't leave your fingerprints around, so there was little chance of you contaminating the crime scene."

"You truly thought of everything, didn't you?"

She sounded surprised by that fact. Surprised ... but impressed.

It was hard to miss the way she appraised him as if she were seeing him for the very first time again. "Does that satisfy your curiosity?"

"Not even close."

"You'd have all the time in the world if you came to Paris with me."

"And why, Uilleam," she said with a little shake of her head, "don't I think that's a good idea?"

"That's the question I've been asking myself."

"Why this interest?" she asked, her voice a bit softer now. More earnest, somehow. "Why are you being so persistent about this?"

Why, indeed.

That, too, was a question he asked himself repeatedly.

Why this time?

Why *her*?

What was it that made his thoughts run in circles? Why did she make him want to seek her out when he knew little good could come of it, considering what she did for a living.

He didn't have an answer any more than she did.

❧ 20 ❧

YOURS

Karina was running out of reasons to stay away.

When he wasn't around, he was all she could think about. When he *was* around, nothing else in the world mattered other than him.

Uilleam wasn't awful to her. Quite the opposite, actually. He was charming, a little mischievous, and had the sort of face that made her wonder how many women threw themselves at him on a daily basis.

Which was why when she received a text from an unknown number with only an address, she went.

No questions asked.

She still hadn't figured out whether that made her an idiot or not.

But as she let herself into the building and followed the directions listed in the text, she couldn't bring herself to care either.

The door was unlocked, so she let herself in, scanning over everything before she walked inside.

She found Uilleam sitting at a rather large round table, waiting for her.

"You wanted to have dinner?" she asked, looking from him to the table where he sat.

"That comes later. For now, I want to play a game."

If he meant to make her speechless, he succeeded. She stood

there, rendered mute, unable to fully grasp what he was saying. That he didn't seem concerned at all about anything outside of this room.

Their polar opposite careers.

The reason they had even crossed paths in the first place.

But she had always been attracted to dangerous things. "What sort of game?"

Almost to the moment she finished her question, a butler appeared carrying a tray.

No, not a tray, a board. With thirty-two pieces on top. She easily recognized the checkered pattern, though this particular set was made of clear and frosted glass. Each piece looked hand carved, so intricate that she marveled at the price someone must have paid to have it commissioned.

She remained standing, drawing her own conclusions as the man finished setting up the board in the middle of the table before turning to leave. "You want to play a game of chess?"

He nodded once. "Have you played?"

She thought of one of her old tutors who'd had a love for the game. The matronly woman had tried, on various occasions, to teach her how to play, but she had never been very good. Though if she were honest, she didn't know how anyone could be good at a game like this.

"Have you?" she asked, turning the question on him, wondering if he would answer.

He was very good at not answering questions about himself. So much so that even she would forget what she had asked him until much later when she realized he had never actually given her an answer.

His smile was slight. "On a few occasions."

"Your humble way of saying you're good at this, right?" Which wasn't much of a surprise. "Why do you want to play is a better question, I think."

"I thought we could make a wager."

"Hardly seems fair. If I had to take a guess, I'd say you would win each time."

"Which is why we're not playing to win." He gestured to the

board with a wave of his hand. "For each piece of mine you collect, I'll answer one of your questions."

The rules sounded simple enough, so much so that she found herself sitting, resting her elbows on the table. "And you? What do you get?"

"You."

He said it so casually that she couldn't help but look up and try to read his expression. To see if he meant those words the way she took them. "I can tell you now that you won't win my body through a chess game."

"No, I want that freely given, poppet. I've told you that. This is merely a way for you to learn more about me. That's your reason for not coming to Paris with me, no? Because you don't know me."

That was what she had told him, and she'd even meant it at the time. But she hadn't expected anything more to come of that. She thought he would get bored, or at least move on to easier prey—even as the thought made her stomach turn—she hadn't, for a second, thought he would do *this*.

"You don't even know what questions I would ask."

"I'm not a shy man."

"I'm a journalist."

"And if you planned to do a story on me, you would have done it by now. At least one that was worthy of a second read," he amended, remembering what she had already written.

But they both knew that had only been a means to get his attention and nothing more.

She also knew, despite his words, they were betting on more than a few innocent questions. The only question now was what she was willing to give to sate her curiosity.

"What are the rules, exactly?"

Apparently, she was *more* than willing to go along with what he wanted.

"For every piece you collect," he said with a nod of his head to his side of the board, "I'll answer one of your questions. The more value the piece is worth, the harder the question could be."

That sounded easy enough, and fair on both sides.

"And you?" she couldn't help but ask. "What do you get out of it?"

His smile was his answer. "Should I explain the rules?"

Though she was fairly sure she knew them all, she nodded for him to continue, listening closely as he explained what each piece was and how it moved around the board.

This, she realized, was a little bit more than just a ploy to get her interested in him. The detail in which he spoke, the way a small fire seemed to be burning inside him, made it so clear that chess actually meant something to him.

"Confident enough?" he asked as he placed the king's piece back on its square.

Even if she wasn't, there was no way she was walking away from that table until she got what she wanted.

Karina moved closer to the table, looking from him to the board. The first move felt like it should have been easy, effortless even, but if she had any chance of having her questions answered, she needed to think about every move she would make.

After careful consideration—and a calming breath—she moved her first pawn forward two spaces.

"What made you suspect someone else was involved with Paxton?"

She looked up in surprise, taken off guard by his question.

"I said you could ask me anything you wanted should you capture a piece, I never said I wouldn't be questioning you."

"Semantics."

He winked. "Keep up, poppet."

"It wasn't any one thing you did," Karina answered, pausing when he reached forward to move his own pawn forward, this one several spaces away from her own. "I'd heard about the merger, thought maybe it was one of his competitors, but when that didn't add up, I figured it had to be someone who was trying to make it look as if he was guilty."

Over the past few weeks, she had kept most of her thoughts to herself, only asking questions of a certain few. She didn't realize, until this moment, that she had never shared just how she had reached the conclusion she had.

More than once, she found herself peeking up at him as they played, trying to gauge his reaction from his emotionless face as she spoke.

By the time she finished, she almost suspected this had been his plan all along, to learn the faults in his actions so that he could be careful not to repeat them again, but once she trailed off, watching with a bit of annoyance as he easily captured one of her pawns almost as an afterthought before finally meeting her gaze.

"Your mind must be a beautiful place."

Because she thought like him, she reasoned, but she accepted the compliment all the same.

The reason didn't matter entirely. Not when it still made her feel jittery inside.

How she found herself ducking her head and tucking her hair behind her ear.

When he took her knight, she asked, "What's your next question?"

"I want your hand."

"My what?"

He stretched his arm across the length of the table, turning his palm up, giving her a peek at the scar that lanced across his hand. As if someone had dragged a knife across it.

"Your *hand*," he said, taking hers.

His thumbs rested across the back of her knuckles, his other fingers beneath. Two pressed softly against the underside of her wrist.

"Continue," he said, going back to the game as though this weren't remotely out of the ordinary.

"What was I saying?" she asked, still distracted from her hand in his.

"How did you learn about me?"

Here, she hesitated. "Debra Tucker," she said, glad when she saw the recognition light up in his eyes. "Her pupils were dilated." She smiled as she knocked his bishop aside. Another question for her then.

She hadn't realized Uilleam was staring at her until she looked back up. "What?"

"How do you know about her? What's the connection?"

"She was a beautiful woman in her fifties. I imagined if she was anything like they said in the magazines, her beauty routine would be extensive. Which got me on the topic of these eye drops I remember"—she caught herself before she said *my mom*. The last thing she needed was him asking questions along that vein—"a woman I knew who had talked about these special eye drops that were controversial because of their belladonna content."

The idea of it sounded so ludicrous to her—that anyone would want to risk putting poison into their body was astounding—but a great many people had done drastic things in the name of beauty.

"But there was no mention of any belladonna anywhere. Not in police reports or anything that I could find. And considering the cost of them, I doubted the boy they suspected could have bought them. So where did they come from?"

"And that brought you to me?"

"To someone." She'd had no idea it would be anyone like him. "There were pieces to the story that didn't make sense, just like with Miranda."

He remained silent for a long while, just studying her.

"Final question," he said with a nod of his head at the board.

She needed to make this one count. "Why me? Why do you want me to come on this trip so badly?"

It wasn't as if this were the first time he had sought her out. And after she had denied his request the first time, he still came back time and again. It didn't make sense for the man he was.

"I can't help it?" he said, his voice softer now.

His brows drew together as he asked the question, his fingers briefly tightening around her wrist. A flush of awareness swept through her, her focus straying onto the contact between them.

"I want to hear every whisper and sigh and gasp. I want to feel you make those sounds." His expression was almost pained. "It's driving me insane. So to answer your question, I want to indulge my curiosity as you indulge yours."

She swallowed past the lump in her throat. "Are you always so forthcoming?"

"Honesty usually gets me what I want."

She didn't have an answer for that. "It's your move."

He barely glanced at the board before taking her final knight, leaving her with very few options. "I'd love to give you a slow and methodical explanation for what I want to do to you when I get you in my bed, but I'd rather show you."

Her heart galloped at the thought, and she couldn't help but wonder if he noticed. If he could feel it from where his fingers were pressed against her skin.

"Is there a question in that?"

"Your blush was enough."

She focused back on the board, scanning over each piece until she saw something she couldn't quite believe. At first glance, it didn't look as if there were an opening, but if she took the rook sitting right next to his king, she would checkmate him.

He would lose.

"No, I do have one final question for you," he said, interrupting her train of thought.

"Ask," she answered, confident now in her chances of winning this game.

"Will you come with me to Paris?"

The smart, logical part of her said to turn him down. To walk away before things got out of hand. Walk away while she still had the chance.

But the rest of her wasn't agreeing with what her brain was telling her. "Yes," she finally answered. "I'll go with you."

She grabbed her queen and moved it across the board, replacing his rook with her queen and caged his king in.

Checkmate.

"Beginner's luck," he said with a nod of his head.

"You were distracted."

His mouth jerked up in a smile. "Maybe so. I'll have my rematch."

She was pleased with herself, for as long as it took her to realize just how gracious he was being about her winning at a game that was, as he'd said, his favorite.

She stood, looking from the board to him. "You let me win."

He arched a brow. "Did I?"

"So I would say yes to going on the trip with you."

"You were going to say yes regardless," he answered confidently, "which was why I didn't wait until after you took my rook to ask you to come with me."

Maybe the man in him had always known that she would say yes, but she couldn't help but think the notorious fixer had ensured no matter how this game ended, he would get what he wanted.

The world was like a chess game to him, and he was exceptionally good at it.

21

ANOTHER LIFE

Nine months ago, when she had been sitting on the floor of her apartment with a cup of tea in one hand and a pen in the other, thinking about a man without a name or face, she hadn't imagined she would be here now, packing to go away with him.

It didn't seem plausible.

She wasn't the sort of girl who ran off with a man—especially a man like Uilleam Runehart.

Yet there was no mistaking the sound of her zipper as she yanked it closed on the smaller of her two suitcases. She lugged it over to sit in front of the front door next to the other one, returning to her bedroom to make sure she didn't forget anything.

She'd thought packing for a vacation, even if only for a weekend, would be easy—something she didn't have to give much thought to. That, at most, she would need to toss in a few dresses, stockings, jeans, and a coat or two, considering the rapidly cooling weather over there, but ever since she had requested time off from the paper, she had been giving this *too* much thought.

No matter what she selected, even if it was something she had worn on numerous occasions already, she still tried it on and checked her reflection in the mirror, gazing at herself critically from every angle. She wasn't just considering how she thought she looked.

She was also thinking of Uilleam and his thoughts.

Whether he would think this particular shade of cerulean blue complemented her skin tone, or if the hem of her skirt was just short enough to make the view of her legs tantalizing as opposed to scandalous.

Not for the first time, she realized she was thinking about this too much.

By the time she finished, she had enough to wear for a week, and she was prepared for practically any scenario.

The only thing she had to do now was meet him at the airport hangar.

She had considered briefly, after he'd extended the invitation, whether he was making it a point *not* to offer to drive her. If only because he wanted the choice to be hers.

That her presence, there or not, would be answer enough since she would be going of her own volition.

But she also found that it was much easier to worry about what she was going to wear rather than what would happen once she was actually in Paris with a man whose motives were murky at best.

Not that she minded really.

She rather liked the mysterious side to him. No matter how many layers she attempted to pull back, there was another one waiting.

He was a puzzle she was having far too much fun trying to piece together.

But now was her chance.

This was more than just a trip to one of the most romantic cities in the world—it was a date.

One of the few life skills she didn't have much practice in.

Growing up the way she did—sheltered from the world during boarding school, then at Ashworth Hall with Mother as she learned more about what it meant to be an Ashworth woman—she had never had the opportunity really to talk to boys.

The ones she'd known at school were either incredibly boring, all chasing after the three most popular girls at her school, or were focused on sports and other matters.

That wasn't to say she had been completely hopeless in the dating department. After moving to New York, she'd gone on a couple of dates and even made out with the first one, but with the way her work was set up, that came first for her.

Not a lot of people understood that.

But Uilleam might.

Of course, she didn't know that completely—she would only now be spending any extended time alone with him.

But what she felt for him all the same … it was too complicated and indiscernible to simply be considered a crush. That word felt too juvenile while lust felt too singular.

That was what this weekend was for, however. Feeding that curiosity that was burning like fire whenever she thought of him.

It was time to do something she wanted.

DESPITE THE COPIOUS AMOUNT OF CLOUDS OBSCURING THE EARLY morning sunlight, it was still beautiful outside. Cool enough that she was sure fall weather would be right around the corner, while warm enough that it was clear summer was still hanging on.

It was the perfect backdrop to the sight of Uilleam standing next to a private jet on the tarmac, his phone to his ear as his gaze was trained off in the distance, having not noticed their approach yet.

She wished her heart didn't try to beat right out of her chest when she saw him, taking in his striking appearance.

For once, he wasn't in one of the three-piece suits she'd grown accustomed to. Instead, he was in a pair of gray trousers tailored for his height, and a white shirt with the top two buttons left undone.

She expected him to quickly usher her onto the plane, to say they were running late or something, but what she *didn't* expect was for him to just stand there staring, looking as if he was surprised she was here at all.

His smile came slowly, taking over his entire face and transforming his look of indifference to something else entirely.

"Afraid I wouldn't come?" she asked, tucking wispy strands of hair back out of her face.

His expression betrayed how he really felt even as he said, "You, more than anyone, continue to surprise me."

"I'll take that as a good thing."

He circled around to the back of the car to assist the driver in grabbing her bags, toting them over to the jet where a flight attendant was waiting to receive them.

Uilleam turned back to her then, and asked, "Any last words?"

Was she backing out, he was really asking.

Even if she had wanted to, and there was no part of her that did, she had come too far now to walk away before she got answers to her questions.

THE FIRST TIME KARINA HAD EVER BEEN ON AN AIRPLANE, SHE'D held the armrests tightly, her fingernails digging into the leather as she counted down the seconds until they were in the air. Even after, she still waited several moments for the disorientating feeling of being in the air to fade.

Each time after had only been marginally better.

Those times had been on commercial airlines. Never on a jet.

Especially not one that looked like this.

Everything was done in shades of beige and white, and even the carpet matched the buttery brown of the seats.

She expected there to be some awkwardness between them. They weren't lovers going away for the first time together. She wouldn't even go so far as to say they were friends.

This was new, uncharted territory for her.

There was a strong chance she was making a colossal mistake, and that she would live to regret it by the weekend's end. But like a moth to a flame, she was willing to take the risk.

Just as she was about to list reason number sixty-three why her coming here was both wonderful and terrifying, Uilleam returned, looking far less annoyed now than he had before he disappeared to the back of the plane.

It didn't make sense, the way her senses seemed to come alive whenever he was near. The way she was anticipating the moment his attention turned to her. And when it did; she wasn't disappointed.

With just a look, he managed to make her feel like the only woman in the world.

SOMETHING TOLD HER THAT WHEREVER THEY WERE GOING, IT WAS going to be just as over the top as the car they were riding in once they had landed in a private airfield hours later. Much of her time on the jet had been spent sleeping, and she had only woken up when she felt Uilleam sweeping his fingers through her hair as they started their descent.

At first she had been disappointed she'd wasted a perfectly good opportunity to find out more about him, but now that she was able to stay awake during the car ride through the city, she didn't mind it as much.

Medieval architecture gave way to more modern buildings, including one that stood out among the structures surrounding it.

Uilleam pulled in front of a gated side street where he had to step out to not just enter a passcode into the security box, but to also press his palm against the green screen before the gate made an audible groan as it rolled open.

Karina didn't speak, not as they drove down the alley and around to the back of the building, the gate slowly closing behind them. It wasn't until they reached the fountain—an angel with its wings spread, her graceful face tilted toward the ground as water rained down around her—that one word slipped out.

"Wow."

Thick patches of grass bisected tiles of concrete, the landscaping just as beautiful as the house itself.

But that didn't sound quite accurate.

Despite its proximity to the city, the place was a *mansion* with so many windows that she wondered how the view would look in the spring when the flowers bloomed again.

"Is this yours?" she asked, unable to help her awe as she looked around at the garden and the towering tree in the very center of it.

Fall had already begun to transform the color of the leaves, changing the rich green they had once been to a rustic shade of yellow and orange. Against the white brick of the mansion and the tiles of cement, it looked as if she was walking across a sea of color.

"Would you believe me if I told you I bought this recently?"

She turned quickly, trying to read his expression. "Not for me, surely ..."

His smile was a touch clever. "Are you impressed?"

"I'd find it alarming."

Uilleam's laughter echoed as he pulled a key from his pocket. Opening the large ornate door, he stepped to the side to allow her in first.

She thought she was prepared for opulence when she stepped inside—something that reminded her of a museum more than anything else—but instead, she got the complete opposite.

Art hung along all the walls, sculptures tucked in corners, and the sofas that she could see weren't made out of leather or some other impossible fabric that meant it could get damaged very easily. The living room itself looked open and inviting—as if it were well-lived in rather than a room meant for show.

"Would you like a tour?" he asked, setting her bags aside, rolling up the sleeves to his shirt as he walked over to her.

But before she had a chance to answer, his phone rang again. This was something she needed to get used to when dealing with him. His phone was rarely off, and even if it was, like on the plane, he still had it in his hand constantly.

"After," she said when he glanced from her to the device in her hands.

There was an apology in his eyes before he took the call and stepped off to the side.

Trying to offer him as much privacy as she possibly could, she took her time looking around the exterior, breathing in the Paris air, still a little shocked that she was here at all.

And with *him* no less.

Unbidden, her gaze moved over to him, lingering on his back as he faced the opposite direction.

It was hard to imagine that someone as young as him was not only filthy rich—evidenced by the way he traveled and the Rolls

Royce they'd climbed out of—but held enough power and prestige that people *actually* feared him.

And not even because he was violent in any way. Despite all the rumors she had heard, not a single one of them had ever mentioned that he harmed people physically.

He played with people's minds, even manipulated their lives at will, but he didn't *hurt* them.

As quickly as he had been conducting his phone call in English, he switched to what sounded like German, his tone changing as he turned back to face her. It was obvious that he was growing more annoyed by the conversation the longer he went on, but he had yet to end the call.

She was almost becoming annoyed with herself that she liked seeing him this way.

Maybe she just needed to admit to herself that she liked *him*.

He gestured for her to follow him, giving up the pretense that his conversation would be over anytime soon.

He removed a set of keys from his pocket and fit one into the lock, letting her enter first before he came in behind her.

Karina had never been the sort to be easily impressed by material things and the abundant wealth she saw around her.

Though not many knew this about her, she had lived in homes that cost more than one million dollars and had even been in others that cost a fraction of that. Both had their positives and negatives, but she had always found she rather liked quaint places.

Sometimes family portraits and knickknacks reflected far more beauty and warmth than a place that was pristine without a single piece of furniture out of place.

But this place ... it fell somewhere in the middle.

It wasn't merely a penthouse he was renting in the city or a temporary home where he intended to sleep for a mere few days before moving on. It felt lived in.

She could feel *his* energy surrounding her.

Paintings hung on the walls, some abstract—made up of harsh brush strokes in bright, vivid colors—while others were more classical, beautiful, and incredibly old.

With Uilleam still distracted for the time being, she left him in search of a bathroom to freshen up, using that as an excuse to tour the rest of the place on her own.

As far as she could tell, there were three bedrooms on this floor alone and just as many bathrooms, but as she swept through the back hallway, she found another spiraling staircase that led down instead of up, and the closer she came to stand by it, the better she could smell and even hear the water below.

There was a pool down there. Somewhere she would definitely need to explore while she was here, but that would come later.

22

EVENINGS

WHILE SHE COULD HAVE STOPPED ON THE MAIN LEVEL THEY'D come in on and waited for Uilleam to return from wherever he had disappeared off to, Karina instead chose to venture up the winding staircase to the next level.

If he asked, she would say she had come looking for him, which was partially true, but she also wanted to sate her curiosity where he was concerned.

Now that they were actually here, she felt a little unsure.

If nothing else, she knew of *one* thing that had brought them here —their connection.

The feeling she had wondered if she felt alone before he made it abundantly clear he felt it too. There was still the question of whether or not they would be sharing a room—something she still wasn't giving much thought to though she definitely needed to.

It wasn't that she was expecting him to jump her bones the second they were near any horizontal surface, but even she felt that desire.

The want and need.

It didn't matter that she hadn't been with anyone else before. It wasn't as if she could ignore what she was feeling.

The third level had the same appeal as the first—large paintings on the wall, a satin covered bench in front of a bay window, and a rather interesting looking bust sitting on a marble pillar. She wondered again whether he was behind the décor or if he had delegated the job to someone else.

The first closed door she reached was a half bathroom. The next, an office of sorts that could have doubled as a library, considering the sheer number of books inside. She lingered inside, gaze drifting over the spines of books before she spotted a lone title sitting on the ebony desk across the room.

The Art of War.

She picked it up, running her fingers over the cover and then turned it back over in her hands. Though Isla had always said the book should be required reading for everyone, Karina had never actually picked up a copy.

Now, she was curious about it again.

"Do you like sushi?"

The question couldn't have come at a worse time, considering she was snooping just a little, but that didn't stop a smile from gracing her face as she turned to look at him.

"I've never had it, so I wouldn't know."

She didn't mention that the idea of putting raw fish in her mouth, actually chewing and swallowing it, made her stomach turn. But she had always wanted to try it all the same.

She was a glutton for punishment.

"An associate of mine has invited us to dinner."

"Us?" she asked curiously.

His answering smile was warm as he further entered the room, eyeing the book she held in her hands.

"I wouldn't very well leave you to fend for yourself our first night here."

She shrugged.

Truthfully, she had come prepared for anything. While she was naïve about many things, she also knew there would be certain information he wouldn't share with her. She doubted he would be giving her an all-access pass to his criminal empire, no matter if he thought she looked nice in a dress.

"So this business dinner is with …?"

"Haruto Nakamura. He's mostly involved in imports. Has one of the best shipping routes across the globe. If you need something moved, he's the man for the job."

"And you're sure you want me there?" she asked, a little surprised he was even offering.

While one of the conditions of her coming along with him to Paris was that she wanted to see the other side—the shady businesses he dealt in as well as the way he operated—but she only thought he would show her quite innocent things. Or as innocent as anything connected to Uilleam could possibly be.

His smile was a little less charming now and more cunning. "I always like to have a plan B."

"I'm not sure if I should take that as a compliment."

"Everything I say about you is meant as one."

The man had a way with words.

———

STARING INTO THE MIRROR, KARINA ADJUSTED THE SKIRT OF HER dress again, eyeing her reflection critically before she started back on her hair. She hadn't been sure, after leaving Uilleam upstairs so she could shower and dress, what she had wanted to wear for dinner.

It wasn't every day she had dinner with international criminals.

Or Uilleam, for that matter.

Which was why she had selected a dress in a jade green color that was modest along the front with a back that dipped very low. With open-toe nude heels and a matching bag, she looked less like the journalist she was, she thought, and more like someone who would be on Uilleam's arm.

By the time she came back upstairs, Skorpion had arrived, his phone in his hand even as an absent smile had graced his rugged face. A woman, she guessed. Men always got that expression on their face when they were talking to someone they liked.

More than once, she thought she had seen it on Uilleam's face.

"Do you always attend meetings with him?" she asked, though her question really was, had he been around on the days when Uilleam had sought her out.

He shook his head, briefly looking up from his phone. "I'm only here as a reminder."

"A reminder of what?"

"That just because I have a beautiful woman with me doesn't mean I'm going to be distracted," Uilleam's voice came from behind her. "Though I might be wrong about that," he finished before she felt the brush of his fingers along her spine. Quick enough that she almost missed it, but the lingering sensation reminded her it had been all too real.

"Have you always been this charming?"

"*Une si belle distraction—Such a beautiful distraction,*" he continued with a smile.

Uilleam led them to a black Range Rover, and with one click of the key fob, the tail lights blinked twice before he opened the passenger door and gestured for her to climb inside.

With the dim street lights, it was hard to make out much of the city as they drove away from the house with Skorpion trailing them.

"Is there anything I should know?" she asked, turning to look at him and enjoying the way the moonlight spilled over the side of his face.

"Both his wife and mistress will be there. His wife's name is"—he paused, seeming to think over his answer—"Aiko? Or is that the mistress? No, I'm certain Emika is the mistress. It would be best if you didn't mix up the two—they get violently aggressive if you do."

She couldn't help her look of astonishment. "Is this some sort of test?"

It sounded like one.

Would she be able to figure out which one was which without jeopardizing the business he had come to conduct?

"You have to give me more than that. Otherwise, you're just setting yourself up for disaster."

He didn't appear nearly as concerned as she felt. "Or a more entertaining dinner," he countered with a light laugh.

"You get far too much enjoyment out of manipulating the people around you."

"Life would be undoubtedly less mundane if people weren't so easily manipulated."

Remarkably so. "Go on then. Give me a clue."

"Aiko grew up on a horse ranch from my understanding. Her father was an honest worker with very little money. She was married off at sixteen to a businessman in Hong Kong, but a rival had him killed—or something unfortunate like that. Eventually—though this was never shared with me—she found herself in Haruto's bed."

That could have been either of them realistically.

Both wife and mistress would be sleeping with him.

"On the other hand, Emika is unlike any woman I've ever met. Conservative, yet ruthless. She'd be an asset if she wasn't so unpredictable."

There was genuine admiration in his voice, she thought. And maybe it was for that reason that she wanted to meet this Emika—to see whether she could gauge what Uilleam saw in her. It wasn't jealousy, she reasoned. That wasn't it at all. Not even a little.

Before she had the chance to question him further, they arrived at the restaurant, the valet speaking rapid French, then happily taking the keys from Uilleam before he drove off.

Uilleam's hand slid down hers, his thumb brushing the palm of her hand before he intertwined their fingers. His slightly calloused skin was warm, his grip firm. There was not a bit of awkwardness as she fell into step beside him, walking through the restaurant's front doors.

The atmosphere was quaint but lavish. Gilded fixtures and Renaissance paintings hung along the walls, and if she had to guess, no one in this room was worth less than six figures.

The hostess took one glance at Uilleam and sprang into action, guiding them through the cluster of tables toward a private area in the back of the restaurant that was sectioned off by gauzy curtains, preventing anyone from seeing who was on the other side.

Uilleam glanced down at her as if he could sense her nerves and wanted to ensure her, without words, that he fully expected her to pass whatever little test this was. Even if she wasn't so sure.

He stepped out of his shoes first, leaving them tucked into a corner, then gladly offered his hand as she bent to unbuckle her heels and place them alongside his. She felt more at a disadvantage now that she'd lost six inches in height.

Unlike her, Uilleam was still towering at over six feet tall.

"Mr. Runehart and his guest have arrived," the hostess announced as she swept the curtain aside for them to go through.

The robust man seated at the table was the first person Karina's gaze was drawn to.

Haruto got to his feet without preamble, greeting Uilleam in heavily accented English.

Karina wasn't sure what to do with herself as she watched the two interact. Finishing school ensured that she remained standing with her back strait and her posture impeccable, a light smile gracing her face.

But as quickly as she had felt out of sorts, she remembered Katherine's lessons.

She greeted both of Haruto's women, not calling either by a name since she didn't have very much to go on yet. She still needed time to observe the two before she made a decision.

"Lovely girl," Haruto complimented Uilleam, as if he were responsible for the way she looked.

Men in his position were amusing.

Karina didn't speak any of the problematic thoughts in her head, merely smiled as she was meant to and let the man kiss the back of her hand.

"Let's eat!"

They all took their seats at the table before Haruto picked up the tiny bell from the table and gave it a ring. Mere seconds passed before the door slid open again and waiters bustled in carrying food and drinks.

She had thought, since this was essentially a business meeting, Uilleam would forget her presence beside him. Haruto certainly seemed to have forgotten that he hadn't come alone with the way he talked to Uilleam.

He hardly glanced at the two women sitting on either side of him.

But Uilleam ... he was different.

Even as he flawlessly carried on a conversation with Haruto, he still managed to whisper in her ear whatever dish was brought out.

He wordlessly asked if she were enjoying herself when he looked in her direction. And if he thought she didn't like something, he wouldn't hesitate in switching dishes with her, or ordering her something else entirely.

Uilleam was *thoughtful.*

As time slipped by, she found herself relaxing further at his side, more than happy to be there.

But as dinner slowly started to come to an end, he rested his hand on her knee, the gesture seemingly innocent as he continued his conversation without falter. She might have thought it was a passive gesture until she shifted and his fingers tightened

Not enough to hurt—it was certainly not pain she was feeling— but with enough pressure that she was acutely aware of the hold he had on her.

The way his hand was slowly moving from her knee to the stretch of thigh not concealed by the short dress she wore.

She stifled her reaction as best she could, even reaching for her second glass of wine.

Now the sweet bite of alcohol was exactly what she craved.

Well ... not the *only* thing.

Somewhere between the end of her first glass and the tentative sip of her second, her mind had drifted from the duties of this night to something else entirely.

She'd become entranced by the way his arms looked, the sinew and muscle practically begging to be touched. She grew curious, wondering what he would look like once he shed his very proper clothes.

What did he look like naked?

Did the reality live up to the fantasy?

Of course, she had an *idea* of what was hidden beneath those tailored clothes of his, but she was tired of wondering.

She wanted to see for herself.

And more than anything, she wanted to know what it felt like to be *with* a man.

Her virginity wasn't something she had held onto because she had been looking for, 'the right person to lose it to,' she had just never met anyone she'd wanted to risk being seen by her mother with in high school. And after moving to New York, she'd just been too busy to get out there.

Uilleam couldn't have come at a better time.

And with the way she was feeling now ... she had an idea how this night would end.

No, *focus*.

She needed to pay attention to what was going on around her, though Uilleam seemed intent on making sure that was the last thing she did.

"If you intend to do business with Gaspard, you need to prepare yourself."

She mentally filed that name away, intending to ask Uilleam about it later, but the rest of Haruto's words fell on deaf ears when Uilleam's hand crept its way beneath the skirt of her dress. Thankfully, he was still at the very edge of the fabric—intimate but innocent all the same—but that didn't make it any less indecent. It didn't mean that she didn't know exactly what he would find if he ventured up a few more inches.

"I have Gaspard exactly where I need him. Everything is going according to my plan."

Haruto let out a good-natured scoff, not convinced but willing to let Uilleam believe what he wanted.

Curiosity made her glance over at him. She wanted learn more about the mysterious man who made Uilleam's brow furrow, but while the question lingered in the back of her mind, Uilleam distracted her by finally moving his hand beneath her dress.

She was careful not to react, even as his sudden touch surprised her and caused goose bumps to break out along her skin.

The rest of their conversation was lost on her as she grew distracted by his touch, and the way her skin seemed to come alive. It took every bit of effort to pay attention to everyone speaking around her—especially the women who spoke quietly among themselves.

By the time the dinner came to an end, Karina had her fingers wrapped around Uilleam's wrist, preventing him from making the ache worse.

"Thank you for a lovely evening," Karina said as she accepted the man's embrace before turning to face the woman standing to his right. "And Emika, it was a pleasure to meet you. Aiko, as well."

For only a moment, she wondered if she had gotten their names wrong—if the game Uilleam was playing had come to an end and now she would suffer the consequences. But neither woman reacted violently. They both smiled and inclined their heads.

Even as her mind had been elsewhere and he'd happily attempted to distract her all throughout dinner, she had gotten it right.

Uilleam, who stood mute to the left of her had a small, knowing smile on his face.

As the others turned to walk away, Karina looked at him. "Did I pass?"

"I never doubted you for a second."

"No?"

He shrugged. "You found *me*, didn't you?"

Yes. Yes, she had. "So ... what happens now?"

He brushed his hand over the slight growth of hair on his jaw. "Do you trust me?"

"I ..." She wanted to say she did because that would be the truth.

She knew it wasn't rational. She knew that he hadn't given her any reason to believe a word that came out of his mouth or anything that he did. If anything, she *knew* that nothing was ever what it seemed when it came to him.

But she still didn't care.

"I probably shouldn't trust you, but I do."

"Then we have one more stop to make."

"Oh? Where are we going?"

There was something about the expression on his face that told her wherever they were going ... she wasn't ready.

23

HUSH

Do you trust me?

Such an innocent question coming from anyone else, but when those four words spilled out of Uilleam's mouth, Karina knew her immediate answer should have been no.

He was quite possibly the *last* person on earth she needed to trust, but that didn't stop her from taking his hand when he offered it.

From letting him guide her into the idling SUV to not asking a single question as he drove them through the winding streets of Paris.

They weren't going back home, that much she knew. He was too excited, eager almost, and whatever it was he intended to surprise her with, she doubted he could have hidden it there without her noticing.

But she was *just* tipsy enough not to care where this night would take them.

She wasn't thinking about consequences or anything else.

She wanted the adventure—*craved* it—more than she ever thought possible.

Just the feel of his presence beside her, and the heat of his palm across the back of her hand had her heart thumping away in her chest.

More than once, she found herself peeking over at him, wondering where his thoughts had gone. All during his conversation with Haruto, he had seemed more focused on her. Stroking his fingers along the curve of her thigh, smiling down at her whenever she parted her legs just a little more to give him better access.

But now that they weren't alone, he didn't touch her. And save for when he was actually helping her into the truck, he hadn't looked at her either.

They pulled in front of a gated residence, the seal in the very center of the black iron parting down the middle as it opened. She sat up a little more to see the grounds as they drove up a winding pathway, the cobblestone making the truck sway gently.

Up ahead, past the streaming water fountain and neatly trimmed bushes, was the biggest mansion Karina had ever seen. Track lights lining the front hedge illuminated the white brick, making it seem all the more wondrous in the dark hours of the night.

"Is this yours as well?" she felt compelled to ask, almost afraid that his answer would be yes. She knew his wealth was vast, but this just seemed unnecessary.

"A friend's place of business."

"That sounds decidedly vague."

A corner of his mouth twitched. "It was meant to."

"Why did you bring me here?"

"Testing a few theories."

"Is everything a game for you, Uilleam?"

"Only when it's not."

Which wasn't an answer. Not really. "What kind of theory?"

She knew with some certainty as she took his hand that whatever she thought this was going to be, she wasn't prepared. But she still dutifully followed him.

It wasn't until she made it inside the sprawling mansion that Karina got an idea of what this place was. The heat in her face would have confirmed it even if another waitress in black leather hadn't passed by, carrying a coiled whip clasped in her gloved hand.

She nearly jumped out of her skin when she felt Uilleam come up behind her, his hand resting on her lower back. "Is this some sort of sex club?" she asked, wishing her voice didn't sound as breathy as it did.

"Don't let Laurence hear you say that—he'd take it as a personal insult."

But she didn't know how else to describe it. It was the only word that came to mind to describe not just the attire of the women—and men who walked the floor carrying drinks—but the overall atmosphere.

"What is this place, exactly?"

He urged her forward toward the marble staircase up ahead. Even as she was nervous to peer over the railing to see what awaited her below, she still put one foot in front of the other. Willingly being led into the devil's playground.

"They call it Hush," Uilleam finally explained, filling in more details as they descended a level, the room transforming right before her eyes.

Like how Laurence had been notorious for fulfilling the sexual desires of those with discerning means. How nothing was off limits so as long as it didn't involve children or violence against women. That, Uilleam said, had made him both popular and hated within the same circles.

It wasn't much of a surprise that Laurence didn't sound like a bad man—Orion was a good person too, and still broke the law—but a part of her hadn't expected Uilleam to do business with men like him. She knew the moral line he stood on was gray, at best, but sometimes she thought he teetered over to the darker side when he wanted.

If she had thought the floor above them was obscene with the men and women in various leather outfits, this level ... she blushed the moment the woman in nothing more than a collar and a fox tail walked by her carrying a tray.

Uilleam plucked her a drink from a waiter in a leotard, passing it to her without a word. She downed it in seconds, hoping the alcohol would calm her.

But if anything, it only made her more aware of everything happening around her.

He led her to a door built into the wall, one where he had to press his hand against a particular spot to get it to pop open, then he ushered them inside.

His expression was unreadable as his gaze trailed over her as if he was seeing her for the first time. "Wait for me," he said, "I'll be right back."

Before she could ask where he was going, he walked out, leaving her alone in the dark room with windows that spanned the entire space.

A nearly three-sixty view of everything outside of it.

She wasn't sure how long she was alone, not when she immediately went over to one of the glass partitions and stared out, unable to quell the impulse.

It could have been seconds or minutes, she didn't know.

Nor did she care.

She just simply ... watched.

Everything around her.

The sounds of the club on this level carried through the walls, though this space seemed to be sealed off from everything else.

Perhaps it was the champagne swimming through her veins, warming her up from the inside out — or maybe she just didn't want to admit that he had this effect on her even though he hadn't touched her yet.

She still didn't turn from the glass, however, when she heard the door open again.

She could *just* see his reflection as he moved toward her, wishing it didn't send a chill down her spine.

And as she watched him slip out of his suit jacket and toss it to land on the curved leather couch across the room, she had no question he was going to finish what he had started earlier.

She couldn't say she minded, even as it made her heart race.

After a moment, she forced her gaze away from his reflection and back toward the others standing on the other side.

It was easy to think she could see everything happening outside of this room yet no one on the other side would be able to see her. It took everything in her not to press her hands against the glass, wondering whether her palm prints would reflect on the other side.

She was far too aware of everything going on around her not to notice Uilleam's hands shifting her hair over her shoulders, causing goose bumps to erupt in the wake of his touch.

This close to the glass, not only could they see the scores of couples outside the room but also their reflections in the mirror.

She could see how nervous she looked. How eager. She could almost see the anticipatory gleam in her own eyes as Uilleam stepped closer, not enough that any part of them was touching, but so close that she could *feel* his presence behind her.

Goose bumps were breaking out along her arms, the fine hair on the nape of her neck was standing on end. She was *reacting* to him, and he hadn't even touched her yet.

But she wanted him to. Craved it.

Was counting down the seconds until he shifted, his hand coming to rest on the curve of her hip before sliding inward, tracing the line of her skirt until his fingers hovered over the button and zipper. He didn't thumb it open, nor did he just shove her skirt up to get his hand between her legs. Instead, he just ... waited.

But she wanted him to. She wanted to feel the fabric give beneath his strength more than she had ever wanted anything in her life.

"Afraid yet?" he asked. The first words he'd spoken since he entered this room with her.

Words that coiled down her spine and pooled low enough that she felt them like a physical caress.

"Is that your intention? To scare me?"

"*Tempt,*" he corrected a second later, shifting his body just so that she felt the brush of his shirt-clad chest against her back. "There's no fun in scaring you away."

"No?" she asked, sounding breathless to her own ears, wondering if he could hear it too.

"*No,*" he repeated. "The time for running is done."

He wasn't letting her go.

The unspoken truth hung between them, thickening the air. Making it hard for her to take a proper breath.

At the first brush of his lips along the shell of her ear, she shuddered, her heart thumping so fast in her chest, she was almost positive he could hear it.

Inhaling a deep breath, she watched as his gaze dropped to her chest. Felt the moment his fingers tightened on her.

"Undo this," he ordered a second later, plucking at the fabric of her dress that was tied into a bow at the front, sounding as if the words were forced out of him, his need too great to ask her nicely.

There was no question he was just as affected as she felt.

Even as she readied to obey, she caught his gaze in their reflection. "You didn't want to be the one to do it?"

"I'm seconds away from ripping the fucking thing off you, poppet. Let's not test my restraint lest you leave here in tattered fabric."

She felt those words down in the pit of her stomach.

Her fingers shook as she undid the first button, revealing the very tops of her breasts, imagining what it would have felt like had he ripped her top off. She could almost imagine the sound of the buttons hitting the floor and scattered everywhere.

Just the thought was enough to make her core clench.

But before she could finish the last three, his other hand came to rest on top of hers, preventing her from continuing.

Instead, he merely shifted the fabric away before pressing his lips to the curve of her neck, tracing a path downward until he was nearly at her shoulder, but just before he got there, his lips parted and all she saw was a flash of white before his teeth were skimming her flesh.

Not enough to hurt but surely enough to leave a mark.

To make her jolt.

For her hands to clench tight and a moan to spill from her lips.

But he didn't stop there.

He reached up, his gaze meeting hers through the glass as he curled his fingers around the lace covering her breast and gave it a sharp tug, the undeniable strength he possessed and seemed to be struggling to rein in had her breathing out a heavy breath.

Another yank had it ripping a bit, not that she cared. She was too lost in him and the sensations he was awakening inside her.

The way the cool air of the room brushed over her tightening nipple.

Karina was nearly lost in the moment until a woman on the other side of the glass' gaze caught hers as her partner fisted her blond hair and dragged her face up. She gasped, shifting back a step, not that it did her much good.

Not only because she was still practically bare from the waist up, but because there was nowhere to go. She merely stepped back further into the fold of Uilleam's body. And even as she wanted to be mortified, she thoughts immediately latched onto the hard length of his cock that she could feel through the trousers he wore.

"They can't see me," she whispered the reminder to herself, needing the reassurance.

"Can't they?" Uilleam asked in her ear, making her heart flutter anew. "But you like this, don't you? Observing everything and everyone around you with no one the wiser." His hand had slipped down to the hem of her skirt, slowly dragging it up. "They never see what's right in front of them, do they?"

For a moment, she had been so sure that the room they stood in had a one-way mirror—that she could observe everything while not one single soul on the other side of the glass could see her. But Uilleam had her doubting that.

Could they see her?

The way he had her nearly bare from the waist up, or the crude, filthy way his hand had disappeared up her skirt.

His hand closed tight around her thigh, sparking an ache that made her whisper his name. He was just a hair's breadth away. It would take less than an inch for him to touch her *there*. Feel how wet she was. How desperate and near shameless.

"When you climb into your bed at night, how do you get yourself off? Do you fuck yourself with those dainty fingers of yours? D'you rub your clit in tight, slow little circles? Can you make yourself be patient?"

Each question had her thighs clenching. Not that it did her much good, considering the placement of his hand. God, she was sure if he just brushed his knuckles across her damp folds, she would spontaneously combust.

She was careful, *very* careful to keep her hands on the ledge of the window. The last thing she needed to do was reach for him.

"Your nervous," he whispered next. "Don't be. I want you to enjoy this."

Words were lost on her, hovering just out of reach. The only thing she knew at that moment was that she was willing to give him anything if he kept touching her.

"I'm not going to fuck you here," he said, punctuating those words with a dip of his middle finger into her core, stretching untried muscles. "Not for your first time. That'll come later."

An audible moan left her, and though she didn't know what sex felt like, she couldn't shake the thought that he was going to make it good for her.

Pain and all.

"Now answer my question. How do you get yourself off?"

No one could see her, she reminded herself.

No one but the two of them would know how she reached down and covered his hand, using his fingers the way she used her own.

Reveling in the feeling.

Enjoying it all the more because he caught on quickly. He didn't stop there, though, he gave her more, slowly sinking one finger inside her pussy, still keeping his thumb pressed against her clit.

"I've been dreaming about this," he whispered next to her ear, adding a second finger, grinding them in harder when his name spilled from her.

Her fingers curled into fists, her head falling back to rest on his shoulder, her breasts pushing out, nearly touching the glass.

"Give it to me," he said as he sped up his thrusts.

Rubbing her faster and faster, taking her higher than she had ever been.

Whatever he said next was drowned out by the sound of her own scream as it built and crested with the force of her orgasm. The only reason she was still standing was because Uilleam kept hold of her.

Kept her steady.

But just as she started to descend, he pulled his wet fingers free of her before he dropped to his knees and dragged one of her legs over his shoulder.

"One more," he whispered in French, his gaze on her even as he move closer to the juncture of her thighs.

"I can't."

"You *can*. This is not me asking."

He buried his face between her legs, and if it were at all possible, she saw stars.

She was sensitive, almost *too* sensitive, but Uilleam didn't stop. Not when she was a quivering mess, barely holding on to her own sanity, or when she gave him what he'd demanded and came again, her fingers buried deep in his hair.

God, she *felt* him groan against her, not stopping for so long that she was sure she would pass out from the pleasure of it all.

But finally, only when she was practically boneless and couldn't stand did he pull away and wipe his mouth with the back of his hand.

His pupils were blown, and there was no mistaking the erection barely contained behind his trousers.

He wanted her.

Undeniably.

And she was more than ready to give him everything he wanted.

No matter the consequences.

✣ 24 ✣

TAKE ME

No one made her feel the way Uilleam did.

Wild.

Liberated.

Like she was flying in the clouds and never wanted to come back down.

But that was just because he made her happy even as he exasperated her. She liked the challenge he presented. It was nothing compared to what she was feeling now as she slipped into her coat, taking his hand as he walked her out of the room.

She didn't have to guess whether anyone else knew what had happened in that room. They might not have been able to *see* them, but it was written all over their faces now.

Her hair was no longer polished and in place, and she doubted there was a stitch of lipstick left on her mouth.

But she also couldn't bring herself to care what they must have thought of her.

Not when Uilleam seemed rather determined to get her out of there and back to their place.

"Leaving so soon," Laurence called after them from a booth in the corner, his knowing gaze making Karina blush and look away.

"Expect a call from me," was all Uilleam could bother to say before he was walking them out of the building entirely, gesturing for the valet to bring the truck around.

Desire ran rampant through her veins the moment he had touched her down in that private room, but despite the chill in the air or the long journey home, it was still there. Simmering. Waiting to be stoked.

She was still excited. Eager.

Shamefully desperate.

Because more than anything, she wanted to please him. The thought as foreign as it was welcome.

She wanted to learn what *he* liked and what he didn't.

And as his gaze cut to her across the charged space between them, she would have paid anything to know what he was thinking.

But as she imagined the possibilities, she was also nervous.

Shy, rather—even as she had been all too willing to let him fuck her right there in the back of a sex club where anyone could have walked in at any time.

He wanted it to be special for her, he'd said.

He made it all too easy to fall in love with him.

The headlights illuminated the front gate before they idled there as it slid open, and Uilleam drove inside. Neither of them spoke as he parked in the garage and they stepped out.

Nor when they were inside, but they had barely passed the front door before he yanked her to him and meshed his lips to hers, so sudden that he took her breath away. It didn't end there. No, he had to fist the length of her hair, sweep his tongue across hers. Drag her into the fold of his body until she could feel every hard inch of him.

Only when his phone made another incessant sound did he finally pull away. "Hold that thought."

Turning away, he snatched his phone from his pocket and barked out a greeting in harsh, rapid Russian before disappearing around the corner. She couldn't help the amused smile on her face as she listened to his voice fading.

At his anger at being interrupted.

There was a certain sort of satisfaction that came with the knowledge of knowing a man like him wanted her.

But before he came back, she kicked off her heels and started on the zipper of her dress, tugging it down before shimmying out of it.

All the way up to his bedroom, she left a trail — a challenge.

Her heart was threatening to beat right out of her chest as she waited — the rhythm thrown off again when she heard his footsteps.

When he found her standing there waiting for him, he didn't hesitate.

He pressed her back against the wall, his hard jaw all she could see before she finally looked up to meet his gaze. She'd thought she'd known back at Hush what it meant to have his attention on her.

She thought she was prepared for the intensity of it all, but that was nothing compared to the way he made her feel now.

He held her face in the palm of his hand, his fingers splayed across one cheek as his thumb stroked over the other.

Seeing him now, the way he stared down at her with an expression that sent a chill down her spine and made a shaky breath leave her ... he felt like an entirely different man.

Like he wasn't Uilleam anymore — a man who enjoyed his games and getting what he wanted.

This was the man so many others feared — the man who made deals to further his own agenda.

To reap him more power.

The *Kingmaker* she had written so much about.

She wished she didn't love the sight as much as she did.

He tilted his head down a fraction and instinctively, she raised to meet his lips, already anticipating the moment of contact, her fingers twisting in the front of his shirt.

But he stopped a whisper away from her mouth. His gaze finding hers again. "How much would you pay to be a queen?"

"What?"

She couldn't believe he was asking her this *now*. That he was —

"How much" — he ripped her underwear off with undeniable strength — "would you pay?" He walked her over to the bed and practically threw her on it, dragging her up onto her knees. "To be a *queen*?"

His palm came down to smack her ass, the pain sudden and sharp but sending a molten heat right to her core.

This wasn't like the club.

His touch was too deliberate. Too demanding. Coaxing a reaction before she could even think of one to give.

But that was what he wanted, she thought. Her to be mindless. To focus solely on him. It was impossible not to.

"I have all night," he reminded her softly, his fingers skimming over her belly, then down between her legs.

He might have said one thing, his words a gentle caress over her skin, but he wasn't following his own suggestion with the way he zeroed in on the bundle of nerves screaming his name.

He wanted an answer to his question.

"Anything," she finally said. She would have felt ashamed by how needy she sounded if she hadn't been so into him. "I would pay any price for you."

He smiled. "Good girl. Now, let's learn what you like," he said as easily as if they were discussing the weather. "You seem to love a finger on your clit, don't you?"

He demonstrated the remark without hesitation, reminding her just how good he was at that.

But this time, he wasn't trying to get her off quickly like he had been at the club.

Now, he was taking his time.

Exploring the rest of her.

Making her lose her mind.

Never in her life had she wanted someone to touch her more than she did him at this moment. Embarrassment at the position she was in should have coursed through her—a flush in her cheeks at the feel of him staring at her naked beneath him.

Desire only burned hotter when she heard him shrug out of his shirt, then the unmistakable sound of a zipper being pulled down.

She squeezed her eyes shut. Though tempted to glance back at him, she remained still, remembering his order not to move. But the longer she kneeled in the center of the bed—on display, she thought —the more anxious she became.

She wished she knew what he saw when he looked at her. Or at least, what was holding his attention for so long. Instead of touching her, he seemed content to look his fill.

Unable to help herself, she anticipated the moment he finally touched her. She imagined the caress of his fingers, the harshness of his grip when he grabbed her.

But neither compared to the reality because instead of his hands, she felt his lips. First, at the nape of her neck, sending a shiver racing through her, then between her shoulder blades before he continued a path down her spine, each kiss better than the last.

By the time he reached the small of her back, she was a quivering mess, jolting every time his mouth skimmed her flesh, feeling the wetness between her thighs. It was ridiculous how turned on she was now when he'd barely touched her.

Just like when they were at Hush.

When she had been all but helpless against the feelings he provoked.

He tapped the inside of her thighs, one after the other, in a silent command for her to spread them wider. Even as her cheeks flushed and she was sure her legs quivered with every inch she moved, she did as he asked.

Then with a strength that made her gasp, he flipped her over onto her back, her gaze lifting to his as he moved between her thighs. Pale moonlight slashed across his front—leaving parts of him in shadow, the others standing out in stark relief.

But even as she wanted to take a moment to admire the glorious nakedness of him, it was impossible not to focus on the condom he brought up to his mouth and tore open with his teeth.

She stared transfixed as he removed the latex, then rolled it down the thick length of his erection.

For just a moment, panic sliced through her. Not because this wasn't what she wanted, and not even because she was afraid he was going to harm her in any way. But he was big, and no matter how she tried to work out the logistics in her mind, she didn't think he would fit.

"I'll be gentle with you," he promised, reading the anxiety in her expression.

She nodded, unable to find the right words.

She knew she wanted him—knew she wanted *this*—but that didn't mean she could shake the nerves.

Reaching between them, he gripped his cock and lined himself up with her slit, his gaze dropping to where they were nearly connected.

Very carefully, going slower than she thought he really wanted to, he fed his cock into her inch by inch, flexing his hips gradually until she became *very* aware of him inside her.

A breath exploded out of her at the first burst of pain, her nails instinctively digging into the muscle of his back as she resisted the urge to push him away.

But Uilleam kissed her before she could form another thought, and all too quickly, she was lost in the shape of his mouth—in the way he expertly took her mouth.

Distracting her long enough for him to sink in another inch.

A gradual slide in, a jagged glide back out.

It still *hurt*. She was still very aware of every move he made, the pain fading too slowly.

But she was caught up in the expression on his face.

A look of pained pleasure as he ground his jaw, his gaze dropping to where his cock was buried inside her.

And when she clenched around him, his eyes fell shut even as his hand squeezed the meat of her thigh.

"Let's not do that, poppet." He raised up then, the muscles in his abdomen flexing as he seated himself inside her. "We need to make this last."

A breathless sound escaped her, but even she didn't know whether it was in fear ... or excitement. But it seemed to only spur Uilleam on as his hips kicked forward again, another curse falling from his lips.

The pain faded to something else. Something that had her back arching and her hips rolling.

Something that felt so good, the only thing she could say was, "*More*, please."

He groaned, tilting his lips into a masculine sort of smile that sent satisfaction racing through her.

He had her hair wrapped around his fist, and he pulled, tipping her head back so he could press open-mouthed kisses to her throat.

"I'm not going to last," he said, sounding pained even as his thrusts kicked up a notch.

And God, *God*, he was really fucking her now.

So hard it should have been painful.

But it wasn't.

It was everything she had ever dreamed of.

And when he came moments later after three punishing strokes, she realized she *could*, in fact, come three times in one night.

❧ 25 ❧

PRETTY WOMAN

KARINA CAME AWAKE SLOWLY, SQUINTING HER EYES AGAINST THE sunlight streaming in through the parted curtains.

She knew even before she reached out and felt the sheets that Uilleam wasn't beside her. And judging from the coolness of them, he hadn't been there for quite some time. She vaguely remembered the squeeze of his arm around her waist before his touch disappeared entirely, but the pull of sleep had been too great to ignore.

Drawing in a breath as she arched her back and stretched her arms up above her head, she slipped out of bed, heading for the bathroom.

Even if she could ignore the ache in her thighs where his hands had gripped her or the other, more delicious discomfort, there was no ignoring the trail of clothes on the floor that led up to the bed.

It was impossible not to think of last night.

About Hush and everything that had happened down in that darkened room.

About what had come later once they were truly alone and Uilleam had given her his undivided attention.

The thought was enough to make her breathless all over again. Making nerve endings flare to life again in remembrance.

It was a night she would never forget for as long as she lived.

A part of her was almost afraid that he had ruined her for other men. That if there was ever someone after him, she would have to compare the two, and with the way she felt currently, *no one* could compete with him.

Finished on the toilet, she scrubbed her face clean, getting rid of last night's makeup before she smoothed on moisturizer. Then she donned the white silk robe hanging from a hook in the bathroom, knotting the tie before going in search of Uilleam.

She didn't care that she wasn't the image of grace for once. Her hair could benefit from a comb as opposed to the messy bun she had thrown it up in, and Katherine had always taught her that a no-makeup look still involved a bit of foundation and mascara.

But looking *presentable* was the last thing on her mind at the moment. If there was ever a physical description of what one looked like after having sex all night—she was it.

The warm, fragrant aroma of freshly baked pastries drew her out to the balcony where breakfast was displayed on an ornate, rather large table that took up nearly the entire width of the balcony.

Sitting at the table with a newspaper in his hands and his phone resting silently beside him was Uilleam. She was fully anticipating his immaculate appearance, but instead she found him in a pair of gray sleep pants that hung low enough she could see the sharp indentations at his waist, the V tapering down and making her wish he hadn't bothered to put on pants at all.

Even his hair was a bit unkempt, the strands messy and hanging over his forehead as if he had been running his fingers through it incessantly.

"It really isn't fair that you look like this so early in the morning."

Even when he wasn't at his best, he was still leagues beyond the rest.

His answering smile was playful and mischievous as he tossed the paper down to look back at her. "Good morning, poppet."

He offered his hand, and she didn't think twice before accepting it, allowing him to pull her toward him. Her body didn't seem to care that she was still a little tired and definitely a little sore because the moment she was within mere feet of him, it felt as if her entire body lit up.

This, she imagined, was what it was like to *want* someone.

To feel alive in their presence and never want the sensation to end.

The butterflies had metamorphosed into something else.

He gave her something she thought she'd already had.

Excitement.

"You're up early," she commented thoughtfully even as she got more comfortable on his lap.

"My work is never done," he answered simply, seeming content to just watch her.

Even if that were true—and she suspected it was, considering who he was, what he did, and whom he did it for—it was still only eight here, which would mean it was three in the morning back in New York.

She didn't even know why *she* was up.

"What do you have planned for today?" she asked, plucking a strawberry from the tray and biting into it.

"You," he said.

"*Me?*"

"It's a surprise."

She smiled despite herself. She loved surprises. "What kind of surprise?"

"One you'll get to see as soon as you're ready to leave."

He didn't have to say another word before she was hopping up and off to find something to wear, his laughter echoing behind her.

———

"Shopping, Uilleam?" she asked, looking back at him. "I've always wanted to have a *Pretty Woman* moment."

It was impossible not to see the amusement curling the left side of his mouth. He didn't respond to her remark, but rather, he opened the door and gestured for her to go in ahead of him.

Back in New York, the nicest boutique she had ever entered was the one Isla had sent her to when she'd been looking for a dress for the fundraiser, but even that paled in comparison to wherever she was now.

The floors were white marble with thin gray lines throughout. A crystal chandelier hung over a mirrored table that beautifully reflected the golden rays of sunlight spilling into the store.

A woman of indiscriminate age, wearing a black dress, towering heels, and dark red lipstick stepped out from around the corner, greeting them with a smile and an extension of her hand.

"Mr. and Mrs. Runehart, we've been expecting you."

Hearing her say that name sent a weird pang through her, the feeling strange but not entirely unwelcome. While she slid her sunglasses off her face and peeked over at Uilleam, but he didn't bother correcting the woman's assumption.

"Madeline, nice to see you again."

Karina didn't get a chance to ask if the two knew each other before the woman was looking her over with an appreciative eye. "Mr. Runehart has told me so much about you ahead of our fitting today."

"Has he?" she asked, genuinely curious, considering this was all a surprise to her.

"All nice things, I promise."

They followed her into a separate room, this one only accessed by a pair of opaque frosted glass doors. A long, tufted bench sat across from a trio of mirrors, all providing different angles from one another, and just off to the right was a high wingback chair in the same dark gray fabric as the bench.

"If you'll give us a moment, Mr. Runehart," Madeline said with a gesture of her hand for him to stay put, "we'll be back with the first selection."

Karina wasn't sure what to expect as she followed the woman into a back dressing room, changing into a robe as she waited for the other woman to come back.

It was almost surreal being here with him—living a life she had never expected. If her mother had told her over a year after she had left home for the first time, she would be in Paris with a man like Uilleam, she wouldn't have believed it was possible.

Not like this.

It wasn't long before Madeline was back, pulling a rack of dresses and other assorted clothing behind her.

The white dress hanging at the very end was calling her name—
or perhaps it was because Madeline casually mentioned that it had
been Uilleam's favorite—and she didn't hesitate before plucking it
from the row and quickly stepping into it.

She didn't bother looking at her reflection first before she left the
dressing room to go and find Uilleam. She was more curious about
his reaction. All too quickly, she remembered the night of the
fundraiser and the appreciative look he'd given her.

She wanted to see that expression again.

"You still haven't told me what, exactly, you need from this
Gaspard man," she said, remembering the name from the night
before.

He had been rather quiet on the ride here despite how warm he
had been over breakfast. Maybe he'd known she would have questions for him that he wouldn't necessarily want to answer.

He looked to be contemplating what he wanted to say—or
perhaps deciding whether he would answer her question at all—
before he finally spoke. "In the simplest terms, he's the key to me
getting a seat at the table."

Karina stayed silent a moment, processing that. She had never
imagined any real structure to the way criminal organizations
worked. Mostly, she hadn't thought beyond mafias or gangs where
there was a boss and all the people under them.

She had always assumed that men like Uilleam were only out for
themselves—that they didn't work with anyone else.

She certainly hadn't expected some sort of *commission* behind the
scenes.

Karina stepped off the podium, crossing the floor until she was
standing mere feet away from him. "What kind of table, exactly?"

He sifted his fingers through his hair, his gaze steady on hers.
"Can I trust you?"

"I haven't given you a reason not to," she countered, the words
coming far too easily though they weren't entirely true.

He thought he knew her and what she did—he thought he knew
everything.

He knew *nothing*.

"They call themselves the Coalition," he explained, his voice loud enough for her to hear, but soft enough that no one would be able to overhear their conversation.

She had seen him, on so many occasions, talk candidly about everything, yet when he spoke of this Coalition, his entire demeanor changed.

"The seven most powerful men in the world."

Her brows knitted together. "Like presidents?"

"Men who value their anonymity as much as they value their bank accounts."

Interesting.

And not just because she had never heard of them—though she was sure, if she were to ask Isla, she wouldn't have heard of the Coalition either.

She was more interested in the fact that Uilleam wanted to join their ranks.

"What do you have to do to become a part of it?"

"That's an answer I won't part with."

She blinked in surprise. "Why not?"

"The less you know, the better it is for the both of us. I can't afford any harm coming to you because of secrets I was better off keeping." His expression softened as he spoke but still had an edge to it that made her breath catch. "I don't know what I would do if someone harmed you."

She thought of the lengths he had been willing to go just to have her attention. The way he had repeatedly shown up at her apartment, or the way he had Orion thrown in jail just because he *thought* there might have been feelings there.

She should have been *worried* about those lengths.

Not to mention, the reason they had ultimately crossed paths in the first place.

Uilleam was a villain in every sense of the word. He did deplorable things for his own gain and cared very little about who he crossed to see it done.

Yet she was still drawn to him.

That powerful, relentless pull was too much to ignore.

And what must that say about her, that she was willing to accept the worst bits of him without any promise that he would change.

Why did it make her feel a little flutter in her chest at the mention of what he might do should any harm come to her?

"You can keep your secrets," she found herself saying, "but only for now."

Only until she figured out what this was between them, and whether she actually wanted it.

"You're resourceful," he said, tucking a strand of hair behind her ear. "I imagine you'll learn plenty during our time here."

He could certainly bet his life on that.

His phone chimed, the sound wiping her smile away. Despite how little time they had spent together, she knew what it meant when his phone rang.

Business was calling again.

"I have a meeting." He looked from his phone, then back to her, and mixed in that eagerness was genuine disappointment that he was leaving her.

She couldn't be mad seeing that. "Go on then. I wanted to explore the city anyway."

He kissed her hard and fast before slipping something into her hand. Then he was gone without a backward glance.

Looking down, she saw a black card gleaming and looking entirely too tempting.

A *little* shopping couldn't hurt.

26

GASPARD

At five in the morning, Uilleam found himself tracing the freckles on Karina's back with his gaze, wondering whether the pattern he was noticing was an actual constellation, or if it was his mind trying to attach meaning where there wasn't any.

He found he couldn't help himself.

Fascinated was not a strong enough word to describe the way he felt. He didn't care that he had had plenty of time to explore in the hours after he had returned from a business meeting and found her waiting for him with a coy little smile and a gleam in her beautiful eyes.

He had forgotten everything other than her as he'd carried her upstairs and sated himself with her.

The first time, he had been gentle with her, knowing she would be sore from the night before. He'd had to close his eyes against the sensation — ignore the way her pussy clenched around his cock while he was fucking her. His only goal had been to make it good for *her*.

But the second ... his only concern was just how quickly he could get them both off.

Now, despite how early he had risen the morning before and the few hours of sleep he had been gotten after exhausting himself with her, he was awake again.

Because as much as he wanted to remain right where he was, this trip to Paris *wasn't* just about being with her—he had come here for a reason.

And *that* reason had agreed to meet in just a couple of hours.

This was arguably the most important day of his life. No ... that wasn't quite right.

This was *next* to the most important day, second only to when he was officially accepted into the Coalition.

When he finally surpassed his father's legacy.

It was no great mystery to anyone who knew him that he'd loathed his father and everything he'd stood for as long as he could remember.

The day he'd finally been put in the ground couldn't have come soon enough, and though he'd raised him all his life, Uilleam hadn't shed a single tear for the man.

If anything, he had felt relief—*peace*, for the first time—because his presence on earth would no longer plague him.

But Alexander hadn't gone quietly, even as his death had been short but painful.

No, days before he had succumbed to the horrors he'd unleashed on others—when he'd beaten Uilleam to within an inch of his life—he had made it abundantly clear what he thought of him and what he was capable of ...

"Weak!" Alexander shouted, kicking Uilleam in the stomach, making him curl into himself as he tried to protect his vital organs.

Not that it was doing him much good. He didn't feel ... right. And if he had to guess, even in his delirium as pain radiated throughout his body, there were a number of bones broken and if he sustained any more damage, he doubted he would walk away from this encounter still breathing.

"Just like that brother of yours. Weak! *You're no fucking son of mine."*

He punctuated the remark with another kick, this time using the toe of his boot to flip him over onto his back, the task made all the more easy because Uilleam hardly had the strength to protect himself, let alone resist him.

Dragging in a rattling breath that hurt every single one of his ribs, Uilleam coughed and sputtered, blood spraying from his mouth, droplets spattering the marble floor beneath him.

Through one half-swollen eye, he stared up at the man who had never felt much like a father though they shared so many features.

He didn't see love and compassion in Alexander's eyes—emotions he had always suspected a father should have felt for his son. Instead, he found an emptiness that had stopped being alarming years ago.

And nestled among that nothingness was something else. Something that Uilleam hadn't seen aimed in his direction since Kit had left in the middle of the night with their uncle, never to return.

Hatred.

"You'll never be anything more than what you are right now," he said as he crouched. "Dirt beneath my fucking shoe."

He shook his head as if he were disappointed.

As if the mere sight of Uilleam made his stomach turn in disgust.

He could have gone his entire life without seeing that expression on his face.

The next punch took him by surprise, whipping his head to the side, splitting his cheek open where it sliced across his teeth. He actually saw stars moments before black dots winked in and out of his vision.

He was going to die here.

At the hands of his father on a marble floor that he'd walked along for more than half of his life.

But he wasn't the praying sort.

Nor would he beg.

If anything, that would only prompt Alexander to make this hurt worse.

Instead, despite all odds, he laughed.

It sounded strangled, even to his own ears, and he could even feel the blood spilling down his lips as he grinned, but he couldn't bring himself to care.

Not when he was dying.

And God was he ready for this hell to be over.

"You'll rue this day."

Alexander's boisterous laughter mirrored his own—disbelieving and mocking.

But Uilleam didn't care, not when the world around him was growing dark around the edges.

Alexander shook his head, even as he stood and rolled his bloodstained sleeves up. "I regret nothing."

But he would, *Uilleam thought before the beating started again.*

He didn't know how — a part of him didn't even believe it was possible — but he would.

He would make him regret *every breath he had ever taken in his miserable, unending life …*

Uilleam didn't realize he was squeezing Karina until he felt her protest, murmuring sleepily as she attempted to turn in his arms.

Offering her a wordless apology with a kiss to the back of her shoulder, he released the hold he had on her and slipped out of bed.

He hated that the thought of Alexander always sent him into such a fucking state. That he could lose track of time and himself whenever he got lost in memories better left buried.

It felt as if a lifetime had passed since that night, and the week he'd spent in a drug-induced coma to recover from his injuries.

But sometimes, when he let his mind wander, he could still feel the echoes of that day as if it were happening all over again.

Disappearing into the bathroom, he stepped into the shower stall, not bothering to wait for the water to heat before he let it rain down on him.

The cold helped wake him up — livened his senses.

Thirty minutes later, after he'd showered and dressed, Uilleam was back in his bedroom straightening the knot in his tie, his gaze finding Karina where she was still fast asleep in the bed.

She was still naked as far as he could tell, the sheet only covering her to just about the curve of her hip.

It should have concerned him the way he felt seeing her in his bed. It went beyond typical male satisfaction.

What he felt was too primal. Too selfish.

He wanted her nearly as much as he wanted a seat at the table, and if he could have both, he would do everything in his power to make sure he did.

He deserved as much.

He'd *earned* it.

Leaving her a note on the nightstand promising to return before the sun went down — and leaving his credit card should she want to leave and explore the city on her own — he ventured downstairs where Skorpion was waiting with a cup of coffee in hand.

"Long night?" he asked.

"I have considered firing you, you know."

Skorpion scoffed as he climbed to his feet. "Who else do you know that can do what I do? Not to mention put up with your shit," he said with a pointed look as they walked out the door.

"That's why you've lasted as long as you have."

"Yeah," he said with a grin, "let's go with that. Anyway, what's on the agenda?"

"The meeting with Gaspard."

It was the only thing that mattered.

The single most important meeting of his career.

All his deals and plans and careful schemes had led up to this moment.

Nothing could stand in the way of it.

"And the missus?"

He thought of Karina, still asleep, one hand resting on the side of the bed he'd vacated. "I shouldn't be long."

"Understood."

Skorpion drove them to the recital hall where Gaspard had agreed to meet with him.

Unlike Uilleam, the man he was meeting with had very particular tastes and usually conducted his business in one of two places. The specially designed office with bulletproof walls and armed guards around every corner.

And here.

The theater where the ballet company both rehearsed and performed for the public.

From what Uilleam understood, Gaspard was a major benefactor for the French ballet company, having donated more than a quarter of a million dollars this year alone.

But he *wasn't* sure why he liked to meet here, of all places. He couldn't say whether it was because he actually meant for his guests to be comfortable or to let their guard down.

Uilleam intended to do neither.

"As always, if I'm not out within the hour, you know what to do."

Skorpion nodded, shoving the car into park. "Godspeed."

Buttoning the front of his suit jacket as he exited, Uilleam checked both ways down the street before crossing, bypassing the few pedestrians on the sidewalk as he entered the building.

He followed the signs down the hallway until he reached the private staircase that led up to the balconies overlooking the stage.

It didn't take much effort for him to find where he needed to go, not when two men in creaseless suits stood on opposite sides of the door leading to Balcony 7.

They eyed him momentarily before the one to the left opened the door and gestured for him to enter.

As he walked through the darkened corridor, all he could see ahead of him was a man with graying black hair sitting in the very front row, his attention on the women on stage.

Whether they knew he was here—or perhaps were already used to his presence—they danced as if they weren't being observed.

"Uilleam Runehart. I can't say I ever thought we would meet, but here we are."

One thing about Gaspard? He didn't mince words. He didn't pretend to be something he wasn't.

He didn't like Uilleam, and he made that fact clear.

The cynical part of him admired the man for it.

"Those who underestimate me are often surprised when I surpass their expectations. A character flaw, I imagine."

The thing about Uilleam? He didn't bow before any man.

Not even one arguably more powerful than him.

But Gaspard didn't take offense, merely chuckling as he stood and offered a slightly wrinkled hand where a gold cuff winked at his wrist.

"Nice to finally meet you, Runehart. I've heard wonderfully bad things about you," he said, slipping back and forth between French and English as he spoke. "Not worse than that father of yours, of course."

If Uilleam had hated his father, it was no great mystery that most he had ever crossed paths with hated him as well.

And funnily enough, he had been spared much of his father's wrath for the most part because he was his mother's favorite. She'd doted on him more often than he could count—and though that love had felt suffocating at times, it had also saved him.

He still, even at his age, wasn't sure whether he should be thankful to her because of it.

After all, she had hated his brother for reasons he never understood. And those reasons had made Kit an easy target, even if he *had* been the eldest brother.

"Alexander was an acquired taste," he said with a shrug, helping himself to a seat.

He looked around the room, his gaze skirting over every seat and balcony, looking for faces within the shadows.

Skorpion was hidden somewhere in the room, ready to do whatever was needed should Uilleam need him to, but he was looking for unfamiliar ones who might mean him harm.

He might have wanted to do business with Gaspard, but he didn't trust the man even a little.

His father might have gone mad, but he hadn't been completely flawed in his reasoning.

"Tell me," Gaspard said as he snapped his fingers, prompting the attendant idling in the back of the room to move over to the bar cart and grab two glasses. "Was it your idea to present Paxton with a solution only to snatch it away?"

"Forgive me, but I believe we both know the answer to that question, no?"

Gaspard's smile slipped a bit, betraying the careful mask he had in place. "Clever."

Yes. Yes, he was.

And he had no shame in admitting as much.

He always had a contingency plan—thrived on them, actually.

He even had one for Gaspard, though he doubted he would need to implement it.

"Let's cut to the chase, shall we? You're here because a vacancy has opened up at the table."

"There's no better man to fill the position than me," he returned just as easily. "Or are we pretending you weren't impressed by what I did in New York?"

"Entertained would be the better word, no? You are ... like a magician with a top hat in your hands, and from inside it, you pull a cute little white rabbit."

Uilleam tightened his hand around the arm of the chair, ensuring Gaspard couldn't see the way his fingers twitched at that remark.

It was what he wanted.

A reaction.

He refused to give him one.

"Is *that* what you think?"

Gaspard's gaze briefly landed on him, analyzing and assessing. "I *think* that people overestimate what you're capable of."

Uilleam had never burned a man alive before—a bit grisly for his tastes—but as he stared across the aisle at the man sitting in the leather chair with a condescending smile on his slightly gaunt face, he considered taking the lighter from his pocket and watching the flames eat away at his flesh.

It wouldn't be a quick death nor would it be painless. His clothes would melt into his flesh, a searing heat that he would never have the pleasure of forgetting.

And that was only if he survived the ordeal.

"You're just a small fish in a very big pond, as the Americans say," Gaspard continued, drawing him from his thoughts.

He seemed to struggle with what he wanted to say next, grappling for another insult. "Ordinary," he said after a moment. "I've met many men like you."

After a moment, Uilleam set his drink on the table, making a pointed effort not to shatter the glass. "There is nothing remotely ordinary about who I am or what I'll become."

That was enough to wipe the smile from the man's face, draining his amusement away.

"If you think you're joining my Coalition, you are mistaken, Uilleam Runehart."

"If you think I came here asking permission," Uilleam said as he leaned toward the man, making sure his words were heard, "you'll understand very quickly how wrong you are. And fortunately for us all, your vote isn't the only one that matters in the end."

"Then why come seeking my approval."

"I only needed you to get me here—which you did once you authorized a meeting in exchange for Paxton."

His mouth opened and closed, realization setting in.

He hadn't come seeking Gaspard's permission for anything—he needed only to give others the idea, and the rest would spread.

"Your rules stipulate that should a vacancy open within the Coalition, a replacement will be chosen within six months. In that six months, you haven't held a single meeting with anyone with the exception of yours truly."

Sometimes, the only thing one needed to get what they wanted was making the right impression.

"How am I doing for a little fish?" Uilleam stood before the other man could think to respond. "I understand you may have hated my father, but I am not him. Set your grievances aside."

He looked as if he wanted to curse him or threaten him, surely, but he did neither. Instead, he simply said, "The welcoming party is tomorrow night."

Uilleam inclined his head before heading for the door. "Looking forward to it."

❦ 27 ❦

SWEET NOTHINGS

KARINA LOOKED DOWN, WATCHING THE EXPLOSION OF BLUE AS IT quickly swept through the bath water, turning it from translucent to a soft shade of blue-green. Steam billowed and swayed above the water, but before she stepped a foot inside, she crumbled a few bits from the bubble bar she'd picked up as well and crushed it beneath the water.

The fresh, citrusy scent of lemongrass filled her senses, making her eagerly slip out of her robe and step into the water, pausing a moment to adjust to the heat.

A long sigh spilled from her lips as she sank into the water, the bubbles nearly covering her completely. It didn't take long before her muscles were relaxing and she was content to lie there for as long as possible.

If there was one thing she missed from home, it was being able to sit in the tub and just soak while her mind wandered. She hadn't minded, at first, that her tiny apartment only had a stall for a shower —it made getting out of the house in the morning relatively quick— but moments like these had her wondering whether it might be time to move.

Her mind drifted in a dozen different directions—the work she would be going home to in a few short days, the *other* work that she refused to consider for more than a few moments at a time, and the voice mail from Orion she still hadn't listened to—but even as she tried to focus on anything else, her mind always went back to Uilleam.

To *last night*.

It shouldn't have been possible for her skin to grow warmer, considering the temperature of the bath she was sitting in, but she couldn't help but think she was burning a little hotter at the thought of him and everything they had done.

Truthfully, it was the *only* thing she could think about.

Especially since she had woken up sore in the best way possible and found him waiting with breakfast on the balcony.

Meetings, he'd told her earlier before leaving her to do as she pleased. He'd promised to return as quickly as possible, yet he had already been gone for more than six hours already.

She expected the time to pass quickly, and after visiting the market and picking up a few things, she hadn't realized how much she would miss his presence until she had returned and found he still wasn't back yet.

More curious than she cared to admit, she should have asked what sort of meetings he would be attending—whether they were more of his infamous deals.

Karina had only just closed her eyes after sweeping tendrils of her hair behind her ears when audible footsteps made her shift, her gaze darting to the arched doorway seconds before Uilleam walked inside.

His gaze had appeared concerned for a moment before the expression smoothed away once he laid eyes on her. He looked almost … relieved to see her.

Yet instead of making a coy joke or even bothering to *ask* if he had, in fact, missed her in all the time he was gone, she smiled softly, feeling shy all of a sudden. "Hey."

"*Soyez toujours mon cœur qui bat—Be still my beating heart.*"

The words were said softly, so low that she almost missed them, but there was no mistaking what she had heard, nor could she mask the pleasure she felt at hearing them.

Turning over, she rested her arm against the side of the clawfoot tub, leaning toward him. "You have a way with words, Uilleam Runehart."

"Did you miss me?" he asked with a little tilt of his head as he tossed his phone on the counter and started loosening the knot of his tie.

"Yes," she admitted softly, feeling the blush in her cheeks as she marveled at the fact that she'd actually answered truthfully.

He let his tie fall from his fingers once he got it over his head, then started on the row of buttons down his front next. It didn't matter that she had seen his naked chest in early morning sunlight yesterday or even that she got to run her fingers all over it and the rest of him the night before. It was a different experience entirely when he began stripping out of his shirt.

His shoulders and collarbone, then the flat but ridged expanse of his abdomen, the lean muscles in his biceps, and even the prominent veins that forked up his forearms.

It still felt as if she was seeing him for the very first time.

"Did you think of me?" he asked as he started on his belt, then the button of his trousers, but he didn't immediately step out of those.

Instead, he allowed them to sit at his waist and gave her a tantalizing view of the black waistband of the boxer briefs beneath as he dragged the stool from the vanity and placed it next to the porcelain bathtub.

Her smile was a little coy as she said, "You didn't give me much of a choice."

She was reminded of him every time her thighs rubbed together and she felt the ache there. The way she could so clearly remember the tremors she had felt when he was inside her.

No, she didn't think she would stop thinking about him for a while.

"Where were you today?" she asked softly as he brushed the damp strands of her hair off her face.

Even after he did the intimate gesture, he remained close, his elbows resting on his knees, his hands clasped in front of him.

She didn't miss the way it looked with the two of them sitting like this.

Her naked shape mostly concealed by pale blue water and bubbles, him in a perfectly pressed suit.

As if he were a Lord and she was his lady.

As if he were her master and she his willing, obedient slave.

"Is that really what you want to ask me about?" His question came on the heels of a smile that had finally managed to fight its way onto his face.

He'd noticed where her gaze had gone and lingered.

Of course he had.

She might have only stared at for a mere second, and her facial reaction before she schooled it for even less than that, but for a man trained in reading people, it wasn't a mystery that he had noticed the change in her.

Now, the only question was how to answer his question.

"It'll answer both questions I have," she responded simply.

"Clever."

"I like to think so."

"The meeting with Gaspard."

Right. She was hearing his name quite a lot now. "The French billionaire," she said with a nod, having done a bit of research while he was gone.

She didn't know everything there was to know about the man, only what little had been released in interviews and news articles about his accomplishments and philanthropy. Beyond that, she hadn't found much else.

There was also the little that Uilleam had already told her about him when he had taken her shopping.

"I'd requested a meeting with him. Today was an ... interview, of sorts."

"Him or you?" she asked, noting his smile.

He actually rolled his eyes. "Regrettably, some are more stubborn about accepting my services when I offer them."

"They obviously don't know what they're missing," she said, reaching up to brush her fingers along the hand he now had wrapped around the rim of the tub.

While at first she had meant it as a way to *not* stroke his ego considering her tone of voice, there was also no mistaking the truth in those words either.

They *didn't* know what they were missing when it came to what he could do.

"He's from a different time," Uilleam muttered without inflection as he undid the cufflink on his shirt sleeve and rolled the material up. "When men were only allowed a seat after they'd reached the age of fifty. Only then, in his opinion, has a man really lived."

Uilleam was nearly three decades short of that

At his age, Karina thought, he should have been working for someone else as a recruit, or an underling at best, yet his playing field was vastly different.

He was vastly different.

Not only was he his own boss, but he commanded others.

Whatever rules had been in place before Uilleam came along, before he became a fixer—a *Kingmaker*, as she had dubbed him— they had no place here now.

"Sounds very backward."

"Because of the age limit? I agree."

"Because there are no *women*. Why is it that men tend to forget women can be just as ruthless?"

She expected him to protest, to try to make an argument to excuse it, but he merely laughed.

"Of that, I have no doubt."

Her smile grew by an inch as she turned to better face him, enjoying the look on his face far too much. The way he seemed to be trying to erase the bubbles surrounding her with his mind alone.

It was only right that she help him.

Placing her hands on the edge of the clawfoot tub, she moved to her knees, watching the way his Adam's apple bobbed as he swallowed.

Not even a minute passed before he was reaching for her.

His gaze stayed on hers even as his hand descended down her stomach. "Such beautiful, dangerous creatures," he said with a minute shake of his head. "You never see the danger until you're already wrapped around their finger."

"Oh?" she asked, her voice a little shaky as she inched closer to him, parting her thighs in the process. "Is that how you feel? Do you think you're wrapped around my finger?"

He blew out a breath, his thumb pressing down on her clit before rubbing in achingly slow circles. "More than you could ever know."

"Uilleam —"

"Say my name like that again." His voice took on that low, smoky quality that made her arch into him, spiking the heat coursing through her. "I love to hear you say it."

His name spilled from her again when he curled two fingers inside her, a curse following when he cupped her jaw and forced her to look at him.

"I'm not going to let you come until I'm ready," he said a moment later. "If you have me wrapped around your finger, it's only fair I have you around mine, hmm?"

She didn't have words.

Not that any of them would be good enough.

Because he had her, and there was no denying that.

He owned her right down to her very marrow, and she was done denying that fact to herself.

28

DEAREST ISLA

IT DIDN'T MATTER IF SHE WAS BACK HOME OR, AS IT WERE, enjoying her time in a different country, If there was one person Karina always answered the phone for, it was her sister.

"You know," Isla said once the call connected, "if you took Mum's calls, she wouldn't require me to do her dirty work."

Karina smiled despite herself. "Is that the only reason you're calling?"

"Of course not," Isla returned flippantly. She rarely did anything she didn't want to do. "Tell me about you. What have you been up to besides having murderers put behind bars? Did you love the dress you needed?"

Karina smiled before she even meant to, remembering the night of the dinner very well. It had been the first time she'd ever seen Uilleam's face.

In many ways, that had felt like the beginning of this strange, wondrous thing between them.

She told her of the fundraiser and the many nights that followed. About the joy she had felt once Paxton had been arrested.

"Mother used that to her advantage."

Karina's smile froze in place at those words. "How do you mean?"

238

"Just a few well traded stocks is all," Isla said glibly.

As if it meant nothing.

And really, it should have. She should have been glad that someone else had reaped the benefits of Paxton's incarceration—especially her own family—but while she wanted to see it that way, she also couldn't help but think it wasn't Paxton's misfortune that Katherine had garnered riches from, but rather off the back of Miranda.

The thought made her pluck at the string on her shirt.

"But that's a story for when you finally join the business. Which will be … ?"

"Oh, not you too," Karina said on a sigh, rubbing her brow. Any mention of her time ending in New York and her going back home always brought on the beginnings of a headache.

"I'm only asking the question we're all thinking. When are you coming *home*? We miss you."

Home.

The very thought of it should have made her smile, or at the very least, she should have felt a longing in her heart for a place she hadn't returned to in over a year now, yet … she didn't miss it.

Sure, there were times when she wished she could venture outside and smell the cherry blossom trees that stood tall in front of Ashworth Hall, but the home, itself, she didn't think about, let alone miss.

She thought she *would* have by now because that was what her relocating had been about in the first place.

Moving to the States had been her way of getting away, spreading her wings.

Learning what she was made of without the security, or pressure, of her family.

She'd wanted to explore her passions and decide for herself what she wanted out of life. She'd wanted the chance to experience what she thought it meant to be normal before she committed to venturing into the family business as her sister had done.

"I can't say I've made a decision just yet."

"Why not? What's there left to think about?"

She wished it was that easy for her. That she could fall in line with what Mother expected of her children the way Isla did. In many ways, her sister was the better daughter. There hadn't been any hesitation on Isla's part when it came to the family business.

She had gleefully and quite eagerly joined the ranks without a single hesitation.

She hadn't had the same sort of doubts that whispered in the back of Karina's mind. She didn't wonder what else the world had to offer.

Except Karina *had*.

She had wanted to exhaust every option before she came to a decision.

"You've not met a man at that paper, have you? Someone you fancy?"

A lie sat heavy on the tip of her tongue. "Not someone from the paper, no."

"But you *have* met a man? Or woman?" Isla added with the sort of tone that told her she wouldn't mind the possibility.

Her smile was rueful. "A man, yes."

"You've clearly been holding out on me," Isla said, sounding scandalized. "Who is he? What does he do? Where did he go to university?"

Karina was almost sure if she did give just a name and a significant enough occupation, Isla might very well know who she would be talking about.

Isla knew of most powerful men.

"His name is Uilleam. He's a ..." She stumbled only for a moment before remembering this was her sister, and that she always told Isla the truth. "Uh, fixer."

She waited for the questions she knew would eventually come, but as she anticipated them, Isla stayed quiet.

Too quiet.

No questions about the man or how she knew him. Not even how they had met.

Which could only mean one thing.

She knew of him.

"I'm afraid to even ask what you're thinking," she said a moment later when Isla *still* hadn't spoken.

Some part of her had known this day would come, that she would have to explain her relationship with a man like him. Not because he was a criminal—her mother and sister would probably applaud that fact—but someone who used his name as a weapon and made his presence felt while her family tended to stick to the shadows.

The Ashworths had a tendency to know everyone, yet no one knew them.

"This isn't ... Mother's doing?" Isla asked, her voice trailing off at the end as if she already had an answer but was hoping for another.

"Of course not," Karina said quickly. "She doesn't know about him ... or us, rather."

"He was the one you wrote about then—the one people are starting to call the Kingmaker?"

She hadn't known when she wrote that little piece that the moniker would stick—that it would become something of a title. "I didn't know you kept up with my work."

"I didn't know you were keeping these sort of secrets from me."

While some might have possessed a great poker face, Isla also had a tone about her voice that made one wonder what she was truly thinking.

Karina had witnessed her using it on more than one occasion.

Yet now, she could hear the strain behind those words.

There was more to this than she realized, and that thought was enough to make her heart stutter.

"What is it, Iz? What aren't you telling me?"

"Let's meet."

"What? I'm in Paris," she reminded her. She didn't bother mentioning that she hadn't gotten around to telling Uilleam about her.

"I can have the jet there within a couple of hours—I had business in Brussels," she tacked on, sounding distracted. "This is a conversation better had in person."

"But—"

Isla didn't give her a chance to protest before ending the call, the click in her ear enough to make her curse.

Isla was coming, whether she liked it or not.

And more than that, she was coming with information she probably wouldn't like.

———

It was one thing to sneak out of her apartment in the middle of the night when she was back home. It was something else entirely slipping out in an entirely different country.

Of course, she could explain it away easy enough. She could just say she was going to the shops or maybe the market to cook a meal for dinner as opposed to going out, but that didn't stop her nerves from racing as she left their temporary home.

She walked nearly a mile up the street before hailing a taxi and giving the man behind the wheel the name of the hotel where Isla was waiting for her.

It wasn't that she was nervous—at least not entirely. Truthfully, she was a bit ecstatic at the idea of seeing her sister after so long. Fourteen months might have passed in the blink of an eye, but that didn't mean she hadn't felt homesick.

She missed seeing her best friend in all the world.

That was the thing about them. The three years that separated them in age meant nothing to Isla.

For as long as Karina could remember, it had always been the two of them against the world. They had confided secrets they would never tell a single soul. They had learned and grown together, so much so that their bond was unbreakable.

But even as she was confident in their relationship, she still didn't know what to expect from this meetup. The unmistakable silence that had stretched on for what seemed like ages had already made her worry, even before she heard the way her sister reacted to Uilleam's name.

It was almost funny now, ironic really, how emboldened she had felt at others' fear of Uilleam when they spoke his name, but she had never considered her reaction to someone she knew remaining mute on him.

Not for long, anyway.

Karina checked her phone again, reading the address Isla had texted her twenty minutes ago before looking back out the window at the buildings she passed in the back seat of the taxi, reading the street numbers.

For once, she was glad Uilleam was at a business meeting that he didn't want her privy to—it would make it easier for her to see her sister without having to tell him anything about it.

It wouldn't be a lie, not really. If he asked, she would tell him she went to the market or sightseeing, maybe both. She would just fail to mention one of the stops she made.

Just a little white lie.

But even as the thought of lying to him didn't sit well with her, she knew she didn't have a choice.

She didn't know if she ever would.

The hotel she arrived at was tucked well enough into the city proper that it was easy for her to slip into the middle of a crowd and disappear. She took the elevator up to the eighteenth floor, finding the key under the flower pot as Isla had told her.

As she entered the room, the floral scent of her sister's favorite perfume hit her.

At first glance, no one would have thought she and her sister were related. They might have shared the same mink-colored hair and stood the same height, but that was where the similarities ended.

Isla had the sort of model good looks that could have landed her on the cover of a fashion magazine or gracing a runway in Milan, while Karina believed she resembled their father more.

And she considered herself more of a practical dresser, only putting in more effort when it was absolutely needed, but Isla was different. From the way her hair was always curled and groomed to the subtle but glamorous makeup she wore daily, her outfits, as much as her personality, made a bold statement.

But beneath the glamour of it all, Isla was a woman that no one wanted to mess with. It was often too late by the time someone realized this little fact about her, though.

A pair of crystal encrusted Louboutins rested in front of the couch, one of the first signs that her sister was there, even before she heard the rattle of ice cubes hitting glasses. Isla rounded the corner a moment later carrying a chilled bottle in one hand and the glasses in the other.

There was a moment when she saw the relief on Isla's face, knowing it was probably reflected on her own too. They were just sisters then who hadn't seen each other in far too long.

The way she had been years ago when Isla was away at school and wouldn't return until the winter holidays or summer break. Or when she had finally come home only for Karina to be the one to attend school far across the country.

But as quickly as that relief had settled over the both of them, it only took one glance around at where they were to remind them why they were here together.

"This is the part," Isla said as she sat gracefully, pouring a drink from the tumbler into both glasses, "where you tell me everything."

She wished she could say there was nothing to tell really—the relationship, if it could truly be called that, was still new—if only so that Uilleam could remain solely hers for a little while longer, but she had already said too much already.

And a large part of her wanted to know what her sister knew about him ... while a smaller part wanted to know what she thought of him.

For a moment—just a moment—she tried to imagine what this conversation would be like if Uilleam hadn't been who he was. If he had been an ordinary man who did honest work, would she still feel the same amount of trepidation she felt now?

But the answer to that question didn't matter in the grand scheme of things because whether he was or wasn't wouldn't matter because she was still the same person.

"I don't even know where to begin."

"Anywhere," Isla replied with dainty shrug, lifting her drink to her lips. "The beginning is always helpful."

But what she didn't understand was that the beginning was subjective. It could have been the moment they crossed paths that very first time at the dinner, or even when she had guessed his involvement in Miranda's death.

Or even the story that had alerted her to his existence entirely.

She didn't know where to start.

So it all came pouring out of her before she could stop and form coherent thoughts. Everything.

From the middle to the beginning to the end and around again, purging everything she possibly could until she finally had to pause long enough to take a breath.

She hadn't realized in the midst of her word vomit that Isla hadn't actually taken a sip of her drink yet but merely held it in one jeweled hand. There wasn't judgment in her expression, that much she could see, but the silence stretching on again worried her all the same.

"Now will you tell me?" Karina asked as she reached for her own glass, needing the sharp bite of the alcohol to dull her nerves.

"Tell you what?"

"Why the very mention of his name prompted this visit."

She could tell just from the expression on her face that she wished she didn't have to, but the pact between them always demanded that they stay honest with each other if no one else.

"He's, well … of course, I've heard of him," she said, switching from whatever she had been about to say. "Even before you dubbed him the Kingmaker."

"How have you heard of him?" she asked. As hard as it had been for her to find anything on the man with the way people were so nervous to talk about him, she found it almost impossible to believe.

"His family is notorious." When Karina remained silent and continued to stare at her, Isla went on. "His father, Alexander Rune-hart, was something of a criminal mastermind. They called him the godfather of crime. It's a mantel Uilleam has made very clear he's trying to pick up."

Another gulp of her drink. "And how do you know of him?"

"He's, uh …" she hesitated again, uncertain whether she should answer.

That only made Karina's fears worse. "Tell me."

"He's on the list. Rather, his father was on the list, and his name replaced his once he was dead."

Not only was she learning that Uilleam's father was dead from someone other than him, but she also heard the last thing she wanted to hear.

"Not Mother's list."

Isla's expression was grave. "I'm afraid so."

Mother's list was the most precious thing she owned, if anyone asked Katherine. A little black book with a number of names written in delicate cursive. Each one as important as the last. Some had been crossed out over the years—usually accompanying a great scandal, or if it came to it, death—but others still remained.

Names of people who proved a threat to Mother's empire.

Names of people she would do anything to get rid of.

And somewhere, whether on the first page or the last, Uilleam's name was in it.

Before the thought could send her into a panic, her phone chimed with a text. Uilleam, asking about her day, wanting to know what she wanted to do with the rest of their evening now that he was free.

She let that text, that promise of something later, ground her in the present.

"Iz, I have to go. We'll have to talk about this later."

"Very well. So long as you realize that we will have to talk about it."

"Of course," Karina said with a nod, distracted.

"Better with me than with Mother, no?"

That was enough to make Karina look up, to recognize that everything was beginning to change again. And with that thought came a niggling of something else. Something she couldn't quite put words to.

"Text me when you're back in Brussels." Karina turned to leave.

"Do you love him?"

The question shouldn't have felt as much like a punch to the stomach as it did, but Karina felt it all the same. Such a simple question with a complicated and uncertain answer. "I don't know," she answered, because for once, she didn't know.

The answer to this particular question eluded her.

Isla's expression was slightly strained as she reached between them to rest her hand against her knee, unconsciously offering comfort for her next words. "Don't fall in love, Karina. It only ever ends one way."

❦ 29 ❧

WORTH

DESPITE ISLA'S REVELATIONS, KARINA COULDN'T LET THAT distract her from why she had come to Paris.

One thing she was very good at was pretending.

Pretending as if she wasn't still thinking about what Isla had said.

Pretending as if she knew nothing about the man currently standing opposite her as they waited on the dock, preparing to board the yacht where glowing lights lit up the interior and a party was in full swing.

And in a glance, she could quite clearly see it was a *man's* party.

It was the only thought that came to mind as she stepped on board the luxury yacht idling on the water.

She'd come expecting the sheer luxury of it all—from the white leather bench seats and dark polished wooden floors, and even the crew that were all in crisp white uniforms, all perfectly groomed and manicured—but what she wasn't expecting was the sheer number of women in bikinis.

Especially when the temperature was steadily dropping as the sun had all but disappeared.

Sure, those bikinis might have been made from some sort of fur as far as she could tell—and there were even a couple who strolled past her in long fur coats as well (though their bikinis were made of some sort of reflective material) — but they were all in some state of undress that made her feel as if she looked like a nun in her simple jewel-toned dress.

They were models, she thought, or at least women who aspired to be. And though there were a few who made their way around the party, most remained in one place, casually sipping from crystal champagne glasses.

As if they were merely part of the party's decorations — meant to be seen and nothing more.

The thought made annoyance creep through her.

It was men like Gaspard that made her do what she did.

The William Paxtons of the world.

Women shouldn't have been mere objects for them to toy and tinker with when they saw fit.

"Let's save that ire in your eyes until *after* the party, shall we?"

Her expression cleared away as she glanced up at Uilleam, feeling the weight of his palm on the small of her back. "Am I really that transparent?"

"Only when you're visualizing prey."

A startled laugh left her as he guided them below deck, down to where the heart of the party was.

If she had thought the top was extravagant, this was something more.

Golden light reflected off paneled walls, and there was a certain newness to everything that made her wonder whether this particular vessel had been purchased specifically for this event.

The men milling around the floor certainly seemed the type to spend in abundance for something like this.

"Reginald Turner," Uilleam leaned down to whisper in her ear, low enough for only her to hear his words. To anyone else, it might have looked as if he kissed her cheek.

The man in question walked toward them, his portly face lit up as he laid eyes on Uilleam first.

He was a boisterous man with a voice to match, and though she had momentarily thought he would ignore her presence altogether, he nearly took her clear off her feet as he embraced her as enthusiastically as he had Uilleam.

"It's good to see you, old boy! Where have you been hiding yourself?"

"Business and beautiful complications have kept me busy," he returned just as easily.

It took everything in her not to roll her eyes at that.

"So I've heard," Reginald said with a wink of his eye. "Dirty business in New York, was it? What'd they call you—the *Kingmaker,* no?"

A brush of Uilleam's thumb along her spine had her shifting closer to him.

"Has a nice ring to it, doesn't it?"

God, she'd already made a monster out of the man.

It continued this way as they circled the room. Uilleam whispered a name in her ear before the corresponding person came over to greet him. Some acknowledged her as his date—others acted as if she didn't exist at all.

She wondered, at first, why he bothered to tell her their names at all—it wasn't as if any of them went out of their way to introduce themselves to her—but then she remembered his words from the other night.

About how he knew she paid attention to everything going on around her. How she liked to observe and learn others' secrets without them being any the wiser.

No, he wasn't giving her everything there was to know about the people attending this party, but rather allowed her to make her own observations.

He gave her what she didn't know to ask for.

She watched him as he spoke with another man who was some sort of oil tycoon. It would be easy, so terribly easy to fall for a man like him.

To dive headfirst into something foreign and new just to get a little closer to him—to peek behind the veil that was always calling her name where he was concerned.

A commotion on the other side of the room dragged her from her thoughts, bringing her attention over to the couple that slowly descended down the stairs.

Like Uilleam, the man wore a three-piece suit in the darkest black with a blood-red tie. There was a certain air about him that set him apart from the other men in the room.

Not to mention, the woman walking alongside him wore a figure-hugging red dress that reached the floor and trailed a bit behind her. She also seemed to eye the women in bikinis with disdain as she accepted a glass of champagne from a passing crew member.

The pair looked as if they were attending a red carpet event rather than a party thrown by a notorious criminal.

If she had to guess, the two were important. They were greeted just as gleefully, if not more, than Uilleam had when they arrived.

For once, Karina squeezed Uilleam's hand to get his attention. Even as the man in front of them was speaking, clearly impassioned by whatever he was saying, Uilleam ignored him entirely to focus on her.

She couldn't unpack that at the moment. "Who are they?"

He turned his head to follow her gaze, finding the couple she meant, and to her surprise, his mouth curved into a genuine smile.

"Let me introduce you."

He excused them with barely a wave before taking her hand again. They were nearly across the floor when the couple who'd grabbed her attention spotted them.

They, too, smiled at the sight of them.

It was clear, at that moment, they knew each other quite well.

"I thought you were skipping the festivities this year, Carmelo." Uilleam greeted the man, though his words lacked their usual ire.

As Karina looked from one man to the other, she didn't think she could recall a single person who Uilleam had appeared to genuinely enjoy speaking with. He wasn't much of a people person by any stretch of the imagination.

"I couldn't very well miss your debut."

Even if she hadn't known he was Italian from his coloring, she definitely knew the second he opened his mouth. There was no denying the polished, alluring quality of his accent.

"And who is this?"

Uilleam smiled down at her, seeming proud to show her off. "Karina Ashworth. Karina, this is Carmelo Albini, and his wife, Aurora."

She smiled at them both, accepting Carmelo's proffered hand before leaning into Aurora as the woman kissed both of her cheeks.

"It's a pleasure to meet you, Karina."

"Likewise."

They tried to hide it—and had she not been looking for it, she might have missed it—but the pair were surprised to see her. She wasn't quite sure whether it was because Uilleam had brought a date along with him, or whether it was *her*, but she was inclined to believe the former.

"That's quite the dress you're wearing," Aurora complimented with an appreciative glance.

"Oh, thank you," she said, smiling up at Uilleam. It *had* been his choice.

Aurora was kind, Karina found as they talked. Unlike the other women in the room, she made it a point to circle the room, speaking with everyone.

But she wasn't treated the same way the others were. They all spoke to her with respect, their gazes never straying beyond her eyes.

It was easier now to see how divided the room was once she took a step back and looked at it. Each group had a person at the very center.

And if she had to guess, she would assume every one of them were the high-ranking members Uilleam had briefly mentioned.

Abrupt applause drew Karina's gaze back to the stairs leading up to the deck, moments before a rather short man in a slightly too tight suit came walking down the stairs.

Her fingers instinctively tightened around Uilleam's as she felt him stiffen beside her.

She could understand why even as she knew very little about the other man.

She knew men like him.

The sort who thought they owned the world and everyone in it.

He wore a pair of thick black frames, almost comically big, but they seemed to fit him. Even still, he looked nothing like the sort of man who was a part of a criminal conglomerate like the Coalition.

"I'm so glad you all could join me."

He basked in the attention, making quite the spectacle, but no one seemed to mind.

She knew, without having to be told, this was Gaspard. The man Uilleam had come to see.

"And if it isn't the man of the hour ..."

His smile was a little too wide as he greeted Uilleam with a clap on his back. His gaze briefly skirted over Karina, dismissing her just as quickly without saying a word.

One could always measure a man in how he treated those he considered less powerful than him.

"Let's talk," Gaspard said next, already heading in the opposite direction.

She could practically see the restraint as Uilleam didn't respond, merely giving a curt nod of his head.

But there was fury in his eyes, and if he'd been half the man he was, she was sure he would have stabbed the man by now.

"Forgive me," he said next to her ear. "I'll be right back."

She smiled when he pulled away. "I'll be fine."

After a long moment, he turned on his heels and walked away with select men in the room following them.

THIS LATE AT NIGHT, THE OCEAN WAS A DARK, BLANK CANVAS OF glimmering water, as beautiful as it was daunting.

The murmur of voices from the party inside carried through the cracked doors behind her, but Karina was far more focused on the water below to decipher the voices and piece together the conversations.

Sometimes, it could be a bit overwhelming to listen to everything going on around her and keep track of who said what. Trying to make sure she didn't miss any stray details lest it come up later.

It wasn't necessarily because she needed to relay the information to someone else, but just little bits for her to know and tuck away in the back of her mind.

She just wanted a moment of quiet. A moment when she could think clearly without having to process everything around her.

She had to remember that she wasn't just her mother's daughter.

No matter what she did, she couldn't get her conversation with Isla out of her mind. Or everything she had revealed.

It lingered, and no matter how she tried to pretend the conversation hadn't happened at all, it was all she could think about.

"Ah, *madame*. Uilleam's pet, oui?"

The slight quizzical tone to his voice might have made the question come off as more innocent than he meant it had it not been for the expression on his face.

She would have been able to guess, even before Uilleam had told her outright, that the pair weren't particularly fond of each other.

She was also starting to think that he had good reason.

Gaspard was ghostly pale, the color made all the more stark from his dark suit, gloves, and walking cane.

"*Oui, merci. C'est une belle fête. Merci pour l'invitation — Yes, thank you. This is a lovely party. Thank you for the invitation.*"

She only allowed herself the smallest of smiles at his reaction to her speaking flawless French. If he thought she was just a pretty girl on Uilleam's arm and nothing more, she would gladly show him otherwise when Uilleam wasn't around to see.

She still had her secrets after all …

"I trust you're enjoying yourself?" he asked after a beat. "I don't think I've seen very much of you around before."

No, she imagined he wouldn't.

Sensing she wasn't going to respond, he went on to say, "Tell me, how does a nice girl like you wind up with a man like Uilleam Runehart?"

"I guess I'm lucky in that way," she answered, briefly glancing behind them at the party, trying to find Uilleam in the crowds.

"Hmm." He was staring now, his gaze slightly narrowed. "You look … familiar."

A flood of heat swept through her, but she was careful to keep her expression neutral.

Familiar didn't mean he knew her secret.

It just wasn't possible.

But … if he was as powerful as Uilleam had proclaimed him to be, she wouldn't be surprised if he had met her mother once.

She sincerely hoped he hadn't.

"Karina."

She sighed in relief, turning to face Uilleam as he came from around the side of the boat. She could almost *see* the tension easing from his shoulders.

"Lovely date you have here, Runehart."

"Very much so," he returned, the arm he slid around her waist nothing short of possessive.

Gaspard seemed to find the move amusing. "Have a good night."

"You as well," Uilleam returned easily. "I look forward to working with you."

He said it so casually, Karina didn't think anything of his words, at least until she saw the way Gaspard's expression shifted.

His nose turning up as if he smelled something bad.

The slight curl of his lip.

He *very* much hated that idea.

"Quite sure you have what it takes?"

"I wouldn't be here otherwise."

"Despite what others believe, I don't find luck admirable."

"Luck has nothing to do with it, unfortunately. I'm just very good at what I do. It's never too late to teach an old dogs new tricks. You should call and set up an appointment."

The taunt got him exactly what he wanted.

Gaspard sputtered, barking out French curses that had his guard —who'd been standing silent off to the side—shifting on his feet, already reaching for the gun holstered at his belt.

A wolf whistle from the other side of the deck where Skorpion was standing gave the man pause. And when he gave him a two-fingered salute, his smile a little wolfish, the man dropped his hands to his sides altogether.

"You underestimate me at your own peril, Gaspard," Uilleam said a moment later, drawing Karina's gaze to him.

The man she knew was gone.

In his place was the *Kingmaker* again.

Enthralled was the only word she could think of.

It was the only thing she *felt*.

Even as Gaspard strolled away unharmed, she fully suspected that Uilleam could conquer the world if he wanted.

30

WEAR THE CROWN

Uilleam didn't speak for a long time. Not as they were leaving the party, or afterward, when they had climbed into the rental and driven away. But that had been an hour ago.

Karina had wondered, in all that time, what was on his mind. What had caused the tension around his mouth and the sudden silence he had fallen into. Somewhere along the way, she had kicked off her heels and tucked her legs up onto the seat as she shifted as close to him as she possibly could while still wearing her seat belt.

She reached out, brushing her fingers along the scruff of his jaw before sifting them through the thick strands of his hair, watching the lines smooth away along his forehead, some of the tension easing.

After a moment, he reached over and rested his hand first on her knee, then shifted it farther up until his fingers curled around her thigh. Even with the warm air blowing through the vents, she could still feel the warmth of his touch.

It was such a simple gesture, just an absent action that spoke volumes to her.

She expected him to drive them back to their place, but he turned down a street she was sure led in the opposite direction. Beside him, though, she was content to go wherever he took them.

An hour or maybe longer had passed before the pinpricks of early morning sunlight breached the dark sky, and they finally arrived at Uilleam's destination.

Even at their distance, she could see the dark glimmer of the ocean water. At this hour, she wasn't expecting anyone to be out on the beach, but at the edge of the lot where they were parked, she saw a sign that marked this particular beach as private.

Uilleam put the car in park. Leaning back against the seat, his tension returned just that quickly. "Tired?" he asked.

Even if she had been, she wouldn't have told him. She was far more interested in him and what was troubling him. "Not at all." She studied him now, her gaze drifting over his face. "You don't sleep very much, do you?"

She had noticed it already, even in the short time they had been here in Paris. At first, she had thought it was the time change, but not in all the time they had been here had she ever woken up beside him, no matter what time they fell into bed together the night before.

"Hmm. Is it that obvious?"

"No one has a mind as keen as yours," she said softly, a thought that had been running through her mind for a while now.

She'd tried, before she ever agreed to come on this trip with him, to imagine his thought process and work through the intricate web that had surrounded Miranda's death. She tried to piece together what Uilleam had done and the sheer reach he possessed, but it wasn't so much that he had accomplished all this.

But rather that he had predicted it to begin with.

She wondered about the boy he had been before he became the man he was now. Had he always been able to see solutions to difficult situations? Had he excelled in school? Or had it been the opposite? Had he struggled, then turned his weaknesses into his strengths?

"That's not entirely true, though, is it?" he asked looking over at her, his expression unreadable.

"No?" She couldn't think of anyone who rivaled him.

Her mother, perhaps, but a part of her doubted that to be true.

"You see what so many others don't."

She wanted to deny those words—say she just simply paid more attention—yet she remembered where she was and how she had gotten here. That she was part of the reason Paxton was even in prison.

"It must be terribly lonely up there in the clouds," she said, thinking of the various portraits in his Paris home of planes and clouds.

He could read people so easily that she imagined most weren't a challenge for him. As if he were forced to look down at everyone else and observe them living their lives.

"It was," he said—*whispered*. A confession he wasn't expecting to make.

She snapped off her seat belt, glad for how spacious the car was. It made it easier to climb across the gearshift onto his lap. He helped once he realized what she was doing, his arm wrapping quickly around her waist and pulling her the rest of the way over.

It took a bit of maneuvering to get more comfortable, but once she was settled against him, she reached up to cup his face, feeling the prickle of his facial hair against the pad of her thumb.

She liked him like this, more than she would care to admit.

The way his shoulders relaxed when she got close, and the contented sort of smile that spread across his face as his hands settled on her hips.

He had already slipped out of his suit jacket and left it sprawled across the back seat and had even unbuttoned his waistcoat. She carefully undid the buttons down the front of his shirt until the halves spread and revealed tan skin and fine chest hair beneath.

She wanted to bask in this quiet moment with him. To let the night's events slip away, but she felt compelled to ask, "Why would you want to do business with a man like that? You wouldn't have to worry very much about enemies working with him."

"That would be ignoring the purely financial relationship. As long as the parameters are clear, there's no reason for anything to go wrong. I trust the fact that he would try to plot against me, so I would never be surprised the day he actually does."

She thought on that a moment, trying to understand his reasoning and failing. "That sounds exhausting. I'd think that would be less productive. You'd be spending too much time on the defense to actually focus on anything else."

His smile grew a touch, there and gone. He was impressed. "Therein lies the rub."

She shook her head before she turned his face side to side. "How heavy is that head of yours?"

She hadn't expected him to understand what she was implying, but this was Uilleam after all. A man who seemed to know everything.

"Enough to wear the crown."

"So what happens now?" she asked. "Do you pretend as if nothing happened?"

"There's still one final meeting," he said, hands drifting lower to skim over the slits in her dress.

"Are you nervous?"

"Not in the least." His gaze lifted to her face. "Are you worried about me?"

"Why wouldn't I be? You have no sense of self-preservation, clearly."

His sudden laughter made her heart flutter.

"But seriously. Gaspard doesn't seem to like you very much."

"But he does like money, and that's the only motivation most men need."

"Not you?" she asked, genuinely curious. "What's your motivation?"

"The endgame," he said, his gaze never straying from hers.

"There won't be much to enjoy about your endgame if you're too dead to see the end of it."

"Don't worry," he said with a chuckle. "No one can get rid of me that easily."

"Because you won't fail in this?"

"Because I need more time with you."

Those words swept through her, turning her insides to mush. He was staring at her, she realized a moment later as she forced herself to look at him, taking in everything he was saying. She remembered how captivated she had felt, seeing the beginnings of morning light, but he looked just as captivated by her.

"You're staring, you know."

"You're worth staring at."

From anyone else, those words might have made her roll her eyes, but coming from him, they only managed to make her blush brighter than before.

She thought of what Isla had said the last time she'd seen her.

Don't fall in love. It only ends one way.

But how could she not?

It wasn't as if it was something that could be stopped once it started. She couldn't turn what she felt off any more than she could pretend she felt nothing.

She cupped his face before leaning into him.

He slipped his hands beneath the skirt of her dress, fingers skimming over the lace between her legs, but he didn't delve beneath the delicate fabric until he had his hand cupping the nape of her neck and was dragging her down for a kiss. Only then did he yank the fabric to the side, zeroing in on exactly where she needed him most.

A gasp left her, but she didn't let the bliss she was feeling stop her from reaching for his belt buckle and wrestling it undone with one hand.

She could almost *feel* the smile on his face as he lifted his hips and helped her free his erection.

He palmed her hip, squeezing tight as he drew her down, rubbing his cock through her folds.

"*Now,*" she said, her voice needy, her nails digging into his shoulders.

Uilleam whispered something against the curve of her throat, but the words were lost on her, and she couldn't bring herself to care when he finally pushed inside her.

Having him inside her felt *right*.

Nothing had ever felt as good.

She leaned back as much as she could, rolling her hips, her eyes squeezing shut as she focused on the sensations he evoked.

What started gentle turned into something that had her blood running hot and her voice breaking as she screamed his name.

It all became a blur.

The wet friction …

His teeth skimming over her throat before latching on ...

Ragged groans that tore free from them both.

And when she came, an out-of-body experience that had her seeing stars, she couldn't bring herself to loosen the grip she had on his shirt.

Because she never wanted to let go.

31

BELLA BELLA

CARMELO ALBINI WASN'T THE SORT OF MAN WHO TOOK MEETINGS with anyone unless they were of his organization or the Coalition.

And even then, he only met when it was absolutely necessary. He had never been what most would consider a people person and had the rather amusing tendency to say whatever was on his mind, even at the expense of whoever he was speaking with.

That was what the top men in his organization were for. They determined whether something was a waste of his time or if their concerns actually warranted a face to face with the mafia Don.

He was particular that way.

It was a rather well-known fact that Carmelo despised having his time wasted, and if it was, he would happily make an example out of the man foolish enough to do it.

Uilleam, on the other hand, had a standing invitation. He needed only to call, and Carmelo would accommodate him.

He had been friends with Alexander, despite the man. Well ... as much as one could befriend someone who was prone to random acts of violence and savagery.

Even now, he could still remember the days Carmelo would stop by the castle for dinner, bringing his wife and two sons along. It had always been a rather pleasant affair when they came around, thanks in part to the fact that Carmelo's presence had seemed to keep Alexander mellow.

At least in the earlier days.

There had been only a few men Alexander could be around without becoming paranoid that they were trying to encroach on his business.

Carmelo was Italian, part of a long lineage of *Cosa Nostra*, and unless that same blood ran through their veins, there would be no need for him to worry.

To them, family was family—everything else came last.

But toward the end of his seemingly unending life, Alexander had gone too far on more than one occasion and even Carmelo hadn't been able to be around him without wanting to kill him.

Only after the man had died did Uilleam get back into contact with him. And by the time he had started his own ventures while taking over the family business, he would almost consider the man a friend.

So when a problem presented itself that he couldn't immediately solve—this particular problem beginning and ending with Gaspard—Uilleam went to the only person he knew would keep his confidence while also potentially providing him with a solution.

It was only a bonus that Carmelo was in the Coalition as well.

"When you said you wanted me to come with you today," Karina said, drawing him from his thoughts. "I didn't think you meant to *Italy*."

He *had* said he wanted to take her everywhere—that he wanted to show her the world. His interest had always been complex when it came to her, but after last night, he had to admit this wasn't just a casual feeling.

It wasn't merely curiosity anymore.

He wanted to know everything there was to know about her. The good, the obscene, and everything else she didn't share with anyone else.

More than ever, he found himself distracted, wanting to spend more time with *her* rather than the never-ending work that was his empire.

"We were invited to dinner, poppet. It would have been rude to decline."

Besides, it would have been a travesty if he hadn't been able to see her in this dress with its gauzy fabric and high slit that revealed the creamy expanse of her legs beneath.

He was more curious about how long it would take him to unlace the strings along the back of it later.

She tried to hide it as she tucked her hair behind her ears, her gaze falling onto the water as they rode the taxi toward the manor only reachable by this river, but she was pleased.

Carmelo, Uilleam thought, had always had the right idea when it came to his privacy. He refused to stay in the city, and after ensuring that no one could even approach his home unless they were on a boat, he made it vastly harder for his enemies to reach him.

They were nearly to the gates when he spotted the young Albini brothers racing along the side of the property, oblivious to everything around them.

"Oh wow," Karina murmured, drinking in everything around them from the tall wrought-iron gates that opened to the stone stairs.

The villa itself was perched at the very top of the hill, as vast as it was beautiful.

"I've always heard these villas were beautiful, but seeing one in person is utterly breathtaking."

Uilleam smiled as he took her hand and helped her off the boat, nodding toward one of Carmelo's men waiting at the gate. He might have been wearing a suit and polished leather shoes, but the man was also capable of violent things better left unspoken.

He spoke into the wired earpiece a moment before he opened the gate and allowed them through.

Carmelo and Aurora were waiting for them by the time they reached the top.

"Good to see you, Uilleam," Carmelo greeted with a kiss to both of his cheeks. "And Karina, always a pleasure."

He repeated the same gesture with Karina before Aurora enveloped her in a hug.

Aurora was unlike his mother in most ways. She was kind and considerate, welcoming in a way his mother wasn't.

He was glad Karina was meeting her.

"Come, we can talk in my office."

He touched Karina's back briefly before he left her with Aurora, following Carmelo to his office on the opposite side of the property.

"You've brought her here," Carmelo said conversationally, though there was a certain note of curiosity there. "Can you trust her?"

The question was a loaded one if he had ever heard one.

One that he, surprisingly, didn't have to think too much about.

He glanced back a moment, seeing her through the tall windows as she smiled at whatever Aurora was saying to her before they both disappeared into the villa.

"She's given me no reason not to."

Carmelo accepted this with a nod of his head, opening the door to his office. "Good. Let's talk."

His office was a traditional room complete with bookshelves built into the walls and a desk of the same dark mahogany.

A sitting area was positioned just off to the side in front of a fireplace where flames burned bright and the wood crackled from the heat.

Carmelo didn't hesitate to walk over to the gold bar cart and pour them both a drink. Uilleam had never been much of a drinker—he'd seen how it affected his father and never liked the idea of being anything like him—but Carmelo, he indulged.

The man didn't speak until he'd sat in his chair—always to the right and angled away from the door—and taken a sip of his brandy. "Gaspard never did like your father." Uilleam shrugged.

Not many had.

Even before he'd gone mad there at the end, Alexander Runehart had never been a likable man. He was too gruff and blunt—too prone to violence even for the most minuscule insult. He'd had more enemies than anyone Uilleam could ever think of.

"I assume my father slighted him in some way."

A curious quirk curled the left side of Carmelo's mouth. "Shunned is the better word there, I think. As often as Gaspard had tried to go into business with your father for years ... I would be more surprised if he welcomed you with open arms even with all you've accomplished."

Uilleam contemplated what reasons his father might have had to refuse whatever endeavor Gaspard had wanted.

"I shouldn't find it surprising at all that I'm still paying for my father's actions."

He didn't doubt that he would for a long time to come. The only question was just how powerful and numerous his enemies were.

"Is this truly what you want?" Carmelo asked. "You don't need the Coalition, not with all you've accomplished on your own."

It wasn't a question of whether he needed to be a part of the elusive organization, but rather how he could use it to his own benefit.

"It's the next logical step," he found himself saying.

"Then what are you willing to do to obtain it? You have my vote —that you already know. And considering you've not asked about anyone other than Gaspard, I assume you already have the majority?"

On the surface, it appeared quite simple to join the elite group of criminals that made up the Coalition. It all came down to the number of votes a man had, as well as his ability to pay the initial fee and the yearly dues.

Uilleam's fortune was vast, in part because of his own dealings but even more so because of his family's legacy.

Now, it was just a question of the votes he needed.

"I have three," Uilleam said, mostly to himself.

The Coalition was made up of six men.

Carmelo Albini, the boss of bosses.

Haruto Nakamura, head of the Yakuza in the Eastern hemisphere.

And finally, Thomas Callahan, a man who ran a vast criminal network the likes of which the Americas had never seen before.

"I imagine Marko is firmly for whatever Gaspard wants. He always did blindly follow the man."

Uilleam smiled ruefully. "It also doesn't help that he hates you and will likely vote against anything you agree to."

"Russians," Carmelo said with a shrug. "I know no other men

who hold grudges quite as long. I'll … take care of that little problem. Don't worry about him."

"Gaspard won't change his decision."

Carmelo nodded. "As long as you know." He finished off the rest of his drink. "Find what the man covets and give it to him. I'm sure he'd be more amenable to any request should you manage that."

"What does he covet?"

He had been asking himself that very question for a few weeks now.

That was the rub about dealing with men who had more money than they would ever be able to spend. Whatever they wanted, they could usually get themselves.

"I suggest you start looking," Carmelo said with a rap of his knuckles against the arm of his chair. "Your deadline is here."

Yeah … as if he needed the reminder.

"Word of caution," he said lifting a finger into the air. "Don't ever think Gaspard isn't plotting against you … Snakes are very well hidden."

32

CIAO

She was in over her head.

It was the only thing Karina could think about after he had disappeared into a back office with the Italian crime boss, leaving her sitting with his wife.

Aurora had the glamorous appeal of a well-kept woman, but something about the way she sat with her spine straight and hands gently folded in her lap that made Karina think she wasn't just arm candy.

She was certainly more than that.

"I hope you're staying for dinner?" Aurora asked once they were alone again, her arched brows going up expectantly.

Considering he had packed a bag for them before they left Paris, she could guess they were. "Absolutely."

"Perhaps you would like to help me. When those two are alone, it'll be a while before they come out."

Aurora had the sort of kitchen she had always dreamed of having for herself. Quartz countertops, stainless steel appliances, and the sort of rustic appeal that could only be found in Italian villas.

Two pots were already simmering on the stove, the scent of herbs and tomatoes nearly as mouthwatering as the sight of the sauce itself.

Aurora moved effortlessly around, grabbing an apron that

wrapped around her waist from a hook on the pantry door, then going over to the garden sink to wash her hands. Karina found it fascinating to watching her sink into her task, grabbing a platter from the refrigerator, as well a package of what looked like some sort of dough.

Katherine had never been much of a cook. That was one of the few places her strengths didn't lie. Her second husband—the man who'd entered her life once her father was gone—had found it endearing that she couldn't cook. Trying in vain to teach her, he had even gone as far as to hire a chef to come in to teach her.

She had always willingly went along with it, though her skills never improved. But she had smiled through it, poking fun at her own shortcomings—performing my duties, she had told Karina years after—when, after several years, she was just as helpless as she had always been.

Besides, Katherine was the sort who would much rather pay the best to eat their food than whatever she could manage.

Karina, on the other hand, loved being in the kitchen—though she had been turning to takeout far too often lately. She enjoyed finding and testing new recipes, but it wasn't as much fun when she was cooking for herself. And as that thought crossed her mind, her treacherous heart immediately skipped a beat at the idea of cooking for Uilleam.

"How did you two meet?" Aurora asked, her voice soft but curious.

Her interview, Karina thought. These people were close to Uilleam, that much she had known already, but if he was bringing her here, there was a sign in that, she thought. They would want to know more about her and what she meant to him. Before yesterday, she would have said that they were just two strangers who happened upon each other.

But now ... now she wasn't so sure.

Even beyond what she suspected her mother had done, there was still the little matter of how she and Uilleam had met that wasn't exactly conventional.

She even found herself clearing her throat before she murmured a quick, detail-less account of how they had ultimately crossed paths.

She didn't mind mentioning that she was an investigative journalist, figuring Uilleam might have mentioned it well before he brought her here.

It was interesting to see the way her lips quirked as if she found that detail charming, and Karina couldn't help but wonder what she really thought, but she didn't comment on that bit of information.

"And now you're here with him in Paris," she said.

Though not a question outright, Karina could hear what she wasn't asking. Why was she here now, considering where they had started? "He's ... well, he's Uilleam."

"And he's almost impossible to say no to?" Aurora guessed. "He got that from his mother. There wasn't anything that woman couldn't get her hands on if she really wanted it."

Karina filed that information away. The way she spoke in the past tense made her think Uilleam's mother either wasn't in the picture anymore, or she had passed away. And if it was the latter, she wondered when it had happened. How had Uilleam taken it ...

In the short time they had spent together, he hadn't mentioned much about his family. Yet he had brought her here. It felt as if she knew so much about him, so much so that she thought she knew him, but then there were these little reminders that she didn't *really* know anything about him.

That he was still virtually a stranger.

"Outside of us, I don't think there are very many others who are willing to tell him no. His brother, Kit—"

"He has a brother?" Karina asked, the question out of her mouth before she could think to swallow it.

Isla hadn't thought to mention him, though now that she thought about it, she hadn't mentioned any of his family other than the father who had once been over the family empire. Had she done that on purpose?

"Ah, don't worry," Aurora said, mistaking her surprise. "The two of them go through bouts where they stop speaking. This is probably just one of their off seasons. One day, it will feel as if he doesn't have anyone at all, and then the next, it'll be as if the pair of them had never gone a day without speaking. Siblings, you understand."

"Yeah," she said with a light laugh. "I do."

"Mmm."

Karina didn't realize, until that moment, that she had revealed something about herself that could very well get back to Uilleam. Aurora wouldn't know that she hadn't mentioned having a sibling to Uilleam, and they didn't have the sort of relationship where she could ask her to lie on her behalf.

But Aurora didn't mention her slip.

"He's unlike anyone I've ever met," she said softly, pausing over the dough she was meant to be rolling, but whenever she thought of Uilleam, she always grew contemplative.

"Don't worry," Aurora said as she wiped her hands off on a dish towel. "She hasn't shared any of your secrets."

Karina looked over her shoulder to find Uilleam leaning against the doorframe at the edge of the kitchen, a soft expression on his flawless face. He couldn't have been standing there long, but it was also clear he'd heard what she had said about him.

"Would you mind if I stole her for a moment?" he asked, already walking toward her.

"Of course, dinner should be ready in twenty minutes."

"I'll have her back by then, I promise. She's a bit anal about everyone being at the table before anyone eats," Uilleam explained once they stepped outside into the garden.

Karina tried to remember the last time she, Isla, and their mother had attempted to sit down for a meal together. "Sounds reasonable."

"Things are going to get a bit ... complicated," he said as he looked down at her, his expression more strained now. There was something he wasn't telling her, or rather, there was something he wasn't quite ready to say.

"Because of your thing with Gaspard?" she asked.

"It's ... well—"

"Complicated?" she finished for him.

"Precisely."

"You'll never be in implicit danger," he said, sounding as if she had questioned him about it. As if she were the one who was nervous.

But to her surprise, she wasn't. And even she didn't know why.

The only thing she did know was that she trusted whatever

Uilleam had planned. She had seen firsthand what he was capable of when he set his mind to something.

"I trust you," she said a moment later, smiling at the disbelieving laugh that fell from his lips.

"Do you really?"

"In this, of course."

She didn't doubt for a second that Uilleam could get anything he wanted. She found it wasn't very easy to go against him.

Even she hadn't.

He took her hand then, kissing the back of her knuckles. "Should be fun then."

This thing between them could never work, and Isla had said as much.

And considering they stood on two very opposite sides of the spectrum, she couldn't imagine what would become of them.

Either it was going to be the most amazing experience of her life.

Or he would ruin her.

And she didn't think she would ever recover from that.

***

THE JOURNEY BACK TO PARIS WAS A QUIET ONE.

She couldn't say what had Uilleam quiet and staring off into the distance, but her thoughts were occupied by him and everything she had learned over the past forty-eight hours.

She'd always been curious about what he did and how he did it, but that curiosity felt a bit tainted now that she knew what she did.

That her own mother considered him a target.

It was one thing to know he was powerful. Of course it was all impressive to *her* because she had never met a man like him before.

She doubted she ever would again.

But even what she knew had to pale in comparison to what she didn't know. Otherwise, her mother wouldn't be interested in him. His name wouldn't be listed in a black ledger that she kept on her person at all times.

Tomorrow was the day of reckoning. A day Uilleam had been working toward for longer than she'd known him.

A day that would, arguably, make him one of the most powerful men in the world.

And she knew, even as she glanced over at him before reaching to tuck his hand into hers, that once he did, there would be another enemy on his hands.

An enemy she could never, ever tell him about.

Because it wouldn't just disrupt this thing between them.

It would change *everything*.

33

ABYSS

He'd been waiting his entire life for this.

For as long as he could remember, Uilleam had always wanted to be powerful. What had started as a mere thought bloomed into something even he had a hard time truly explaining.

He knew *why*, of course—he was a product of his father's making, after all—but as the years passed and he grew to be in the position he was in now, only one goal had been left to achieve.

And securing a position with the Coalition would make that a reality.

Sure, surpassing his father was a reward within itself, but he was far more eager to cement his place within the criminal underworld. And by the time he was finished, they would all know his name.

He heard the whispers and rumors. The way he was avoided unless the person was in dire straits.

But for a man like Uilleam, it wasn't enough.

He wanted their fear and willing obedience.

He wanted them all to quake at the mere mention of him

His name was already revered—while a new one rose on the heels of it—but what he was trying to accomplish today ... *this*, his seat at the table, would create a legacy.

One last little test stood between him and victory.

He'd met with each member of the Coalition individually, ensured he'd given them ample evidence as to why he would make a worthy addition to the organization, and now today was his last meeting.

An initiation, of sorts.

One where he would meet with them all as a collective to hear their final decision. He expected it to be more of a formality and not too involved.

This final meeting between him and the six standing members of the Coalition had come because of *his* blood, sweat, and tears. His *hunger* for more.

He wouldn't be leaving that room until he had everything he wanted.

"You're not even a *little* worried?" Karina asked from her position in the bed, staring at him with an inquisitive expression.

She tried to hide it, but he could see the worry she felt, and even though he knew it was unwarranted, he could still understand why she might have been nervous about what the day would bring.

"Why should I be?" he asked, finishing with the knot in his tie before turning to face her. "What's there to be concerned about?"

"Well ... Gaspard," she replied rather bluntly. "I don't know him as well as you do, but anyone can see that he isn't fond of you."

That was putting it nicely.

Uilleam would be the first to say the man undoubtedly hated him.

That wouldn't change the outcome of this day.

"His bark is vicious but little else."

He wasn't the sort to get his hands dirty. That wasn't to say he hadn't had a few men killed in his lifetime—inevitable in their line of work—but he didn't often make a habit of it.

She shook her head, her hair shaking with the movement. "My mother always said never underestimate a man's hatred—especially the ones who can still smile in your face."

His brows shot up as he turned to fully look at her. In all their time together, he didn't think he had ever heard her discuss her family or where she had grown up. Sure, he had what little Skorpion could find outside of her biography on the paper's website, but he hadn't gotten anything from *her*.

And now that he thought about it, he hadn't actually *asked* either.

More curious was the fact that he *wanted* to know more about her, and not because he enjoyed learning others' secrets. He wanted to know about the woman herself.

Who she was beyond what he already knew.

Where she had come from.

He wanted everything.

And once this was done, he would have all the time in the world to learn everything there was to know about Karina Ashworth.

"Smart woman, your mother."

If he'd turned back to the mirror a moment sooner, he might have missed the way her expression seemed to freeze on her face, or the way her gaze dropped to her lap, but he didn't understand what she needed to be shy about.

He wouldn't judge or think her less than because she hadn't grown up the way he did.

Sometimes, he wondered if he would be a different man had he not been raised under a tyrant's hand.

Karina cleared her throat as she sat up a little further, holding the sheet to her chest, the dainty gold necklace he had given her the other night still hanging around her slender neck.

"Just be careful," she said after a moment. "I don't think he would want you to be a part of ... whatever this is if he had a choice."

No, he certainly wouldn't.

But it wasn't entirely up to him.

No one in the history of the Coalition's formation had ever been voted in unanimously. As long as the majority agreed, that was all that mattered.

Except ... Uilleam would be the closest. There was only one vote he hadn't been able to guarantee, and that was Gaspard's. The others he had met or spoken with individually as he'd prepared for this day over the past couple of years.

He knew, at the very least, he had their backing.

Which, undoubtedly, made Gaspard despise him more. Because they all knew, though it would never be said aloud, that had Uilleam been anyone else, Gaspard would have happily agreed to allow him entry.

He was only denying him now out of spite.

Which meant he had also succeeded in something even Gaspard hadn't been able to accomplish.

The thought brought a smile to his face.

He leaned over her, his palms sinking into the bed on either side of her. "I like to think you're my good luck charm," he whispered with a smile, enjoying the faint scent of her perfume that lingered on her skin.

She smiled lightly, fingering his tie. "If you make it out of this okay, I might actually believe you."

He pressed his lips to her forehead. "You don't need to worry about me."

She shook her head, her expression turning surprisingly serious. "Someone has to, I think."

He could see she meant that—it was written all over her face. He found her concern endearing and ... cute, if only because he knew it was unwarranted.

She wasn't used to the life he lived and the various meetings he attended, the majority of which ended in one way.

No matter the obstacles—no matter how impossible the odds— he always ended on top.

Uilleam made sure of it.

"When this is done, I have a surprise for you."

That seemed to lighten her mood. "You're full of them."

For her, he could. "I'll call you when I'm on my way back."

"Play nice with the others," she whispered against his lips.

He could practically feel the smile forming even before she pulled back and he was graced with the beauty of it. "There are some deals I *can't* make, poppet."

"Watch Gaspard," she called after him, making him pause when he was nearly out the door. "I don't trust him."

Neither did he, but he didn't bother to voice that thought aloud.

THICK GRAY CLOUDS HUNG HEAVY IN THE EARLY MORNING SKY, briefly obscuring the white glow of the sunlight.

But even as snow was promised, it was still a beautiful day, and though it might have been wishful thinking on his part, he thought it reflected what this day would bring.

"I still think you should have worn the vest."

It was the second time in the half hour they had been in the truck that Skorpion had made that remark. Unlike himself, his mercenary *was* wearing a bulletproof vest over his T-shirt, and probably had enough weaponry on his person to make him a one-man army.

But that wasn't the sort of message he wanted to send to Gaspard.

He wanted the other man to know he wasn't afraid—that he didn't think Gaspard had the balls to try to act against him.

"It isn't necessary," he said again, turning his phone over in his hands, his gaze on the window to his right.

Even if Gaspard *had* wanted to act, he wouldn't do so now—not while Carmelo was still in the city. Though his mentor liked to think he wasn't as transparent as he was when it came to his favoritism, most knew that he and Uilleam had a relationship beyond casual acquaintances.

"Besides, that's why I have you."

Because unlike a lot of men he knew, Skorpion had quick reflexes. Almost as if he sensed what a person was about to do before they actually acted on it. If there was ever a man he needed in his corner should Gaspard try anything, it was the one currently behind the wheel.

"Did you make the reservations?" he asked, changing the subject.

"I did, which reminds me. You need to get a fucking assistant. What do I look like?"

Uilleam made it a point to lean forward and look him over. "Like a very large assistant."

"I *will* shoot you."

"Then who would sign your checks?"

"This could have gone very differently," Skorpion reminded him, briefly glancing at him through the rearview mirror.

"I—"

He didn't get to finish what he was about to say.

Not when the sudden sound of an engine revving far too close drew his gaze to the window, just in time to see the massive truck speeding toward them.

He didn't get a chance to warn Skorpion of what was coming.

He didn't even have a chance to brace.

Not before impact.

Not before the sound of crushing metal and splintering glass filled his ears.

But it was nothing compared to the pain—sudden and sharp, nearly taking his breath away—and as quickly as it came, blackness swooped in on the heels of it.

He wasn't sure how long he was out, but one second, he had been bracing for impact, and the next, all he could see was smoke and smell burning rubber and gasoline.

He reached blindly for his seat belt buckle, trying unsuccessfully to get it undone.

Something warm and wet dripped from his forehead, but he couldn't let himself think of what it was, not if he wanted to get out of this.

"Keanu?" he called, his voice hoarse.

It was hard to tell through the haze and smoke whether Skorpion was still there, though he was somewhat sure he could see the vague shape of his body.

"*Keanu!*"

He swung blindly for the front seat, managing to hit the seat, feeling some relief at the weight he felt.

Skorpion was there, at least.

"We have to get out of the car," he said, the words sounding muffled to his own ears.

Giving up on the seat belt, he swung again at the seat in front of him, the ringing in his ears intensifying, his vision growing more blurred at the edges.

When he heard the sound of Skorpion's groan as came to, he should have felt relief.

But it lasted for as long as it took for him to hear the sound of an assault rifle being racked ...

279

34

GOODBYE

FOR THE FIFTH TIME THAT NIGHT, KARINA FOUND HERSELF glancing up at the oversized wall clock, wondering just how long Uilleam would be gone.

Had she not met Gaspard and had Uilleam not told her stories about the man, she wouldn't have been quite as worried once he left for the final meeting. She might have been able to get lost in one of the programs she had only been half paying attention to over the past couple of hours or even dived into a book to pass the time.

Yet from the moment he had kissed her on her forehead before walking out the door, she had been awake and waiting. And time always passed so much slower when actively watching the clocks.

She didn't know, however, how many times she had picked her phone up only to put it back down again. She knew that if Uilleam had contacted her, she would have known by now, but for the life of her, she couldn't imagine what was taking so long.

Grabbing her glass off the coffee table, she carried it back into the kitchen, snagging the bottle of rosé she had been slowly draining slowly. Even the buzz from the alcohol wasn't enough to completely quiet her mind, but it was helping, if only a little.

She had only swallowed a mouthful before she heard a door open and slam, footsteps following. Her heart galloped in her chest, relief flooding through her as she quickly stepped out of the kitchen, anticipating the moment Uilleam rounded the corner.

Except it wasn't Uilleam.

Over the past few weeks, she had gotten used to Skorpion's presence—not something she ever thought she would say, considering the sheer size of him and the fact that he was paid to do bad things on occasion—but seeing him tonight made her chest feel tight.

And that was before she noticed the spatter of blood on the side of his neck.

It was harsh against his tan skin. A tarnished shade of red that just looked wrong.

She didn't realize he had been talking to her until his hand was on her shoulder and she finally looked away from the blood to meet his gaze. "He's alive," he said quickly, cutting right to the point.

The only problem was that those words were very specific, and she understood exactly what they didn't say. "What happened? Where is he?"

Because he might be alive, but that didn't mean he was okay.

And considering Skorpion didn't have any cuts or wounds on his person that she could see, that made it abundantly clear that the blood on his neck wasn't his.

"He wants you home."

"What? What does that even mean?"

But Skorpion didn't bother answering her question before he was sweeping through the space and gathering anything he thought might have been hers.

She should have been calm and collected—she had to be that way, considering the things she saw and heard for her job—but she was panicking. More than she ever had in her entire life.

"You brought a suitcase, right?" Skorpion asked over his shoulder, still scanning the floor before heading for the stairs.

She should have been alarmed by the fact that he knew his way around so effortlessly, considering he had been staying elsewhere and hadn't stopped by during the week they were here, but Uilleam had probably told him, her mind supplied.

Because he was alive. She had to keep reminding herself—there was no reason to panic just yet. But that didn't stop the worry and fear from manifesting.

That maybe this was—

"Yo." Skorpion snapped his fingers in front of her face, drawing her gaze to him. "You can trust me."

There was a steely sort of earnestness to his voice. She knew she could, and she wanted to, but the other more stubborn part of her demanded visual confirmation.

She needed to see for herself that he was as she'd last seen him.

"But *where* is he?" she asked, the words almost getting lost between them as she swallowed, afraid of his answer.

"You really gonna make me carry you out of here?" he asked, his tone making it quite clear that he was prepared to do just that.

"If you answer my questions, I'll go willingly." But she couldn't bring herself to move or focus on anything other than him. She needed to know more than he was telling her.

Skorpion considered a moment, then seemed to come to a decision. "He's at a safe house that was set up years ago. It's remote and so far off the books, no one would be able to find him there. There's a couple of physicians there looking after him."

"So you're taking me to him then?" she asked, though even to her own ears it sounded very clear that she expected to be with him.

"That's not going to happen."

"Why—"

"Let's say I did, yeah? I take you over there and the same man who shot him chooses to send a team after him now instead. What happens then?"

"You'll—"

Save his life, her mind supplied before she even thought to say the words. And on the heel of them came the fact that Skorpion couldn't very well be in two places at once, and she would have to fend for herself.

After all, his job was to protect Uilleam.

Not her.

Even if Uilleam demanded it.

"But he's fine?" she stressed, wishing that the burning behind her eyes would go away. Crying wouldn't change anything.

It wouldn't get her to him, and it wouldn't change the fact that something, though she still didn't know what, had gone wrong.

"As soon as you're safe, he'll reach out to you himself," Skorpion said, this time with a pointed nod at the room she'd slept in the first night.

There was so much she wanted to say.

So much she wanted to do, but as it stood, she was virtually powerless.

She would just have to wait.

NINETEEN HOURS. SEVENTEEN MINUTES. THIRTY-NINE SECONDS.

Karina had counted down every moment from the time she left Paris until she landed back in New York and made it back to her apartment. She had busied herself with unpacking and putting away laundry to keep from thinking about the fact that she hadn't heard from him.

She had cleaned everything within reach throughout her living room to forget that her phone was so silent.

Only when exhaustion had finally made her pass out on the couch did she finally close her eyes long enough not to think about anything at all.

But when she woke up the next morning, her heart thundering in her chest as the day before's events quickly played on a cycle through her mind. When she found that her phone was still as silent as it had been the night before, she did something she'd sworn to herself she wouldn't.

She picked up her phone and considered calling her mother.

❧ 35 ❧

HELLO MOTHER

Even the gentle snowfall outside her bedroom window wasn't enough to put Karina in better spirits. If anything, her mood only worsened as she stripped her bed of its linens and tossed them into a pile in the corner.

Funny that she had gone nearly her entire life without ever knowing Uilleam's name or about his existence at all, yet two weeks of zero contact with him had her practically climbing the walls.

She'd hoped, with all the optimism in the world, that he would reach out to her once everything—though she still couldn't say what *everything* consisted of—had settled. While she still didn't know what had taken place in Paris, she could guess, at the very least, *something* had gone wrong.

And even after it became clear to her that Uilleam wouldn't be calling, she still hadn't given up quite yet. She called the number she had for him, only to find it disconnected, and no amount of niceties or bribes had helped her at his hotel because, according to them, no one under his name had ever been staying there.

It was as if he had vanished off the face of the earth.

All too quickly, she was reminded that while everyone knew *of* the man, none of them knew *him*. They had no way of getting into contact with him, and even if they were able, Uilleam came to them, not the other way around.

So without any luck, she merely had to wait.

Again.

But this time, she didn't have anger toward him to give her a reason not to think of him and try to push his presence out of her thoughts.

This time, the only thing she could feel was concern. *Anxiety.* Worried that something terrible had happened to him and she would never know it.

It was ridiculous that she had developed such strong feelings for him in such a short amount of time. She hardly knew the man, and that point had been made all the more clear considering she was back in New York and he was ... somewhere.

And when she took a moment to actually think about it, she also realized that she had hardly spent more than a couple of weeks' time in his presence altogether. Hardly enough time to develop *feelings*.

But that didn't change the fact that she lay awake at night thinking about him. Wondering if he was okay. If he was alive ... Whether he was thinking about her.

She wanted *answers*, and she was dangerously close to doing just about anything to get them.

Emotions had no place in her profession. They never led to anything good, she found, and she couldn't imagine that anything good would come from her curiosity.

Which was how she found herself standing in line at her favorite juice bar after a three-mile jog, hoping some of the excess energy she felt would dissipate. The cafe was surprisingly busy for a Sunday morning, especially this early, but it was a beautiful day all the same, and she had nothing but time on her hands.

Work would resume tomorrow, and she wouldn't have time to focus on anything other than whatever story landed in her lap.

Making it to the front of the line, she ordered a green juice and then paid, stepping off to the side to let the person behind her order.

The chime of the bell above the glass door drew her gaze in its direction, foolish hope blooming to life in her chest. She had long stopped wondering—or even caring, really—how Uilleam found her the way he did when he just popped up.

Now, she hoped for it.

But instead of a man in a black suit, she found Isla strolling in wearing a blood-red dress and her signature trench coat, her heels impossibly high.

In the week or so since they'd last seen each other, she'd changed her hair—the dark hair they'd inherited from their father significantly lightened at the ends. What Isla had once called her summer hair.

To her credit, Karina didn't react to seeing her sister *here*, of all places, though a part of her was anxious at the sight of her. The rules they lived by stipulated that they never cross paths—especially since Isla was currently on an assignment.

Not because they couldn't aid each other—which they often did despite Mother's rules—but because it would only ever take a glance to see their similar facial features and discern their relationship to each other.

It was information they kept carefully guarded.

It was no one's business but their own.

Except they had already broken the rules once while she was in Paris. If Isla was here now, that could only mean things were not nearly as simple as she'd hoped.

Careful to keep a blank expression on her face, Karina accepted her drink once her name was called, then headed outside before Isla could get a word out. The last thing she needed was their conversation to be heard by anyone.

"Does Mother know you're here?" she asked once they were outside.

"Of course," Isla returned just as easily. "Who do you think sent me to fetch you?"

Her day, even this early, was going from bad to worse.

She closed her eyes a moment, trying to tamp down the swarm of emotion that was threatening to take her over. "Why?"

Isla turned brown eyes on her. "You already know the answer to that question, I'm afraid."

Yeah ... unfortunately, she did.

With Uilleam, everything had been terribly simple.

She didn't have to second-guess her hair and makeup, the way she dressed, or even how she carried herself. She was just that —*herself*. It all came naturally, but as the meeting with Mother drew ever closer, Karina knew her appearance was not up to standard.

It didn't matter that her hair was swept back into a neat and elegant knot, or that her pencil skirt and blouse didn't have a single wrinkle or imperfection. She'd even taken an extra minute to ensure her eyeliner was as even as she could possibly make it.

But it didn't erase the fact that she looked tired, and that she hadn't been sleeping well since she'd returned from Paris. And no amount of concealer would prevent Katherine from noticing.

Ever since she and Isla had arrived at her apartment and she'd disappeared into her bedroom to get ready, she'd wondered and worried what Katherine wanted to speak to her about.

Unlike her sister, she wasn't *officially* on any assignment here. If anything, New York was meant to be a sabbatical of sorts before she made a final decision on whether she actually wanted to join the family business.

Hell, even the thought of it was enough to make her reach for the delicate charm resting at the hollow of her throat and worry it back and forth, wishing it could offer more comfort, or at least a bit of clarity.

Because, if she knew nothing else, she knew this meeting Katherine had called began and ended with Uilleam.

"So," Isla called from the other room, "what's he like?"

Karina paused where she stood, glancing out the bedroom door to find Isla standing near her dining room table, her gaze riveted on the vase of blue roses sitting in the center of it.

"I've heard the rumors, of course, but those are only worth so much. I'm not all that interested in the business side of him—what's the *man* like?"

Interesting, Karina thought.

Complicated.

So much so that she doubted she could explain the complexities of Uilleam Runehart.

He was, in a word, different from any man she had ever met before.

"Whatever you've heard," Karina said as she turned off the light and closed her bedroom door as she walked out, "he's probably worse."

Isla turned to look at her then, her gaze appraising. "We all like what we like."

Yeah, she was learning that the hard way.

CLOSING HER EYES, SHE LET THE GENTLE ROCKING OF THE CAR lull her into a sense of false calm as she pictured Uilleam in the back of her mind. His smile. The way his laughter made the corner of his eyes crinkle. How he looked at her when they were alone as if no one else in the world mattered.

It was *that* feeling she clung to as they arrived at the boutique hotel in lower Manhattan. It might have been small, with no more than a dozen rooms if she had to guess, but it had the rustic, old-world charm about it that reminded her of home.

Before she could climb out, however, Isla reached over and grabbed her hand, her expression changing a little. "It's only a moment."

To anyone else, those words wouldn't mean anything at all, but to her, they meant everything. They brought her back to a time when she had been particularly nervous about talking alone with her mother.

Even now, she could remember the many occasions when she had stood afraid outside of Mother's office, chewing on her nails as she contemplated running away so she wouldn't have to face whatever mood Katherine was in, but Isla had always been there to take her hand and do very much what she was doing now.

Calming her. *Reassuring* her.

Everything would be fine, no matter what happened.

These meetings, and the ill feelings that usually came with them, would only ever last a moment.

"Call me once you're finished."

Karina could only nod before she climbed out of the car, smoothing the front of her skirt as she stepped up onto the sidewalk and smiled at the doorman who gave her a short bow and gestured for her to go on inside.

She stopped by the front desk and picked up the key she'd known would be waiting for her, eyeing the room number written across the back of it in black Sharpie. She rode the elevator up to the third floor, drawing in a much-needed breath as the doors slid open and she stepped out into the brightly lit hallway.

All of the doors on this floor had Do Not Disturb door hangers fastened to the doorknobs with the exception of room 394.

Though she already had a key card and needed only to press it against the sensor to let herself inside, Karina still found herself hesitating all the same.

A moment, she reminded herself. *It'll only last a moment.*

Reluctantly, she pressed the key card against the electronic pad, then waited for the green light to flicker before she pushed the door handle down and shouldered the door open.

It amazed her still how quickly she reverted to the little girl she had once been. One that had desperately hoped for her mother's approval.

She'd always thought of herself as the good daughter. The one Mother didn't have to worry about or clean up after. She did what she was told, when she was told. Unlike Isla, who had a tendency to rebel when the mood struck her.

Except this—her new place here in New York—*was* a small act of rebellion.

If Mother had had her way, she wouldn't be here at all.

"A fresh pot of tea would be lovely, thank you," came a voice from across the room. The soft, elegant prose as distinctive as it was deceptively friendly.

Just hearing her made Karina stand a little straighter, her shoulder going back a fraction.

"Mother."

Slowly, as if she hadn't a clue that Karina would be popping up today—as if she hadn't specifically requested her to—Katherine Ashworth turned on her more moderate heels, her lips only curving the slightest bit as she smiled. She looked younger than she actually was, her blond hair well maintained without a gray hair in sight, but Botox had always done wonders for her, even if it meant making it impossible to read her.

"Darling, it's so good to see you. I was afraid you wouldn't have time to see me."

Karina's smile felt brittle even as she forced one onto her face. "Of course. I wouldn't miss this for the world."

Because Katherine would have made her life a living hell if she hadn't.

The bellhop she had been speaking to excused himself and left the room so quickly, Karina hardly had a chance to see the poor boy's face, but if his haste was any indication, she wasn't the only one dying to get away from her.

"How are you, Mother?" she asked, accepting Katherine's embrace, pressing her cheek to either side of her face so as not to ruin her lipstick.

"Better now that I see you're not involved in that unfortunate incident in Paris."

Whatever doubt that had existed in her about what this meeting would be about fled at those words, and before she could check the impulse, she found herself asking, "You know about Paris?"

Her smile was a bit more indulgent now. "Surely, you know it's my duty to know what's happening in your life."

Once, she had thought it was sign that Katherine loved her. That she *cared*. The other girls at boarding school had always complained that their mothers didn't ask about their studies or how their time was when they were away from home.

They were too busy, they'd say, being the perfect housewife.

They all had loved the idea that Katherine wanted to know the sort of friends Karina made. Who their families were. The connections they had ... the last, of which, was never spoken aloud.

They didn't understand the burden there.

"What have you heard?" she asked, unable to keep her emotions in check long enough to pretend she didn't really care about the answer.

The only thing she could think about was Uilleam and whether or not he was okay.

"Oh, just this and that. Come and sit. Let's catch up. I'm sure you have loads you'd like to fill me in on."

The remark might have been uttered politely, but Katherine's gaze was a little sharp as she led her over to the settee by the fire and patted the cushion beside her. This conversation had been inevitable, but that didn't mean she was going to enjoy having it.

"Where would—"

"Let's start at the beginning, shall we?"

Karina swallowed past the knot in her throat and told her, in the simplest of terms while lacking crucial details, how she had come across Uilleam and their time together. She didn't mind, so much, the details of the game they played or how Paxton had ultimately ended up in prison awaiting his trial, but once she got closer to the end and the invitation to Paris, she trailed off, leaving her to fill in her own details.

But Katherine was a clever woman and able to read between the lines far better than anyone she knew. "Oh, sweetheart. You were supposed to use this opportunity to learn, not do something as foolish as falling in love. Have you forgotten everything I've taught you?"

A retort sat on the tip of her tongue about how she wasn't in love with him—that it was too soon for a feeling as strong as that—but the rest of what she was saying finally processed inside her mind.

The implications behind them. "What does that mean, exactly? This opportunity?"

Katherine folded her hands in her lap, her nude nails matching the shade of her heels. "You didn't truly believe it was a mere coincidence that you happened to stumble upon him, did you? Had I not given you a nudge, you would have still been writing enlightening articles about what socialite is screwing whom."

That quickly, her mind took her back to that day when she'd gotten the phone call—the one that had made her wonder about Uilleam and just what he did. Before he'd ever had a name.

The voice hadn't been familiar—she would have recognized Katherine's voice straight away—nor was it one she thought she had ever heard before or since, but with Katherine's connections, she could have easily paid the person to call and pass on the information.

Karina hadn't doubted the caller for a second.

"It was you then who told Camilla to let me have that case," she said, speaking the truth aloud to help her brain catch up with all that was being revealed. "You *wanted* me to meet him."

"Don't misunderstand, darling. You were doing quite well on your own, but our window was short. I couldn't afford another six months of waiting."

Because had she not looked into that first case, she would have never made the connection between Uilleam and Paxton. And this, all of it, would have turned out vastly different.

"Besides," Katherine went on, seeming oblivious to Karina's sinking mood. "Had I not helped things along, you wouldn't have been able to get close to him at all, would you?"

She was shaking her head before her mother could even finish. "It was never about his business."

"I'm aware. That was your first mistake," Katherine returned sharply, his tone dripping with disapproval.

But she couldn't focus on that.

All her brain seemed to be able to process was the fact that without her mother, she and Uilleam would have never crossed paths.

She would have never pushed as hard against Paxton because she wouldn't have thought for a second that someone else had been involved. That someone else had been pulling the strings.

Just as Katherine had been pulling hers.

"So what was this?" she asked, furious that her voice was shaking there at the end. "Why did you want me to meet him?"

"Because I have a job for you."

No other words had ever filled her with quite as much dread as those did.

More than anything, she hated being manipulated by those who proclaimed to love her. Which was why Isla always, no matter how it might make her feel, told her the truth.

It was also why Katherine told only lies.

"I never told you I wanted to work for you," Karina said as she climbed to her feet. *Needing* to do something. Pacing the floor was a welcome alternative to what she *really* wanted.

"You're an Ashworth, Karina. Don't be silly."

You're an Ashworth, she said, as if the name itself led credence to inevitability. As if she had always been destined to be the creature Katherine had wanted her to be.

Men liked to call women like her black widows.

Other times, something a little more derogatory.

That was what Katherine had wanted from her.

Nothing as honest as a journalist for an American paper — helping innocents get justice and ensuring the guilty paid for their crimes.

While Katherine didn't mind the latter so much, she didn't just want the men of her choosing to lose it all. She wanted to be the one to gain what they had lost.

"Oh, do sit down, dear. Our tea has almost arrived."

"Why?" Karina asked, ignoring her demand. "Why him? Why Uilleam?"

But when Katherine issued a demand, she expected it to be followed.

Only when Karina moved to reclaim her seat did she speak again.

"Your sister always said you were a bit young," Katherine said with a mild shake of her head, "that you weren't ready to do what we did. I had to remind her that she was seventeen the first time I sent her on an assignment. Now, look how well she's doing."

Karina didn't have a response to that, but she did wonder about that conversation. Isla had never told her a word of it.

"I didn't anticipate that you would fall in love with the first man you met."

Then she couldn't have known Uilleam, Karina thought, even as her stomach twisted.

Because how could she not ...

"It was because of her that I even allowed you to come here and pursue this little hobby of yours. I thought once you realized how ridiculous you were being, you would see the error in your judgment and finally accept your place in the family."

She paused as a knock sounded at the door, a butler entering with a cart topped with a pot of tea, saucers, and little sandwiches cut into triangles.

Only once she was gone again did Katherine continue. "I just wanted you to have a little taste of what it felt like. The Runehart boy should have been easily dealt with. Sure, he's amassed a bit of respect and power amongst the right circles, but nothing I couldn't get rid of with a snap of my fingers. But somehow, you, my dearest daughter, managed to fuck that up."

Karina flinched, squeezing her hands together as she looked away from Katherine and down to her lap.

"Instead of coming to me, as you were *taught*, or even your sister, you somehow made him more powerful than he already was. You turned him into something ... something—" She gestured with her hand, seeming unable to find the right word.

But Karina knew exactly what she couldn't say. "The Kingmaker. I turned him into a kingmaker."

In many ways, she had birthed this new identity of his.

"Ah, yes. The title you gave him. Have you forgotten that words have power, Karina?"

"I wasn't thinking," she whispered, more truthful than she realized.

She *hadn't* been thinking about anything other than Uilleam. Of how he would respond when he saw it.

"It doesn't matter now," she said, ignoring her last question. "He's gone."

"Licking his wounds, no doubt. Gaspard *did* do quite a number on him."

That quickly, her head jerked up and she stared at her mother as Katherine poured her tea the way she liked before plucking one of the sandwiches from the plate and biting into it. "Did something happen to him?"

"Powerful men don't reach their position unscathed. You'd do well to remember that."

Those words went in one ear and out the other. "Where is he?"

"Does it matter?"

Yes, she wanted to say. The affirmation right there, needing only to be spoken, but she couldn't bring herself to say it.

"What happens now?" she asked instead.

There was, after all, a reason Katherine had made an appearance here in New York. And she knew, even before she heard her answer, that she wasn't going to like what she said.

"Now," Katherine said, her gaze moving to her, "you make a choice. Are you going to choose him or your family?"

A question with an impossible answer.

❧ 36 ❧

AWAKE

IF UILLEAM COULD REMOVE HIS USELESS RIBS WITHOUT consequence, he would dig the fucking things out of his chest with his bare hands. It would undoubtedly feel better than the hell he was already suffering with them still *in*.

Every breath was a chore and brought a new wave of pain whenever his lungs inflated.

If that had been the *only* thing that hurt on him, he might have suffered in silence, but every inch of him felt like an open wound refusing to heal.

Ever since he had come to in the back of a racing ambulance, his head thick with fog and his nerve endings alight with agony, the only thing he had wanted to do was pass out again. At least he knew he wasn't dead.

Death wouldn't hurt *this* much.

Gritting his teeth, he planted his hands on either side of his body and forced himself into a sitting position, the pain nearly too great to ignore. But if he gave into it now, he would stay vulnerable, and that was the last thing he needed after Gaspard's attempt on his life.

Fucking Gaspard.

He'd known the man was bold. He hadn't gotten to his position in life without being willing to cross a number of lines to get what he wanted, but Uilleam hadn't actually expected the man to do *this*.

This was beyond bold—he was declaring war.

And when there was war, others came out wanting their pound of flesh.

Not that he blamed them. He was an equal opportunity offender, and if he had been standing on the other side of this, he would have done the absolute same and not thought twice about it.

But even as he understood their motivations, he had also made sure word had gotten out that should anyone attempt anything against him, his retaliation would be swift and undeniable.

Whether on bed rest or not, he was not a man to be fucked with.

A knock sounded at the door, distracting him from his thoughts long enough that he could finally sit up the rest of the way and rest his back against the plush headboard. He might have had to clutch at his ribs and a hiss spilled from him as he attempted to move again, but at least he was upright.

A nurse in light blue scrubs entered the room, her dark hair tied up in a bun. She wasn't one he was familiar with, but if she was here, Katt—the doctor he kept on his payroll for occasions such as this—trusted her.

And that assurance, for the moment, was all he needed.

"Good evening, Mr. Runehart. I'm Rebecca, and I'm assisting Dr. Katt. It's good to see you're awake. I'll need to change your bandages, but I'll save that for after I check your vitals."

He sat through her ministrations without complaint, his gaze riveted to the mirror across the room. She was proficient at her job, doing her best not to cause him any pain, but even as careful as she was, he could feel every second of her unwinding the bandage wrap from around his torso.

It was one thing to feel the pain, but it was something else entirely to *see* the reflection of it.

He was a mess of bruises, so much so that it looked as if he was still suffering from internal bleeding with how purple his side was. The very edges had faded the tiniest bit, and even a spot beneath his collarbone was a muted shade of yellow.

He looked like roadkill and felt like it too.

Before he could let the sight of himself send him spiraling, his mind shifted to another direction—one that was less painful.

One that actually brought him some semblance of peace.

Of balance.

Karina.

She was safe, that much he'd ensured before Katt had drugged him long enough to fix the damage Gaspard had wrought. But even as he *knew* she was back in New York and out of harm's way—Skorpion had made sure of this—the fact that he couldn't *see* her made his chest feel tighter than it already did.

He wanted, no *needed*, to see for himself. To at least explain his sudden and unexpected absence.

But that was a liability he couldn't afford to risk.

Not to mention, after he'd woke up in this room, Skorpion had taken away each of his phones and only ever relayed his messages—though never any from Karina. He was sure from the way the man avoided bringing her name up at all that she had called at least once.

Safety precaution, he'd said.

As soon as he was able to move without feeling as if he would keel over with every step, he would put an end to that.

"Where's Katt?" he asked as she pulled the blood pressure cuff from his arm and stepped away from him.

"Speaking with your security," she said with a slight nod of her head toward the door. "I'll let him know you're awake."

She snapped her gloves off, tossing them into a wastebasket as she left the room. With the door slightly ajar, he could just make out her shadow, and the others that lingered there, even before soft voices carried.

Before anyone could walk in, however, he shoved the sheets off his legs and twisted his body to plant his feet on the floor. He hated how long it took him to get to his feet, and how it took even longer for him to shuffle his way over to the bathroom and get inside while also closing the door.

He'd taken this all for granted—something as simple as getting up and crossing a room without feeling as if he was running a marathon.

And worse, seeing the damage to his body up close in the mirror that spanned the entire east wall of the bathroom was sickening. In mere weeks, he looked as if he had lost a few pounds. His face a touch more gaunt and a thinness to his arms that he didn't like.

If only because he looked like shit, he wanted to make Gaspard pay for what he had done.

By the time Uilleam came back out of the bathroom, he was no longer alone.

Skorpion's massive frame took up the entirety of the armchair next to the bed.

While Uilleam had been in a drug-induced haze for the first few days after the shooting, he'd still been out of it for quite a while after, but even when his thoughts had been hazy, he *did* recall Skorpion sitting in that very spot on more than one occasion.

He would have to find a way to repay him.

"What's the word?" Uilleam asked as he gingerly climbed back into bed, feeling far too much relief as he relaxed back against the pillows.

Gaspard might have taken his pound of flesh, but he wouldn't give anyone else the opportunity to do the same.

"It's been pretty quiet as far as I can find. Those who know aren't talking, and those who don't are none the wiser."

Good enough for the moment. "Where is she?"

He didn't have to elaborate on the *she* he meant. There was only one woman he would be asking after.

"Safe. I have someone watching her place—says no one has come and gone but a woman with blond hair."

No one of notable interest, he figured. "I need to see her."

"That's a stupid fucking plan."

"Careful."

Skorpion's gaze cut to him. "In case you forgot"—he gestured at him with a flick of his hand—"Gaspard tried to have you killed. It wouldn't be unreasonable to think he'd try again if given the opportunity. You took her *with* you to meet him, so he knows her face. If he can't get to you directly, you know he would use her."

Of course he would.

Uilleam would do the same—had even done so in the past—but that didn't erase the desire that was eating at him.

It had taken a number of years for him to find balance in his life, and though Karina had tipped the scales at one point and disrupted everything he thought he knew, she had also righted it again.

And threat or not, he had no intentions of remaining in this room for much longer.

He refused to hide and cower.

His father had taught him better than that.

A message needed to be sent.

"What would you have me do?" he asked. "If I let this go unanswered, he wins."

And that was something Uilleam couldn't allow.

Not just because he wanted to see the end of the man and everything he had built, but because he couldn't afford to look weak.

Not after he had come so far.

He was standing at the precipice of who his father had been and the man he had hoped to be.

"If you answer prematurely, he wins anyway because you'll be dead."

Feeling both tired and frustrated, Uilleam raked a hand down his face. "What would you have me do?"

Skorpion shrugged, not offering an immediate response. "You got a call your first night here," he said, pulling the mobile from his pocket. "I suggest you return it."

He caught the device Skorpion tossed at him, his brow furrowing as he read through the list of various numbers, stopping once he reached the one he was looking for.

A missed call from a man he'd least suspected, but the one he needed most at this moment.

His day was starting to look up.

TWO MORE DAYS OF BEDREST AND MEDICATION MADE ALL THE difference in the world.

He might have still been badly bruised, but at least it didn't take a concentrated effort to make even the slightest move now.

At least it felt as if he could breathe again without wishing he wasn't.

Besides, he was glad for it. Being idle made him antsy—his mind rebelled at stagnation.

He needed something to keep him stimulated.

Katt had already come and gone for the day, his presence not really needed now that Uilleam was on the mend.

He could actually pull on a shirt without feeling as if the material was abrasive against his skin. That it didn't *feel* like a weight on his chest.

But even as he felt better, he should have been resting and regaining his strength because he still wasn't back to one-hundred percent, but instead, he was awake and sitting in front of the trio of televisions on the other side of his room, watching the news.

He wished it calmed him enough to make him feel less ... on edge, but he was teetering on the edge of a break, and if something didn't change soon, he feared he would turn to more drastic measures.

Heavy footsteps sounded, so loud that his gaze skirted in the direction of his bedroom door.

No one was supposed to be here after Katt had come and gone. Not to mention, Skorpion wouldn't be arriving for at least another two hours.

Carefully, Uilleam leaned across the side of the chair he was sitting in, pulling the Ruger from its hidden position beneath the chair.

He might not have made it a point to use guns, but that didn't mean he was unprepared.

As soon as the door opened, Uilleam turned and aimed, his finger resting beside the trigger, at least until he saw who entered the room.

Anyone else might have reacted to having a gun pointed at them, but Zachariah Runehart wasn't just anyone. His reflexes were keen and well honed, and four decades of living the way he did ensured he knew when and if his life was in any actual danger.

Or perhaps he didn't see Uilleam as a threat, considering he had been in his life since Uilleam was in diapers.

"Uncle Z. You're the last person I was expecting to see."

His uncle might have been many things, but sentimental had never been one of them. He was far more straightforward that Uilleam's father had been and possessed considerably more tact.

"It looks like I'm digging you out of a hole you seem determined to bury yourself in."

Uilleam scratched at his whiskered face, knowing he was in desperate need of a shave, but for the time being, he couldn't be bothered.

There were quite a few things he needed to see to, and his facial hair was at the very bottom of that list.

"I'm handling it."

"I made a promise to—"

"My father was never one to hang on such sentiment," Uilleam interrupted before he could finish.

If he thought to guilt him that way, it wouldn't work.

Alexander would have sacrificed his own family if it meant he got what he wanted—had done so once before, in fact.

"It wasn't to him," Zachariah continued before sitting on the opposite chair, his gaze briefly flickering over to the many televisions Uilleam was sitting in front of. "To Kit."

Uilleam frowned—a reaction that was almost standard when he heard his brother's name. It hadn't always been this way in the beginning, back when they were living together at Runehart Castle during the months he was home from boarding school.

Those had been some of the best days of his life when he took a moment to think about it. If he'd had no one else to confide in—to look up to—he had Kit.

At least until Kit had turned seventeen.

Something had changed about him that year.

Something Uilleam had never been privy to. He had seemed more reluctant to be home and acted as if he would rather be anywhere but there.

Which, considering the idol worship Uilleam had once felt for him then—thankfully that hero worship had simmered down—it had still hurt to think his brother hadn't wanted to be around when he was all Uilleam had.

It was somewhere in the midst of that time that Uilleam grew out of it and became less disillusioned where his brother was concerned.

And though he would never admit it to himself, it was after his brother's departure that his resentment for him grew as well.

"So is that why you deigned to call me after all these years?"

Unlike his brother, Uilleam didn't consider himself particularly close with his uncle. His particular occupation wasn't one that he was interested in.

He trained assassins.

Molded and shaped them into calculated, cunning killers.

It was his specialty.

Kit's specialty.

Uilleam had never been overly fond of killing—he'd much rather have someone else dirty their hands with the job.

Even as his own were just as stained.

"You decided to make an enemy of Gaspard Berger."

Uilleam didn't offer a response as the other man took a seat beside him. There wasn't much he could say—not when he wasn't wrong.

"They're not going to stop just because you're down," Zachariah said with a shake of his head, his expression grave. "If anything, they'll try harder. There's no easier prey than a man already on his knees."

"I know," he answered, even if it was a bit of an overstatement.

He wasn't on his *knees* just yet, but Gaspard had almost accomplished that.

"What you need to do is prepare for it. Tell that big Samoan to teach you how to use a damn—"

"I had something else in mind."

Zachariah arched a brow, his skepticism clear.

It was a thought he'd contemplated for quite some time now. He had known, long before Gaspard took his shot at him, that he had enemies, but he'd also thought he'd have more time before someone struck out against him.

Not to mention, he'd thought his notoriety would help him in the same manner.

And while it had deterred some, he needed to make sure

everyone knew that acting against him wouldn't be in their best interest.

To implement that plan, it had to be more than him.

"Go on then," Zachariah said with an impatient gesture of his hand. "What is it?"

"Mercenaries."

He blinked once. "You're not serious …"

"That's why I called you here. You, better than anyone, can help me bring this to fruition."

"What exactly do you intend to do with the mercenaries?"

For the first time since he'd feared he would die in the streets of Paris, Uilleam smiled. "I'm going to make an army."

37

A WELCOME RETURN

ANOTHER GLANCE AT HER PHONE, ANOTHER MOMENT WASTED.

She was still waiting ... still expecting.

Hoping against hope that something would change. *Anything.* She didn't care so long as something did.

It didn't matter that she was starting to develop a routine that wasn't doing her the least bit of good. She didn't know why she was still checking at all considering *nothing* had changed, and there was very little reason to think that anything would.

But the part of her that had always made her different from her mother and sister refused to think that Uilleam had brought her along with him to Paris simply because he wanted to have sex with her.

That could have happened at any time, if she was being honest with herself. Hell, it had nearly happened on more than one occasion before Paris had ever been mentioned.

So the time she spent there with him wasn't black and white.

There was more to it than that.

She had to believe that.

Because otherwise ... these feelings that had her stomach twisting into knots would be for nothing.

But it still didn't change the fact that she had yet to hear *anything* from him.

Not a call.

Not a text.

He hadn't even sent Skorpion back around to let her know anything.

Now, without any way of getting into contact with him, she had to settle for waiting. She certainly wasn't going to ask her mother for assistance, though she had briefly entertained the idea.

Katherine had never been the sort to do anything out of the goodness of her heart. Her favors came with strings, and having witnessed the sort of things she asked for in return, Karina would rather take her chances elsewhere.

Forcing her mind off Uilleam, her mother, and everything else that had her distracted from the articles she was reading online, Karina tried unsuccessfully to focus back on work.

"You've been really quiet since you got back," Samantha said conversationally as she came from the office kitchen, leaning one shapely hip against the side of her desk. "How was your trip?"

Karina might have been back for nearly two weeks now, but mentally, she was still in Paris—in a mansion just outside of the city.

At the time, she hadn't realized she'd been taking her time there with Uilleam for granted. If she'd known then what she knew now, she would have savored every moment with him.

Spent more time lying beside him, enjoying the contentment she felt in his presence. The peace that always settled over her when she was with him.

Just the thought of him made the pang in her chest worsen. "It was good … fun. I'm just tired, you know? Jet lag."

It was the best excuse she could think of. The truth was far too complicated to explain to anyone.

Samantha sighed, looking off into the distance as if she could imagine a more beautiful place. "I've never been out of the city. First chance I get, I want to go to Spain. No … Australia. Somewhere warm, definitely."

Karina tried to listen to whatever she was saying, she really did, but it was hard paying attention as her mind was somewhere else.

The only hope she had of not driving herself crazy with thoughts of Uilleam was if she buried herself in her work.

"Sam, I—"

"Ashworth!"

Saved by the bell.

She offered her an apologetic smile as she stood. "The editor calls."

"No worries, we'll chat later."

Lord help her.

But as she walked toward Camilla's office, she was reminded that there *was* one person she could talk to without worrying what sort of price she had to pay in return.

Though even as the thought filled her with hope, she wasn't so sure whether the meeting would go at all the way she was hoping.

———

FOR ONCE, ORION DIDN'T LOOK HAPPY TO SEE HER. HIS EASY expression was pensive now, his brows pinched as he tossed back the last of his drink and pushed the glass to the edge of the table before raising his hand to signal for another.

She didn't like this look on him.

The indifference.

Something akin to bitterness, though she couldn't read it quite right, and with her current mood, she wasn't sure she wanted to.

She had her own issues to deal with.

"I can't say I'm not surprised you agreed to meet me," she told him as she placed her purse in the booth opposite him before sliding in.

He gave an absent nod of his head, having yet to actually look at her. "Yeah? Well, when have I ever been able to say no to you?"

Karina fell silent, not quite sure what to say. She doubted anything she *could* say would be good enough.

"So ..." he started, tapping his thumb against the table, still not looking at her. "What's brought you around here? I thought you had a thing with the fixer."

Had she actually thought this would be easy just because she *knew* Orion? If anything, it was worse.

With him, she couldn't pretend as if Uilleam was an innocent man, or that something good was buried beneath the surface. Orion knew all about him, probably more than she did.

Not to mention, Uilleam had had him arrested and thrown in jail simply for *knowing* her. She couldn't imagine he was his favorite person.

If she had to guess, he was probably public enemy number one at the moment.

"You hear things, more than anyone I know."

A muscle jumped in his jaw. "And you want to know what I've heard about him."

Karina nodded, not trusting her voice.

"Yeah? And what do I get in return?"

She … hesitated, though only for a second. "You've never asked for anything before."

"It was never about fucking Uilleam Runehart before. It was different then."

"Different because of who he is, or different because I'm the one asking?"

The question slipped out before she could contain it, and she knew within seconds that it was the wrong thing to ask. It was written all over his face.

But before he could respond, the bartender came over, eyed him sharply—undoubtedly looking for telltale signs of his drunkenness— before refilling his glass and carrying on.

Orion didn't toss this one back like he did the other. Instead, he turned the glass round and round in his hands, staring down at the amber liquid as if it held all the secrets in the world.

She wished she knew what he was thinking.

She also wished it wasn't because of her that his expression was so grim.

"What do you care?" he asked after a while, pale eyes finally lifting from the tabletop to her. "Why do you give a shit what happens to him? 'Cause the way I see it, he doesn't give a shit about you."

"Orion—"

"What, you think I'm wrong? If he did, where the hell is he? Huh? Because a little bird told me he's alive and well despite the odds, and if you're here with me and not him, looks to me like he didn't want you to know."

This time, he lifted his drink and swallowed half, grimacing against the burn. "The motherfucker just won't die already."

With the way he grumbled those words, she wasn't sure he had meant for her to hear them.

All the same, she ignored the remark and focused on the rest. "So he *is* alive?" she asked, wishing that didn't make her feel better.

Why *should* it?

It wasn't as if Orion was wrong.

She *didn't* know where Uilleam was, or if he was okay, or even what had happened to him. Sure, he had wooed her with flowers and that irresistible Welsh charm, but in the end, hadn't he just gotten what he wanted?

He'd had her in nearly every room of the place, not to mention in Hush. He'd been *insatiable*, but in the end, he had merely had his guard fly her home without so much as a goodbye.

And now that it was abundantly clear that he was alive and well, she had to acknowledge the fact that Uilleam hadn't been the one to tell her as much.

And in two weeks, he hadn't even attempted to reach out at all.

Orion gave a harsh shake of his head. "You deserve better than what he's offering you."

Now, it was Karina's turn to sit back with a sigh, signaling the waitress that was already heading in their direction. "Yeah ... I'm not so sure about that."

The admission surprised even her.

She had always been careful, not just with her words, but with her speech—with the way she carried herself in general.

For more than a year now, she had become the best actress she could possibly be. She'd donned a mask and made sure it was pristine.

Now, even she saw the cracks.

Orion's hand suddenly covering hers made her look up at him.

His hand was rough with calluses, but there was also a comforting warmth to it that reminded her why she had always liked being around him.

"Maybe you don't see it, babe, but I do."

Because it was all an illusion, she thought sadly. Everything he thought he knew—everything she had shown him of herself since they had met was a carefully constructed reality.

It didn't matter that she had always had good intentions—that her work for the *Post* was every bit as important to her as she proclaimed it to be—it was still all a lie.

She turned her hand over until she could feel the heat of his palm against her own before she squeezed his hand, then pulled away. "You don't know the first thing about me, Orion. I'm not at all who you think I am."

He looked down at where her hand had once been. "No? What does it matter one way or the other? I like what I *do* know."

Maybe he did ... but even she couldn't say whether the parts of her that *he* knew were real, or if they were a part of the image she created.

In the beginning, she had tried to keep her two identities separate. The Karina who had grown up at Ashworth Hall, learning the art of manipulation and world domination ... then there was the Karina who had come here, wondering whether an ordinary life was what she wanted more.

In the end, however, she couldn't help but think she was some hybrid of the two, and considering the world she was living in, that wasn't a very good combination.

One day, she would have to choose.

Either she was all in, or she walked away from every bit of it.

She couldn't have it both ways.

By the time she had her drink ordered and the fruity concoction was sitting in front of her, Karina wasn't sure whether she was thankful she could avoid talking for a little while longer, or if the alcohol would soon drown away the bad feelings in her heart.

Orion twirled his keys around his finger. "Need a ride?"

"No," she said, her smile coming a little bit easier now. "And I don't think you're in any state to be driving either."

A corner of his mouth tugged up in that little half-grin of his, reminding her why she had always enjoyed being around him so much.

"Wasn't planning on it, but if you're going uptown, we can share a taxi. Least I could do since I got you a wee bit drunk."

She laughed, feeling lighter than air. "Not even close."

But that didn't mean she wasn't feeling the effects of the alcohol.

The first drink had taken her the longest, at least until her throat had become numb to the burning vodka and she could swallow it all down with no problem.

She'd hardly finished that one before he was buying her a second. Their conversation might have started tense, but by the end of it, they were laughing again—spending time together as they always had.

More than anything, she was glad she was able to find a distraction.

It had felt like ages now that she had been in a constant state of anxiety, worrying about Uilleam and where he could be, but by the time she got to the bottom of her second glass, that worry had turned to anger.

Because Orion was the second person who told her that Uilleam was okay. That he was alive and breathing and, even as he wasn't out of the shadows quite yet, he was still doing what he did best.

Making deals.

Manipulating others.

Being the *Kingmaker*.

She almost wished she could hate him—she was sure that would be easier than the confusing, convoluted feelings she was currently dealing with.

"So how about it?" Orion asked, digging his hands into his pockets, his gaze trained on her in that sleepy, content way that made him all the more attractive, and he probably knew it. "Want me to take you home?"

Being with Uilleam, she understood the allure of sex now.

How easy it was to fall into it.

To want it.

Crave it.

To give herself over to her desires and think of nothing else.

But ... when she thought of that, she could only picture Uilleam. She saw him leaning over.

Remembered the way his voice sounded in her ear.

Felt the way his fingers dug into the flesh of her thighs when he was close.

She *only* saw him.

"I don't think that's a good idea," she whispered, wishing the blush she felt staining her cheeks would go away.

But Orion didn't get upset by the rejection. "Maybe next time when you're not ... distracted."

He let out a whistle, pulling one of his hands from his pockets to signal the taxi idling a block down. It flashed its lights before pulling toward them.

"You'll call me when you're home, yeah?"

"I promise I will," she said with a nod.

He pulled her into his embrace, holding her tight against his well-muscled chest.

Orion was ... safe.

And maybe, in a different life, she could have changed her mind right then. Told him he *should* make sure she got home safely himself.

But that was only a stray thought.

Instead, she pressed a quick kiss to his cheek and climbed into the back of the cab, waving at him through the window as it pulled away.

Whether she liked it or not, her heart, if nothing else, still belonged to Uilleam.

After rattling off her address to the cabbie, she rested her head against the cool glass of the window, closing her eyes momentarily as she let the gentle rocking of the car lull her.

Soon, this night would end and a new day would begin.

And starting tomorrow, she would have to make a concentrated effort *not* to think about Uilleam or what they had shared. It was time to move on, and she couldn't do that if she spent her every waking moment concerned about him.

She had to let him go.

By the time she made it up to her apartment, her buzz was starting to wane and she was looking forward to stripping out of her clothes, throwing on some comfortable pajamas, and climbing right into bed.

She could already imagine the cool, softness of her sheets—the downy pillow that never lost its shape. The prospect sounded far too enticing to ignore.

Wrestling with her key, she finally managed to get the door unlocked and stumbled her way inside, silently reminding herself why she didn't drink on nights when she had to be at work the next morning.

She fumbled for the light switch, nearly managing to trip over her own two feet before she finally got it turned on, pale yellow light flooding the small space.

She tossed her purse aside and stepped out of her heels, too busy thinking about her bed to realize she wasn't alone ...

"Is it that easy for you?"

That *voice*.

Even with the two drinks she'd had, Karina wasn't drunk enough to mistake the man standing within the shadows of the building.

She could *never* mistake Uilleam for anyone else.

Turning, she trained her gaze on that shadowed corner, needing to know—needing to *see* him for herself. Some part of her had wondered whether Katherine had been wrong about the information she had heard.

Whether Uilleam *had*, in fact, been fatally injured back in Paris and she would never know.

She'd even hoped that it was Orion's hatred of him that made him want her to stay away from him.

But she was wrong on both counts because sitting in her armchair as if no time had passed at all was Uilleam.

❧ 38 ❧

IN THE LATE HOUR

UILLEAM COULDN'T COUNT ON ONE HAND THE NUMBER OF TIMES he had been betrayed.

From his parents, who had taught him that the unconditional love they should feel for a child was all but nonexistent. To his brother who'd saved himself and left him at the hands of their father *knowing* what the man was capable of.

And that was just family.

Legion had come after him.

Business associates.

Enemies—though this wasn't as much of a surprise as the others had been.

And countless others who had come and gone …

But Uilleam took that as his due. He expected it from everyone, which was why he rarely let anyone close enough to do him harm.

Yes, he trusted Skorpion with his life and would do just about anything for the man as payment for his loyalty, but that didn't mean he wasn't prepared should he ever act against him.

He had safeguards in place for such a reason.

Yet even knowing this—even being the person *he* was—he wasn't prepared for the way he felt when he'd been sitting in the back of the SUV, watching Karina with Orion.

He'd left nearly as soon as he'd arrived.

He *needed* to leave, or else he wouldn't be responsible for what he would do next.

Afterward, he should have gone back to his hotel as Skorpion had told him. There was no reason for him to risk any more exposure, but instead, he went to her apartment and settled there.

Waiting.

Waiting ... for this moment.

The gentle scraping of the key as it was being forced into the lock. The creak as the door was finally pushed open and Karina came stumbling inside, a wistful sort of smile on her face.

That smile set him on edge.

He watched as she stepped out of her heels, seconds from pulling the band from her hair before he finally spoke.

"Is it that easy for you?"

She whipped around to face him, relief flooding those brown eyes of hers. It was written all over her expression and the way it looked as if her shoulders sagged at the sight of him.

But he couldn't bring himself to focus on that reaction. The only thing he could see in the back of his mind was her standing there with a man he already despised.

"Uilleam ..."

She didn't seem to know *what* to say, but he did. He had enough words for the both of them.

Slowly, he moved to his feet and walked over to her. "Why were you with him?"

"*Him*? What? What are you talking about?" She seemed genuinely confused for a moment, but it fled as anger at him surfaced. "That's not even important. Where the hell have you *been*? You disappear for weeks and now you show back up as if nothing has happened and *you're* upset with *me*?"

"You—"

"Have you lost your *entire* mind?"

That was up for debate.

But he wasn't thinking about anything other than the red-hot jealousy currently coursing through him.

"Did you ever consider for a moment that I was trying to protect you?"

Her eyes widened, her anger only getting worse as color infused her cheeks. "How could I possibly know that? I thought you were dead!"

And it was as if those words echoed in her ears because her expression broke then—tears welling that made his chest feel tight.

He would do anything to stop her tears, he realized.

"Karina—"

He caught her wrists before she could shove him, feeling far too much satisfaction now that he had her here.

That he could feel her.

Touch her.

Breathe her in.

"Do you even understand what that was like?" she asked, her voice breaking at the end.

He had a thousand excuses, most of them legitimate, but he doubted any of them would be good enough.

They wouldn't be for *him*, if the situation were reversed.

"You didn't—"

He kissed her because it was the only thing he could think to do.

The only thing he *wanted* to do.

He missed her. The feeling she gave him. The way he felt at peace when he had her close.

He missed the connection he had never had with another person.

And when she wrapped her arms around him, holding tight, he carried her into her bedroom and showed her just how much he'd missed her.

39

IDLE CONVERSATIONS

"I THOUGHT HE WOULD HAVE TOLD YOU," UILLEAM SAID HOURS later, his fingers skimming up her bare spine as she laid across his chest.

"Well, he didn't, and I'm angry with him for not saying anything."

It wasn't as if he didn't know where she lived or had her number.

He could have slipped her some sort of covert note if he thought maybe someone was watching, but he hadn't said a word.

"Perhaps he knew you wouldn't have been satisfied by just knowing."

"He wouldn't be wrong," she grumbled, knowing herself far too well.

She would have wanted to see him and taking no for an answer had never been her strong suit.

"Well, there's no reason for you to worry any longer," he said with a sigh. "I'm not going anywhere again."

She almost made him promise that to her.

It was sitting there on the tip of her tongue, but she didn't.

She didn't want him making a promise he couldn't keep.

"What happens now?" she asked, turning so she could see his face.

"Now, I make sure Gaspard Berger understands quite well what it means to feel pain. And when I do, I'll be putting him in an unmarked grave."

His tone didn't shift, nor did his voice change.

He could have been discussing the weather for all the care he put into those words. It certainly didn't sound like a man who wanted to *murder* someone.

"Uilleam—"

"Don't worry yourself about that," he said, leaning over to kiss her lips. "It won't affect you, I promise."

That ... that he could promise.

"Are you forgetting that I'm a—"

"The body would never be found," he said casually. "There would be no story to write."

She couldn't believe she was hearing him correctly. She couldn't be. "Uilleam, you can't just *kill* the man. What if someone finds out it was you?"

"They wouldn't."

"Right ... because he didn't try to kill *you* not that long ago."

He might have been enthusiastic with her tonight, but she could still see the bruises. The careful way he held himself.

There was only so much he could hide.

"Karina ... it's not something you need to concern yourself with."

"If it's about you, then of course it concerns me! What the hell did you think I would say? Yes, go on and put an even bigger target on your back?"

He must have realized she was serious as his easy demeanor faded away. "You don't have to worry about losing me."

"But I almost did," she whispered.

And it had managed to turn her small world upside down.

He swallowed before scrubbing a hand down his face, turning to look at the clock on her nightstand. "It's late. We should sleep."

He didn't give her much of a choice before he hauled her up against him and turned off the light.

His arm looped around her waist, holding her against him.

For a long while, she lay there in silence, waiting for his hold to loosen.

After Uilleam had drifted off, his breathing slow and even, she slipped out of bed and grabbed her phone as she went.

She closed the door behind her, making sure she had as much privacy as possible.

Even as she was both mentally and physically exhausted, she was still too wired to sleep. Too busy thinking of everything Uilleam had revealed.

His plans and intentions.

What it would ultimately mean for them.

Katherine would have told her to cut her losses and get out before the blowback affected her as well.

Isla would have told her it was time to let Uilleam go because there was no reasoning with stubborn men like him.

But she couldn't do either.

She didn't *want* to do either because when she pictured her life — when she pictured what the next few years would bring her — she couldn't imagine it without Uilleam.

Without his smile and charm.

Without the games he liked to play that were both exasperating and exhilarating.

She couldn't — she *wouldn't* — let him go.

Which meant it was time for her to make a choice.

A decision that had her hands shaking as she turned her phone over in her hands and pulled up her messages, scrolling until she found her mother's number.

She couldn't call. She didn't think she had the fortitude to call and actually voice the words aloud.

Instead, she texted them, counting every second it took her to type out those three words, because she knew everything would no longer be the same once she did.

That she could never take back this moment once she pressed send ...

But for the second time ever, she put what she wanted first.

She made a decision for herself and told Katherine the truth.

I choose him.

ANOTHER DAY, SHE MIGHT HAVE BEEN PLEASED BY THE AUDIBLE sound of the door closing, signaling Uilleam's return, but not today.

This time, she only felt ... worry.

Anxiety.

Fear.

Because she knew, just as she'd known the night before when they'd wound up in bed together, that nothing was ever going to be as it had been before Paris. Back when their biggest obstacle had been a man who'd murdered his mistress.

He didn't stop walking until he reached the bar cart across the room and poured himself a healthy amount of whiskey into his glass, drinking it down without needing to take a breath. Even as his face twisted up at the burn of it, he still poured another. This one, he drank a little more slowly.

She was almost afraid to ask him what had happened in the time he'd been gone. Whether he had found an answer to his looming problem. But she didn't.

Merely staring at him standing across the room, she wondered what would come next.

He strolled over to her, glass in hand, his gaze briefly flickering to the TV she had playing in the background just to have some noise in his suite. "Anything of interest?"

She shook her head.

Even if there had been, that would be the last thing she wanted to discuss. Not after everything he had told her the night before.

It didn't matter that they were now in a hotel in the middle of the city instead of her apartment, or that it was more secure, she couldn't forget.

Not only would Gaspard be in the city—*this* city—but Uilleam also fully intended on killing him.

On making him answer for cutting their time together in Paris short.

All night and morning, it was the only thing she could think about. And what made it worse was that Uilleam didn't seem to understand why she was nervous.

Why the thought of him acting prematurely made her worry.

"Why?" she asked, feeling as if her heart was mere seconds from beating out of her chest.

She wished she could identify the emotion running rampant inside her, but she couldn't put a name to it. The only thing she could do was *feel*, even if it felt as if she was being torn up inside. "Why me?"

Never had she seen the look of frustration that crossed his face before. Uilleam didn't *get* frustrated. He was always in control of everything and everyone around him.

But not now.

"Is this really a conversation we need to have *now*?" he asked, his irritation leaking through.

Ah, she knew that tone of voice. The one that said she needed to back off before he snapped. Before he reminded her why so many people feared and revered him.

"I won't give you a second chance to have it."

He looked as if he wanted to argue further, or better yet, avoid the conversation entirely, but whatever he saw in her face right then caused him to walk over to her, standing so close that she could see the golden flecks in his dark eyes.

"You have nothing to fear. I—"

"*Me*, Uilleam Runehart. Why did you pick *me*?"

"Because you didn't *break*," he hissed back at her, his hand slapping down against the wall next to her head. "You didn't run and hide or beg like a child. You *smiled* at the challenges. You walked headfirst into them without a second thought." He sighed, his brow furrowing. "As delicate and beautiful as porcelain, but you refused to break. How could I not choose you?"

Those words drifted into her heart and planted themselves there. She knew how impossible it was to feel what she did for a man like him. Someone who had shown her how ugly the world could be, but he'd also shown her how marvelous it was at times.

These past few months had completely turned her world upside down.

Changed everything she thought she knew, and she had him to thank for it.

"Then you know that I won't stand here and let you do something stupid that will get you killed."

That quickly, the mask fell back into place. "I have it all under control."

She couldn't help but wonder if he truly believed that … or if he didn't have a choice. "What happens after?"

"We move on and—"

"Uilleam, please. We both know better than that."

This time, she wasn't asking for pleasantries or clever words. She wanted the truth. She was *worried*, even if he wasn't.

"Karina—"

"Let's say it happens as you say," she went on before he could finish. "By the end of your meeting with him, you get exactly what you want. Gaspard dies. You have to know there will be a price to pay for that."

"There's a price to pay for everything, didn't you know."

"Now you're being deliberately obtuse."

"What would you have me do, hmm?"

"Not go out there and get yourself killed, for starters."

"That's not telling me anything."

"I'm just saying there's another way!" she snapped, annoyed that he seemed intent on misunderstanding what she was trying to tell him, and annoyed by how difficult he was being.

Something changed then.

Not just with his demeanor, but in the way he held himself as he pushed off the wall and took a step away from her. It was as if he turned into an entirely different person.

"And this clever way you presume to know so much about. What exactly do you expect to come of that? Do we all sit in a neat little circle, discuss our grievances, and go on about our business? Do I have that correct?"

"I suspect there won't be a legion of Gaspard's men pissed off and wanting to kill you if you take out their boss."

"What is life without a little war?"

"I don't know," she answered honestly. "I suspect it's like whatever you were feeling when they nearly killed you in Paris."

A muscle jumped in his jaw. A testament to his darkening mood, but if he thought that was going to deter her, he clearly didn't know her very well.

"And it wasn't just you, was it? It's not just your life that would be on the line for the choices you make. Or do you truly believe I'm stupid enough to think you had Skorpion bring me home personally because you were feeling chivalrous ..."

"If you think that if I spare his life there won't be any repercussions, you're not nearly as intelligent as I thought you were. But I find I'm often blinded by those closest to me."

She had always figured he was good at cutting with his words, but she didn't give him the satisfaction of a reaction.

"Yet I'm intelligent enough to know that you're a dead man if you kill someone who *everyone* knows you hate. Are you sure *your* endgame can handle that, Uilleam? Do you truly believe you're smarter than *every* single person in the world? Because even if you were, unless you're tracking every single member in his organization at all times and you have the security of a fucking *army*, someone will get close to you, and guess what? I don't want to fucking *bury you*."

Uilleam stared at her for a long while, and with each passing second, his irritation faded.

"I'm ... sorry," he said a moment later.

It sounded rusty coming from him, as if he didn't make it a point to apologize to anyone, but the fact that he uttered those two words was enough for her.

"He *should* answer for what he did to you," she said more gently, stepping closer to him. "But find another way. I don't ... I don't want to lose you, Uilleam. Not right now. Not ever."

Not when she had only just gotten him.

Not when she had decided to keep him and forsake everything else.

40

SPARK

GRIPPING THE HANDRAIL, UILLEAM STOOD ON THE BALCONY outside of his bedroom, staring down at the city below him.

He should have been at peace. He knew what needed to be done —he even had a solution to ensure he got everything he wanted in the end—but instead of peace, he only found more questions.

For once in his long life, he was doubting himself.

All because of *her*.

Karina.

His poppet—his *bane*.

Even as he wanted to dismiss her words of caution—he would have already done so had it been anyone else—but because it was *her*, because he cared what she thought of him, her warning had lingered with him.

Playing over and over again in his thoughts until he had no choice but to actually consider what she had said.

Gaspard deserved to die—he deserved everything Uilleam had planned for him and more ... but did he truly need to die *now*?

Was his death truly worth the hell that would be rained down upon him?

He might have put up a good front when Karina had asked as much, but he knew that Gaspard's organization was legion.

If he was half the man Uilleam expected him to be, he would have safeguards in place that ensured should he die, someone would not only take over his position, but his death would be avenged.

He had to find a way to circumvent that.

THREE DOTS FLICKERED ON THE SCREEN, RINGING FOR SEVERAL moments before tapering off again.

A part of him was almost afraid that Carmelo wouldn't answer. That he would have to find the answer for himself, even if time wasn't on his side. But as he was about to ring off, the screen went black before it lit up with color once more, the Italian's face taking up much of the screen.

Carmelo took one glance at him and shook his head, appearing far too amused. "You are your father's son, as they say. He never knew when to die either."

Usually, Uilleam would have a ready response—it wasn't as if this was the first time he had ever heard those words—but in his current mindset, he couldn't think of anything else but the task at hand.

"I need your help," he said instead, leaning back in his desk chair, steepling his fingers in front of his face.

Carmelo nodded once. "What can I do to help?"

"How do I kill a man who can't be killed?"

The question seemed to stump him as he blinked once, considered the question a moment, then blinked again. "Speak English."

The only problem with that was he didn't know *how* to explain his intentions.

Killing was easy—that would solve his problem on a more permanent basis. But it *would* cause more problems than he currently needed.

And while he might have been back in the game, he still wasn't at one-hundred percent. His ribs were still tender, and he still had to rest more frequently because of it.

Should Gaspard have the safeguards in place that he suspected, there was only so long he could go on before one of his men caught up with him.

And as Skorpion liked to remind him, there was only so much he could do. There was only one of him.

For now.

"I ... can't kill him," he finally forced himself to say—*making* himself acknowledge that fact.

The sooner he recognized it as the truth, the sooner he could move forward and shape it to be what he needed.

Carmelo didn't respond immediately, but Uilleam could see that he agreed. Which meant, if he had to guess, he knew the consequences if he struck too soon.

"Killing someone isn't the only way to get rid of a problem."

No, it wasn't. But it *was* far more convenient.

And more satisfying.

"I don't have to tell you to watch where you step, Uilleam. You know better."

"What's worse than being dead?"

That answer was exactly what he needed.

Now he just had to think of a way to implement that plan.

WHEN HE WAS A BOY, WATCHING THE WAY HIS FATHER RULED OVER everyone around him—making sure his presence was felt as much as it was seen—Uilleam always wondered what sort of man he would be.

Whether he would ultimately turn into his father, or if he would be worse.

Monsters bred monsters.

He wasn't disillusioned enough to believe that he would leave his childhood unscathed.

He had always been rather knowing of that fact.

But he could never say that he had anticipated this moment in his life.

When everything was about to change.

When he would become the one to change it.

By this day's end, he would be a different man in more ways than one.

Entering the spacious room, mindful of the woman walking two paces ahead of him, Uilleam kept his hands tucked into his trouser pockets.

If nothing else had come of the attempt on his life, he was far more conscious about the people around him, even more so than he had been before.

It was always a bit odd, seeing a 3D rendering of a room, and then entering that very place in person. It was foreign still, but familiar all the same.

The twin gray couches that faced each other. The knit rug that ran between the two of them. Even the priceless art had been written down and documented, as well as the built-in safe behind the one on the left.

The woman stopped in the middle of the floor once they reached the open space where a media room had been converted into an indoor spa.

Only men with far too much money and not enough taste had a waterfall running into a pond in the middle of their living room. It seemed like a waste of space to him. Then again, this was Gaspard, and the man wasn't known for his subtle demands.

The man in question sat in a white robe on a black chair, two women standing behind him, kneading their fists into his back. He didn't stir at Uilleam's appearance in the room, though he was sure from the way his guard in the corner had cleared his throat at the sight of him, he knew he was here.

"The penthouse in Time's Square," Uilleam said as he stepped forward past the retreating woman. "That's a bit predictable for a man of your standard, no?"

From the way he looked up with a smile, he recognized his own words reflected back on him, but while they had rankled Uilleam, Gaspard didn't look bothered at all by them. Why would he? In his mind, he had won.

The game was over.

Men always underestimated those they saw as the dark horse.

"I figured you were alive somewhere, licking your wounds. Your father was a hard man to kill you know, so I didn't expect it to be easy to get rid of you. I'd pay a fortune in gold to learn who finally killed the old bastard."

Oh, if only he knew the answer to that question.

"I do, at the very least, appreciate an honest man. I'd hate for you to insult my intelligence and pretend it wasn't you who tried to kill me."

"You cost me a lot of money," Gaspard said sitting up, waving his hand to dismiss the women who quickly turned and left.

The guard in the corner of the room shifted on his feet, his gaze scanning the area around them.

"I'd like to think so," Uilleam said with a shrug. Anyone who came after him could expect his retaliation to be swift and painful as possible. It was better not to risk it. "It would be unfortunate if you didn't actually have to *work* for it, especially with the amount of effort I've put into *you* these past few days."

He tried to hide it—and Gaspard was better than most at keeping his expression neutral—but Uilleam didn't miss the confusion in the man's eyes.

"Curious thing, those drinks," Uilleam said with a casual nod of his head at the cup in his hands. "They use a special ingredient in those, don't they, Gaspard? Elderberry, isn't it?"

He didn't think he had ever seen a man swallow as harshly as Gaspard did at his remark, and had he not been in a rapidly declining mood, he might have reveled in that look of surprise. Taunted him with the knowledge that he knew something he shouldn't have.

But with his current mood, he wanted to see this done.

Because he wasn't worth more than that.

"I thought about just having you shot. Easily done and virtually untraceable considering who I wanted to hire, but then I thought, what would your men do at your sudden passing? I would be a fool if I didn't think they would target me for it, especially after that unpleasantness in Paris."

Gaspard set the drink away, as if that would change anything at this point. He had already consumed enough to make sure the contents fully went into effect. "What have you done, boy?"

"It was simple really. I wanted a seat at the table, as was my due. Your insulting little tests and demeaning comments should have been enough to ensure my entry, considering I tolerate that from no one, but you're not just anyone, are you, Gaspard? You're like my father in that way. A stubborn bloody tyrant."

A man he hated as much as he had hated his own father.

Gaspard dragged in a rattling breath, his eyes widening as he coughed, trying to clear his throat. The more he panicked, the faster his blood raced—the faster the poison swept through his system.

"You would have gotten by with your slights for as long as it took to kill you in some other sort of grisly fashion, but instead of doing what a corrupt bastard should have done, you tried to kill me." Uilleam moved to his feet then, advancing on him. "And I really don't appreciate attempts on my life."

"What did you do? What did you do to me!" Gaspard demanded, his face turning an alarming shade of purple.

"They're called miracle berries," Uilleam said calmly, carefully, making sure he understood every word. "Should you consume one, it'll make the taste of sour foods sweet. Fortunately for you, I'd wager. I don't imagine the taste of belladonna is a pleasant one."

Gaspard's eyes widened, and Uilleam knew he wouldn't have to explain the significance behind his drug of choice.

It had all been by design, after all, but only because he was enjoying this far too much did he do exactly that.

"I couldn't kill you—there would have been too many questions —but put you into a coma first ... Well, I didn't prepare your drink, did I? Nor would anyone know I was here, because you planned to kill me again, didn't you?"

A shadow moved in the corner of the room, Skorpion coming out from inside a room where he closed the door after him, snapping off bloody gloves. Looking far too comfortable at having done so.

But that was why Uilleam kept him.

Because he was good at what he did.

Uilleam did what he did best—he manipulated the truth until it appeared as he wanted it to.

No one would ever know what happened here.

"Sneaky little poison, that one," he said conversationally. "It attacks the nervous system, so I promise this won't be painless. And I have all the time in the world to watch you slowly eat away. But the best part is that when the day comes that I finally put you out of everyone's misery, you'll never see it coming. As far as you'll ever know, I killed you this day. And there's fuck all you can do about it."

Gaspard gave a jerky shake of his head, his coughing fit sounding worse as the seconds creeped on.

"Because I have everything I want."

He had Karina waiting for him, and once Gaspard was no longer around to interfere, he would have his seat.

A pleased smile lifted the corners of his lips as he returned to his seat, staring at the man slowly dying in front of him.

Yes, he had all the time in the world when he was king.

❧ 41 ❧

CONSEQUENCES & CHOICES

As she tucked the necklace Uilleam had given her in Paris away inside the jewelry box, she carried it out into the living room and placed it on the mantle above the fireplace.

The start of something new, she thought.

Out with the old, in with the new.

Everything else she had stashed away where Uilleam would never come upon it.

In the grand scheme of things, the action didn't mean very much. It wasn't as if her mother was here to see what she had done—or that she would be moved in any way *had* she been there—but it still meant something to Karina.

The reasoning behind it.

The symbolism.

She was her own person, with her own ideals and dreams and thoughts, and even if she wasn't completely sure what all she wanted —or how any of this would end—she still had to try.

She still had to see what she was made of outside her family.

She had to believe there was more to life than the life and role Katherine wanted her to step into.

There was no better time to try than now.

Otherwise, she knew she would regret it for the rest of her life.

And one little secret wouldn't hurt too much.

Since she'd been home, she'd been doing a lot of that. Thinking. Rearranging. Taking little bits that reminded her of her old life and tucking them away.

Though she was ready for a fresh start—a *real* fresh start this time—she wasn't quite ready to let them all go yet.

One day, maybe … but not now.

Instead, she tucked it all away to deal with another day.

As she was finishing, a sharp knock sounded behind her, a moment before the lock turned and the door opened.

"Since you have a key," Karina reminded him without looking behind her, "you don't have to actually knock when you come in. You just … *come in.*"

She'd meant the words as a joke, already smiling, at least until she saw the rather serious expression on Uilleam's face.

In the weeks since Gaspard, a lot had changed while remaining the same.

Uilleam took frequent trips, sometimes for days at a time, but when he left now, he made sure she knew.

He didn't provide her with details most times—something she was still trying to change—but he shared, and that meant more to her than anything.

But he wasn't supposed to be back for a couple of days more, yet here he stood with an expression that worried her.

"Uilleam, what's wrong?"

He stood in the entryway holding a single blue rose. The color was just as impeccable as the others he'd given her, but it still seemed better somehow.

As if it were freshly cut for this moment.

"What are you …?"

He opened his mouth, but no words came out. He just continued to stare at her with an expression that made her worry.

The intensity of his gaze made her break the silence stretching between them. "Uill—"

"I need you."

He said it so bluntly. Without inflection or the slightest hesitation.

He said those words like he meant them.

Those three little words meant everything to her.

It almost felt as if they burrowed themselves inside her and planted themselves right in her heart.

"I can breathe when I'm with you," he continued, stepping further into the room. Closer to her. "I can *sleep*. I ... I feel everything I never thought I would. You make me a better man."

She was struck mute, unsure what to say. *How* to say it.

When she imagined how this conversation would go, she thought she would have some sort of clever response. That she would know exactly what to say, but she was fighting the ridiculous urge to cry, so for once, she didn't have all the right words.

She only had the unflinching truth.

"I need you too, Uilleam."

More than she ever thought possible.

More than she would ever accurately be able to put into words.

She'd chosen him, after all. "I ... love you," she whispered, fighting past the lump in her throat.

"Then give me a chance," he said, reaching for her hands. "Let me give you the world."

A deal he offered so many ...

And now, it was her turn to accept.

TO BE CONTINUED ...

ACKNOWLEDGMENTS

Wow!

There were some days when I wondered if I would ever get to this point. Five years ago, when I first had a spark of an idea for Uilleam and Karina, I knew, even then, that I would absolutely *love* telling their story. They both have captivated me so much over the years, but I also knew they had to wait their turn—that it wasn't time yet for their story to be told.

Now, I can finally, *finally*, say that the Kingmaker is here and it's time for his, and Karina's, story to be told. I really hope you enjoyed reading the first installment in their series as much as I enjoyed writing it.

And speaking of writing, I wouldn't have been able to finish this book without two very special people in my life. H, thank you for all of your love and support, and especially for letting me wake you up at two in the morning whenever I needed plot advice. You're the best, Lol.

Kris, my fave human ever—the Niklaus to my Luka—I literally don't know where I'd be without you. I can't count how many times you talked me off the ledge while writing this book while simultaneously making sure I was still actually *writing*. I'd probably be lost without you, so consider yourself my best friend for life.

And to my readers, you guys make my job so easy. Your enthusiasm for this book and this couple kept me going. If you think you're ready for White Rabbit: The Fall ... trust me when I say, you're not.

It's going to gut you.

xx LM

ABOUT THE AUTHOR

London Miller is the author of the Volkov Bratva series, as well as Red., the first book in the Den of Mercenaries series. After graduating college, she turned pen to paper, creating riveting fictional worlds where the bad guys are sometimes the good guys.

Currently residing in Atlanta, Georgia with her husband and two puppies, she spends her nights drinking far too much Mountain Dew while writing.

For more information:
www.londonmillerauthor.com
london.millerauthor@gmail.com